The
Saturday Evening
POST
Stories 1962

The
Saturday Evening
POST
Stories 1962

SELECTED FROM
1961

Doubleday & Company, Inc.
Garden City, New York
1962

PRELUDE TO DOOM is a chapter from the novel,
TRUST IN CHARIOTS by Thomas Savage, published
in 1961 by Random House, Inc.

Contents

The
Saturday Evening
POST
Stories 1962

Paris Is the Place for You!

WILLIAM SAROYAN

Dear old Katey kid: Come to Paris as soon as you can. Don't put it off until you are a year older, because Paris may be different in a year, and I don't think you ought to miss the way it is now.

Everything is people in Paris. The people keep saying "Ah" and "Oh la-la" to one another all day and all night. No matter what time you go to bed you will hear somebody in the street saying "Ah" or "Oh la-la" in a loud voice to somebody else. I wish I knew a little more French than I do, so I could begin to guess what this is all about.

I know it's about tomatoes now and then, because I saw a little old lady buying fifty francs' worth of little old tomatoes from a young movie star at a pushcart on a narrow street, and after the little old lady had come out with her "Oh la-la," the movie star put back a bad tomato and put in a slightly better one. The little old lady wagged her head at his audacity in trying to give her a bad tomato, handed over her coin and went down the street, whereupon the movie star said "Ah" and made a famous French face. I call him a movie star because I've seen him in the six or seven French movies I've seen so far.

All of the people in the French movies appear to have side jobs selling tomatoes from pushcarts in the streets. The French people want their movie heroes that way. And that's one of the things I want you to come over and enjoy.

The French seem to believe that if there is anybody who isn't handsome enough to be in a movie, then there isn't anybody who *is* handsome. They don't like their movie heroes to be better-looking than the rest of the people.

Everybody in Paris believes he either is in a movie or could be if he wanted to, and everybody acts as if he had just turned down a big part in a movie because it wasn't as much fun as being in the full-time movie he has always been in.

I think this particular movie, which is a very pleasant one, is coming to an end, though, and may be over next year about this time. And who knows what the next movie is going to be like?

You're not a kid any more, although I've got to call you "Katey kid" because I've always called you that, and my Della has been dead five years, and your Edward has been dead two, and our kids have all grown up.

I don't mind saying I'm sixty-six, although I can't understand how I ever got to be so old all of a sudden. Wasn't it just last year that both of us graduated from Fremont High School in the same class?

I'm not asking you to come over and be my bride, either, in case you're thinking that that's what's in the back of my head. The only thing in the back of my head is that for all of my sixty-six years, Paris has got me thinking I'm sixteen again, and I believe it'll get you to thinking you're sixteen again too.

Now, as you may remember, when I *was* sixteen, I spoke to you about our getting married, and you asked for a little time to think it over. You felt there was plenty of time—and, of course, there was. There were fifty years of time for me, for instance, but now all of that time has been used up, but at least once a year—in October, because that was when I brought up the matter the first time—I've thought it over. *Old Katey kid, what's she up to now, I wonder?*

This time I would rather you didn't ask for time to think it over, because I have this feeling that the movie is going to change, and I don't think you ought to miss this part of it, which seems to be the best part.

It's late September now, and October will soon be here. Bring your money, of course. It would be silly for me to pretend I could afford to pay your way and then pay your expenses after you got here. I live like a king on thirty dollars a week, which is what I get in the mail the first of every month, the retirement pay of an ex-English teacher at Fremont High School, and I just couldn't pay for anything else out of that. But I know you get more than that in the mail the first of every month from Ed's insurance. With that extra money, you could buy some of the things that Paris is famous for—hats, shoes, perfumes. I know you could live like a queen on your money.

I live a little down the hill from a place called Pigalle, in what you might call the slums, only nobody here does that. Everybody believes he is in the same movie that everybody else is in, and everybody believes his own neighborhood is the best in the city.

The name of my street is *Rue de la Victoire*, and I am at No. 127, third floor, front two rooms, no elevator, but you don't need an elevator. The people in the building are all fine people who say "Ah" and "Oh la-la" to one another all the time. I haven't learned any real French yet, but after all, I've been here only six months. I wanted to be sure I wanted to stay before trying to learn the language; but now that I know I want to stay, I'm taking lessons from the old man who lives on the floor just below mine, who used to be a gardener but has been retired for more than twenty years.

He wrote his age on the back of an envelope the other day, and it was eighty-eight. I couldn't believe my eyes, for he doesn't look that old at all, except for his big white mustache. He gets around nicely, too, although he doesn't take the Metro very much because he doesn't like crowds. The Metro is short for *Métropolitain,* the name of the subway.

You can get around very nicely for a very small amount of money and you can get there much swifter than by a taxi, for instance. I take a taxi once in a while, but not too often. Why waste the money? The people of Paris don't like to waste money.

The man's name is Lebeque. The first thing he wanted to teach me was to count, which I am now able to do. And then he taught me the days of the week. I always know what day it is. Today is *samedi,* for instance. Saturday.

The two rooms cost me, furnished, three hundred francs a day, or about sixty cents. Well, they're worth it. They're not exactly enormous rooms, but I have all the room I need and then some. The kitchen is small, but it *is* a kitchen, and I get out some pretty good cooking in there.

Now, the other day, the lady who occupied two other rooms on this floor, also overlooking the street, was taken at her own request to a home because she didn't want to look after herself any more. Since her departure I've visited her rooms and I know you would love them and be perfectly at home in them. The rent, I am sorry to say, is a little higher than mine—three hundred and fifty francs a day, or seventy cents; but the rooms are really worth the difference—better furnished, more suitable for a lady, and just a little more spacious too, with more light, on account of an extra window.

So if you came to Paris and liked the rooms and took them, there you'd be at that end of the third floor, and there I'd be at this end; and if it was October at the time, we might just take it into our heads to walk to the Opéra—not to go inside or anything, I mean to the place where the Opéra is—and from there we could walk on to the Louvre, where all the great paintings are, but again we wouldn't need to go in. I think it costs half a dollar, but once you are in there, there is enough to see to keep you there all day. We might do the Louvre together, starting early one morning and leaving at closing time. We'd take our lunches, of course, as many people do.

But if we didn't go in, we could visit the Tuileries, which is a famous garden, full of chestnut trees, little lakes with kids sailing boats on them, and a lot of statues of various kinds. We could walk around in the garden—it's very big, you understand, and we could sit and talk and notice the statues and watch the kids and the other movie stars or we could just listen to them and try to guess what they're saying.

At the other end of the garden is the famous *Place de la Concorde*, where there is an Egyptian obelisk that is always nice to see from far off or from very near, and then comes the famous *Avenue des Champs-Elysées*, a great place for promenading.

We could have fun, Katey kid; and don't think for a moment I don't know I'm being a little forward about it. But why shouldn't I be? I don't believe you'd rather I weren't, as a matter of fact. You only live once, and there comes a time when it just doesn't do not to be forward, or at any rate a time when it is no longer necessary to be overcautious. That time came for me five years ago when Della died.

I really didn't know what kind of a time I had come to, but little by little I began to find out. I don't blame my kids for being busy with their own lives. When they were little I was pretty busy with mine, I guess, but as long as Della was there with me they visited us regularly. The wives of my three boys were always bringing stuff along, and the husbands of my two girls were always doing that too, and even some of their kids, my grandkids, brought stuff along—a little painting, or something made in shop at school, book ends or something.

For all I know, it may be that way with you too, now that old Ed has been gone for two years, or maybe it's only *beginning* to be that way. Well, take my advice and don't wait until it goes too far. Just remember our talk in October fifty years ago and come to Paris. Just remember I remember you as if you were the pretty girl you were then, which you are.

But why Paris? Why not California, for instance, or Florida? Well, I really don't quite know how to put it, but if you're going to go away, I say go away, go far away and be gone, be truly gone.

I didn't write to anybody for a month, because I didn't want anybody to misunderstand—which is easy for kids to do. But after a month, I decided to write to every one of them—sons, daughters, their wives, their husbands, and their kids. I even wrote to kids I know can't read, and every letter went into its own private envelope, because that would please each of them. And I believed soon the replies would begin to come. Just a letter in the box downstairs with my name on it, instead of only the check every month. Nothing fancy—"Hello, Pop, got your letter; glad to hear all goes well. Good-by, Dan." Or Dorothy.

I wrote a new letter every day describing life in Paris in a kind of humorous vein, and so by the time I had written to everybody, more than two weeks had gone by, and I believed the replies would begin to appear in the box downstairs.

Every morning I looked into the box. At last one letter came, from my grandkid Helen, who is now eleven, I think. George's second kid. They say she's a little slow, only they put it another way, but I'm not going to put it that way at all. She wrote the letter in print, and it must have taken her a long time. "Dear Grandpa: Thank you for your letter. I love you. I miss you.

Come and visit me tomorrow, please. Helen." I never received a letter that made me prouder.

I'm crazy about the people of Paris, of course. They are really a lot of fun—so enthusiastic, so full of noise and life, so outspoken, so charming, really, and every one of them is like a hero in a movie; but at the same time I miss my own people a little. The trouble is, so many of the people I miss—well, they're gone. I even miss some of the people I never cared for, because if they *weren't* gone and if I happened to see them, I would at least remember that we knew one another long ago, even if we didn't care for one another.

Now, with October coming on, I just don't want to be quite so far away from everybody I ever knew, and the one person I want most of all to be not too far away from is you. So come on over, and let's start October together; let's have the whole month together. I know Paris is the place for you, just as it's the place for me, and we'll have nothing but happy times all over the whole great city.

Of course, I'm not going to mail this letter, just as I haven't mailed the other six or seven I've written to you during the past three months, but that's only because the letter's not quite good enough.

But one of these days, I'll write a letter that I know *is* good enough and I *will* mail it; and even if you don't come to Paris, or even if you don't answer it, I'll be glad you received it and read it, because the fact is, Katey kid, I love you, I have always loved you, I will always love you. Your old rejected suitor.

JOHN COPLEY

Dr. Blanke's First Command

C. S. FORESTER

Malcolm Blanke, M.D., was in a state of mental turmoil when he came back into the room where he had undergone his oral examination. Two stupendous things were happening to him at once. He was about to learn if he was to be granted a Ph.D., and he had just joined the United States Navy. About the Ph.D. he would hardly have worried at all if that had been the only factor in his present life. He had every confidence in his thesis on the Histology of the Peripheral Neural Plexuses.

It had broken new ground; it had disproved one theory and established another, and it opened the way to a fresh series of important researches. It had called for four years of hard work —four years of the most slavish concentration, the most accurate laboratory technique, the most painstaking observations and the most ingenious theorizing regarding the deductions to be made from them. The examining board could hardly deny him his Ph.D. now that they had studied his thesis.

Incidentally, it was more than likely that the end result of his work would be the alleviation of a good deal of human suffering, which was a strange thought in a world at war— Blanke could think that way now that he was emerging from four years of total abstraction and now that he had joined the Navy. In fact, as he went back into the room to hear the decision of the examining board regarding his Ph.D., another absurd human thought came up into his mind—at some rare frivolous moment in his youth he had read about the procedure at Naval courts-martial, and how the accused coming in to be told the finding was warned in advance by the position of his sword on the table; the sword point toward him meant a verdict of guilty. Blanke remembered this as he remembered everything he had ever read because he had the fantastic memory of the true scholar, but the clearest proof that he had been jolted out of a purely academic state of mind was that he actually found himself sparing a glance at the council table to see if there was a sword there.

"I must offer you my heartiest congratulations on your thesis, Doctor Blanke," said the chairman of the examining board.

"A very definite contribution to human knowledge," said another member.

"Thank you, sir. Thank you," said Blanke vaguely in acknowledgment.

"I understand we should address you as Lieutenant Blanke, and not as Doctor Blanke, in the future," remarked the chairman.

"I suppose that's so," agreed Blanke. "I've just received my orders."

"At any rate, you have your Ph.D.," said the chairman, "but I don't expect it will be much use to you in the Navy. Undoubtedly it's your medical degree that interests Uncle Sam at the present time."

The day the last word of the thesis had been typed, the last reference checked, Blanke had sent in his application to join the Navy. Less than a week later the Navy had asked for a copy of his M.D. degree, something he had almost forgotten about during four years of research. And now he was a lieutenant (j.g.) USNR—for years, he knew, that would be far more important than just being a Ph.D.

He went back to his home, and his mother awaited him as he let himself in at the door. She was Doctor Blanke, the same as he was; her vocation had been mathematics, but she had years ago reconciled herself to the fact that her son had chosen to be a mere scientist.

"Well, dear?" she said.

"It's all right, mother."

"I'm glad, dear," she said. "Of course, I never had any doubts."

She might have been expected to discuss his Ph.D. further, but she was a woman as well as a Doctor of Philosophy, and there was something else she could hardly wait to mention.

"There are about a dozen big packages for you, dear," she said.

"My uniforms, I expect," Blanke said.

"Well, aren't you going to open them?" demanded his exasperated mother.

"Of course I will, mother," said he. "In fact, I seem to have heard somewhere that it's illegal for a member of the armed forces to wear civilian clothes now that there's a war."

"I'll help you, dear," said his mother.

Over some of the packages there was a shade of disappointment. "You didn't need any more underclothes, did you, dear?" asked his mother.

Blanke came over and looked at the contents. "That," he decided, "must be the 'six undershirts and six pairs of drawers' they spoke about."

"Your present things are much more suitable," sniffed his mother.

"Here's the khaki," said Blanke, opening another package. He unfolded the coat and held it up for inspection.

"Don't you think you'd better try it on, dear?" said his mother.

She left him while he put on regulation shirt and coat and trousers and tied the regulation tie. When he called her in again, he was standing before the mirror, trying to appear unconcerned at the first sight of himself in uniform.

"You look quite handsome, dear," she said, and only a mother could have thought that the gangling Blanke, with his laboratory pallor and scholarly shoulders, was "quite handsome." Blanke turned back to the mirror.

"Just a minute," said his mother, diving into one of the packages. "Here's something else you have to have." She produced the shoulder boards with their gold stripes.

"Yes, of course," agreed Blanke. "They show my rank. Let's put 'em on."

He buttoned them on his shoulders, and his mother handed him the regulation Navy cap. Blanke did not find much reassurance in the reflection that stared back at him out of the mirror. The United States Navy cap of 1942 did not sit well over a long, intellectual face; the coat was startlingly new and did not fit him very well. A more objective eye than Blanke's or his mother's would have thought he looked less like a Naval officer than like a scarecrow that had oddly acquired a new Naval uniform.

To be out in the street was a little disturbing; it seemed as if every eye were on him, even though he assured himself that by now Naval officers were common enough to attract no notice. After he dismounted from the bus in the vicinity of the Naval District Headquarters, he realized that uniformed men were saluting him as they passed. As he entered the doors, he wondered if he should take off his cap. He knew that the Navy had odd customs to which he would have to conform, so he drew himself up to the full height of his gangling six feet three and spoke stiffly down to a seaman's stocky five feet four in what he decided was a peculiarly inefficient way of asking where he could find the transportation officer.

He said, "Thank you"—surely Naval discipline did not ban that minor politeness—and turned away to follow the instructions given him. And then he entered into an encounter which was, in time to come, to save his life and the lives of fifty other men. A burly figure in khaki had intercepted him.

"Excuse me, sir."

"Yes?" asked Blanke.

"Could you spare me a minute before you go to the transportation desk, sir?"

"Yes, I suppose so." Blanke remembered to look at the shoulder boards; these were decorated each with a thin band of alternate blue and gold, and Blanke had no idea what rank this indicated, but he was reassured by the fact that he was being addressed as "sir," even though the man who spoke to him had snow-white hair. This individual looked around as if considering what action to take.

"This way, sir," he said, making up his mind. He led Blanke to a small office at the side of the entrance hall, and at a jerk of his thumb the three seamen sitting there at desks got up and left. When the door closed behind them, Blanke found himself being looked at with a sort of kindly forbearance that puzzled him.

"You've just joined, sir?"

"Yes."

"You haven't been to indoctrination school yet?"

"No," replied Blanke, who had never even heard of indoctrination school.

"Are you on your way there, sir?"

"No. I'm going to join my ship."

"Your ship, sir!" The astonishment was profound. "Well, you must excuse me, sir, but you can't go there like that."

"Why, what's wrong?"

"Everything, sir, if you'll excuse me. Those shoulder boards. You're wearing 'em the wrong way round, sir. You should have the points inward so the stripes aren't up under your neck. Here, let me do it for you, sir. . . . That's better. And these buttons—you keep them done up, all the time. And the pocket flaps should be out, not in."

By the time everything had been twitched into position, even Blanke was aware of the improvement.

"Thank you," he said with genuine gratitude. He knew he had much to learn, and this would be as good a time to start as any. "Who is it I'm thanking? What do those stripes mean?"

"Warrant bo'sun, sir. Warrant Bosun Dean. Thirty-seven years' service, but they won't let me go to sea now. You don't mind me speaking to you like this, sir?"

"Mind? I'm grateful to you, of course. I have to learn sometime."

"It's too bad they're sending you to sea without any indoctrination at all. But I know they're short of doctors. What ship, sir?"

Blanke had to stop and think, for one name meant no more to him than another. "The *Boon*."

"*Boon*? DD."

"DD?"

"Destroyer, sir."

Dean tried to conceal the pity he felt for a man who did not know what a "DD" meant and yet was going to be pitchforked into one.

"That's one of the smaller ships, I take it," said Blanke.

"You're darn right, sir," agreed Dean. "Let me show you the way to the transportation desk."

Blanke was learning fast; when he arrived at the desk he was much relieved that the glance the transportation officer gave him was very different from the glances he had received so far. He was looked at as if he were just one more raw lieutenant in the medical corps, and that was an immense step upward.

"Priority Four," said the transportation officer, examining Blanke's orders. "You could be here for weeks if we try to fly you out. But you've got to go. They want doctors."

He opened first one file and then another and ran through them without result. Then another idea struck him, and he reached for a third file.

"That's it," he said. "We can kill two birds with one stone. You're ready to go on board, I suppose?"

"Well, yes," said Blanke.

"Tonight?"

"Of course, if it's necessary."

"It's necessary, all right. *Wilhelmina*—Dutch registry, chartered transport, Dutch officers, Javanese crew. She's taking an antiaircraft-artillery outfit out to Nouméa. They haven't an Army doctor with them, and we can fit you in all right. I'll get your orders endorsed. Come back in ten minutes."

Blanke walked away a little dazed, but trying to appear as if he were perfectly accustomed to being ordered to sail at a moment's notice with a Javanese crew to a place he had never heard of. He was grateful when bosun Dean appeared.

"Did they give you any orders, sir?" he asked, and Blanke told him. "*Wilhelmina*. She's a fast transport—one of the ships that got away when the Japs overran the Dutch East Indies. Look here, sir, would you care to come and wait in my office while they type out your orders?"

Blanke was glad to accept, was glad to take the proffered chair and the proffered cigarette. The transition was continuing. The eagle powers of observation that for four years had expended themselves down the tube of a microscope were beginning to devote themselves now to the human beings and the material things that constituted his new world. He was aware of the concern, almost paternal, with which Dean was regarding him.

"It's only now that they've decided to put doctors into every destroyer, sir," explained Dean. "Only one in four in peacetime. But now the DD's have twice as many men on board. And those ships fight—more likely to fight than the battle wagons are."

"I see," said Blanke.

He would have to study the technique of naval warfare—and make plans how best to give rapid care to a crowd of wounded men in a shell-torn steel hull. Dean was shaking his head with something of sorrow—no, sympathy—in his expression.

"You don't know *anything*, do you, sir?" he said.

"I'm afraid I don't. I'll have to do some reading."

"I wish we was going to be in the same ship, sir," said Dean. "I could teach you a lot, quick."

"I wish we were," said Blanke with sincerity.

Dean's eyes strayed to something on the desk before him. Then he took the plunge.

"Look, Doc," he said. "I won't have the chance to make a Navy man out of you, but here's a book. Take it and learn something about the Navy." It was a largish, bluebound book that he offered.

"That's very kind of you," said Blanke, taking it; he did not know yet that his life depended on his taking it. It was the *Bluejacket's Manual*, and as he ran through the pages, all sorts of headings met his eye—"Uniform Regulations," "Types of Navy Ships," "Routines Aboard Ship" and more advanced subjects, like "Communications and Signaling" and "Boat Seamanship."

"Thank you again," said Blanke. "This must be just what I need."

"You're very welcome," said Dean. "I hope you find it useful. You'll have plenty of time for reading in the *Wilhelmina*—and your orders'll be ready by now, I expect, sir."

Those orders took Blanke on board the *Wilhelmina* that night. He walked down the gangway onto the first deck—except for ferryboats—that he had ever trodden in his life. There were soldiers and packing-cases everywhere. Someone with dark skin—Javanese, Blanke guessed—passed him on to a harassed individual who said, 'Dis vay, pliss' and led him to a cabin where a fat Dutchman in shirt sleeves sat at a desk and read Blanke's orders and groaned.

"O.K.," he said at length. "You slip here."

"Here?"

The little cabin seemer to be completely full, with a desk and a bed and miscellaneous packages, but a wave of the fat Dutchman's arm indicated that there was an upper bed against the wall.

"I'm de purser," said the fat man. "I slip here." He indicated the lower bed, then said, "I am busy."

Blanke went quietly, nor was he averse to seeing something more of this first ship of his. As he entered a corridor, a door opened, revealing an Army officer who noticed his uniform and politely stood by the door for him to enter. It was a small room full of tobacco smoke and crowded with men who made him welcome and introduced themselves, the officers of the antiaircraft unit whose enlisted men thronged the deck.

"Glad to find we have a doctor with us after all," said one of the captains, and Blanke forbore to comment on the remark.

He was content to sit silent, for the officers, he was glad to observe, were as excited as he was and soon left him out of the conversation when he offered no contribution to it. After a time one of the lieutenants, at a nod from one of the captains, left for the purpose, as he said, of "seeing the boys into bed." Blanke saw his opportunity to say good night, made his way back by a miracle to the purser's cabin and entered it to find the purser stretched out on the lower bed, still checking through papers and not in the least inclined to conversation.

Dr. Blanke's First Command

Blanke discovered how to lower his bed, just as he would
have found out the principle of some novel piece of laboratory
apparatus, and he climbed up and in. He glanced at the three
books he had taken to bed with him, put down the *Bluejacket's
Manual,* picked up and discarded *Wounds and Burns,* did the
same with *Preventive Medicine in Tropical Climates,* and
went back to the *Bluejacket's Manual* again. He was tired
enough to go to sleep quite shortly, with the light on and the
Bluejacket's Manual on his chest.

So it was in this way that Malcolm Blanke went to sea for
the first time, a queer introduction to Naval life, and yet one
that early enough made plain to him the salient characteristics
of life at sea in wartime—monotony, overcrowding, lack of
privacy. In the *Wilhelmina* the United States officers shared
the quarters of the Dutch officers, which meant that three
men lived where one lived before; the sergeants shared with
the ship's bosun and the stewards, about four men to one pre-
war berth, while the soldiers, 200 of them, could spread themselves where twelve passengers had once lived in comfort. And
through all this the Javanese crew flitted like ghosts, going
about the ship's business as if all these others did not exist.

There was little to do; there was very little that could be
done in those cramped conditions. Twice a day there was boat
drill and abandon-ship drill; there was physical drill; there were
classes in the theory of antiaircraft gunnery, and not even the
blue Pacific sky could brighten those. For twenty-four hours
the prospect of arriving at the romantic Hawaiian Islands lifted
the pall of boredom, but the pall closed down all the thicker
when the *Wilhelmina* steamed out again into the endless Pacific after only eighteen hours' stay, during which not a soldier
set foot on shore.

The one man in the ship who was free of boredom was,
naturally, Blanke. He was a true scholar, and here he was
congenially employed in study; and the tasks he set himself

had the unusual quality of being planned for practical ends. He had to make himself ready for a new life; there would be fantastic demands made upon him, and he had to prepare himself to meet them. With the intense concentration of a scholar, he read the books he had with him; to achieve that concentration he spent most of his time stretched out in the upper berth of the purser's cabin, for the purser was a man of few words who left him alone and allowed him a privacy impossible to find in the crowded wardroom or on the noisy deck. He read his professional books with care, calling up memories of his life as a hospital intern to fill in the gaps. He would lay his book down, gaze up at the deck beams overhead and take himself, step by step, through an emergency appendectomy, for instance. That was easier then trying to picture himself handling casualties in a destroyer under fire, but he rigorously made himself visualize those possible situations as well.

Naturally he was methodical about all this; no one without method could have devised the scheme of research which had resulted in his Ph.D. thesis. He spent his mornings in study of his professional books, with a break for sick call, which he attended at the request of the officer commanding the troops, but at which nothing ever showed up which could not have been safely left to the medical corporal. Two hours in the afternoon he devoted to acquiring a tan, with nicely judged proportions of shade and sunshine, because he knew he would be much exposed to tropical suns in the future. And the rest of his time he read the *Bluejacket's Manual,* and this was the hardest work of his day. It called for an effort of will to concentrate on the thousands of new facts presented in those 800 crowded pages. But he made himself learn them, conscientiously setting himself to answer the quizzes at the ends of the chapters to test his knowledge.

Some of the knowledge was obviously advantageous; he learned about specialty marks and insignia, and in the few moments when he could be alone, he taught himself to salute in the prescribed method. He read about Personal Hygiene and First Aid to inform himself about what the Navy thought officially about these things; that was easier than the Manual of Arms and Close Order Drill, but he worked through those before applying himself to the more interesting chapters on Types of Navy Ships and Shipboard Routine. It was hard to study the technique of Cleaning and Painting, but the General Safety Precautions, of course, had a direct bearing on his future duties. He read everything and he conscientiously stored everything away in his remarkable memory. When he reached the glossary at the end, and admitted to himself that he knew the meaning of every term in it, from "abaft" to "yoke," he felt an actual sense of loss in that he had no further difficult work to occupy his mind—and the *Wilhelmina* was still not due to arrive at Nouméa for another four days.

That was when tragedy struck; that was when Blanke learned that those long periods of tedium that characterize Naval life in wartime can be terminated in a single second.

Blanke was in his bunk dozing, his open book on his chest, when the torpedo exploded. He woke, only conscious that something violent had happened. The thundering noise he heard next second he could not explain to himself; it was the sound of the water, flung hundreds of feet into the air, bursting over the upper works of the *Wilhelmina*. Then there was a momentary silence, a dead, dead silence, in the midst of which the *Wilhelmina* lay suddenly over toward one side, rolling him against the bulkhead. He found the light switch and pressed it, and there was no result; he clicked it twice more before he realized that the electric power was off. Down below him the purser was talking volubly yet quietly in Dutch, and then Blanke heard a whistle blowing outside, its staccato notes bearing a message of great urgency.

He knew now that the *Wilhelmina* had been torpedoed, that

she was lying helpless, without power, without even steam for the siren, and that she was heeling over in her death agony. He hauled himself up against the list out of bed. Those urgent whistle notes outside conveyed something of panic, and for two or three seconds that panic infected him; he was blundering frantically in the darkness of the cabin before he pulled himself together. He had learned by painful experience in the laboratory and operating theater that haste and carelessness brought disaster—that reaction came fast, and pride came only second. He was the only Naval officer in the ship and he was not going to show fear. He forced his mind into its usual orderly way of thought, only incidentally observing—like a footnote to a thesis—the physiological symptoms of tension manifesting themselves as he found his shoes and his life jacket. Then he made his way up the sloping deck to the door on the heels of the purser, and out into the windy darkness toward his station for "abandon ship."

For many years after the torpedoing of the *Wilhelmina* he was able to recall clear-cut details of the abandoning of the ship; his mind, trained to observation, noted these details of a strange and new experience and stored them away. He learned about discipline. There were voices in the darkness; there was the tone of bravado in which unseen soldiers cracked jokes about their desperate situation, and there was the note of hysteria in other voices, and the stillness that ensued when the voice of one of the artillery lieutenants—cracking a little with strain and yet under control—ordered silence.

"Don't act like kids," added the lieutenant. "You're men." Blanke at thirty-one felt, even at that moment, an odd twinge at hearing someone of twenty-four speaking like that to soldiers of twenty.

The voice of the Dutch third mate, stumbling over his English, could now be heard.

"All right, thank you," said the lieutenant, and then to the soldiers, "Get into the boat."

Several flashlights made a pool of light in the darkness, and out of the pool the men climbed in, hastily but with hardly a sign of panic, although another rasping order from the lieutenant was necessary to impose silence again as the crowding began. Blanke stood waiting his turn beside the Army officers. He felt someone plucking at his sleeve. Someone—the second mate, he thought, but he could not be sure in the darkness—thrust a piece of paper into his hand.

"Position and course," said the man and then hastened off again toward the next boat before Blanke could reply. He put the paper into his pocket, ready to hand it over to whoever would be in command of the boat, and then there was a ridiculous moment of politeness as to whether he should climb in before or after the lieutenant. Then they sprang in together, pushing in among the soldiers, and after them came two of the Javanese deck hands, silent as always and insinuating themselves between the close-packed bodies on the thwarts.

There were Dutch orders shouted from the deck, and a clanking of machinery. The boat lurched and swung hideously in the darkness, crashed against the ship's side, swung and hit the invisible water with a splash amid yells from the soldiers, and then came soaring up on a black invisible wave and rolled horribly, as if she were going to turn over, righted herself at what seemed the last possible second, and then sank down again more unpleasantly than any elevator Blanke had ever experienced. Not until much later did he come to realize how fortunate they were to have reached the water at all without capsizing; the Javanese deck hands had done a neat piece of work at bow and stern.

It was the blackest overcast night anyone could imagine; the *Wilhelmina* was already out of sight, the more so as the soldiers who had flashlights in the boat were using them freely

—one shone straight into Blanke's face and left him quite blinded.

"What do we do next, sir?" asked the artillery lieutenant beside him.

"I can't see a thing," was all Blanke could say at the moment.

The lieutenant lifted his voice in a bellow as he ordered the flashlights extinguished. "Save 'em until you need 'em," he said.

The boat lurched and rolled again, soaring up and then dropping down, the abrupt descent marked by wails from the soldiers. The Pacific swell which the *Wilhelmina* hardly noticed had free play on the small boat; moreover, the brisk trade wind was turning her round slowly in a series of circles, so that each successive swell met her at a different angle, and her rolling and lurching were unpredictable in the darkness.

"Parm me," said the lieutenant, with a blurry attempt at politeness, and then he was horribly seasick—so, judging from the sounds, were most of the soldiers. So was Blanke, after struggling with his symptoms for several minutes. He had never known such misery as overcame him then. The world was utterly pitiless, and he was hopeless and useless, and death would be welcome when it came, especially when the boat rolled wildly again, from far over to one side to far over to the other; a good deal of water slapped in, calling forth startled cries from the men it wetted.

Luckily for everyone concerned, that scientific mind of Blanke continued to function. It could not help analyzing the reasons for that uncontrolled and unpredictable motion of the boat. It was unpredictable simply because it was uncontrolled. The boat was spinning, slowly but helplessly, under the influence of the wind and should be brought under control so as to meet the rollers end on. Blanke's mind went back into the high-school physics and mechanics he had studied fourteen years before, picked out the relevant facts and proceeded to build up suggestions upon them. If something could be put up to catch the wind at the tail end—at the stern—the boat would turn like a weathercock and point into the wind and, presumably, into the waves. That would be a good idea, but he did not see how it could be done in the dark. Similarly, if something could drag in the sea at the other end—at the bow— the boat would trail back from it, with bows to wind and sea. That might work very well if it could be done, but Blanke was not too sure how to set about it; it was the crowding and the darkness, in other words, which prevented Blanke from reinventing the sea anchor that night.

The rudder, of course, would only function if the boat had some motion of its own through the water. Of course! The boat had an engine. If that were set running, someone could hold the rudder and steer her so as to meet the waves properly. He remembered that while he was waiting his turn to get into the boat, he had heard one of the other boats, with an engine running, leaving the ship.

"Hadn't we better get the engine started?" he said to the artillery lieutenant and realized as he said it that the lieutenant was too far gone with seasickness to be rational.

Blanke would have to deal with it himself. With the need for instant action, he put aside the temptation to follow up a new line of thought regarding the effect of military discipline on the young men crowded into the boat; they were used to receiving orders and drilled into obeying them. No time for such thoughts now. Blanke got cautiously off his thwart and began to push his way in the direction in which one of the Javanese deck hands had disappeared when they got in the boat. He had to climb over shoulders; he trod on bodies lying in the bottom, bodies that hardly resented the pressure of his foot.

"Where's that sailor?" he demanded. "Where's that Javanese?"

"Here, sir—back here," croaked a voice.

Blanke shook the Javanese's shoulder. "Motor. Engine," he
said.

The Javanese said something in reply. Blanke felt his wrist
held and his hand guided; that was the tiller—he knew the
word from the glossary in the *Bluejacket's Manual*—a short
piece of iron or wood used to turn the rudder. It swung unre-
sisting in his hand; of course, that would be the case if the boat
had no motion through the water. The Javanese had left his
side; Blanke had the impression that the seaman was climbing
forward by the route he himself had followed, over the heads
and shoulders of the crowded soldiers. He waited tensely; he
heard the Javanese call out something to his compatriot, who
answered. He heard noises and expostulations which indicated
that soldiers were being heaved out of the way; he heard a
clatter and clanking of metal—during this time the boat had
pitched and rolled excruciatingly a dozen times, and three
times water had slopped in over the sides.

There came a sudden roar of the engines, and Blanke felt the
rudder come to life under his hand. The roar ceased; the rudder
died, but then the engine roared again, confidently, with every
promise of permanence, and the water over the stern boiled,
and the rudder bit. They were frightening, those first few seconds; it took Blanke that long to grasp the technique of turning the tiller the opposite way—during those seconds the boat
slithered precariously along a crest and came nearer to capsizing than ever before, amid cries of dismay from the passengers. But by the time the boat had completed the circle, Blanke
had matters almost under control. He met the next wave bows
on; there was infinite satisfaction at first in doing so, in feeling
the boat climbing the slope, but when they reached the crest
and put their bows down and their stern up, and shot down the

farther side, it was not so comfortable—in fact, it felt hideously dangerous.

He wanted to saw at the rudder, but restrained himself with the thought that that would be more dangerous still, but then his doubts were resolved by a sudden drop in the pitch of the engine's roar. He could feel the speed moderate, and the boat breasted the next slope more satisfactorily still and pitched over the crest in a manner quite restrained, so that some sort of small cheer came from the passengers capable of any sensation at all. Blanke guessed that the Javanese at the engine had throttled down, and he was grateful, even though he had little attention to spare for them; he had to concentrate on the feel of the wind on his face, on the lurch of the boat and on reminding himself to pull the tiller to the left—to port— when he wanted to head to the right—to starboard.

In a few minutes it was becoming second nature to him. Seasickness was forgotten; there was actually something exhilarating in handling the boat like this as she chugged valiantly forward in the dark. Where he was going he did not know, but he reconciled himself to that by telling himself that until daylight should come and new arrangements could be made, he was doing the only safe thing. Thinking along that line, he realized why there was no ship's officer in the boat—this was the chief engineer's boat, and he could guess what had happened to the chief engineer. The instant helplessness of the *Wilhelmina* after the torpedo struck told of a hit in the engine room; the chief engineer had died for his country.

That gloomy train of thought was interrupted by his overhearing a fragment of conversation among the soldiers just in front of him.

"There's lockers under these seats. Let's have your flash a minute, Joe."

"Leave those lockers alone," snapped Blanke; strain and excitement put an edge on his voice.

In four years of research he had had painful experience with overenthusiastic, or stupid, or inquisitive laboratory assistants, and he could guess at what disasters might ensue if prying fingers got to work on those lockers. But he was astonished at the intensity of his speech—he would never have snapped at technical assistants in that way, but then his life was not in danger.

The fact was that the steadying of the boat's motion and the comforting thought circulating among the soldiers that the Navy was now in charge, were encouraging the more active of the young soldiers to indulge their innate restlessness.

"Move over, can't you?" said a voice.

"Get off my feet, you big slob," said another.

"Wish I had a drink," said a third.

It seemed as if in no time at all the unseen passengers were beginning to surge about in the boat; Blanke, keyed up to the highest pitch, was acutely conscious of variation in the trim, even if he did not use that word to himself. He only knew that it felt dangerous when the boat went down on one side and that it was likely to interfere with his steering. He opened his mouth to expostulate—and then shut it again while he rehearsed what he was going to say. He had to give an order; he had to shout into the wind, so that he would have to use all his lung power. He took a deep breath, told himself that he must display no agitation and then let himself go.

"Sit still, all of you!" he yelled.

It was gratifying that he made so much noise, and the result was gratifying, too, in that there was quiet in the boat and that someone, presumably the lieutenant, endorsed his order.

"Sergeant, see that the men keep still over there."

"Yes, sir."

There was much to be said for discipline when it produced such results. But, on the other hand, the cessation of the bustling in the boat and his growing familiarity with the handling of the tiller gave Blanke an opportunity to think again. He began to wonder what would happen next, and what he ought to do—if anything. He was the biggest fraud who had ever held a tiller. When daylight came, decisions would have to be reached. They would have to set that course which was written on the paper in his pocket. "They"—whom did he mean by "they"? The Javanese? The artillery lieutenant? He had an uneasy feeling that by "they" he really meant himself.

There must be a compass in the boat—otherwise there was no reason for the paper with the course written on it. He presumed he could set a course. He had no idea where he was—the word had gone round the ship that they were four days from Nouméa, and four days would mean what? A thousand miles, fifteen hundred miles? There certainly would not be gasoline to last all that time. They would have to use the sails—he had seen masts in the boat and presumed that there were sails. He found himself hoping devoutly that the Javanese deck hands knew something about sailing a boat. There was a chance that daylight would reveal one or more of the other boats near them, but Blanke could guess how small a chance that was; he could work out in his mind how limited was the horizon from a small boat and how widely dispersed the boats could become during several hours with a brisk wind blowing.

As he reached that conclusion it became borne in upon him that he could now see something of the boat and its crowded passengers; he could see the heads and shoulders in front of him as dark masses in a lighter medium. Daylight was actually coming, and he stirred in his seat to discover he was horribly stiff, and his hand ached from its viselike grip on the tiller, and he was shivering with cold.

"Well, there it is, boys," said a voice in the boat, and everyone started chattering at once—at least, everyone who was not too cold or seasick to chatter. The light increased rapidly, and he could see the unshaven cheeks and the drawn features of the packed crowd. He could see the two Javanese crouching by the engine, and the young lieutenant perched on a thwart near them. The lieutenant rose with infinite stiffness and pushed his way to the stern of the boat and into a minute space beside Blanke.

"What do we do now, sir?" he asked, speaking in a muffled tone in an effort not to be overheard by the soldiers crowded all round.

The question, and the manner of asking it, confirmed Blanke in his certainty that the artillery lieutenant, although perfectly qualified to command an antiaircraft platoon, had not the least idea what to do when adrift in the Pacific with fifty castaways.

"Let's look round," said Blanke, temporizing.

The lieutenant agreed without making any move to follow up the suggestion, and Blanke knew he had to act. He caught the eye of one of the Javanese by the engine and beckoned to him. Then he handed over the tiller and prepared to stand up. It was not going to be easy.

"Prop me up," he said, coming erect on his aching legs and preparing to mount on the thwart. Half a dozen hands were raised to hold him as he stood, wobbling dangerously in the heaving boat. There was nothing to see; he shifted his feet precariously as he turned to sweep the horizon. There was only the sea, only the long rollers marching toward them. The motion of the boat became more pronounced, and Blanke saw that half, or more than half, of the soldiers, carried away by his example, were scrambling to their feet to look around too; he ought to have expected that. He nearly missed his footing and exclaimed loudly, and the lieutenant had the sense to appreciate the danger.

"Sit down, you men. Sit down, all of you!"

He was obeyed, and Blanke stepped down and reseated himself.

"Nothing in sight," he said, and now he had to think quickly —rather, he did not have to think, but had to implement the decisions which the meditations of the night had forced upon him. He took the scrap of paper from his pocket and studied what was written on it: "Course 222° True. Var 11°E." He could interpret that, all right, thanks to the *Bluejacket's Manual.*

"I have the course here," he said. "I think we'll have to get under sail."

He was painfully conscious that fifty pairs of eyes had him under their scrutiny and that fifty lives might depend on his decisions. The Javanese beside him had caught the last word he said.

"Sail," said the Javanese and then pointed toward the engine. "Motor—stop."

The Javanese backed up his words with an eloquent gesture; he was clearly implying what Blanke had already thought of— that gas was likely to run short any moment.

"You see we'll have to ——" said Blanke to the lieutenant; he was having to struggle against a curious constriction of the throat as he spoke. Then to the Javanese, "All right. Sail."

The Javanese nodded—he even smiled. He returned the tiller to Blanke, stood up and shouted in his own language to his fellow seaman. The two of them became immediately active, and Blanke was relieved to see that their movements were entirely purposeful and that they did not have to refer to him. They scrambled up and down the length of the boat, pushing the soldiers out of their way when necessary; the soldiers watched their actions with dull interest. There was a good deal of upheaval while the Javanese moved the soldiers off the lockers along the sides of the boat and dragged out grimy rolls of canvas and then busied themselves with the lines that came with them. There were two masts laid lengthways in the boat, and the Javanese raised first one and then the other—Blanke

37

noted that they lay in opposite directions, sensibly, so as to call
for the least movement to set them up. Each mast in turn had
its base passed down through holes in the thwarts, and was
settled down with comforting solidity into what Blanke knew
—thanks to his scholar's memory—were called the "steps" below. The wire ropes attached to the tops of the masts were led
out to the sides of the boat and hooked onto these; Blanke
dived into his memory again to come up with the word "stays."
Things were really moving too fast for his mental comfort. Already the Javanese were looking to him for orders, ready to set
the sails. There must be a compass somewhere in the boat,
otherwise he would not have been given that scrap of paper.
Then before him he saw a small varnished trap door, which he
raised in desperation, and underneath it was a compass. There
were the words U. S. NAVY. BuSHIPS. No. 1 COMPASS, engraved
on the ring—these lifeboats, of course had been supplied by
the Navy when the *Wilhelmina* had been chartered.

"I was wondering about a compass," said the artillery lieutenant, and Blanke forbore to say, "Not as much as I was." Instead he devoted himself, gratefully, to the deviation card inside the lid.

He plunged down into his memory again and, like the diver
in the old ballad, came to the surface again with a pearl. "Can
Dead Men Vote Twice?": Compass, Deviation, Magnetic,
Variation, True—that was what the initial letters of those
words stood for; the *Bluejacket's Manual* had told him so. He
could perhaps have worked out the compass course from first
principles, but the mnemonic saved time and trouble, besides
reminding him forcibly of the need for correction. A few seconds' study of the deviation card revealed the huge importance
of it, for it was a cumulative and not a self-canceling correction.
He had to subtract no less than 27 from 222.

With the pencil he had taken from his pocket he wrote
down the resultant figure 195, on his scrap of paper, and then

checked through his working again, swallowing hard with excitement as he did so. An uncorrected error of twenty-seven degrees in the course could mean a difference of dozens of miles in their destination, the difference perhaps between life and a lingering death out in the wastes of the Pacific. It was almost inconceivable that a man should be facing that grim possibility when less than three weeks earlier his chief doubt had been whether he would be awarded a Ph.D.

Now everybody was waiting for him again. Now he had to reach fresh decisions. He pinned his faith on the Javanese and beckoned to one of them and then gestured toward the tiller; to his relief he received a nod in return. They switched off the engine, and the man he had beckoned to came scrambling aft, where they made room for him at the tiller. Blanke showed his written 195 and pointed to the compass, and was reassured again by a nod. The Javanese understood and shouted in his own language to his compatriot and was answered in a rapid-fire conversation.

It was a moment of tense excitement—now that the engine had ceased running, the boat was beginning to wallow aimlessly again over the rollers. The other Javanese was pushing his way through the crowd and putting ropes in the men's hands; and then with gestures he called on them to pull.

"Heave ho!" shouted someone, apparently thinking that was amusing.

With a creaking and groaning the sails began to rise up the masts. There was a moment of chaos, a moment when Blanke felt consuming doubt which later he realized was fear. The sails flapped with a thunderous din, and the boat lurched and pitched horribly. The Javanese at the sails was leaping about the boat, over heads and shoulders, attending to this and that. The boat lay over momentarily worse than ever, and then the Javanese at the tiller pulled it far over and she steadied herself. The sea bubbled round the rudder, and inconceivably, order emerged from the chaos. The Javanese at the sails was still leaping about, pulling at ropes, but obviously he was only making minor adjustments.

Blanke looked at the compass, and there was the lubber's line swinging close about 195 degrees. He looked up at the sails, and they were bellying out, but under restraint, and the Javanese attending to them was hauling them in to a slightly closer angle, with the help of soldiers, into whose hands he was putting the ropes. He was pushing and gesticulating at some of the men to induce them to move across the boat and sit on the other side—that made an appreciable difference to the feeling of stability. For the boat was lying over, with the wind coming sideways at them; Blanke's mind promptly grappled with the deduction that on a course of 222 degrees True, in an area where the southeast trades prevailed, the wind would naturally come in over the side; he looked up at the sails again and down at the boat and thought about the triangle of forces at work which would drive the boat in a direction different from that of the wind.

And it was surprising, too, to see how differently the boat was behaving. Even though she was not heading directly into the waves, she was not lurching so wildly nor so menacingly as she did when not under control. Her behavior was actually purposeful; under the steadying influence of the sails, she was yielding to the rollers in a measured fashion, with a rise and a roll and a pitch that actually had some aesthetic quality about it. The water—the "wake," that was the word—bubbled behind him; a few fragments of spray were flying from the bows. Blanke was astonished at the discovery that this might almost be thought of as pleasant; and when, some moments later, the clouds parted sufficiently to allow the rising sun to shine on his back, he contrasted his previous feeling of despairing misery with what might almost be described now as well-being. He caught the eye of the Javanese at the tiller; busy though this man might be, darting vigilant glances up at the sails and down at the compass and over the side at the rollers, he yet could find a moment to grin at him in a sort of conspiratorial confidence.

There was a perceptible change in the soldiers too. Except for two unfortunates who were still far gone in seasickness, they were all talking at once. Cigarettes were being smoked in such numbers that the wind was carrying off a small trail of smoke—to "leeward," that was the word. And already there were cries of despair as cigarettes were counted up; there were men with none and men with a few and none with many. Every soldier in the boat was cursing the suddenness of the alarm which had set them adrift without a chance of gathering up precious possessions. Then, almost immediately, there were remarks made loudly by one and another, and questions asked of the sergeants, obviously intended to reach the lieutenant's ears. The soldiers were hungry and thirsty and they wanted to eat and drink.

The lieutenant turned to Blanke. "Any orders, sir?"

Blanke could not answer immediately. The difference in the size of his collar insignia—smaller than that of the Army— marked him as the only Navy officer in the boat. But that no more qualified him for the command than did his greater age. If by chance there had been present the lowliest, most newly joined seaman second class, that seaman would legally be in command. The oak leaf and acorn on Blanke's collar specifically disqualified him: the *Bluejacket's Manual* was quite definite about that. Yet, despite all this, Blanke could not close his mental eyes to the obvious fact that the course of previous events had conferred the command on him. And reluctantly he faced the next fact, which was that if he were to disclaim all responsibility and throw in his hand, the result might easily be disastrous for all on board. There were many long difficult days ahead, and the occupants of the boat had come to look on him as possessed of all the technical knowledge necessary. That confidence, baseless though it might be, was an asset of supreme importance. He could not evade the trust reposed in him; yet he still longed to temporize.

The boat corkscrewed over a roller, and the water that had entered the boat surged over the bottom boards and slapped against his ankles—it had done that a hundred times already and had ceased to attract his notice until now, when he was looking for an excuse to evade decision. He seized on the chance; and that brought to his notice what the bottom of the boat was like, after that horrible night.

"Don't you think the first thing to do," he said mildly, "is to clean up? Look at all this."

The lieutenant might be a man who feared responsibility, but he was open to suggestion. "Quite right, sir," he said and then he lifted up his voice. "At ease!"

It was interesting how the commotion died away—interesting to notice the easy manner of the lieutenant, accustomed to command and expecting to be obeyed.

"We're going to get the boat cleaned up," the lieutenant went on. "Sergeant Schwartz, I want everyone at work."

Discipline, not too deeply rooted among those young soldiers, had a hard struggle against the complete novelty of the situation. The buzz of talk reasserted itself, but the lieutenant was ready for that.

"No breakfast until the boat's policed," he said. "Sergeant Schwartz, you heard my order."

So now, while the soldiers were at work bailing out and clearing up, the lieutenant turned to Blanke to discuss the next problem, which he had already raised by his last speech.

"What do we do about that, sir?" he asked. "What about food and water?"

Blanke was already turning over in his mind what the *Bluejacket's Manual* had to say about Survival Afloat and he supplemented that with what he had learned during his medical training. He opened the locker beside him and saw with relief that it was filled with small cans—he really had not doubted that it would be, but he was relieved, all the same.

"How long before we're rescued, sir?" asked the lieutenant.

Blanke felt acute irritation. He wanted to turn upon the lieutenant and point out that he did not know where he was, had only a vague idea of where he was going and could form no estimate of the speed between these points. The violence of his feelings surprised him; it was really shocking to find that there was something alluring about the prospect of losing his temper and flaring out, uncontrolled, in a wild outburst to compensate himself for the things life was doing to him and for the responsibilities piling on him.

The realization steadied him; it was the more easy to maintain his self-control because he was interested in the discovery that he was liable to such fits of rage even though he could not remember ever having had one before. Lastly, he remembered the *Bluejacket's Manual* again. There were a few lines there about the initial feeling of "relief and elation" when finding oneself in a lifecraft away from the sinking wreck, followed by a warning that these attitudes might "worsen into irritability and preoccupation." That book was certainly accurate. He almost smiled at the thought and, in consequence, could make himself talk with studied calm. He posed as if he had been accustomed all his life to dealing with problems of death and survival.

"We'll have to go carefully right from the start," he said heavily and unemotionally.

"Of course, sir."

"Each of these cans is a day's ration for one man. We'll have to halve that. Two meals a day—one can between four men at each meal."

"Yes, sir."

Blanke looked round again; his mind recovered another word from the glossary—those small barrels were called "breakers," but whatever their name, there were not too many of them.

"Of course, water's more important still," he said, in the same emotionless voice. "One pint a day—a quarter of a pint four times a day."

"Yes, sir. We'll start as we mean to go on," said the lieutenant helpfully.

That was indeed how they went on. By the second meal all novelty had worn off, and the healthy twenty-year-old appetites of the soldiers were insulted at the attempt to satisfy them with four sugar tablets and two malt tablets and one stick of chewing gum. A quarter of a pint of water went in two gulps, almost unnoticed. There were signs of that depression and reaction which the *Manual* warned against. The sun, which had so gratefully warmed them at dawn, turned into an enemy, fierce and unrelenting.

It was lucky for everyone in the boat that Blanke's orderly and active mind—the mind of a trained observer, seeking always a vent for its activity—was in charge. He noted at once that it would be impossible for the two Javanese to attend all the time to the tiller and the sails; moreover—grim thought—one of them might die. It was necessary to train replacements, so every half hour a fresh man came back to the tiller and studied how, under the grinning tuition of the Javanese (those Javanese stayed miraculously cheerful and were always ready with a polite grin as a substitute for words) to keep the boat steady on her course and to stand by what Blanke doubtfully called the "sheets"—he could not be quite sure of his memory regarding that word.

There was the horrible cramped discomfort of sitting up in the boat. Blanke realized that it was hardly necessary for the life jackets still to be worn. Removing them added considerably to the available room, and, as well, the life jackets could be used as a mattress in the one available space in the middle of the boat, whereon nine men at a time—nine out of fifty-four—could indulge themselves in the unspeakable luxury of stretching out straight and going to sleep.

Three hours of sleeping stretched out was very comforting and refreshing. Blanke chose that interval because then the cycle shifted through the day and gave everyone an equal chance of sleeping in the dark or in the daylight.

Naturally it was not very long before the survivors wanted to know how long the voyage would last, and Blanke, warned by his experience with the lieutenant, managed to decide upon an answer.

"Let's say a thousand miles," he said. "It may be more, but let's say that to start with."

At once everyone wanted to know at what speed they were traveling. No one could be sure, and even in the steady trade winds their speed was obviously variable. It took Blanke half a day to come up with the solution. Probably it was not an original reinvention of the old-fashioned ship's log; more likely some scrap of schoolboy reading had survived in Blanke's memory. At any rate, he took one of the long lines in the boat, knotted it at six-foot lengths (Sergeant Schwartz was just six-feet tall, he said), attached a couple of empty ration cans to the end and let it run out astern while timing it against the second hand of his watch.

So that was another item in the routine, one in which everyone was interested. Every half hour the log was cast, and the calculation made while everyone waited breathlessly. There were groans of despair when the speed was announced as being only 2.1 miles an hour; there was elation when it was 3.9—and another figure added to the column Blanke kept on the back of the deviation card, mounting up toward the arbitrary thousand that Blanke had selected, and only Blanke gave a thought to the fact that each result might easily be 50 per cent in error.

There were other breaks in the day. Early in the very first afternoon one of the Javanese rose hastily from where he was sitting, like a statue, in the middle of the boat, and called the attention of his colleague to something on the horizon. At the sight of what they saw, one of them came hastily back to the tiller while the other went to tend the sails. Blanke saw the squall approaching; he had seen similar ones from the deck of the *Wilhelmina* and had observed them with interest; but if it had not been for the Javanese, he would not have attached the importance to it demanded by an overcrowded small boat.

They dropped the big sail in the middle, which surely must be the mainsail, and they reduced the little triangular sail in front, leaving undisturbed the little rectangular sail on the mast in the stern. By that time, the squall was close upon them. When the boat rose on a wave, Blanke could see a gray line on the surface of the water, straight as if drawn with a ruler, advancing close upon them. Even before it reached them, preliminary gusts of wind roared at them, laying the boat over amid cries of alarm from the soldiers until the Javanese pulled the tiller over, turning the boat into the wind, and then she rode more steadily, while the wind howled about them, and the spray flew in sheets, and finally the rain came deluging down. The sail at the stern produced the weathercock effect that Blanke had already thought of. He ran through the glossary in his mind; what they had done was to "heave to"— an expression with an odd old-time flavor. Yet, with that wind howling and the sea screaming around them, to heave to meant to live; not to do so meant to die. He noted the rigidity with which he was sitting, the intensity with which he felt the greater gusts, his quickened heartbeat and the dryness of his mouth. This was fear again, intense physical fear.

There was a man over there—there was another—as frightened as he was, or even more. Fear could grip sturdy boys who had not completed high school just as much as it could Ph.D.'s. One of them was looking at him with staring eyes as if appealing to him, looking to him for safety or reassurance. Blanke made a huge effort. He told his muscles to relax, he forced his limbs into an easier attitude, he made himself turn toward the Javanese at the tiller with a nod and a smile which he hoped did not appear like the death's head grin he felt it to be. Then he glanced back at the scared soldier with every appearance of casual confidence he could manage. It seemed to help, even though at that moment the squall burst into its final paroxysm, changing direction several times, slightly but sufficiently to lay the boat over, horrifyingly, before she swung to it. Then a final roaring Niagara of rain, and the squall was over. On the far side of it the sun shone, and the sea was blue again, with the great rollers marching mechanically and predictably toward them.

"Say, cap'n," said a voice. "Cap'n."

Blanke realized with an effort that it was he who was being addressed by this title. "Yes?"

"That rain's salt. I've been trying to drink it."

Blanke tried to explain that with the spray flying, any rain would be tainted with sea water. He devoted thought to the question of devising a means to collect pure rain water during a squall, but in all that voyage he never succeeded. It never rained, as it happened, without wind and spray.

But the squall called more forcibly to his attention the problem of "leeway"—so he called it, self-consciously, to himself. The boat would move sideways to some extent with the wind over the side, and when they were hove to, she would drift considerably stern first before the wind. Allowance must be made for that. Blanke drew mental pictures of the triangle of forces at work on the boat, and arbitrarily selected ten degrees as a suitable correction. His announcement of the revised course was received without comment. The new course

47

brought them closer to the wind, and that accentuated the odd aesthetic pleasure of thrashing along with the spray flying from the "weather bow." It was stimulating even to the most faint-hearted and depressed of the passengers.

So depression and despair were combated during that voyage. There was the half-hourly relieving of the tiller and sheets, and the half-hourly heaving of the log, the three-hourly change-over on the life-jacket mattress and the occasional hasty heaving to when squalls approached. They had to heave to each evening as soon as it was too dark to have adequate warning of squalls. Sergeant Schwartz came up surprisingly with a remarkable plan during the dark evenings, for he started a spelling bee. Only a few men agreed to play, but the competition soon grew keen, and the onlookers were interested in spite of themselves. It was inevitable and highly significant that Blanke should be called upon as arbitrator over disputed points of spelling. There were language classes—in other words, attempts to teach English to the two Javanese, while the soldiers listened with amused interest to the polite efforts of the Javanese to explain to them the intricacies of their own language and of Dutch.

Any distraction was better than crouching idle in the boat, waiting for the moment when two sips of water per man was to be rationed out, waiting for four sugar tablets and two malted-milk tablets. Anything was better than to sit in black despair, in melancholy moodiness that might change at any moment into a flare-up of murderous rage. The pettiest, most trivial, most infantile distractions were of help.

Blanke came to learn quickly enough that the fifty young soldiers in the boat were fifty individuals, and not an undifferentiated mass of bristly faces. He came to know all of them, and in the long dark nights he came to know all the hoarse croaking voices, too, one distinct from another. Within a short time he knew the cheerful and the helpful, and the surly and the depressed.

Besides hunger and thirst, there was hideous physical discomfort, sitting eternally—with one blessed interval of stretching out on the mattress every eighteen hours—on unyielding seats. Damp salt on the skin and in the clothes as the spray dried made a man feel as if he would willingly tear off his skin. By the fourth day boils began to appear; nearly every man on board suffered from them. The sixth evening was marked by the presence of enough moon to make it possible to keep sail set for an hour and more after sunset and add a few more daily miles toward that absurd goal of a thousand miles which Blanke had set, and each successive night the period lengthened.

On the thirteenth day at noon they were still heading on their course. The sun was almost exactly overhead, blazing down upon them, the boat was maintaining its monotonous rise and fall, heel and pitch, with all the crowded heads and bodies swaying in unison as it did so. Then Private First Class Sanderson in the bow raised his head.

"Listen, you guys!"

They listened.

"What d'you think you can hear—harps?" croaked a voice.

"Listen!" repeated Sanderson.

Then another man heard it, and another.

"That's a plane!"

Everyone began to scramble to his feet, even the men on the mattress.

"Sit down! Sit down!" shrieked Blanke, his dry throat seeming to split with the effort.

It was one of the most dangerous moments of the voyage; it called for the united influence of the more levelheaded to restrain the excitement and to make the men sit down, fifty heads turning, fifty pairs of eyes searching the sky.

"There it is!"

The little speck was visible to them all.

"Maybe it's a Jap," said Marx the pessimist, but that suggestion could not prevail long with an antiaircraft unit trained in plane identification.

"It's a Kingfisher!"

"Is he going to see us?"

They watched with terrible intensity; some men were uttering prayers, and others blasphemy.

At 2000 feet the plane was heading a little away from them. Then the plane altered course.

"He's seen us!"

They tried to cheer; they started to stand up again.

"Sit down!" shrieked Blanke again—he had a memory of one piece of research wasted and ruined and necessitating restarting, all because of excited haste in the final technique. But if the boat overturned, there would be no restarting.

Straight for them came the plane. It dived and skimmed close above them, then wagged its wings and circled and made it obvious that they had been seen; it was also obvious that the plane would be unable to land on the rough water. Then it turned and headed back the way it had come; the prayers that followed it were prayers of thankfulness now, and the blasphemies were expressions of joy. Then every eye turned upon Blanke, the man who knew everything, to learn how soon they would be rescued.

"Not until tomorrow," said Blanke, doing hasty mental calculations based on the most fragile of data. "Not until tomorrow evening at the very earliest. But we can all have an extra ration of water this minute."

Seeing how utterly ignorant he was regarding the radius of action of a Kingfisher, and what shipping there might be at whatever base the plane had flown from, if it had flown from a land base, the guess was reasonably accurate—it was exactly twenty-four hours before the mine sweeper showed up on the horizon, and twenty-five hours before they were being helped up onto her deck, nearly twenty-six hours before Blanke was cautiously sipping at the cup of coffee which had haunted his unspoken thoughts for fourteen days.

"*Boon?*" said the mine sweeper's captain when Blanke gave the name of his ship in answer to the captain's question. "She's in at Tongatabu this minute—came in as escort to a torpedoed cruiser. You'll be able to join her at once."

Blanke was still too utterly weary to mention the fact that he had believed all this time that he was steering for Nouméa and had never heard of Tongatabu in his life until now. But he had sailed the lifeboat 400 miles straight toward Tongatabu all the same, 400 miles that made the difference between life and death.

So it was at Tongatabu that Blanke first set foot on the deck of a destroyer. It was there that he reported to the officer of the deck in the words he had rehearsed repeatedly after the mine sweeper's captain had taught them to him.

"Lieutenant Malcolm Blanke reporting aboard for duty, sir. I regret to report I have lost my orders while en route, sir."

The officer of the deck smiled politely and—to his credit— not the least broadly.

"We've been expecting you, doctor. But not in this condition. No baggage, I take it? Then I'll take you to the skipper right away."

The Kingfisher had spread the news of the sighted lifeboat the day before, and Commander Angell, captain of the *Boon*, did not need explanations of Blanke's presence. He made Blanke cordially welcome. Then he went on to say, "I'm certainly glad you've arrived, doctor. We've a plague of cockroaches on board, and I expect you to turn to right away to get rid of them."

The First Day of School

SHIRLEY ANN GRAU

The two painters were first. They came—early in the morning while that side of the school was still in the shade—in a rusty Ford truck. They took out one small ladder and a couple of buckets and carried them wearily up the front steps. Swallows flew out, twittering, from their perch on top of the lintel. The painters stretched, sighed, had a final cigarette and began work. They did not bother sanding, though the doors faced west and had blistered and cracked under the fierce heat of the setting suns. The painters wiped off the summer's spider webs and brushed off the dead bugs. Then they put on another coat of blue paint.

They took their time, moving their arms slowly up and down, not talking, but whistling, each a different tune. The paint was lumpy and too thin. It dripped and splattered on the concrete steps. When they had finished, there was a pattern of blue dots drying in the sun, their color a bit brighter than the ones that were spilled last year. A week later the janitor came, swept the floors with sawdust and got a hose and squirted a little water on the grass in the plaza. That grass had been planted in June. The Garden Club had bought it, the very best St. Augustine grass, and planted it in the little front plaza around the flagpole. But the rains hadn't come, and the tufts of grass turned brown and dried. By the first week of September they were still spotted there, like polka dots.

Behind the school was the playground, an open stretch that the WPA had leveled years ago, back in the '30's. It was just 100 yards or so of bare flat space. Then the bleak face of the hill reared up, thirty feet high, its crest trimmed by the straggling picket fences and the privy-shaped tool sheds of adjoining houses.

There wasn't a single speck of grass on the slope of the hill, and there wasn't much more on the playground itself, just hard-packed mud, cracked like china in the sun and flooding like a tide basin in the rain.

On that particular morning in early September a little breeze was lifting up whorls of red dust, and the sun was hot and bright overhead behind a cloudy sky. The crowd had begun gathering early. At first it was just kids. They stacked their bicycles in little groups against the lamp poles at the corners. Some of them, mostly girls, climbed up the trees and worked their way out to the ends of the limbs, the way they would do if they were waiting for a parade.

After a while, when it was a little past seven, others came— men mostly, only a few women. They parked their cars several blocks away and walked down, singly and in little groups, until they were directly in front of the school and across the street. They didn't stand on the sidewalks. They drifted up on the porches of the nearest houses and loitered there.

Sometimes those people came out to join them, and sometimes the front doors were closed and locked firmly in their faces. When that happened, they sat down anyway in the cane-backed porch chairs and rocked themselves slowly.

Perched in a chinaball tree a girl wearing a bright-yellow dress began singing, "Down in nigger alley . . ."

The people on the porches stopped rocking briefly and

glanced up at her. Her voice drifted off, and everybody sat silent, waiting. Mrs. Louise Vandiver parked her car at the town square. The lawn sprinklers were going. She could see the little tin things dancing up and down like children. The two Confederate cannons, the four pyramids of cemented cannon balls dripped and shone under the cloudy sky. Beyond the reach of the sprinklers the cinder paths and the lines of benches were dusty and dry and empty.

Mrs. Louise Vandiver heaved her heavy body out of the car. There was a yellow-painted parking meter in front of her, but she did not bother with it. All of the meters were broken. When they had first been put in, several years ago, people had objected, particularly the country people. So they had banged into them with their trucks until they were twisted into crazy angles and broken. It would have cost too much money to repair them and too much to take them up, so they stayed, a raggedy picket line around the square.

Mrs. Vandiver walked rapidly so that her chins jiggled and beads of sweat popped out on her face. At the side of the city hall she turned down a shady urine-smelling brick path. POLICE DEPT., the letters were so faded they were almost impossible to read.

She stepped inside, saying emphatically in a clear voice, "Albert!"

The man at the desk looked up. "For heaven's sake, Louise."

There were two other men in the room. She nodded to them. "George Fred. Henry." She eased into a chair and took a couple of deep breaths. The room was very hot. She noticed that the windows were closed and the shutters fastened across them. "Anybody back there?" She pointed to the door at the corner of the small room, the door decorated with a plaque done in bright-red gothic script: JAIL. Her son had done that, one year when the sixth grade studied printing in its art class.

"We moved 'em," Albert said wearily, "early this morning." He took out his handkerchief and wiped his bald head. "Still going to tell me you don't expect trouble?"

"Louise," he said, "go home."

She ignored him. "You going to phone the governor?"

"Listen," he said, "I got enough to do without those s.o.b.'s loose in town."

"You and George Fred and Henry—you going to do it alone?"

"Wallace is out there. And I reckon I can get more."

She shook her head. "Nobody in the square this morning."

"I seen that, Louise."

She turned cheerfully to the others. "You boys going to have a busy day."

They grinned uneasily. George Fred said, "I don't like it much."

"Go home, Louise," Albert said.

"I'm leaving," she said. "Reckon I know what I came to find out."

Michael Sanborn kicked down the stand of his bike and went over to join the group of kids sitting under a big hackberry tree. "Hey, man," he said to no one in particular, "beats school, huh?"

John David McConnell rolled over slowly and stared up at him, his pale-blue eyes glinting in the light. "Does your mother know you're out?"

Michael ignored the insult. He sat down in the circle. "Anything been happening?"

The other kids didn't seem to want to talk, so John David said, "Six people got killed, and then they went and got the dogs and turned them loose on the niggers."

"Aw, nuts," Michael said, "come off it, will ya, alligator?"

A very blond boy with a shaved head giggled.

"See him?" John David asked Michael out of the corner of his mouth.

"Who?"

"Who him." A thumb jerked toward the blond boy. "He got a headful, and they shaved him off."

The blond boy only scratched the mosquito bites on his shaved head and stretched out full length, rubbing his stomach on the ground.

"When are the niggers coming?" Michael asked in an impatient voice.

"Going to drive up with machine guns, in big cars."

"Aw, nuts," Michael said.

They stretched out on their backs then, feeling a little aimless and lost, and watched the hot sky through the arching branches of the hackberry.

All of a sudden John David sat up. "Look, there's the cops!"

The patrol car turned the corner and stopped directly in front of the school.

"Jeezam," John David said, "and there's the old fat slob."

Albert Vandiver, leaning against the car, quietly lighting a cigar, trying to pretend he just happened to be standing there.

"Where's the niggers?" John David said. "Man, I want to see them come."

Phil Holloway banged into the kitchen, where his wife was feeding the baby. "Stubborn old fool!" Betty Holloway did not look up; she kept spooning the strained peaches into the open mouth. "She may be your aunt, honey, but she isn't going to pay any more attention to you than to anyone else."

"Do you know what she told me?"

Betty did not answer. She wiped off a crusty smear of peach.

"I have been teaching school for forty-three years, Philip," he mimicked in a high voice, "and I will be teaching this morning."

"She doesn't understand, honey."

Phil said, "She's just plain crazy."

"At six this morning she asked me for a piece of sandpaper."

Phil scratched the back of his neck furiously. "You know why?" Betty said. "The stopper of the perfume bottle was stuck."

"Oh," Phil said. "That's just great."

"Listen to me, honey. She wanted to open it, but it was stuck because she'd sealed it up with wax from last year."

Phil got himself a cup of coffee from the stove.

"Every opening day," Betty said, "she uses it—and I never noticed her to wear any scent the rest of the year. She had on her opening-day dress too. Did you see that?"

"I didn't look at her," Phil said.

"That dress is older than I am, and she put it on this morning."

"Hell," Phil said, "look at this cup. It's got lipstick on it."

"Well," Betty said, "that's because you took it from the pile of dirty dishes. Get a clean one in the cupboard."

"I've got to get to work. Are you sure you're going to be all right?"

"Over here?" Betty smiled. "The school is miles away."

"Well," Phil said, "if I hear of anything, I'll come right home."

"For heaven's sake, it's not going to be as dramatic as all that."

"You don't know," Phil said. "If the Negroes try to enter that school, or even if they get to the front steps, there'll be trouble, and all Albie Vandiver's yelling won't stop it. You mark my words."

The baby's mouth began to sag open. Betty put down the spoon and tucked a bottle between the smeary lips. "I don't know," she said wearily.

"Way I heard it," Phil said, "they're going to try just one

57

girl, and they're going to walk her right up to the front door, right up to those big blue doors."

"Oh," Betty said.

"Some people've been saying they're going to send her up alone to pound on that big blue front door."

"Oh," Betty said. She stared at the baby's lips pulling on the nipple, and she wanted to cry, though there was nothing to cry about because that wouldn't happen to her child with its blue eyes and fair skin.

"It'll make a real fine picture for the photographers," Phil was saying. "They can call it, 'Child knocks at door of future,' and then they can take pictures of the riot."

"I've got to change her," Betty said. "She's dripping wet."

She fled into the bedroom. In a bit Phil followed her. "I don't want to scare you, honey," he said, "but stay inside, will you? If you really have to go anywhere call me—don't go by yourself."

She put the baby in its crib and stood looking out the window at the paved street, empty and hot. "I've got to put the wash out," she said weakly, "the diapers and things for her."

"Let that go," Phil said. "Just for today. I'll put the dirty stuff on the back porch so the smell won't bother you."

"That's silly."

"Honey," Phil said, "there's people on the streets today looking for trouble. Now lock the door after me when I go."

He checked the lock from outside and waved to her through the window. She watched him drive away. The street was still empty. She walked around the house, slowly, uncertainly, wondering what to do. Finally she remembered. She went to the hall closet and found the shotgun that Phil used to hunt ducks with. She dragged it out and held it crosswise to her body, looking at it. It was greasy, and black smears came off on her hand. There would have to be shells for it, she thought. Somewhere. Those were harder to find. They had got pushed way back on the top shelf, under Phil's Army muffler and his heavy gloves and her brother's old Navy watch cap. She found the box finally and turned the smooth cylinders over and over in her fingers. Finally she picked up box and gun and started for the living room. As she turned the corner, the stock banged into the wall. A large chunk of plaster fell on the polished floor. She did not even notice. She put the shotgun on a chair and the box of shells beside it, then picked up the phone. She would have to call Phil and ask him how to load it.

Miss Ethyl Holloway drove down the street at her usual careful pace, her 1940 Plymouth rattling and creaking over the ruts. The brakes were not especially good, and Miss Holloway pumped them a bit to get up pressure for the long slow slope that ended at the school corner. With one hand she settled the collar of her dress a bit more comfortably about her neck. She was upset; she was angry. She had lost her temper—not more than ten minutes ago—with her nephew Philip.

She almost never got angry. She had trained herself not to. It was the very first thing she had learned in her years of teaching the second grade. She had been teaching when all the children were together in one schoolhouse, and there were only four teachers. Now the children stayed here for the grammar grades only, and then the school buses came, buglike yellow things, and carried them off to high school at Greenfield. But the second grade stayed the same, of course.

So little had changed in her life. She still lived in the house her parents had built in the '80's, sharing it now with her nephew and his wife. She kept her part unchanged, just exactly the way it had been when her mother died. Miss Holloway smiled to herself as she began the long coast down the hill. If her mother were to come back, she would be right at home. Then sometimes it seemed that she had not left, not at all. Seemed as if she had just stepped around the corner to Miss Margaret Lee's for a cup of coffee on a cool morning. *Wait lunch for me, Ethyl, I won't be gone long.*

She came out behind the school, turned the corner cautiously as she always did, entered the school grounds and coasted to the spot behind the east wall, where she had parked every morning since the school was built.

There were no other cars there. She thought, *My clocks are early again.* That happened sometimes. She had got casual about setting them as she grew older. They didn't seem so terribly important any more. It was just as well to be early, though, on the best day of the year. By the end of the week she would have divided her class into children she liked and those she didn't. But the first day, the first day now, she loved them all equally. The ones who were dressed so carefully, hair slicked back wet, hair braided tightly. The ones who weren't, dirty overalls, matted hair, maybe even a bug or two—poor little things couldn't help it. After a few weeks she would be barking at the very sight of their dirt-creased skins, "Go down the hall and wash your face and hands. Keep scrubbing them until they're white, you hear me?"

Miss Holloway picked up her pocketbook from the seat beside her. She also picked up her brand-new roll book, the one she had just taken from her supply. She kept some twenty or thirty books on hand, piled back of her bedroom armoire. She did not trust the stores to keep a supply. After all, you just could not start a class without a roll book. And classes had to be started.

As she opened her door, she noticed Albert Vandiver. She smiled politely at him. "Miss Holloway," he said, "I don't reckon this is a very good place for you to be."

"Albert, what in the world are you talking about?"

"Look," he said, "there won't be any school today."

"Nonsense."

"They're sending one Negro girl," he said, "and there's going to be trouble."

"I've never had a Negro in my class."

"Yes, ma'am," he said. "Why don't you go home?"

"Albert," she said, "you are too old to be so silly."

She got out of her car, purse in one hand, roll book in the other. She walked along the cinder path to the side door. It was closed. *How careless of the janitor*, she thought. *It will be terribly stuffy in the halls.* She pulled on the brass handle. Nothing happened.

Albert Vandiver called, "It's locked."

She walked around to the front of the building, passing the flagpole plot and the half-dead planting of grass. She marched up the broad concrete steps to the newly painted bright-blue doors. She put her hand to the knob, slowly this time. It did not turn. She peered through the small glass panes. The hall with its rising flight of worn wooden stairs was empty. She twisted the handle again, rattling it with increasing strength. Finally she turned around and looked across the open stretch of ground to the street and the houses lined up on the other side, the little neat houses that she had been seeing every single day. Old houses that had been there when she first came to teach.

The wind blew gusty and hard, and the dust spun in great slow whorls. She could feel grit brush her cheek and sting her lips. The people on the other side of the street seemed to be shrinking away. It wasn't like any other day ever had been. Ordinarily they came streaming toward her, the children, all those future years, running to her. And off in the distance, like sheep dogs, there would be the mothers, some of them swollen with child. And they would be her children; she could feel herself teem with life.

The ground in front of her was empty now. She was standing alone with a pile of brick behind her and concrete steps beneath her and the sun a hot yellow moon through the dust.

She stumbled down the steps, around the building and back to her car. Albert Vandiver was still there.

"My nephew told me"—she was conscious that her voice was trembling and old—"and I didn't believe him."

"Yes'm," Albert Vandiver said.

"They can't close the school."

He shook his head. "I'd drive you home if I could, but I got to stay here."

She felt so strange. Maybe she was going to have a heart attack or a stroke or something. Her mother had died like that, in the back yard between the beds of cosmos and tomato plants.

"No school," she said more to herself than to the sweating fat figure that stood beside the car. "There's always been school."

She backed the car, turned slowly around the corner. A little group of men were coming down that hill, walking in the street. They stepped to the curb to let her pass. She looked at the thin sun-scarred faces, the light-blue eyes; she saw the bones of their thin shoulders through the faded cotton of their short-sleeved shirts.

I've seen them before, she thought, *when they were little. I've seen them over and over again, year after year. Stomachs swollen with worms; bodies creeping with lice.*

Those children, grown now, looked back at her. She saw them clearly, saw the necks, crinkled with wind burn, the hands huge and scarred—the hands of dirt farmers, turpentine workers. Saw the lives spent in pine-slab cabins or corrugated-tin shacks—where razorbacks and chickens ran loose during the day and slept at night under the unsteady foundations of the houses. The smells of cabbage and beans and sweat and filth and poverty.

She looked into the long, thin faces and the heavy-lidded

blue eyes beneath the sweat-stained, black-felt hats. And the eyes had the same look she saw year after year in the second grade: hate and fury and blood lust. Those boys had stomped nestlings into the ground, caught rabbits and pulled them into pieces and threw the bloody bits of fur on the schoolroom floor. These men now, what would they be going to tear apart, with more light and life in their eyes than they had had for years?

She thought of all this as her 1940 Plymouth labored up the hill, slowly passing them. She said loudly, distinctly, out of the open window, spitting her words into their cold bright eyes, "White trash."

She drove home, drove into the yard and stopped carefully at the end of the gravel. Then—because she was old and confused by a world she no longer understood, a world her little children had taken over, had grown up in and taken over—she fainted very gently, falling across the steering wheel.

The very few seconds before, when the rising cold began to envelop her and she knew she was going to faint, she felt a tremendous relief. By the time her head touched the wheel she was feeling quite happy. The darkness was no more frightening than the daylight.

Albert Vandiver walked along the sidewalk, mopping his sweating face with his handkerchief. Quiet, casual. At the corner of Jefferson Street five men waited in the shade of a camphor tree. Two were hunkered down, studying the ground between their knees, two leaned against the tree, and one sat with his legs crossed. They didn't look up from under their floppy black-felt hats when Vandiver stopped by them.

He stood very quietly for a few minutes, being sure they knew he was there, being sure he did not startle them. "You all from around here?" It wasn't so much a question as a statement.

63

Nobody answered. Vandiver went along, speaking more slowly than he usually did. "But I don't reckon you are, because I know most people, long as I been living here."

Nobody seemed to have heard him. Vandiver sighed. "Hell of a hot morning. Anybody send you in? Or you decide to come on your own to see the fun?"

One of the men spat a stream of yellow tobacco juice.

"Now I'm right lucky that didn't hit me," Vandiver said pleasantly, "account of then I'd had to do something about it, and I don't want to. I like you boys."

The head of one of the squatting men lifted and looked at him. "You all look enough alike to be brothers," Vandiver said calmly. "You related?"

"No," the squatting man said.

"Be a lot better you all left town."

One of the standing men said, staring at him, "We done nothing."

Vandiver reached for his handkerchief again, slowly. "I like you boys," he said, "and I'm right sorry to hear about your car." He waited, to be sure they understood. "I know you come in a car, because you wasn't around yesterday, and there won't be a bus until one o'clock."

The men shifted. One took off his hat. His hair was whitish blond.

"Kids in this town are bad," Vandiver said. "They been known to put sugar in gas tanks. Especially when it's out-of-town cars—always tell them by the county number on the plates."

They were standing now.

"If that car ain't out of town inside fifteen minutes," Vandiver said, "that's what's going to happen."

He walked away, his fat thighs making him roll as he went.

George Fred Carpenter waited for him at the patrol car. "You get rid of them?"

"They'll go all right."

"Expect more'll be coming."

"Hell," Vandiver said, "can't stop 'em all. I'm just scaring off the ones I can." He reached inside the car, got himself a cigar, began tearing off the cellophane wrapper methodically.

"Lots of kids," George Fred said. "Want me to try and get rid of them?"

"They wouldn't go if you took a blowtorch to 'em."

"What you want to do?"

"Nothing," Vandiver said. "Ain't much we can do except wait and see."

"You hear that just one kid's going to try coming?"

Vandiver nodded. "Heard something like that."

"Hell," George Fred said, "this is just plain a lot of fuss for one nigger kid."

"Yea," Vandiver said as he lighted the cigar, "seems that way."

The cotton curtains matched the pink-and-green pattern of the wallpaper in the small kitchen. The curtains were drawn—although daylight glowed behind them—and the overhead light, a single globe cased in shiny brass, was burning. There were six persons in the kitchen, five men and a woman, and they sat at the chrome yellow table. There was an enamel coffeepot in the center and a neat tray of cups, but no one seemed to be drinking. The men—each had a thin mustache—wore coats and ties, even in the heat, and their dark faces were serious.

Their heads swung to the slight sound of a door.

She was nine or so, and she was carefully dressed in a new blue-and-red print with two starched petticoats under the full skirt. Her hair was done in plaits with curled bangs on her forehead. Her brown face was calm and unsmiling.

The woman sitting at the table got up. "We were waiting

for you, Ruth." She crossed to the child and began to fix her dress, settling it at the shoulders, fluffing out the petticoats, arranging the skirt more precisely on them. The odor of boiled starch drifted through the room.

"Now," she said, "she's ready, Harry."

A short, slight man in a gray suit said, "All right."

One of the other men asked gently, "Do you want to go, Ruth?"

"Yes, sir," she said.

Harry and his daughter got into their car and backed out slowly and headed for the school. It was only a dozen blocks or so—one block to the edge of the Negro district, then through the white streets.

Harry Mitchell could feel the straight little body sitting beside him. Once he sneaked a look. The small face was set, the eyes great and luminous. It wasn't fear. He didn't know what it was. He just had an uneasy feeling that this was not his child at all. It was the eyes, he thought; she had her mother's eyes.

His hands sweated on the wheel. The girl did not move. She sat looking straight ahead, her skirts fluffed out around her. He asked, "Your mother been telling you about the crown of stars?"

She looked at him politely, not quite understanding.

"Nothing," he said. They came to the top of the hill. The school lay in the hollow below them. A half-dozen blocks now. He inched the car along.

"Mother said let me out a block ahead." They had agreed on that. "It will be better for me to go alone."

And where did she get phrases like that, he wondered. Somebody had told her. They were not her words. He could see the school now, the brilliant blue square of the doors. He could see the people lining the sidewalks.

They did not see his car until he came to the beginning of the last block. Then someone noticed. He could see the sudden

flurry as they turned and faced toward him, watching. He had
half expected that they would come streaming toward the car.
They did not. They only strolled out, blocking the street, forming a thin raggedy line, topped by dusty black hats. Always
those hats. His mother had told her children stories about a
black-hatted bogeyman—they had shivered in their beds and
dreamed about him.

Ruth got out. Very quietly she began to walk toward them.
Harry Mitchell watched her thin dark legs, moving beneath
the ruffled dress. And then he did just exactly what he had
been afraid of doing, did just exactly what he knew all along
that he would do.

He jumped out of the car, leaving the motor on. He ran,
faster than he ever had in his life. He could feel the force of his
legs throwing him into the air. He reached her in a moment
and grabbed her around the waist, the starch crinkling against
his sweating hand. He raced back to the car, the concrete
throwing his footsteps back at him. The child started to cry.

He spun the car around and headed up the hill, tires leaving
black marks on the street.

Ruth was still screaming when he turned into his driveway
and carried her into the house. The men were still in his
kitchen. They did not look surprised. He wondered if they had
doubted him all along.

He put the child down. Her mother took her quickly, silently. Doors opened and closed. Then all he could hear was
muffled crying off in a corner of the house. He took off his coat.
His shirt was plastered tightly to his body with his own sweat.

The four men were sitting at the table, waiting. He had to
say something. "Not her," he said finally, and the words that
had been running around his head all morning came tumbling
out, "Why is it always kids?"

They stood up, these men he had known all his life, and they

walked around him and out of the door as if he had not been
there.

The house was quiet. Ruth had stopped crying. He took off
his tie and his shirt. And he was opening the curtains when he
heard his wife come back. "I hate them closed," he said.

She was standing in the door, and her beautiful dark face
was set and hard. "Not Ruth," he said. And then, "You didn't
see them."

She was looking at him steadily, unblinking. She was looking through him with her great, fierce, shining eyes. He sat
down abruptly, wondering if it was true what his grandmother
had told him: that he had white blood. Wondering if that was
what made him do it. And what would white blood be? A drop
in your veins. Maybe it was enough to make you a traitor. It
didn't show, but maybe it was enough.

His wife had not moved. He lifted his head finally, because
there was nothing else to do. "You didn't see them," he said.
"You didn't see the way the street looked down there."

Again the glitter, the terrible glitter. He felt frightened, as
if his skin were white.

By noon Al Vandiver had cleared the streets. The people
who had come to town specially for the day found themselves
with nothing to do, so they got into their cars and went out
into the country, looking for corn whisky. By the middle of the
afternoon the housewives were hosing their porches and sweeping their walks and trying to gather up the bits of paper the
crowd had left. By five o'clock it began to rain, great gushing
downpours that drove the tinfoil and the cellophane and the
cigarette packs into the mud. In the morning when the sun
came up bright and hard and yellow, the town looked washed
clean.

The Captive Outfielder

LEONARD WIBBERLEY

The boy was filled with anxiety which seemed to concentrate in his stomach, giving him a sense of tightness there, as if his stomach were all knotted up into a ball and would never come undone again. He had his violin under his chin and before him was the music stand and on the walls of the studio the pictures of the great musicians were frowning upon him in massive disapproval. Right behind him on the wall was a portrait of Paganini, and he positively glowered down at the boy, full of malevolence and impatience.

That, said the boy to himself, *is because he could really play the violin and I can't and never will be able to. And he knows it and thinks I'm a fool.*

Below Paganini was a portrait of Mozart, in profile. He had a white wig tied neatly at the back with a bow of black ribbon. Mozart should have been looking straight ahead, but his left eye, which was the only one visible, seemed to be turned a little watching the boy. The look was one of disapproval. When Mozart was the boy's age—that is, ten—he had already composed several pieces and could play the violin and the organ. Mozart didn't like the boy either.

On the other side of the Paganini portrait was the blocky

face of Johann Sebastian Bach. It was a grim face, bleak with disappointment. Whenever the boy was playing it seemed to him that Johann Sebastian Bach was shaking his head in resigned disapproval of his efforts. There were other portraits around the studio—Beethoven, Brahms, Chopin. Not one of them was smiling. They were all in agreement that this boy was certainly the poorest kind of musician and never would learn his instrument, and it was painful to them to have to listen to him while he had his lesson.

Of all these great men of music who surrounded him the boy hated Johann Sebastian Bach the most. This was because his teacher, Mr. Olinsky, kept talking about Bach as if without Bach there never would have been any music. Bach was like a god to Mr. Olinsky, and he was a god the boy could never hope to please.

"All right," said Mr. Olinsky, who was at the grand piano. "The Arioso. And you will kindly remember the time. Without time no one can play the music of Johann Sebastian Bach." Mr. Olinsky exchanged glances with the portrait of Bach, and the two seemed in perfect agreement with each other. The boy was quite sure that the two of them carried on disheartened conversations about him after his lesson.

There was a chord from the piano. The boy put the bow to the string and started. But it was no good. At the end of the second bar Mr. Olinsky took his hands from the piano and covered his face with them and shook his head, bending over the keyboard. Bach shook his head too. In the awful silence all the portraits around the studio expressed their disapproval, and the boy felt more wretched than ever and not too far removed from tears.

"The *time*," said Mr. Olinsky eventually. "The time. Take that first bar. What is the value of the first note?"

"A quarter note," said the boy.

"And the next note?"

"A sixteenth."

"Good. So you have one quarter note and four sixteenth notes making a bar of two quarters. Not so?"

"Yes."

"But the first quarter note is tied to the first sixteenth note. They are the same note. So the first note, which is C sharp, is held for five sixteenths, and then the other three sixteenths follow. Not so?"

"Yes," said the boy.

"THEN WHY DON'T YOU PLAY IT THAT WAY?"

To this the boy made no reply. The reason he didn't play it that way was that he couldn't play it that way. It wasn't fair to have a quarter note and then tie it to a sixteenth note. It was just a dirty trick like Grasshopper Smith pulled when he was pitching in the Little League. Grasshopper Smith was on the Giants, and the boy was on the Yankees. The Grasshopper always retained the ball for just a second after he seemed to have thrown it and struck the boy out. Every time. Every single time. The boy got a hit every now and again from other pitchers. Once he got a two-base hit. The ball went joyously through the air, bounced and went over the center-field fence. A clear, good two-base hit. But it was a relief pitcher. And whenever Grasshopper Smith was in the box, the boy struck out. Him and Johann Sebastian Bach. They were full of dirty tricks. They were pretty stuck-up too. He hated them both.

Meanwhile he had not replied to Mr. Olinsky's question, and Mr. Olinsky got up from the piano and stood beside him, looking at him, and saw that the boy's eyes were bright with frustration and disappointment because he was no good at baseball and no good at music either.

"Come and sit down a minute, boy," said Mr. Olinsky, and led him over to a little wickerwork sofa.

Mr. Olinsky was in his sixties, and from the time he was this boy's age he had given all his life to music. He loved the boy, though he had known him for only a year. He was a good boy, and he had a good ear. He wanted him to get excited about music, and the boy was not excited about it. He didn't practice properly. He didn't apply himself. There was something lacking, and it was up to him, Mr. Olinsky, to supply whatever it was that was lacking so that the boy would really enter into the magic world of music.

How to get to him then? How to make a real contact with this American boy when he himself was, though a citizen, foreign-born?

He started to talk about his own youth. It had been a very grim youth in Petrograd. His parents were poor. His father had died when he was young, and his mother had, by a very great struggle, got him into the conservatory. She had enough money for his tuition only. Eating was a great problem. He could afford only one good meal a day at the conservatory cafeteria so that he was almost always hungry and cold. But he remembered how the great Glazunov had come to the cafeteria one day and had seen him with a bowl of soup and a piece of bread.

"This boy is thin," Glazunov had said. "From now on he is to have two bowls of soup, and they are to be big bowls. I will pay the cost."

There had been help like that for him—occasional help coming quite unexpectedly—in those long, grinding, lonely years at the conservatory. But there were other terrible times. There was the time when he had reached such an age that he could no longer be boarded at the conservatory. He had to give up his bed to a smaller boy and find lodgings somewhere in the city.

He had enough money for lodgings, but not enough for food. Always food. That was the great problem. To get money for food he had taken a room in a house where the family had consumption. They rented him a room cheaply because nobody wanted to board with them. He would listen to the members of the family coughing at nighttime—the thin, shallow, persistent cough of the consumptive. He was terribly afraid—afraid that he would contract consumption himself, which was incurable in those days, and die. The thought of death frightened him. But he was equally frightened of disappointing his mother, for if he died he would not graduate and all her efforts to make him a musician would be wasted.

Then there was the time he had had to leave Russia after the revolution. And the awful months of standing in line to get a visa and then to get assigned to a train. It had taken seven months. And the train to Riga—what an ordeal that had been. Normally it took eighteen hours. But this train took three weeks. Three weeks in cattle cars in midwinter, jammed up against his fellow passengers, desperately trying to save his violin from being crushed. A baby had died in the cattle car, and the mother kept pretending it was only asleep. They had had to take it from her by force eventually and bury it beside the tracks out in the howling loneliness of the countryside.

And out of all this he had got music. He had become a musician. Not a concert violinist, but a great orchestral violinist, devoted to his art.

He told the boy about this, hoping to get him to understand what he himself had gone through in order to become a musician. But when he was finished, he knew he had not reached the boy.

That is because he is an American boy, Mr. Olinsky thought. *He thinks all these things happened to me because I am a foreigner, and these things don't happen in America. And maybe they don't. But can't he understand that if I made all these efforts to achieve music—to be able to play the works of Johann Sebastian Bach as Bach wrote them—it is surely worth a little effort on his part?*

But it was no good. The boy, he knew, sympathized with him. But he had not made a real contact with him. He hadn't found the missing something that separated this boy from him and the boy from music. He tried again. "Tell me," he said, "what do you do with your day?"

"I go to school," said the boy flatly.

"But after that? Life is not all school."

"I play ball."

"What kind of ball?" asked Mr. Olinsky. "Bouncing a ball against a wall?"

"No," said the boy. "Baseball."

"Ah," said Mr. Olinsky. "Baseball." And he sighed. He had been more than thirty years in the United States and he didn't know anything about baseball. It was an activity beneath his notice. When he had any spare time, he went to a concert. Or sometimes he played chess. "And how do you do at baseball?" he said.

"Oh—not very good. That Grasshopper Smith. He always strikes me out."

"You have a big match coming up soon perhaps?"

"A game. Yes. Tomorrow. The Giants against the Yankees. I'm on the Yankees. It's the play-off. We are both tied for first place." For a moment he seemed excited, and then he caught a glimpse of the great musicians around the wall and the bleak stare of Johann Sebastian Bach, and his voice went dull again. "It doesn't matter," he said. "I'll be struck out."

"But that is not the way to think about it," said Mr. Olinsky. "Is it inevitable that you be struck out? Surely that cannot be so. When I was a boy——" Then he stopped, because when he was a boy he had never played anything remotely approaching baseball, and so he had nothing to offer the boy to encourage him.

Here was the missing part then—the thing that was missing between him and the boy and the thing that was missing between the boy and Johann Sebastian Bach. Baseball. It was just something they didn't have in common, and so they couldn't communicate with each other.

The Captive Outfielder

"When is this game?" said Mr. Olinsky.

"Three in the afternoon," said the boy.

"And this Grasshopper Smith is your bête noire—your black beast, huh?"

"Yeah," said the boy. "And he'll be pitching. They've been saving him for this game."

Mr. Olinsky sighed. This was a long way from the Arioso. "Well," he said, "we will consider the lesson over. Do your practice and we will try again next week."

The boy left, conscious that all the musicians were watching him. When he had gone, Mr. Olinsky stood before the portrait of Johann Sebastian Bach.

"Baseball, maestro," he said. "Baseball. That is what stands between him and you and him and me. You had twenty children and I had none. But I am positive that neither of us knows anything about baseball."

He thought about this for a moment. Then he said, "Twenty children—many of them boys. Is it possible, maestro—is it just possible that with twenty children and many of them boys? . . . You will forgive the thought, but is it just possible that you may have played something like baseball with them sometimes? And perhaps one of those boys always being—what did he say?—struck out?"

He looked hard at the blocky features of Johann Sebastian Bach, and it seemed to him that in one corner of the grim mouth there was a touch of a smile.

Mr. Olinsky was late getting to the Clark Stadium Recreation Park in Hermosa Beach for the play-off between the Giants and the Yankees because he had spent the morning transposing the Arioso from A major into C major to make it simpler for the boy. Indeed, when he got there the game was in the sixth and last inning and the score was three to nothing in favor of the Giants.

75

The Yankees were at bat, and it seemed that a moment of crisis had been reached.

"What's happening?" Mr. Olinsky asked a man seated next to him who was eating a hot dog in ferocious bites.

"You blind or something?" asked the man. "Bases loaded, two away and if they don't get a hitter to bring those three home, it's good-by for the Yankees. And look who's coming up to bat. That dodo!"

Mr. Olinsky looked and saw the boy walking to the plate.

Outside the studio and in his baseball uniform he looked very small. He also looked frightened, and Mr. Olinsky looked savagely at the man who had called the boy a dodo and was eating the hot dog, and he said the only American expression of contempt he had learned in all his years in the United States. "You don't know nothing from nothing," Mr. Olinsky snapped.

"That so?" said the hot-dog man. "Well, you watch. Three straight pitches and the Grasshopper will have him out. I think I'll go home. I got a pain."

But he didn't go home. He stayed there while the Grasshopper looked carefully around the bases and then, leaning forward with the ball clasped before him, glared intently at the boy. Then he pumped twice and threw the ball, and the boy swung at it and missed, and the umpire yelled, "Strike one."

"Two more like that, Grasshopper," yelled somebody. "Just two more and it's in the bag."

The boy turned around to look at the crowd and passed his tongue over his lips. He looked directly at where Mr. Olinsky was sitting, but the music teacher was sure the boy had not seen him. His face was white and his eyes glazed so that he didn't seem to be seeing anybody.

Mr. Olinsky knew that look. He had seen it often enough in the studio when the boy had made an error and knew that however much he tried he would make the same error over and over again. It was a look of pure misery—a fervent desire to get an ordeal over with.

The boy turned again, and the Grasshopper threw suddenly and savagely to third base. But the runner got back on the sack in time, and there was a sigh of relief from the crowd.

Again came the cool examination of the bases and the calculated stare at the boy at the plate. And again the pitch with the curious whip of the arm and the release of the ball one second later. Once more the boy swung and missed, and the umpire called, "Strike two." There was a groan from the crowd.

"Oh and two the count," said the scorekeeper, but Mr. Olinsky got up from the bench and, pushing his way between the people on the bleachers before him, he went to the backstop fence.

"You," he shouted to the umpire. "I want to talk to that boy there."

The boy heard his voice and turned and looked at him aghast. "Please, Mr. Olinsky," he said. "I can't talk to you now."

"Get away from the back fence," snapped the umpire.

"I insist on talking to that boy," said Mr. Olinsky. "It is very important. It is about Johann Sebastian Bach."

"Please go away," said the boy, and he was very close to tears. The umpire called for time out while he got rid of this madman, and the boy went to the netting of the backstop.

"You are forgetting about the Ariosol!" said Mr. Olinsky urgently. "Now you listen to me, because I know what I am talking about. You are thinking of a quarter note, and it should be five sixteenths. It is a quarter note—C sharp—held for one sixteenth more. *Then* strike. You are too early. It must be exactly on time."

"What the heck's he talking about?" asked the coach, who had just come up.

The boy didn't answer right away. He was looking at Mr.

Olinsky as if he had realized for the first time something very important which he had been told over and over again, but had not grasped previously.

"He's talking about Johann Sebastian Bach," he said to the coach. "Five sixteenths. Not a quarter note."

"Bach had twenty children," said Mr. Olinsky to the coach. "Many of them were boys. He would know about these things."

"For cripes' sakes, let's get on with the game," said the coach.

Mr. Olinsky did not go back to the bleachers. He remained behind the backstop and waited for the ceremony of the base inspection and the hard stare by the pitcher. He saw the Grasshopper pump twice, saw his hand go back behind his head, saw the curiously delayed flick of the ball, watched it speed to the boy and then he heard a sound which afterward he thought was among the most beautiful and satisfying he had heard in all music.

It was a clean, sharp "click," sweet as birdsong.

The ball soared higher and higher into the air in a graceful parabola. It was fifteen feet over the center fielder's head, and it cleared the fence by a good four feet.

Then pandemonium broke loose. People were running all over the field, and the boy was chased around the bases by half his teammates, and when he got to home plate he was thumped upon the back and his hair ruffled, and in all this Mr. Olinsky caught one glimpse of the boy's face, laughing and yet with tears pouring down his cheeks.

A week later the boy turned up at Mr. Olinsky's studio for his violin lesson. He looked around at all the great musicians on the wall, and they no longer seemed to be disapproving and disappointed in him.

Paganini was almost kindly. There was a suggestion of a chuckle on the noble profile of Mozart, and Beethoven no longer looked so forbidding. The boy looked at the portrait of Johann Sebastian Bach last.

He looked for a long time at the picture, and then he said two words out loud—words that brought lasting happiness to Mr. Olinsky. The words were: "Thanks, coach."

The Arioso went excellently from then on.

The Last Rendezvous

ROBERT STANDISH

It was one of Mark Willaston's little idiosyncrasies—and he
had not many—that he feared the embarrassment which might
have been occasioned at the office if he produced an otherwise
clean pocket handkerchief stained with lipstick. It was because
of this and for no other reason that when Jane, his wife of
three years' standing, dropped him at Guildford railway station on five mornings weekly, the parting kiss they exchanged
before he went on to London and she returned to the chores
at Rosemary Cottage, was little more than a perfunctory peck
on the cheek. A stranger witnessing this each morning and
knowing nothing of Mark's little idiosyncrasy might have been
tempted to believe that their marriage had entered the dol-
drums, that sadly prosaic stage when young couples, without being fully aware that it has happened, take each other
for granted. But in the case of Jane and Mark Willaston, the
observant hypothetical stranger would have been wrong.

These two were gloriously, blissfully in love. Their life together had been one of unclouded happiness, for already their
honeymoon had lasted three years, one month and four days.

On this morning in late July—note the date, please, it was
July twenty-eighth—when we first meet these two outside the
railway station, their behavior merits our close attention. There

were three minutes before Mark's train, the eight-thirty-one, was due to arrive. "What are you going to do today, darling?" he asked.

"Just wait for this evening when you come back to me," replied Jane. "Maybe I'll have some news for you then. And I've some odds and ends of shopping to do. It's possible that I might even buy you a present."

"What do you plan to use for money?" he said.

"Not the housekeeping money," replied Jane. "You've got such an appetite that there's never any left. If I buy you a present—and I'm not sure that I will—I shall draw it from my bank. I've never touched Aunt Edith's legacy, you know."

There was no time for more and, even if there had been, the whistle of the approaching train would have made their voices inaudible.

Then something strange happened, something which tempts one to believe that in those swiftly passing moments Mark and Jane were permitted, in some way beyond our understanding, to anticipate time and to catch a glimpse into the uncharted future. To say more than this would be foolish, while, on the other hand, to say less would be to deny the power of love.

They had exchanged their railway-station peck. Jane had opened the door of their small car, while Mark had turned his back and was walking through the station entrance when he stopped dead in his tracks, turned and retraced his footsteps. There, in front of scores of hurrying people making for the train, Mark threw his arms around Jane and, oblivious of the eyes upon them, kissed her lingeringly on the lips.

There are as many kinds of kisses as there are kinds of people, while their nuances are far more subtle than any spoken word. Jane, as she drove away from the station, and Mark, as he leaped onto the train while it was moving, tried in vain to analyze just what kind of kiss that had been and just what it had said. That there had been some special meaning in the kiss neither of them doubted, but it did not occur to either that it had been their last. It was minutes before Mark, his newspaper unopened, wiped his lips clean of lipstick and folded the otherwise spotless handkerchief so that the smear was invisible.

Mark Willaston, who was twenty-seven years of age at this time, held a responsible position with a city firm of insurance brokers, whose principals were so well pleased with his work that they had held out the inducement of a junior partnership. Happily married and with material success already within reach, he seemed to be a man singled out by the gods for special favor.

At twelve minutes after six that same evening Mark emerged from the railway station to look for Jane, who, in the absence of a phone call to say that he would be late, always met the same train. The shadow of disappointment crossed his eyes when he realized that she was not there. Perhaps the car had broken down. He blamed himself for not having cleaned the distributor, which might have been the cause of a slight hesitancy in the engine which he had noted the previous day.

At six-thirty, when Jane still had not reached the station, Mark put in a phone call to Rosemary Cottage. There was no reply, which suggested that she was on the way. At seven there was still no reply. A neighbor, seeing him apparently stranded, and not knowing when he himself might be glad to be saved a six-mile taxi fare, offered Mark a lift, which he accepted.

There were still two hours left of the long summer evening when Mark entered the garden of Rosemary Cottage. The first thing that he saw was that the car was not in the garage. Within a few seconds of opening the front door with his key, he went into every room and verified that Jane was not there. Although perplexed as to what was best to be done, he was

not seriously worried. Jane, he concluded, had had a break-
down somewhere, had telephoned, or would telephone shortly.
The obvious thing to do was to stay where he was, which was
where Jane would expect him to be. Needing some exercise,
Mark changed into shorts and an open shirt, and mowed the
small lawn. This done, he opened a bottle of beer, showered
and changed again.

At nine o'clock when pools of violet shadow were deepen-
ing in the valley and the owls were hooting in the coppice
which adjoined the isolated cottage, Mark made himself a
sandwich of cold meat and lettuce. He had skipped lunch
that day and he was conscious of the gnawing pains of hunger.
But before he ate he phoned a neighbor about some trivial
matter. He wanted to be sure that the phone was working.
When full darkness had fallen, Mark became seriously worried and determined to do something. But what? What was
the intelligent thing to do? Action, any kind of action, seemed
preferable to waiting and worrying. Mark's perplexities were
ended abruptly by the ringing of the telephone.

"Mr. Willaston?" asked a gruff voice. "Just a moment, sir.
This is the Amblesham police station. The sergeant would like
a word with you."

Then another voice said, "I'm afraid, Mr. Willaston, you
must prepare yourself for some bad news—very bad news. Mrs.
Willaston has met with an accident. As you have no car, I'll
come to fetch you. Expect me in six or seven minutes."

"A bad accident?" asked Mark thickly, for his mouth had
gone dry. "You mean she's been killed?"

"I'm afraid that's just what I do mean, sir." The line went
dead.

The horrifying impact of the words had its own kind of
mercy, for to Mark there was an unreality about them, as
though they were intended for the ears of some other Mark
Willaston. When the police car arrived and the sergeant urged

him to put on clothes suitable for a long drive, he obeyed in a daze.

The sergeant was a kindly man, tactful, and made no small talk as they drove south and west for about an hour. At a sign which read COTTAGE HOSPITAL they slackened speed, turning right into a laurel-bordered drive. Nothing about the place was familiar to Mark, who was led into an officelike room where a nondescript man with a stethoscope round his neck peered at him over thick-lensed glasses. "We did our best for her, Mr. Willaston, but there was never any hope. Would you like to see her?"

Jane was in a small room alone. There was a screen round the bed. They moved this and pulled back the sheet. Except that her eyes were closed and her lips bloodless, she had changed very little. "Be thankful that she did not suffer at all," said a middle-aged woman who might have been the matron.

Then they led him away and into just such another room where, minutes, hours or aeons later, he felt the prick of a needle before the curtain of oblivion dropped. It was three days before the doctor-in-charge deemed it wise to allow Mark to leave, and then only because his presence was required at the inquest.

There were no surviving eyewitnesses to the accident. Police witnesses established that Jane's car had been traveling along a minor road leading from the village of Wingfield toward its intersection of the London-to-Chichester road, about five miles from the latter town. She had braked violently a few yards before the intersection. The tire marks revealed this. She then had skidded across the path of an oncoming sports car which, a few moments previously, had overtaken another car at, according to the driver, at least seventy-five m.p.h. The two people in the sports car—a man and a woman—were killed instantly, while Jane had reached the hospital alive, dying about an hour after admission without recovering consciousness.

Although offered hospitality by several friends, Mark elected to return alone in dry-eyed grief to Rosemary Cottage, unable yet to endure the sympathy which was showered upon him. All he was able to grasp at this time was that the accident had occurred soon after five o'clock. By driving fast Jane could have been at Guildford station just in time to meet the six-twelve train on which he had arrived. Foolishly the realization of this gave him a sense of guilt and responsibility.

As Mark discovered over the next days, hearts do not break. Scar tissue formed over his. People were kind, but there was no comfort in their kindness. Alone and surrounded by familiar things which were a link with Jane, he began almost methodically to adjust himself to the terrifying loss he had sustained, trying to understand why he had been singled out by fate for such a cruel blow. Grief is of its essence selfish.

Mark went for a long walk in the woods while Margaret, Jane's sister, cleared the cottage of all Jane's clothes, her toilet articles and other personal belongings. Then, having put Rosemary Cottage into the hands of an agent for sale, he went back to work. The daily journey to and from London helped him to regain some equilibrium. He plunged into work with a furious intensity, hoping to find in it a way of shaking out of the mood of self-pity which, he was only too well aware, would solve no problems. Life was for the living, and he knew that Jane, who had loved life and laughter, would not have wished him to mourn for her too long.

A few weeks after Jane's funeral, when Mark's critical faculties were beginning to function again, he asked himself a question to which there seemed to be no reasonable answer: Why had Jane been where she was when she was killed? On the morning of her death she had said that by the evening she might have some news for him. What news could that have been? "I may even buy you a present," she had said.

It suddenly became tremendously important to Mark to know what had taken Jane to the village of Wingfield that day. The first time he had ever heard the name of the village had been at the inquest. They had had no friends there or anywhere near. They had driven through Chichester a couple of times together, but they knew nobody there either. An easy explanation might have been that Jane, having nothing particular to do, had gone for a drive. Plenty of people went for aimless drives, especially in the summer when the countryside was so lovely. But not Jane. She did not enjoy driving a car for its own sake. To her a car was a means of transportation, not a pleasure vehicle. Some definite purpose had taken Jane to the neighborhood of Wingfield that day, and Mark was determined to find out what it was.

On the following Saturday he drove to Wingfield in a hired car. It was a pleasant enough village with no great character. It had an enormous church which must have dated from a time when a much larger population had been served, suggesting that Wingfield had once been a more important center. There were three pubs and the usual village shops. Mark spent an hour in the post office thumbing through the telephone directory in the hope of seeing a familiar name which might have accounted for Jane's presence there on the last day of her life. Only one name rang a bell. Listed with a number on the Calthorpe exchange was a man with the unusual name of Larbelastier, which, Mark knew, was a Channel Islands name. Jane, long before he had met her, had had a boy friend of that name. Mark racked his brains to try to remember the man's first name, but it eluded him.

Among Jane's belongings had been an address book. Mark drove thoughtfully homeward, making a wide detour so as to call on Jane's sister, who lived with her husband about eight miles from Rosemary Cottage. Without asking why he wanted it, Margaret handed Mark the address book, urging him to stay on to an evening meal. He made his excuses and returned home to the lonely cottage.

In Jane's address book there was a Peter Larbelastier with an address in Devonshire. The entry was in a schoolgirl hand-writing, suggesting that it had been made before Jane's had become formed. The address had been deleted and no other substituted. Peter was the first name of the Larbelastier who lived at Calthorpe. Since he obviously could not inquire of Margaret or her mother without offering some explanation, Mark drove to Calthorpe early the next morning. He was now obsessed by the need to resolve all the doubts which bubbled and fermented in him. A brief study of the road map showed him that the most direct route from Rosemary Cottage was by the road which passed through Wingfield. Why had Jane been on that road? He would know no peace until he had the answer to the question. Even if the answer were to destroy the picture of Jane which was enshrined in his heart, he must have it. If this Peter Larbelastier, by coming back into Jane's life, had been, however indirectly, the cause of her death, Mark believed himself capable of killing the man, whatever the cost to himself.

Calthorpe was a larger village than Wingfield. In reply to Mark's inquiry, the owner of a filling station on the outskirts told him that the Larbelastiers ran a poultry farm about a mile on the other side. He volunteered the information that young Larbelastier was usually to be found before lunch on Sundays in the saloon bar of The Wheatsheaf, where, he added for good measure, the beer was the best for miles around.

At noon, a pint of draught bitter beer beside him, trying to control and conceal his impatience, Mark was at the saloon bar of The Wheatsheaf, listening to the broad Sussex vowels and studying the weathered, bucolic faces around him. Then, just as he was beginning to believe his vigil hopeless, he heard the barmaid say, "Good morning, Mr. Larbelastier. The usual?"

The newcomer was a handsome man of about Mark's age, clad in rough corduroy trousers and a leather jacket. Had the circumstances been otherwise, Mark would have been predisposed in his favor.

The ebb and flow of men at the bar brought Mark closer to the object of his interest, who seemed popular, for he was several times addressed by name by new arrivals. While Mark was turning over in his mind various methods of joining the conversation of which Larbelastier was the center, he saw that the other was aware of his scrutiny. This, he decided, was no time for subtlety, even if he could think of a way of being subtle. "Excuse me for staring at you," he began abruptly, "but didn't I see you a few weeks back with Jane Willaston?"

"No, you didn't," was the curt reply, "and even if you did, what business is it of yours? Are you the chap who's been making inquiries about me at Bert Hatcher's filling station?"

Mark's brain was not functioning as quickly as it might these days, or he would have thought of a more adroit reply than, "Yes, I am. Any law against it?"

"Who and what are you? Don't make mysteries. Ask your questions and get out of my sight."

"Then you don't know Jane Willaston?" Mark persisted. "The question seems to embarrass you. I wonder why."

Other conversations at the bar died away. The edginess in the voices of these two and the mention of a woman's name suggested the excellent possibility of a fight to enliven a dull Sunday. "Seconds out of the ring!" a man's voice said from a table at the rear.

"If you want to fight, fight outside," insisted the landlord.

"Jane Willaston. . . . Jane Willaston," a woman's voice said reflectively. "Where have I heard that name before?"

The situation was getting out of hand. Larbelastier turned

angrily to Mark. "You've said too much, or not enough," he said loudly. "What's it all about? Let's have it. I don't want to have to spend the next week trying to explain who this Jane Whatsisname is to my wife. My name's George Larbelastier. What's yours?"

"George Larbelastier—not Peter?" asked Mark weakly. "I'm sorry," he added. "I've made a mistake. My name's Mark Willaston. Please excuse me."

"My father's name is Peter," said the other less aggressively, realizing there was the possibility that an honest mistake had been made. "Maybe he can help you. I've a brother named Peter, too, but he's in New Zealand. Are you feeling all right?"

Mark felt his head swimming. He clutched the bar counter to stop himself from falling. Two men helped him out into the fresh air. As though from a great distance, Mark heard the woman's voice again: "Jane Willaston . . . now I remember. That's the name of the girl who was killed down at the crossroads a few weeks back. That chap is probably her husband."

"Poor devil!" said a man. "Maybe the shock has sent him round the bend."

In a few minutes Mark felt well enough to drive himself home, with the words of the last speaker ringing in his ears. Were shock and grief driving him mad? Such things did happen.

There was a car in the lane when Mark returned to Rosemary Cottage. A young couple sent by the local agent wanted to see inside. Sunday, they explained by way of apology, was their only free day. Before they left, after nearly an hour spent making notes, they said they liked the cottage and would make an offer next day.

It was as they drove away that Mark suffered the first twinge of conscience. The sale of the cottage, if it materialized, would be a symbolic act, cutting the last link which bound him to Jane. How would she regard this? They had restored the cottage together, much of the work having been done with their own hands. They had bought the furniture piece by piece from antique dealers scattered all over the southern half of England. It had been a labor of love, the most important single thing in their lives—except love itself. Now, for a price, he was proposing to turn house and contents over to strangers. Was this hideous disloyalty?

A strange but logical train of thought was set up by these reflections. Mark had just opened a can of soup. He was about to eat this and some fried eggs off a cleared space on the kitchen table when he realized how deeply Jane would have disapproved of this way of living. Sheepishly, as though under observation, he set a place for himself at the head of the old refectory table in the dining room. There was a bowl of dead flowers in the center of the table. He threw these away, renewed the water and brought in fresh flowers from the garden. There was dust everywhere. The clock had stopped. Cigarette ends littered the inglenook fireplace. One had burned a hole in the rug, a Persian rug which they had bought together instead of a refrigerator, because at the time they could not afford both. He winced as he realized how unhappy this would have made Jane.

Mark toiled for an hour, strangely conscious of Jane's approval, as he restored the dining room to something approximating the cleanliness and order in which she had always kept it. Then he ate his simple meal. It was, he recalled, the first meal he had enjoyed for weeks. Was this, he wondered, the outcome of having earned Jane's unspoken approval?

Alone in the darkness of the garden after eating his meal, trying to piece together the fragments of the tragedy which had been enacted and to make a coherent whole of them, Mark began to laugh mirthlessly at his own inconsistency. Out of some curious blend of deference to Jane's ideas and loyalty to her memory, he had just spent an hour setting the dining room to rights, forgetful altogether of the larger, shameful disloyalty of which he had been guilty. For days he had poisoned himself with ugly suspicions, assuming that just because he did not know why Jane had been in the neighborhood of Wingfield on that fatal day, her reasons for being there were unworthy. Was this all he had to show for three years of happiness, devotion and mutual trust? Merely because he did not know why Jane had been at the Wingfield crossroads at the time of the accident, did any single thing in his knowledge of her entitle him to suppose that her presence there had any other than an innocent explanation? These questions answered themselves as Mark felt himself go hot with shame.

Mark was still in the garden when the clock of a distant church chimed midnight. The air was redolent of the sweetness of night-scented stock, which Jane had sown. She had loved the night too. The chirrup of crickets, the croaking of bullfrogs and the contented rumblings of cows on the other side of the hedge—these had been the background music of the happy years with Jane.

There was a locked drawer in Jane's small writing desk, the key to which he had not yet found. Would this yield some information? Using the claw of a hammer, Mark forced the lock. The first thing to meet his eye was a bundle of his own letters, written before they were married. No guilty secret there. Then there were diaries going back to school days, the last entry being for July twenty-seventh, the day before Jane's death.

Study of the diaries confirmed his belief that Jane was a scrupulously truthful person, for the diary entries of a score of little incidents tallied so exactly with the accounts he had heard in the past from her own lips. Occasional mean little things were set down as mean little things, without the smallest attempt to make them appear noble or even justified. In one entry she admitted having taken advantage of an undercharge by the butcher. "I wonder how often it has been the other way?" was her comment. This must have rankled in her mind, for, three weeks later, there was another entry: "Simpson got his four shillings back today and another eightpence. That makes us almost quits."

Jane's honesty was the real kind, not the kind that is paraded as a showpiece. It was, as Mark well knew, altogether inconsistent with a young woman capable of the duplicity involved in leading a double life. The whole idea was absurd, but —his thoughts went full circle—what had she been doing at Wingfield that day?

It was the last entry in the diary, the entry for July twenty-seventh, which drove Mark back into the private hell he had allowed suspicion to create for him. It read: "G.H. McA. 9:30 tomorrow. I am sure M. suspects nothing."

The drawer yielded little else of interest. On the hall table Mark found a pile of letters, mostly bills, which he had not been interested enough to open. A few were addressed to Jane. One of these, a thick envelope marked PRIVATE in the left-hand top corner, he opened. It contained Jane's bank passbook. Two years previously she had inherited six hundred pounds from her Aunt Edith. This sum, with accrued interest, had lain untouched until the very day of Jane's death, when she had withdrawn fifty pounds in cash.

No such sum had been in her handbag when it had been handed to Mark by the matron at the hospital. What had she done with it? Or had it been stolen by someone who arrived early on the scene of the accident at the crossroads? But, leaving that aside, why had Jane withdrawn the sum in the first place? Was this withdrawal made to pay for the present she had said at the station she might give him? If so, where was it? Jane had always been so emphatic that she would not touch this nest egg except for some very special purpose, and it was not like her to change her mind in such a matter. Less than a year previously the purchase of a TV set had not been considered by her sufficiently "special" to weaken.

Who was the mysterious G.H.? What was Jane sure that Mark didn't suspect? How could that be construed innocently?

The penciled words burned themselves into Mark's consciousness as though written with a hot branding iron. Wave after wave of suspicion rolled over him. She was right. Mark, the poor dupe, had suspected nothing. He remembered that last passionate kiss they had exchanged outside the railway station. What had that meant? Was it some kind of apology in advance for an act of deceit and disloyalty she was even then contemplating?

Mark regretted now that he had allowed Jane's sister Margaret to take away all her personal effects, for these might have yielded the key to the mystery. By now Margaret had probably stumbled on something and destroyed it.

The first light of the false dawn was in the sky when Mark again went out into the garden to wrestle in solitude with the doubts and fears which would not be stilled. Somehow, if he were ever to become a normal man again, he knew he must resolve those doubts. If, blinded by love, he had built up in imagination an altogether false picture of Jane, the sooner he destroyed it the better. To have spent three years worshiping a false image was idolatry in a vicious form. All he wanted was the truth, that same truth to which he had always believed Jane was so devoted. If the truth revealed that Jane to the end had been what he had always believed her to be, surely her love for him would have been strong enough for her to forgive his doubts. It was the kind of poisonous logic which could come only from the sick mind of a bewildered man. On the other hand, Mark found himself arguing, if it should transpire that the web of circumstance in which Jane's memory was caught was incapable of an innocent explanation—and this would surely justify his base suspicions—the truth became even more vitally important to his own sanity. What a fool he would be to go on mourning the loss of someone who had never existed—except as his own false concept of her!

It is easy for an onlooker, with no emotional involvement in Mark Willaston's perplexity, to view his doubts and heart-searchings through jaundiced eyes, forgetting that doubts, however unworthy, are uncontrollable. They come, they go, always unbidden. Doubts can be stifled. They can be side-tracked, put away in some remote corner of the psyche to ferment in darkness, but there is no formula for destroying them except by resolution. Ugly, disloyal as Mark's battle in the garden may seem to us, he had to taste the bitterness of remorse. It was his life, his loss. He had to free himself, cast off the chains which weighed him down if he were to go on living, and he realized that only the truth could make him free.

The chill of the dawn mist was entering into Mark's bones. He shivered, less for this than for the chill which clutched his heart. A sound, muffled by the mist, recalled the description of a scene in another garden two thousand years ago:

. . . this night, before the cock crow, thou shalt deny me thrice. . . . And immediately the cock crew.

While he stood there listening as a cock saluted the advent of another day, hot tears of shame ran down Mark's cheeks. He turned and went into the cottage. Kneeling beside the bed which he and Jane had shared since they returned from their wedding trip to Paris, his soul groped blindly out into the infinite to find her and beg her pardon for having allowed the cloud of suspicion to come between them. It seemed as he kneeled there, his cheek pillowed on the eider down which was still fragrant with the perfume she had used so sparingly, that a gentle hand lay across his shoulders and another smoothed his brow. It told him what he wanted to know above all else—that Jane from wherever she was had not withheld her forgiveness. Still kneeling there, Mark fell into a dreamless sleep.

Awakening to find the sun high in the sky, he felt descending upon him, like some healing balm, a tranquillity he had not known for weeks and with it a calm certainty that this would be a day of discovery, which would end his perplexities.

The postman had left two letters in the box while Mark slept, one of them addressed to him and the other to Jane. The former contained a bill from Dr. James McAlister from the General Hospital, Guildford, for five guineas "for professional services rendered to Mrs. Mark Willaston." On the bill was annotated the dates of two consultations, one of July first and the other on July twenty-eighth.

Jealousy and suspicion had magnified "G.H." into a clandestine lover and Jane, by implication, into a faithless wife. Now, it seemed, she had been ill and, so as not to cause him undue worry, she had kept it from him.

Mark telephoned the hospital, asking to speak to Doctor McAlister, only to be told that he was on leave and would be returning two days hence. The earliest date for an appointment was a week ahead. Mark asked the secretary to book it.

His pulse quickened when he saw the Wingfield postmark on the letter addressed to Jane, and with self-discipline he did not immediately open it.

The bees were humming in the garden. The sweet scents of new-mown hay came from beyond. A lark was trilling in a blue sky, and the world was bathed in golden sunlight. The sense of tranquillity deepened as the memory of cockcrow faded.

Mark's fingers trembled as he opened the letter, as though they knew how important it was. A pulse beat madly in his throat, threatening to choke him.

The letter, written in a spidery handwriting belonging to another age, was from Joshua Meggeson, Antiquary, Church Place, Wingfield, Sussex. It read:

Dear Madam: Further to your esteemed order of July 28th, I beg to inform you that the satin canopy is now completed. I enclose my own certificate of authenticity which, you may believe me, would be endorsed by any reputable authority on Tudor furniture. I trust that the work of restoration will meet with your approval.

In addition to the £50 paid by you on July 28th, the cost will be £8. I trust you will not find this excessive. Yours faithfully,

JOSHUA MEGGESON

P.S. As I am frequently away from the shop, will you kindly advise me by letter when you intend to call for the cradle.

The Phantom Setter

ROBERT MURPHY

Not long after Jack Barlow rented a small house and moved into the pretty, little mountain village to run a timbering operation, he was standing at his back door late one afternoon when a big, gaunt blue-ticked setter trotted through the yard. He wondered to whom it belonged and whether it would be any good on grouse. He had always loved grouse shooting and hadn't been able to do any of it for five or six years; now that he was back in grouse country and hadn't a dog, he wanted to meet someone who did have one with whom he could shoot until he could get one of his own.

It was the first setter he had seen in the village, and he called to it. The dog stopped, turned its head toward him, looked at him for a long moment in an oddly speculative way, wagged its tail slightly and went on.

This piqued him a little, for he had a way with dogs. They liked him at sight, and any dog which didn't hate the human race always came to him when he called it. This was the first one within his recollection that hadn't, and certainly the first one that had seemed to sum him up, make a gesture of friendliness and then dismiss him. It had seemed to say that it had more important things to do than pause for a pat on the head, no matter how pleasant this might be.

He was still thinking about the setter when he walked down the street to the little hotel where he had most of his meals, for he hadn't found a housekeeper yet. After he finished his dessert, he went into the living room, sat down and waited until the proprietor—a tall, middle-aged man named Gibney—had finished his dinner and joined him. They talked a little about the weather and the lumbering, and then Barlow asked, "The grouse season opens pretty soon, doesn't it?"

Gibney gave him a rather odd look. "Grouse?" he asked. "Oh, yes, it starts in about a week. You a grouse hunter?"

"I've been one since I could carry a gun," Barlow said, "but I've been in the wrong kind of country for the past five years. I'd like to start in again. There was a big setter in my yard a while ago, and I thought I'd ask you—"

Gibney interrupted him. "Is that why you came here?" he asked.

This seemed like a strange question to Barlow. Here?" he asked. "What do you mean?"

"I mean, is that why you came to town? Grouse?"

"I came to town for the lumbering. Surely you know that."

"Why"—Gibney said and blinked—"why, yes, so I do." He got up, gave Barlow another odd look and said, "Well, make yourself comfortable. I've got to write some letters."

He turned to go out of the room, but Barlow wasn't through with him yet. "I wanted to ask you who owned the setter," he said, "and if it was any good on grouse."

Gibney took a few steps, stopped and half turned. "Nobody owns him," he said, "and nobody ever will. From all I hear he's as good a grouse dog as you're liable to find. But if I were you I'd let him alone."

Gibney started to walk again. He went out of the room, his footfalls fading down the hall, and Barlow stared after him. He couldn't imagine what had got into the man, who had always seemed friendly and sensible enough before. He was apparently still friendly; his tone hadn't been hostile or unpleasant; but it was hard to find him sensible. Why would a sensible man warn him against a dog that was both ownerless and good at his work? Was there some rivalry over the beast in the village, with trouble in the offing for anyone—any stranger, especially—who got interested in him? Barlow was well aware that there were occasionally some strange characters in out-of-the-way mountain villages, but what did that have to do with Gibney's question as to why he, Barlow, had come there? Gibney knew—and had known all along—that he was getting out timber. Gibney had even advised him, when he had first started, what local men to hire and what men to leave alone.

None of it made sense. Barlow shook his head and went out of the hotel. When he was on the street he paused for a moment, looking about, wondering what to do with himself. He didn't want to return to his house; it was too early to go to bed, and he didn't feel like sitting in the little old-fashioned living room wondering what Gibney had meant. There was a fog now, and the few lights along the street were haloed and dim. The eaves along the porch roof of the hotel dripped in a melancholy way, and the village—which was only a few scattered houses, the hotel and a store—seemed to have withdrawn into the mist and partially disappeared. Half a block away there was a diffused reddish glow, and Barlow remembered then that he previously had noticed a bar sign in that direction. He had stayed away from it, not being much of a drinker, but tonight he thought it would be better than his empty house; he walked down the street and went in.

It was not much of a place, made by knocking down the wall between two rooms in an old house. There was a homemade bar with a dirty mirror and a few bottles behind it, several battered tables and an old jukebox; the light was dim. He had met the man behind the bar, so he nodded to him,

99

moved to the bar and asked for a beer. When it came he picked it up and looked around. At the other end of the room three men were seated around one of the tables, and Barlow was surprised to see that they didn't look like most of the natives he had seen around the village.

Their clothes were better; they looked more like retired city men, and not poor ones either. Each one had a drink in front of him, and they were talking in a desultory way. He was so bemused at seeing them there, in that dingy place, that he stared at them. They looked back at him uninterestedly, and after a moment he remembered his manners and turned away.

"Do those men live here?" he asked the bartender in a low voice.

"Them?" the bartender asked, inclining his head slightly. "No. They all got little houses—fancy cabins, sort of—outside of town and come up about this time of year."

"What for?" Barlow asked. "What could they do here?"

"They say they hunt them grouse," the bartender said. "But nobody sees them doing it very often."

"Ah," Barlow said and walked over to their table. "Gentlemen," he said, "my name is Barlow. I don't want to intrude, but I'm a grouse hunter, and Jerry tells me that all of you are too. Would you mind if I sat down?"

The three of them seemed to withdraw into themselves. They looked at him somewhat stonily, with an obvious lack of enthusiasm, for a long moment; then the tallest of them spoke up. "Ah," he said in a grudging tone. "Yes. Do sit down. My name is Roberts. This is Charley Deakyne, and that's Bill Farley to your right."

Deakyne was a chunky, sandy-haired man, and Farley had a square, ruddy face; all three of them wore good tweeds and had an executive look about them. They nodded to him with no change of expression, with no warmth whatever, and Barlow was suddenly thoroughly fed up with them.

"I'm sorry," he said. "I seem to have come along at an inopportune time." He turned away, went back to the bar, swallowed his beer, paid for it and with a nod at the bartender walked out of the place. As he went out the door he glanced quickly back at the three men; none of them had moved.

The fog was, if anything, thicker than when he had gone in and, as he walked through it back to his house, he began to simmer with an anger that was half bafflement. What the devil, he wondered, was wrong with everybody? The three deadpan executive types, he was sure, had manners if they felt like using them; the hotel proprietor didn't make sense. It seemed to happen when he mentioned grouse—which, in his previous experience, had always brought men together for lively and pleasant talk; for grouse hunters were a dedicated lot and had much to say to one another. It was certainly different in this place.

The rest of the week he was busy, running about in his jeep to the four places where he had men working in the bright autumn woods and seeing to the sawing up of his logs after they were trucked to the sawmill. He kept a sharp eye out for grouse as he moved around or bumped over the logging roads, but saw only two or three of them. It looked as though the shooting was going to be very poor, and he began to feel discouraged about it; in the old days, moving about as he had been moving, he would have seen dozens of birds. A good dog would have been a godsend to him, and he saw no chance of getting one.

On Sunday afternoon, at loose ends and still feeling discouraged, he got his gun out of its case and took it out on the back porch to clean the grease out of it. He was working with rags and cleaning rod when he looked up and was startled to see the big setter sitting ten feet away in the grass with its head cocked to one side, looking at him. It waved its tail gently. It was rather old and ribby, bigger than people want setters any more, and there was a ring around its neck where the hair was very thin, as though a collar had chafed it badly. Barlow stopped rubbing the gun; he almost stopped breathing. His head was instantly filled with wild schemes to get the beast into the house or the garage, and he frantically cast about in his mind to remember where there was something he could use for a leash. The dog somehow seemed to sense what he was thinking, moved off several steps and, as some dogs do, raised its upper lip slightly and grinned at him.

This manifestation, at once sardonic and as plain as words would have been, brought Barlow back to earth again. It indicated to him that the dog knew perfectly what he had been thinking, that such things had been tried on it many times before and that it didn't intend to be taken in. Barlow stood the gun in the corner of the porch and grinned.

"All right," he said. "We won't try to fence you in. All grouse hunters are crazy, but this one isn't as crazy as all that." He stepped off the porch. "Come on," he said, "let's take a walk."

The dog watched until he reached the back of his lot, where the woods began. There he stopped and waved an arm, calling it on. It came past him at a run and, as they got into the woods and moved on, it began to hunt, quartering back and forth in front of him, never too far away. It was a delight to Barlow to be in the woods again, moving through the crimson and gold of maple and beech and the somber gloom of the hemlock thickets with a dog working in front of him.

It was like the one or two really good dogs he had owned years ago, covering an extraordinary amount of ground at a fast and steady pace, never beyond his view. It made him feel, as he had felt with those fine dogs of the past, as though there was a sort of empathy between them. No word need be said; the dog acted as a part of the hunter, a more sensitive extension of the man, never out of touch.

Presently he saw how good it really was; at the edge of a witch-hopple thicket it suddenly stopped, crept forward with its belly low for a few steps and stopped again. Barlow stopped himself, for the dog was not pointing yet; either the bird was still stirring a little or the dog wasn't quite sure of its location. Suddenly, with great caution, the dog moved off to the right and, taking a wide half circle, faced Barlow again from the other side of the thicket and froze. The bird had been running in front of them, and the dog had swung around it, headed it off and stopped it. It had been a beautiful performance.

Barlow began to walk in, tingling with expectation. When he reached the middle of the thicket, a big, old grouse rose from under his feet with its booming thunder of wings, angled up through an opening in the trees with its tail spread wide and disappeared. To see a grouse rise again in the autumn woods, after the dog had handled it so well, brought a lump to Barlow's throat. With the curious dichotomy of the hunter he loved both the bird and the hunting of it; and he had neither seen the bird nor hunted it for a long time.

He called the dog; it came without hesitation and sat down beside him. As he gently stroked its head, he knew that he wanted it more than he had wanted anything for years, and that he couldn't have it. There was no way to bind it to him; its actions in his yard had shown him plainly enough—even if Gibney, the hotelkeeper, hadn't told him—that it would go its own way and come to him when it wanted to. He wondered if that was why he had been warned against it. Had Gibney seen people make fools of themselves over it before and warned him out of kindness, or was there more? He had a sudden, inexplicable feeling that there was, that he had been seduced by a strange, masterless dog into an experience that he would be sorry for. He put his hand under the dog's jaw to raise its head and look into its eyes, but it broke away from him and started to hunt again. He watched it for a moment, rather disturbed but unable to leave it, and followed.

They found no other grouse, which didn't surprise Barlow; he hadn't expected that they would find any so close to the village. He was beginning to think of turning back when they came out onto a road, which Barlow recognized as the one which wound around the hills and finally went through the village. There was a car parked 700 or 800 yards away, and it started toward them. When it reached them it stopped, and Barlow recognized the driver as the man named Roberts, whom he had seen in the bar.

"Good afternoon, Barlow," Roberts said. "I thought I'd find you about here. Someone saw you leave the village with the dog, and from your direction I guessed your course." He smiled slightly at Barlow and then switched his attention to the dog, which turned its back on him and sat down.

"Ah, yes," Barlow said. "Kind of you to go to all the trouble. I suppose there's a phone call at the hotel, or someone wants me."

"Not that I know of," Roberts said. "I wanted to talk to you."

Barlow looked at him in surprise. He was still looking at the dog, and there wasn't any more warmth or friendliness in his voice than there had been in the bar. "Talk to me at home then," Barlow said in irritation. "I'm usually there in the evenings."

"I want to talk to you here," Roberts said, and his glance swung to Barlow, cold with hostility. "Before——" He caught himself. "I don't want you around here, Barlow. I'll buy you out and give you a very good profit."

Barlow stared at him. "Will you, now?" he asked, checking his rising temper. "Good. Bring a hundred and fifty thousand dollars in cash to my house tonight at eight, and I'll go. Otherwise, stay out of my way. I don't like you."

He turned away, climbed the bank beside the road and started into the woods. The dog stood up and followed him. He had gone about fifty feet when Roberts shouted, "It's as much for your good as mine, you fool! Go while you can! Go before that accursed beast—— Go! Go!"

Barlow increased his pace and didn't turn around; the dog moved out, and the shouting from the road diminished behind him and finally ceased.

The dog left him shortly before he got back to his house. One moment it was quartering about in front of him and the next it had vanished completely. He didn't whistle or call; he knew it wouldn't be back that day and wondered with a pang whether it would ever be back again. The shooting season started on the morrow and, now that he had seen what the dog could do with an old grouse smart enough to make a fool of an ordinary bird dog and live for a long time so close to the village, a feeling of depression descended upon him. This depression deepened when he thought of Roberts, who had acted almost like a madman. Roberts, with his ridiculous offer —to which he had got an equally ridiculous reply—and his shouting, was certainly a disturbed character; but the more Barlow thought over what Roberts had said, the more it seemed as though the dog was the cause of it. It seemed obvious that he wanted Barlow out of the village because of the dog and had met him on the road to get ahead of the two others with an offer, but why had he called the dog an accursed beast?

Barlow was so engrossed in his puzzled thoughts when he entered the back door that at first he didn't see Farley, he of the square, ruddy face in the bar, and jumped when Farley said "Hello!" from the door of the living room. "I didn't mean to startle you," Farley went on. "I thought you saw me. I say, I'm sorry I acted such an ass the other night."

Barlow had gathered himself and prepared to give Farley the same treatment he had given Roberts, but this approach disarmed him. "It's all right," he said. "Won't you sit down?" Farley took a chair, and Barlow studied him. He was still wary, despite Farley's belated politeness, and said, "Have you come to buy me out too?"

"Buy you out?" Farley asked. "Why would I try to buy you out?"

"Roberts offered to," Barlow said. "He waylaid me on the road."

Farley showed some signs of agitation; he half stood up and then sat down again. His face hardened. "Why, that——" he began and stopped. Then he smiled, a painful, unhappy grimace. "He obviously didn't succeed," he said. "He was always too jumpy, too gruff, not diplomatic enough. He probably meant, at first, to ask you what I'm going to ask you and somehow got put off it."

"And what is that?"

"To let me shoot with you."

Barlow simply stared at him; it was the second one of them he'd stared at. "Let you shoot with me?" he asked. "Why?"

"The dog likes you," Farley said. "He went for a walk with you. Believe me, Barlow, I'd give almost anything. It might work. Just once, just once more." He was almost pleading now; he leaned forward in his chair, and his hands twitched on the arms of it. "Just once. Please."

Barlow was astounded; maybe this one was mad too. "Look," he said, "all of you treated me as though I had cholera, and I've got to like the people I shoot with. You all begin to show up after I'd been seen walking the dog. I don't know what this dog's got that any really fine dog hasn't——"

"You don't?" Farley almost shouted at him. "You don't? You're lying! When you came in here, you were so bemused that you didn't even see me, and that's proof enough. Barlow, it's worth a thousand dollars to me, I tell you!" He came out of his chair and started for Barlow, but Barlow put up one hand and stopped him.

"That's enough," he said. "I want no part of any of you. Go get yourselves dogs with your thousand dollars and let me alone. Now, if you'll excuse me——"

Farley got a pleading look on his face and held up his hands. "No!" he exclaimed. "You've got to listen to me, Barlow. I'll give you two thousand. What other use do I have for money any more? I loved grouse shooting, and it's been thirty years since I've had any like that. There isn't any like it any more. I've come back and come back, it won't look at me and——"

His voice had been rising; he was like a man pleading for an extension of a loan or something else he needed very badly, and Barlow turned away from him, went out through the kitchen and headed for the woods. As he entered the edge of them he turned and saw Farley at the back door. He pointed his finger at the man and said, "Go away. I won't talk to you. And find that other one, Deakyne, and tell him to stay away from here."

He turned again and walked rapidly on, considerably upset by the scene and even more confused.

The next day the grouse season opened, and Barlow was up early. He had bought a supply of meat, and he put a big pan of it out by the back porch. As he cooked his breakfast he made a number of trips to the back door to look out and see if the dog had come, but there was no sign of it; it still hadn't appeared by the time he finished his breakfast. Feeling like a fool, he took his gun and coat out on the back porch and sat there, hoping it would come, but it didn't. He waited for an hour, feeling more foolish all the time; then he swore, got into the jeep and drove off to where he had seen a bird or two in the past.

He hunted until the middle of the afternoon and didn't see a grouse. Like most men who are accustomed to hunt with a good dog, he had the feeling that he was possibly passing birds that froze at his approach and that a dog would have found, or that there were birds which had run on ahead of him like the one the setter had stopped. Having seen the dog work, he missed it all the more.

It was a day of mounting frustration, and the day following was just like it except that he heard a grouse fly off and never saw it; he began to wish that he had never seen the dog. On the third morning, discouraged and glum, he slept an extra hour and finally got up as grumpy as a bear fresh out of hibernation; when he looked out the back door, more out of habit than of hope, the dog was sitting on the back porch. His grumpiness evaporated; he ran about and got the pan of meat and took it out. The dog grinned at him before it began to eat.

"Ah, you devil," he said to it, half in delight and half in exasperation, "you should have lived in the days of the Spanish Inquisition. You'd have been the chief torturer."

The dog had finished eating by that time; it sat down and looked at him. For a moment its eyes held an odd, cool expression of satisfaction. *Just as though it has me exactly where it wants me*, he thought. He had never seen a dog look quite that way before, and a little shiver went up his spine. He shook it off, went into the house and came back with his gunning coat and gun. The dog followed him to the jeep, and they drove off.

Barlow drove six miles to a very wild stretch of country he had marked long before as a likely spot, parked the jeep off the road and started into the woods. The dog began to quarter back and forth in front of him, its pale body flashing through the sunlight patches of the autumn woods, and Barlow followed happily. They went deeper into the woods, crossed a rocky, swift stream and got into a high, golden beech woods dotted with somber patches of hemlock. It was a good place for grouse, and Barlow began to feel the fine anticipation again.

Suddenly he realized that the dog was not in front of him, that it had disappeared. He stopped to listen for it, disturbed. As he stood there a cloud covered the sun, and the woods darkened; a mean, cold little wind sprang up, rattling the dry leaves and sighing in the hemlocks. The darkness increased, and Barlow heard a distant rolling like thunder, and then suddenly the sun came out again and the wind fell. The woods were sunny and still once more, and off to his left he saw the dog again.

He followed on. Presently it was borne in upon him that he had got into an area which had never been timbered, a thing he had never expected to see. The trees were huge, towering up around him; he had never seen their like except in one or two small parks where the primitive growth had been carefully preserved. Here, all around him, as far as he could see, there was not a sign that man had ever been this way. He was so amazed by this, to find such an area in a country which he knew had been thoroughly cut over forty or fifty years ago, that he forgot for a time to watch the dog. He recalled it with a start and looked around. Forty yards in front of him, in an opening piled with a tangle of deadfall timber, he saw it standing on point.

He moved in. As he stopped a little behind the dog, a grouse got up and, although it flew straight away, he missed it. The dog didn't move, and he took another step. A second grouse rose from the deadfall, half climbing and half flying, with its tail spread wide. As it straightened and began to fly off, he knocked it down. The dog still held steady and, as he stood there, staring, with an empty gun, twelve more birds came up in singles and twos and threes and boomed away.

He was still standing there in disbelief when the dog brought in the dead grouse and laid it in front of him. He picked it up, the bird he would rather hunt than any other, soft and beautiful, big, of a gray cast, with the wide, banded tail and the black ruffs on the neck. He held it for a moment, still unbelieving, for no one had seen fourteen grouse together in that country for thirty years. He looked at the dog, which had turned away to hunt again. It seemed younger, somehow; its coat seemed shinier in the sun; it moved more smoothly, and the worn ring around its neck was harder to see.

A queer feeling of unreality took hold of Barlow as he moved off after it through the great, ancient trees, a feeling that didn't seem to have validity, because he could feel the weight of the dead grouse in his game pocket and the fading warmth of it against his back. He didn't have much time to think about it, for the dog soon pointed again. This time he took the first bird out of a flock of ten and watched, with the sheer pleasure of a dedicated grouse hunter who loves to see birds fly, while the remaining birds took off as the first flock had done.

The rest of the morning was like that; there were grouse everywhere, in flocks and by twos and threes and occasionally a single. It was like a grouse hunter's dream of heaven, like the remembered days of his youth when there were still plenty of birds. Sometimes he watched them go for the pleasure of watching; occasionally he shot at a difficult single, passing up the easier ones. When he had six birds he took the shells out of his gun and stopped shooting, whistled to the dog and turned back. The dog came in and followed behind him, as though it, too, was satisfied.

It had been—with the birds, the shooting, the perfect work of the dog and the wild beauty of the country—the happiest day he had spent for many years; he had long since forgotten the feeling of unreality that had descended upon him at first. It was recalled to him suddenly, with a sense of shock, when he found a cougar's tracks in the sand along a small stream. He had never seen the track of a cougar, the catamount of the early settlers; the beast had been gone from the country before he was born, but there was no question in his mind, from the size of the footprints, that that was what it was. He stood looking at the tracks for a long time, trying to believe that he saw the actual evidence of a living creature that he knew for sure had been exterminated in that country by the turn of the century. All around him grew the great trees that had been long gone, too, and, thinking confusedly of these things, he suddenly realized that he hadn't got into a section that had somehow been spared the attentions of white men, but that they hadn't got there yet. He had gone back in time.

The cold little shiver once more ran up his spine, and he looked quickly about. The woods were still, dreaming quietly in the sun, and the dog was gone. He whistled and called; a wild turkey gobbled from far away, and that was all.

And then there was a rising roar all about him, and the sunlight was dimmed; a dark and flickering shadow fell all around him, and he looked up to see a wide, dark river of birds, seemingly without limit or beginning or end, between him and the sky. He could pick out, here and there against the great river of bodies, some pigeonlike shapes and the swift, pigeonlike beat of their wings and knew that he was seeing what no man of his generation had ever seen: one of the great flights of the passenger pigeons that were gone from the earth.

Any remaining doubt that he may have had was wiped from his mind; a sudden fear that he would never get back again, that he was lost and alone in a world that was now gone, a fear that turned him cold all over, suddenly came upon him and he started to run. He struggled up the steep side of the stream bed under the roaring torrent of pigeons and ran up toward the crest of the mountain that he had been descending a short time before, desperately fighting his way through deadfalls and stumbling over rotting, fallen timber. When he reached the top, scratched and bruised and dripping with sweat, he had to stop; there was a pain like a knife in his side, and his heart sounded like a drum.

He leaned against a tree until his breathing returned nearly to normal and his sight cleared and saw the second-growth timber all around him; as far as he could see, back over the way that he had come, there were no more of the great ancient trees, and the pigeons had gone as if they had never existed. His sigh of relief was more like a sob, and he started to walk again. In ten minutes he came out on the road and saw the jeep parked where he had left it. He went up to it, thumped it to make sure that it was real and got in. His bulky game pocket pushed him forward in the seat, and he got out again. He took the six grouse out of his coat one by one and laid them carefully and unbelievingly on the floor. Only then, as he looked at them, did he recall that the limit was two a day now and wondered what he would say if a game warden stopped him. He shook his head, got in and started the engine.

He was a good deal calmer by evening, but he had no desire to eat anything; after the dinner hour he walked to the hotel and found Gibney in the living room by himself. Gibney glanced at him. "You look shaken up," Gibney said, "so I guess you did it."

"Yes," he said, "I did it. Maybe you can tell me now why you warned me."

"Sit down," Gibney said. "You won't believe what I'm about to say; witchcraft isn't very popular any more."

"Witchcraft? I don't——"

"I don't know what else to call it," Gibney said. "That's why I never talk about it when another grouse hunter comes along. I don't enjoy being called a fool."

"Another grouse hunter?" Barlow said. "You mean they hear about it and come here—come here——" He realized he was repeating himself and stopped. "I didn't hear about it," he said. "I wanted to hunt grouse again, and then the dog came into my yard, and then Roberts and Farley——"

"They've been there," Gibney said. "And they want to get back. They'll do anything, almost anything, to get back again."

Barlow stared at him. "You mean the dog takes them?" he asked. He was beginning to see now.

"The dog took them," Gibney said. "He takes everybody once. Listen now. Ten years ago that dog belonged to a man named Micheals. He was a perfectionist, a strange man, mad about grouse hunting. He trained the dog, and one day the dog did something that put him in a rage. So he hanged the beast."

"Hanged him!" Barlow exclaimed, aghast. "Good heavens, man, whoever hangs a dog?"

"Micheals had spent some time among the Eskimos, hunting polar bear, and Eskimos hang dogs they don't want. So Micheals hanged him. Didn't you see that ring around his neck? By the time somebody cut him down he was, to all intents, dead. But he wasn't dead, as a matter of fact. He came around again, and six months later it was Micheals who was dead. His gun went off accidentally and killed him."

Barlow didn't say anything.

"Pure accident maybe. But after that the dog waited for grouse hunters. He'd appear and get into their good graces, take a walk with them and show them how good he was and then——"

"Yes," Barlow said.

"Did the dog disappear for a while, and the sky darken and all that?"

"Yes," Barlow said again.

"And then after it had taken them into the past somewhere, on the best hunt of their lives, it would never have anything to do with them again."

"Never?" Barlow asked. "Never? There isn't any way to——"

"Do you want to be like Roberts and Farley and Deakyne?

Coming back and back, hoping, waiting? There's no future in it, Barlow. Believe me, I know. I've heard it all."

Barlow was silent for a long time, staring at the floor, remembering the impossible flocks of grouse, the great trees, the pigeons, the day. He wasn't frightened of that place now; he wanted, more than he had ever wanted anything, to go back.

"'Sorrow's crown of sorrow,'" Gibney said softly, quoting Tennyson, "'is remembering happier things.'"

"Yes," Barlow said once more. By a great effort of will he dispelled his longing and his hopes. "Thank you," he said and stood up and walked out of the hotel. The mist had come again, giving what he could see of the village an eerie and ghostlike air. He could see the diffused glow of the neon sign on the bar, where Farley and Roberts and Deakyne were doubtless sitting together, and he shivered and turned from it and walked on.

Image of a Starlet

GEORGE BRADSHAW

AUTHOR'S NOTE. Miss Agnes Fury has a good idea. She is, I had better explain, an actress, or rather, a potential, an aspiring actress, and as such she has noticed with a calculating eye the very large number of biographies of performers which have recently been published in magazines and as books. However, she has an objection to almost all of them: they are written when the actress is old—in her thirties or even forties—and when her memory, to judge by the results, has begun to fail. Too much is skipped over, glossed over or just plain left out, so that you get nothing much more than a catalogue of success—unless, of course, the book is one of those in which everybody is drunk, which is another story.

(It is Miss Fury's conviction that an artist's early life and struggles are quite as interesting and important as her later life and triumphs—Miss Fury is twenty-two. She also believes there is no time like the present to set things down—when events are new in your mind; that in no other way can you preserve the fresh, sweet scenery of the moment. Of course, like any actress, Miss Fury is too busy to do this herself, and so must resort to "—as told to."

(Miss Fury's plans for herself are rather grander than most actresses'. She feels she does not want to limit herself to simply one ghost writer. She is certain that as an actress she will run into many authors, and she expects to extract a chapter from each of them during the time he is in her confidence. And I believe she imagines that as she gets older the authors will get better. In her dreamy eyes I think she already sees the cover of her book—*The Life of Aggie Fury*, by Arthur Miller, John Steinbeck, Tennessee Williams, Ernest Hemingway, William Inge, Lillian Hellman, William Faulkner, and so on. I sometimes wonder uneasily whether in such company there is going to be space for my name, the author of Chapter Five.

(The first four chapters, incidentally, are not yet written. I suggested that maybe I should begin at the beginning, but Miss Fury thought not. For Chapter One, the history of her family, her birth, her early childhood and what the world was like generally in those far-off mythical days of the Nineteen-forties, she wants an Akron author—she was born in Akron, Ohio. And for Chapter Two—"Beginnings of an Education," including her eye-opening experience of first setting foot on any stage in a high-school production of *Mourning Becomes Electra*—she will probably need an Akron author too.

(Someone, in other words, who knows Akron thoroughly, although she is not quite sure yet who this will be. But for Chapter Three—a long chapter of at least a hundred pages describing her college days in the Drama Department of Carnegie Tech—she has several candidates. There were many, many playwrights among the students in her day, and it doesn't seem too much to hope that one of them will turn out to be famous, and so oblige her.

(And for Chapter Four—the descent upon New York with a diploma, a thousand dollars, youth, beauty, talent, ambition and hope, all the blue-sky, white-cloud hope of twenty-one —she has a candidate, a poet. His name is Iago Jones, at least that is the name he writes poetry under and the "Jones" obviously is real enough, and she has known him since the first week she arrived in town. They both lived in the same romantic, ratty little rooming house on Leroy Street in Greenwich Village. He would certainly seem to be the perfect candidate, for he writes well—in fact, very well—I have read some of his stuff—and he saw her constantly all during the time she had the thousand dollars and afterward when she had to go to work: perfect, that is, except for one circumstance.

(The Ford Foundation, in what seems to be an officious, interfering way, thrust upon Iago Jones the sum of ten thousand dollars on the theory that with it he could write in peace. Well, you would think the Ford Foundation would know what any normal, well-adjusted, American poet of twenty-four in this day and age would do when he got his hands on ten thousand dollars. Iago Jones did it. He went out and bought himself a business.

(It was a coffeehouse—Espresso Shop on Cordelia Street, and with all that money Iago was able to fix it up handsomely, and since he was already a kind of figure in the Village, the place was a success from the start.

(That of course brought its own problems. So busy was Iago ordering coffee, hiring waitresses, making change, going to the bank, engaging guitar players and firing chefs, that there was no longer ten minutes a day left for writing. While this naturally didn't bother Iago—as any poet will understand—it did upset Aggie and, for all I know, the Ford Foundation. With Aggie it was personal. What about Chapter Four?

(So we come to Chapter Five. When she was in high school, Aggie's father had insisted that between bouts with Euripides and Noel Coward, she learn shorthand and typing, just in case.

(Well, I need a typist, not daily, but a couple of times a week. I am always losing them because of the irregularity, so when someone told me about Aggie I called her up. She said she would be delighted to come.

(What did I expect? In my day an actress if she felt low went to Lily Daché's and bought herself a hat, but I know this is no longer the case. Nowadays she calls up her psychiatrist, and poor Miss Daché can starve.

(Aggie was a great surprise. She did not wear black tights or those fierce pointed shoes or white lipstick: her hair, medium blond, was brushed and brushed, her stockings were nylon, her suit looked like Chanel, although I don't suppose it was, and just to make sure we weren't living in grandma's day, she had a slash of green make-up across her eyes. It looked fine, I am surprised to say, and altogether she was the sort of secretary you dream about and never, never get.

(I will not bother you with how I happened to write Chapter Five; only remember that beautiful young girls have persuaded elderly authors to accommodate them before this. All references made to people and places will be self-explanatory, I think, except perhaps for "the Class." This is the acting school she went—and goes—to, run by Alex Rhodes; it is very well known among the young.

(So I, who have been a close observer of Aggie now for seven months, write down as told to me. . . .)

CHAPTER FIVE

It was in that winter of 'Fifty-nine—'Sixty that (A) I got my first job in the theater and (B) fell in love—and in that order. I didn't really have time for either, but what could I do? I made time.

I hadn't a cent. All the graduation money that I had brought to New York was gone, so whatever I used for rent and food and clothes and tuition I had to earn. Of course, I couldn't take a regular job because the Class—which I was determined to keep on with—ran from one until four every afternoon.

But there are odd jobs in New York. One of mine, on Tuesday, Thursday and Saturday mornings from nine until twelve, was reading to an old lady. My dear old lady, Mrs. Miller, was almost blind, but she was a bright woman in her seventies and she liked to keep up. So three times a week I went through magazines, newspapers and books and she picked out what she wanted to hear. For this she paid me twenty dollars.

The other three workday mornings I worked for an author, typing manuscripts, trying to make sense out of his checkbook and doing his personal—sometimes appalling personal—mail. That was twenty-five dollars.

And then, thank heaven, there was Iago!

I must confess that I had for a little while misjudged Iago. When I had money and he had none, I fed him, night after night, week after week. And gladly. He was wonderful and he seemed to bring with him whenever he came in all the news of New York—that fine, fascinating news I had been so longing for in Akron and Pittsburgh. And oh, his talk! He used words so differently from everybody else; he saw things so differently, felt so differently—well, he was a poet, no mistake and no apology.

Then suddenly came the *wow* of the ten thousand dollars, and Iago disappeared. I was, I am afraid, slightly bitter. It was a blow to my ego, my poor little trans-Appalachian ego, which at that moment needed all the bolstering it could get. I had no words to say what I thought of Iago, and I used them.

But then suddenly, after six weeks, came a telegram summoning me to the opening of the coffeehouse.

I don't know why I went, but I did. Curiosity, pique, something, but I went. And there was Iago in his element—in a big new clean white sweater, smoking a long thin black cigar, sitting behind an old-fashioned cash register he had painted scarlet.

I suppose I must have appeared pretty astonished, standing

there looking at him, for he said, "Poetry is for squares, miss. Food is in. Poetry is out."

He forced on me sandwiches and cakes and five different kinds of coffee. He behaved as if nothing had happened, as if we had seen each other the day before. "You know how much carpenters get, miss? Eighty dollars an hour. Forget the theater, miss. Go to carpenters' school."

"I might as well," I said. "I've run out of the stuff."

"Have a job, miss," Iago said.

"I have one," I said. I already had Mrs. Miller then.

"Have another."

So I did. I became a waitress for Iago. He gave me a dollar a night and tips and whatever I wanted to eat. I averaged fifty dollars a week and too many éclairs. And the hours were perfect—every night from about ten-thirty till one-thirty.

Well, that sounds like a lot of money, doesn't it? Ninety-five dollars a week. But my rent was twenty, tuition twenty-five and it cost me five a week for buses and subways to get around to my various jobs. That left me forty-five for food and clothes and telephone and cleaning and toothpaste and entertainment. Not much in New York. For entertainment I laughed at myself.

That first night before I left, Iago took a hunk of important-looking paper out of his pocket and handed it to me. "For your portfolio," he said. "Necessary equipment, miss. Share in the future of your country and all that."

I unfolded the paper. It was one share of Loew's Theaters common.

"Closed at sixteen and a half," Iago said. "My favorite reading, miss. Poetry is out. Stocks are in."

"Iago," I said, "you shouldn't have."

Everything happens at once. Within three weeks I had my first job in the theater. Didn't really have time for it, did I say? I was kidding.

Image of a Starlet

It was this I had been aiming at, for as long as I could remember. It was this I had dreamed of, slaved at, starved for. A place on the stage. There was time.

And it happened so easily. One of the teachers at the Class, a director, said to me he was doing a play and he thought I'd be right for a part in it and to come around and read. It was off-Broadway, of course, but these days everything is off-Broadway. So I went around and read and got the part. When I came out of the theater onto the street, the whole city, just as I had expected, had changed from gray to gold.

Luckily we rehearsed in the evening from half past seven till half past ten—the director, like a lot of us, had other work in the daytime. None of my jobs, therefore, was interfered with.

Interfered with? As a matter of fact, I got another.

A model agency I was registered with called me and asked if I wanted a job from five till seven every afternoon. Before I said no, I said, "Doing what?"

"Reading a magazine in Grand Central Station," they said.

"Are you mad?" I said.

They shook their heads. "It's a women's magazine. Promotion. You have to sit and read the magazine on that platform where the automobiles used to spin around. Fifteen dollars an hour."

"Fifteen dollars an hour?" I multiplied rapidly. A hundred and eighty a week. Practically twice my entire income.

"Well, yes," I said. "What do I do?"

What I did was to go to Grand Central Station, where I met a woman from the promotion company, who took me to a dressing room and fixed me up in a wonderful negligee and explained the situation. I was one of several girls who worked during the day, and the agency had been right—all we had to do was sit in the middle of Grand Central and read that magazine.

One girl was dressed as a bride and was obviously so fascinated by her reading that she forgot to go to her wedding. Another was neglecting her housework. What I was to do was just sit across the breakfast table from my "husband" and read the magazine while he read a newspaper.

At five o'clock exactly the promotion woman took me out to the platform, helped me up and sat me down opposite— opposite Bill Anderson.

Good heavens! How can I describe Bill Anderson? I divide men into two categories: Yes, and The Rest; well, let me say Bill was a great big YES. He was large and well put together, with black hair and blue eyes; there was nothing pretty about him—he looked as if he might actually be a husband; I guess, without being conscious of it, Bill was just what I had had in mind all the time.

The first thing he said to me was, "Can you talk without moving your lips?" and I said, "I can try." I did and I could.

I don't say I fell in love with Bill that first moment I sat down, but it didn't take long—two or three days. Bill said he knew from the first instant—but you know, men lie. Anyway, at the end of the third day there wasn't any question for either of us.

We were lucky. We had two whole hours a day sitting opposite each other all alone, except for the ten thousand people in the station, but we didn't see them. I still have the impression the station was completely empty—and we got paid thirty dollars for doing it.

Those two hours, of course, were all we had. Think of my schedule: As soon as I got out of bed I had to tear up town to my old lady or the author, then I had to tear down again to the Class, then up to Grand Central, then down to rehearsals, then over to the coffeehouse and finally home to bed. On Sundays there were six hours of rehearsals, and besides that I had to do my washing and ironing, clean the apartment, write a letter home, wash my hair, do my nails and spend at least ten minutes trying to remember who I was.

Things weren't much better for Bill. He was working his way through Columbia; so he had classes all morning, and after lunch he tutored some rich kid over on the East side in English history, then he went back to Columbia for an hour's basketball practice, then down to Grand Central, then up to 100th Street, where he played drums in a combo in a Chinese restaurant from eight till midnight. It's true he didn't have anything much on Sunday, but as he said, "I have to study sometime."

Oh, we were lucky! We talked and talked and talked and it was wonderful. I don't remember really what we said—I who have total recall—but it was wonderful. I guess we would have sounded pretty odd if anyone could have heard us, because when you talk without moving your lips, you can't, for example, use "b" or "m" or "p," so when I called Bill "my beautiful basketball player," it came out "y eautiful asketall ayer." But we understood.

Of course, I couldn't keep Bill all to myself. I had to tell someone. First I told Mrs. Miller, my old lady, and she reacted exactly as I had hoped she would. She kissed me and cried a little. But then I told my author. He said, "That's the damnedest way to meet cute I ever heard of. What have you got for an encore, Macy's window?" which I didn't think was very funny.

For some reason I didn't say anything to Iago about Bill. I don't know why I didn't, I just didn't. Maybe it was just as well, because one night they met.

Bill said to me in the afternoon, "There's a big banquet at the restaurant and they're having Chinese music, so I have the night off. You couldn't squeeze a couple of hours, could you?"

I frowned. Of course I really couldn't, but I said, "Well. I have to go to rehearsal. But afterward maybe I could arrange at the coffeehouse——"

So that's what happened. We bought hot dogs in Grand Central and ate them in the subway going downtown—it was our first subway ride together—and then while I was in rehearsal, Bill went to a movie. Afterward he picked me up and we went over to Iago's.

Iago was agreeable. "Why not?" he said and shrugged. "Sit down and have a cooky on the house, miss. Entertain your business friend."

We stayed. It is so warm and pleasant there, and I guess too I wanted to show Bill off. He looked so different from most of the characters I knew.

There was an incident, I now realize. Iago came and sat with us for a while, and Bill was his most charming, I thought. Except he said, "This is a very interesting place you have here. Very interesting." At that word "interesting" I saw Iago's eyes narrow. He pulled out one of his long thin cigars, lighted it and got up. That was all.

Until the next night. When I came to work, he called me over to him and said, "Be advised. Don't bring your square friend around here any more."

The only thing I could think of to say was, "He's not square."

"He's square," Iago said.

"No," I said. "No. He plays drums."

Iago said, "In a world as big as this, miss, there are squares even on drums. He's dangerous. Keep away from him."

That was silly. And I guess what I said was silly too. "He's a gentleman."

At that Iago gave up. "Gentleman. The girl doesn't know what I'm talking about."

I didn't. But I was to learn.

Well, that didn't seem like much. Not enough to put a blot on that happy time. I think that if you are young and in New York and things are going well, you have the best of everything in the world today. I know that in that winter I loved the snow, the slush, the dirty rain, the dark days; for I had Bill, I had a job in the theater and I was making two hundred and seventy-five dollars a week. *Me.*

And it was going to last. Bill was graduating in February; he had already been in the Army, so that was taken care of, and he would get a job and—— We hadn't made any real plans beyond that. He didn't seem to worry about the job; he said what he had been studying would fit him for a junior-executive position in management relations or maybe it was management problems—something like that, but good, anyway.

Everything was good. Perfect. Too perfect for me to see the flaw in it.

I was working hard. Besides the three hours of rehearsal at night, the director also worked with me and one of the boys during the three hours every day at the Class. I had plenty of time, therefore, to concentrate on my part.

It was a wonderful feeling, creating something new, not just re-creating old roles in classroom that had already been done by Helen Hayes or Julie Harris or Shelley Winters and probably done better. This part was mine.

But I must admit that in some way I was not fully conscious of what was happening. Perhaps because we rehearsed so long, seven weeks, I was lulled by the rhythm of the days and nights; perhaps because I was still being taught in the Class I was not absolutely aware that this was "for real." It's hard to explain; but I know I only finally woke up to facts one night at the coffeehouse.

Iago said to me in a very offhand way, just for something to say, "When is this little drama of yours going to open, miss?"

And I said, just as casually, "Tuesday."

But then I stopped dead. *Tuesday.* I put my hand to my throat and grabbed on, hard. This was Friday. Tuesday was——

Tuesday. The play was going to open Tuesday.

It was and it did.

I got thirty-two telegrams. Old Mrs. Miller sent a basket of fruit, my author sent a bottle of champagne—authors think champagne is appropriate to any occasion—Bill sent flowers (he had to work, of course, and couldn't be there), and there were other flowers, too, and Iago gave me a chain with a topaz heart on it.

It was a fine electric night, all right. The director stopped in my dressing room ten minutes before the curtain and said the house was packed, that lots of critics had come, even a man from *The New York Times*. You could feel the tension in the air. I don't remember my first scene too well, but after that I quieted down and did all the things I was supposed to do.

And then—oh, before I was prepared—it was over. Yes or no, it was over.

There was a party given at an apartment of friends of the producers afterward and we all went. There was lots to eat and drink, but, of course, we were there for only one reason, to wait for the papers and find out what they said. At about one o'clock we found out.

In all the papers the play got good notices—they were more than good, they were exciting. But in none of the papers did I get a notice—except one: *The New York Times*. And in *The New York Times* I got a bad notice.

I won't put down what it said, word for dagger word; that would be too much, but it was bad. I, Aggie Fury, got a bad notice in *The New York Times*. After all the years of waiting, hoping, working, that is what happened. In an instant.

I went home and fell into bed and stared at the ceiling all night.

I got through the next day. I am naturally healthy, but three aspirins and four cups of black coffee helped. I went to my author and then I went to the Class. I felt I had, just *had* to face everybody right away. But I needed all my strength.

I hope I am going to be able to make myself clear about Bill and Grand Central. So little was said, and so much happened. He was on the platform when I arrived, as usual.

I said, "Did you see the *Times?*"

He had.

I tried to sound light. "It doesn't have a very big circulation," I said.

"Yes, it does," he said.

He was silent for a moment. Then he said, "Aggie, you mustn't go back to that theater."

"What?" I said.

"I mean it." And he began to tell me what he meant.

Bill had a job. He hadn't told me because I had been so deadly concentrated on the play. It was a good job with an electronics manufacturing corporation in San Diego. San Diego, California. He was to report there a week after he graduated.

He wanted me to come with him. He wanted to get me away from this—this thing that had happened to me in the *Times.* San Diego was a beautiful city. There would be plenty there for us to do. We would have our own house and be happy and forget all this.

"Forget all this——"

"Bill—Bill——" I said.

I could not say more. How could I tell him, after such a speech, that my whole life now was dedicated to making *The New York Times* eat its words?

I felt awful—my lowest. I couldn't speak because, without my being able to do anything about it, big fat tears kept forming in my eyes and splashing down my cheeks.

I don't know what people thought. I hope they thought I was reading a very sad story in the magazine. A lot of them looked. We weren't alone in Grand Central Station any more, Bill and I. There were ten thousand people around us, and a lot of them looked.

I could think of only one thing. Iago. I must get to him, I must find him, I must tell him what had happened.

And that took time. First I had to get to the theater and play the performance; but the moment that was over I ran to the coffeehouse.

He wasn't there. I decided to ask one of the girls, but she was no help. She shrugged, and then she said, "Something kookie's going on. I heard he sold this place."

"Sold it?"

"I heard."

I tore out. There was a bar he sometimes went to. He wasn't there. I tried two or three of the other coffeehouses. No luck. And then I thought, *Could he be at home?* I went along to his street and looked up. His lights were on. He was home.

When he let me in at his door, he said, "I thought I was shed of you, miss. Play's a hit. You can relax."

"Iago," I said. "Listen——"

"Sit down."

"Listen. You were wrong."

"I often am."

"About Bill. He isn't a square."

"So?"

"It's me. Me. I'm the square."

"Sit down," Iago said. "Go ahead."

I sat down. "Listen," I said. Then I told him what had happened at Grand Central, all of it, every word of it, what Bill had said, what I said, how I had cried. "So you see," I said, "Bill isn't a square. He's good and he's decent. That isn't square."

"No," Iago said.

"It's me," I said. "I was the wrong one. Thinking I could have everything the easy way. Love, money, a career. Without any trouble. And what do I have?"

"Take it easy," Iago said.

"What do I have? A career? I'm giving a bad performance. I know that as well as *The New York Times*. Love? I simply don't love Bill enough to go to San Diego with him."

Iago came and sat down on a stool in front of me. "Money?" he said.

"Not much of that. Oh, Iago, only one thing good has come out of this." I forced myself to go on. "When I sat there in Grand Central Station with tears splashing over ten thousand people—one thing—one thing I wanted to do, one thing I knew I had to do. And that was come and tell you."

Iago took my hand and held it in his. "About time," he said.

At that I drew the first easy breath I had drawn in a long time. "Why didn't I know before?" I said.

Iago tilted his head. "You're not very bright. Is that it?"

I nodded.

"I knew, of course," Iago said. "A long time ago. But—well, let's——"

"Let's what?"

"Let's talk about now."

In about an hour Iago said, "Are you hungry?" And I said, "Starving."

"Come on," he said, "we'll go to the place. We can't for much longer."

"Did you—" I said, "—did you sell it?"

Iago nodded.

"But why?"

"Something you taught me. A poet can be a coffeehouse owner, but a coffeehouse owner can't be a poet."

I laughed. "Say," I said, "we're learning."

"We're learning, miss."

"I like it."

We went out and it was snowing. It was white and quiet and New York. We walked along slowly and looked at everybody and saw everything, and kicked the snow together.

Hit and Run

JOHN D. MACDONALD

Twenty-eight days after the woman died, Walter Post, special investigator for the Traffic Division, squatted on his heels in a big parking lot and ran his fingertips lightly along the front-right fender of the car which had killed her. It was a blue and gray four-door sedan, three years old, in the lower price range.

The repair job had probably been done in haste and panic. But it had been competently done. The blue paint was an almost perfect match. Some of it had got on the chrome stripping and had been wiped off, but not perfectly. The chrome headlight ring was a replacement, with none of the minute pits and rust flecks of the ring on the left headlight. He reached up into the fender well and brushed his fingers along the area where the undercoating had been flattened when the fender had been hammered out.

He stood up and looked toward the big insurance-company office building, large windows and aluminum panels glinting in the morning sun, and wondered where Mr. Wade Addams was, which window was his. A vice president, high up, looking down upon the world.

It had been a long hunt. Walter Post had examined many automobiles. The killing had occurred on a rainy Tuesday morning in September at 9:30, in the 1200 block of Harding

Avenue. It was an old street of big elms and frame houses. It ran north and south. Residents in the new suburban areas south of the city used Harding Avenue in preference to Wright Boulevard when they drove to the center of the city. Harding Avenue had been resurfaced a year ago. There were few traffic lights. The people who lived on Harding Avenue had complained about fast traffic before Mary Berris was killed.

Mr. and Mrs. Steve Berris and their two small children had lived at 1237 Harding Avenue. He was the assistant manager of a supermarket. On that rainy morning she had put on her plastic rain cape to hurry across the street, apparently to see a neighbor on some errand. It was evident she had not intended to be gone long, as her two small children were left untended. The only witness was a thirteen-year-old girl, walking from her home to the bus stop.

Through careful and repeated interrogations of that girl after she had quieted down, authorities were able to determine that the street had been momentarily empty of traffic, that the death car had been proceeding toward the center of town at a high rate of speed, that Mary Berris had started to cross from right to left in front of the car, hurrying. Apparently, when she realized she had misjudged the speed and distance of the car, she had turned and tried to scamper back to the protection of the curb.

Walter Post guessed that the driver, assuming the young woman would continue across, had swerved to the right to go behind her. When she had turned back, the driver had hit the brakes. There were wet leaves on the smooth asphalt. The car had skidded. Mary Berris was struck and thrown an estimated twenty feet through the air, landing close to the curb. The car had swayed out of its skid and then accelerated.

The child had not seen the driver of the car. She said it was a pale car, a gray or blue, not a big car and not shiny new. Almost too late she realized she should look at the license number. But by then it was so far away that she could only tell that it was not an out-of-state license and that it ended, in her words, "in two fat numbers. Not sharp numbers like ones and sevens and fours. Fat ones, like sixes and eights and nines."

Mary Berris lived for nearly seventy hours with serious brain injuries, ugly contusions and abrasions and a fractured hip. She lived long enough for significant bruises to form, indicating from their shape and placement that the vehicle had struck her a glancing blow on the right hip and thigh, the curve of the bumper striking her right leg just below the knee. The fragments of glass from the lens of the shattered sealed-beam headlamp indicated three possible makes of automobile. No shellac or enamel was recovered from her clothing. It was believed that, owing to the glancing impact, the vehicle had not been seriously damaged. She did not regain consciousness before death.

For the first two weeks of the investigation Walter Post had the assistance of sufficient manpower to cover all places where repairs could have been made. The newspapers co-operated. Everyone in the metropolitan area was urged to look for the death car. But, as in so many other instances, the car seemed to disappear without a trace. Walter Post was finally left alone to continue the investigation, in addition to his other duties.

And, this time, he devoted more time to it than he planned. It seemed more personal. This was not a case of one walking drunk lurching into the night path of a driving drunk. This was a case of a young, pretty housewife—very pretty, according to the picture of her he had seen—mortally injured on a rainy Tuesday by somebody who had been in a hurry, somebody too callous to stop and clever enough to hide. He had talked to the broken husband and seen the small, puzzled kids, and heard the child witness say, "It made a terrible noise. A kind of—thick noise. And then she just went flying in the air, all loose in the air. And the car tried to go away so fast the wheels were spinning."

Walter Post would awaken in the night and think about Mary Berris and feel a familiar anger. This was his work, and he knew the cost of it and realized his own emotional involvement made him better at what he did. But this was a very small comfort in the bitter mood of the wakeful night. And he knew there would be no joy in solving the case because he would find at the end of his search not some monster, some symbol of evil, but merely another victim, a trembling human animal.

His wife Carolyn endured this time of his involvement as she had those which had gone before, knowing the cause of his remoteness, his brutal schedule of self-assigned work hours. Until this time of compulsion was ended, she and the children would live with—and rarely see—a weary man who kept pushing himself to the limit of his energy, who returned and ate and slept and went out again.

Operating on the assumption that the killer was a resident of the suburban areas south of the city, he had driven the area until he was able to block off one large section where, if you wanted to drive down into the center of the city, Harding Avenue was the most efficient route to take. With the co-operation of the clerks at the State Bureau of Motor Vehicle Registration, he compiled a discouragingly long list of all medium and low-priced sedans from one to four years old registered in the name of persons living in his chosen area, where the license numbers ended in 99, 98, 89, 88, 96, 69, 86, 68 and 66. He hoped he would not have to expand it to include threes and fives, which could also have given that impression of "fatness," in spite of the child witness's belief that the numbers were not threes or fives.

With his list of addresses he continued the slow process of elimination. He could not eliminate the darker or brighter colors until he was certain the entire car had not been re-painted. He worked with a feeling of weary urgency, suspecting the killer would feel more at ease once the death car was traded in. He lost weight. He accomplished his other duties in an acceptable manner.

At nine on this bright October tenth, a Friday, just twenty-eight days and a few hours after Mary Berris had died, he had checked the residence of a Mr. Wade Addams. It was a long and impressive house on a wide curve of Saylor Lane. A slim, dark woman of about forty answered the door. She wore slacks and a sweater. Her features were too strong for prettiness, and her manner and expression were pleasant and confident.

"Yes?"

He smiled and said, "I just want to take up a few moments of your time. Are you Mrs. Addams?"

"Yes, but really, if you're selling something, I just——"

He took out his notebook. "This is a survey financed by the automotive industry. People think we're trying to sell cars, but we're not. This is a survey about how cars are used."

She laughed. "I can tell you one thing. There aren't enough cars in this family. My husband drives to work. We have a son, eighteen, in his last year of high school, and a daughter, four-teen, who needs a lot of taxi service. The big car is in for repairs, and today my husband took the little car to work. So you can see how empty the garage is. If Gary's marks are good at midyear, Wade is going to get him a car of his own."

"Could I have the make and year and model and color of your two cars, Mrs. Addams?"

She gave him the information on the big car first. And then she told him the make of the smaller car and said, "It's three years old. A four-door sedan. Blue and gray."

"Who usually drives it, Mrs. Addams?"

"It's supposed to be mine, but my husband and Gary and I all drive it. So I'm always the one who has it when it runs out of gas. I *never* can remember to take a look at the gauge."

"What does your husband do, Mrs. Addams?"

"He's a vice president at Surety Insurance."

"How long has your boy been driving?"

"Since it was legal. Don't they all? A junior license when he was sixteen, and his senior license last July when he turned eighteen. It makes me nervous, but what can you do? Gary is really quite a reliable boy. I shudder to think of what will happen when Nancy can drive. She's a scatterbrain. All you can do is depend on those young reflexes, I guess."

He closed his notebook. "Thanks a lot, Mrs. Addams. Beautiful place you have here."

"Thank you." She smiled at him. "I guess the automobile people are in a tizzy, trying to decide whether to make big cars or little cars."

"It's a problem," he said. "Thanks for your co-operation."

He had planned to check two more registrations in that immediate area. But he had a hunch about the Addams's car. Obviously Mrs. Addams hadn't been driving. He had seen too many of the guilty ones react. They had been living in terror. When questioned, they broke quickly and completely. Any questions always brought on the unmistakable guilt reactions of the amateur criminal.

So he had driven back into the city, shown his credentials to the guard at the gate of the executive parking area of the Surety Insurance Company and inspected the blue-gray car with the license that ended in 89.

He walked slowly back to his own car and stood beside it, thinking, a tall man in his thirties, dark, big-boned, a man with a thoughtful, slow-moving manner. The damage to the Addams car could be coincidence. But he was certain he had located the car. The old man or the boy had done it. Probably the boy. The public schools hadn't opened until the fifteenth.

He thought of the big job and the fine home and the pleasant, attractive woman. It was going to blow up that family as if you stuck a bomb under it. It would be hell, but not one tenth, one hundredth the hell Steve Berris was undergoing.

He went over his facts and assumptions. The Addamses lived in the right area to use Harding Avenue as the fast route to town. The car had been damaged not long ago in precisely the way he had guessed it would be. It fitted the limited description given.

He went into the big building. The information center in the lobby sent him up to the twelfth-floor receptionist. He told her his name, said he did not have an appointment but did not care to state his business. She raised a skeptical eyebrow, phoned Addams's secretary and asked him to wait a few minutes. He sat in a deep chair amid an efficient hush. Sometimes, when a door opened, he could hear a chattering drone of tabulating equipment.

Twenty minutes later a man walked quickly into the reception room. He was in his middle forties, a trim balding man with heavy glasses, a nervous manner and a weathered golfing tan. Walter stood as he approached.

"Mr. Post? I'm Wade Addams. I can spare a few minutes."

"You might want to make it more than a few minutes, Mr. Addams."

"I don't follow you."

"When and how did you bash in the front-right fender of your car down there in the lot?"

Addams stared at him. "If that fender is bashed in, Mr. Post, it happened since I parked it there this morning."

"It has been bashed in and repaired."

"That's nonsense!"

"Why don't we go down and take a look at it?" He kept his voice low.

Wade Addams was visibly irritated. "You'd better state your business in a—a less cryptic way, Mr. Post. I certainly have more to do than go down and stare at the fender on my own car."

"Do you happen to remember that hit-and-run on Harding Avenue? Mary Berris?"

"Of course I rem——" Wade Addams suddenly stopped talking. He stared beyond Post, frowning into the distance. "Surely you can't have any idea that——" He paused again, and Post saw his throat work as he swallowed. "This is some mistake."

"Let's go down and look at the fender."

Addams told the receptionist to tell his secretary he was leaving the building for a few moments. They went down to the lot. Post pointed out the unmistakable clues. There was a gleam of perspiration on Addams's forehead and upper lip. "I never noticed this. Not at all. My gosh, you don't look this carefully at a car."

"You have no knowledge of this fender's being bashed since you've owned the car?"

"Let's go back to my office, Mr. Post."

Addams had a big corner office, impressively furnished. Once they were alone, and Addams was seated behind his desk, he seemed better able to bring himself under control.

"Why have you—picked that car?"

Post explained the logic of his search and told of the subterfuge he had used with Mrs. Addams.

"Janet would know nothing about——"

"I know that, from talking to her."

"My wife is incapable of deceit. She considers it her great social handicap," he said, trying to smile.

"You didn't kill that woman either."

"No, I——"

"We're thinking of the same thing, Mr. Addams."

Addams got up quickly and walked restlessly over to the window. He turned suddenly, with a wide, confident smile. "Damn stupid of me, Mr. Post. I remember now. Completely slipped my mind. I drove that car over to Mercer last July. I—uh—skidded on a gravel road and had it fixed in a little country garage . . . hit it against a fence post when I went in the ditch."

Walter Post looked at him and shook his head slowly. "It won't work."

"I swear it's——"

"Mr. Addams, this is not a misdemeanor. In this state a hit-and-run killing is a mandatory murder charge. Second degree. The only way out of it is a valid insanity plea. In either case the criminal has to spend plenty of time locked up. You'd have to prove the date of the trip, show police officers exactly where you skidded, take them to the country garage, find people to back up the story. No, Mr. Addams. Not even a good try."

Addams went behind his desk and sat down heavily. "I don't know what to do. Get hold of a lawyer, I guess. All of a sudden I'm a hundred years old. I want to make myself believe that Gary bashed a fender and had it repaired on his own so he wouldn't lose his driving privilege."

"Why can't you believe that?"

"He has—changed, Mr. Post. In the last month. The teen-age years are strange, murky years, if what I remember of my own is any clue. He's a huge youngster, Mr. Post. They all seem to grow so big lately. I've had trouble with him. The normal amount. If a kid doesn't have a streak of rebellion against authority in him—authority as represented by his male parent—then he isn't worth a damn. Gary has been a sunny type, usually. Reliable. Honest. He's traveled with a nice pack of kids. He's a pretty fair athlete and a B student. His contemporaries seem to like and respect him. Here's his picture. Taken last June."

Crew cut and a broad smiling face, a pleasant, rugged-looking boy, a good-looking kid.

"He's changed. Janet and I have discussed it, and we've tried to talk to him, but he won't talk. He's sour and moody and gloomy. Off his feed. He doesn't seem interested in dates or athletics or his studies. He spends a lot of time in his room with the door closed. He grunts at us and barks at his sister. We thought it was a phase and have hoped it would end soon. We've wondered if he's in some kind of trouble that he can't or won't tell us about."

"I appreciate your being so frank, Mr. Addams."

"I can't, in my heart, believe him capable of this. But I've read about all the polite, decent, popular kids from good homes who have got into unspeakable trouble. You know—you can live with them and not understand them at all."

"Were you here in the office on the ninth?"

"Yes, if it was a weekday."

"What time did you get in?"

Addams looked back in his appointment calendar. "A Tuesday. I'd called a section meeting for nine. I was in at eight-thirty, earlier than usual. I can't believe Gary——"

"A kid can panic, Mr. Addams. A good kid can panic just as quick as a bad kid. And once you run, it's too late to go back. Maybe he loaned the car to some other kid. Maybe your wife loaned it."

Addams looked across the desk at Walter Post, a gleam of hope apparent. "It's against orders for him to let any of his friends drive it. But it could have happened that way."

"That's what we have to find out, Mr. Addams."

"Can we—talk to my boy? Can we go together and talk to Gary?"

"Of course."

Wade Addams phoned the high school. He said he would be out in twenty minutes to speak to his son on a matter of importance, and he would appreciate their informing him and providing a place where they could talk privately.

When they arrived at the high school, they went to the administration office and were directed to a small conference room. Gary Addams was waiting for them and stood up when they came in and closed the door. He was big. He had a completely closed expression, watchful eyes.

"What's up, dad? I phoned the house to find out, but mom didn't know a thing. I guess I just got her worried."

Wade Addams said, "I was going to let Mr. Post here ask you some questions, Gary, but with his permission I think I would like to ask you myself."

Walter Post had to admire the man. The answers he would get would very probably shatter a good life and, unless the kid was one in ten thousand, his future would be ruined beyond repair. Yet Wade Addams was under control.

"Go ahead," Post said.

"You have acted strange for a month, Gary. You know that. Your mother and I have spoken to you. Now I'm desperately afraid I know what has been wrong."

"Do you?" the boy said with an almost insolent indifference.

"Will you sit down?"

"I'd just as soon stand, thanks."

Wade Addams sighed. "You'd better tell us about the front-right fender on the small car, Gary. You'd better tell us the whole thing."

Post saw the flicker of alarm in the boy's light-colored eyes as he glanced sideways at Post. He had hunted a killer, and now he felt sick at heart, as in all the times that had gone before.

"You better clue me, dad. That question is far out."

"Did you repair it yourself? Were you driving or was one of your friends driving when you hit that woman? Does that— clue you enough?" he asked bitterly.

The boy stiffened and stared at his father with a wild, naked astonishment. "No!" the boy said in an almost inaudible voice. "You couldn't possibly—you couldn't be trying to——"

"To what? I'm ordering you to tell me about that fender."

The boy changed visibly in a way Walter Post had seen once before and would always remember. It takes a curious variety of shock to induce that look of boneless lethargy. Once, at a major fire, he had seen a man who believed his whole family had perished, had seen that man confronted by his family. There was the same look of heavy, brooding wonder.

Gary Addams slid heavily into one of the wooden armchairs at the small conference table. He looked at the scarred table and said in a dull voice, "I'll tell you about that fender. The fourteenth of September was a Sunday. You can look it up. You and mom had gone to the club. Nancy was off someplace. School started the next day. I played tennis. I got back about four in the afternoon, dad. I decided to wash the car. I hadn't washed it in two weeks, and I figured you'd start to give me a hard time about it any day. That was when I found out somebody had bashed the right fender and had it fixed since the last time I'd washed it. You wash a car, and you can spot something like that right away."

"But, Gary, you didn't say anything."

"If anybody'd been home, I'd have gone right in and asked who clobbered the fender. You know, like a joke. But there wasn't anybody home. And it—it kept coming into my mind. About that woman." Wade Addams had moved to stand beside his son. The boy looked up at him with a dull agony. "Dad, I just couldn't stop thinking about it. We always go down Harding Avenue. Our car matches the description. And if—if you or mom had bashed a fender in some kind of harmless way, you wouldn't have kept it a secret. I couldn't imagine you or mom doing such a terrible thing, but I kept thinking about it, and it got worse and worse. I thought I was going to throw up. And ever since then, I haven't known what to——"

"Where were you on the day that woman was hit, son?" Walter Post asked.

The boy frowned at him. "Where was I? Oh, a guy picked me up real early, about dawn, and a bunch of us went up to his folks' place at the lake and swam and skied all day and got back late."

Wade Addams spoke to his son in a strange voice. "Let me get this straight. For the last month, Gary, you've been living with the idea that either your mother or I could have killed that woman and driven away?" Walter Post could see how strongly the man's hand was grasping the boy's shoulder.

"But nobody else ever drives the car!" the boy cried. "Nobody else."

Walter Post watched Wade Addams's face and saw the fierce indignation of the falsely accused change to a sudden understanding of what the boy had been enduring. In a trembling voice Wade Addams said, "We didn't do it, boy. Neither of us. Not one of the three of us. Believe me, son. You can come out of your nightmare. You can come home again."

When the boy began to cry, to sob in the hoarse clumsy way of the man-child years, Walter Post stepped quietly out into the corridor and closed the door and leaned against the wall and smoked a cigarette, tasting his own gladness, a depth of satisfaction he had never before experienced in this deadly occupation. It made him yearn for some kind of work where this could happen more often. And he now knew the probable answer to the killing.

When Addams and his son came out of the room, they had an identical look of pride and exhaustion. The boy shook hands with Post and went back to class.

"Now we go to your house and talk to your wife," Walter

Post said. "We were too quick to think it was the boy. We should have talked to her first."

"I'm glad we did it just this way, Mr. Post. Very glad. About the car. I think now I can guess what——"

"Let's let your wife confirm it."

At 3:30 that afternoon Walter Post sat in the small office of Stewart Partchman, owner of Partchman Motors. With him were Partchman and a redheaded service manager named Finnigan and a mechanic named Dawes.

Finnigan was saying, "The reason I didn't let Thompson go, Mr. Partchman, is that he's always been a reliable little guy, and this is the first time he goofs. Dawes drove him out there to bring back the Addams job, around nine o'clock, and figured Thompson was following him right on back into town, and Thompson doesn't show up with the car until after lunch. He had some story about his wife being sick and stopping by his house to see how she was."

Partchman said angrily, "So it gave him time to take it someplace and hammer that fender out, then come back here and sneak the headlamp and chrome ring out of stock and get some paint onto it."

"It was in for a tune-up," Finnigan said, looking at the service sheet on the job, "new muffler, lube and oil change. It got in so late we couldn't deliver it back out there until the next day. I remember apologizing to Mrs. Addams over the phone. I didn't tell her why it was late. She was pretty decent about it."

The mechanic said, "Tommy has been jumpy lately. He's been making mistakes."

"How do you want to handle it?" Partchman asked Walter Post.

"Bring him in here right now, and everybody stay here and keep quiet and let me do the talking," Post said wearily.

Thompson was brought in, small, pallid, worried. His restless eyes kept glancing quickly at Post. Post let the silence become long and heavy after Thompson asked what was wanted of him. At last he said, "How did you feel during those three days, while you were wondering whether she was going to die?"

Thompson stared at him and moistened his lips. He started twice to speak. The tears began to run down his smudged cheeks. "I felt terrible," he whispered. "I felt just plain terrible." And he ground his fists into his eyes like a guilty child.

Walter Post took him in and turned him over to the experts from the Homicide Section and accomplished his share of the paperwork. He was home by six o'clock. He told Carolyn about it that evening, when he was lethargic with emotional reaction to the case. He talked to her about trying to get into some other line of investigatory work and tried to explain his reasons to her.

But they woke him up at three in the morning and told him to go out to River Road. He got there before the lab truck. He squatted in a floodlighted ditch and looked at the broken old body of a bearded vagrant and at the smear of green automotive enamel ground into the fabric of a shabby coat. He straightened up slowly, bemused by his own ready acceptance of the fact it was not yet time to leave this work. Somebody was driving in a personal terror through the misty night, in a car so significantly damaged it would wear—for Walter Post—the signs and stains of a sudden murder.

The Frigid Sea

EDMUND GILLIGAN

On the western edge of the Grand Bank of Newfoundland, a Gloucester dory lay tied up to a trawl buoy, a black keg marking the position of a trawl line that had carried hundreds of baited hooks to the halibut roving forty fathoms below. The two dorymen had set their trawl shortly after daybreak. Now they shrewdly glanced, this way and that, into the fog that streamed gray and thick over their heads.

They were in the worst circumstances known to the Atlantic fishermen. Neither October gales nor December ice caused the fear in their hearts that the fog of springtime created. "Gone astray in fog" had been the epitaph of many a doryman in their time and for generations past. If the fog held, they could not be easily found by their schooner, the *Judith*, that had dropped them there. Nor could they find her. They could barely see a dory's length away. In fact, the trawl buoy vanished at times in the hissing passage of fog.

Worse still, the fog had changed in character. The changes had been so subtle, so difficult to size up, that they hadn't yet figured out their true meaning. The first sign of new trouble had come soon after they had tied up to wait for the schooner to blow a signal that they should begin hauling fish. At breakfast, when the fog had first swirled over the schooner, it had been the captain's opinion that the sun would drive the fog off in no time at all. That opinion had been theirs too. So they had watched without misgivings when the *Judith* sailed off to the northwest, where her nine other dories were to be dropped, one by one. Now, in full morning, the sun had failed to lighten the fog. They had been trying to make out the reason for this failure, most unusual in April.

Garry Bohan, the younger man, was the first to speak of the changes. "This vapor, Simon—it ain't what it was at daybreak. I don't know what it's doing. And it's some degrees colder—the water, I mean." His eyes, gleaming very black in a constant measurement of the fog, were startling in the extraordinary pallor of his face, a natural color in him because sun and wind never stained his skin. He looked more like a lithe, able Spaniard than anything else. He was a man of much strength and the best helmsman aboard the *Judith*. In her swift voyages to the lively Wednesday market at Boston, he could steer her "through the eye of a needle," as the Gloucestermen used to say in those old days, the bygone days when such vessels worked under sail only.

His dorymate answered by a despairing strike of his hands together. A freckled man of more than middle age, seeming huge in his black oilskins, he wore an odd bit of dress—a muffler of white wool, roughly tied under his chin. In that foggy dusk, the cloth set off his face clearly and thus showed the gauntness caused by illness. That was the reason for the muffler—he had nearly died in November of pneumonia that had knocked him out during the last trip of the season. The schooner had laid up since.

"More to it," said Garry. "I figure this vapor is wetting up a little—not much, but a little." He ran his hand down his frost-scarred cheek and looked closely at his glove, the white cotton glove of their trade. He raised his arm and examined the tiny drops gathering in the wrinkles of his yellow oilskins.

He waited a while, not exactly in deference to the older man, but because he really didn't want to say anything more just then. There was still a chance that the schooner would come to pick them up or, at least, that she would blow a warning signal that they should leave their trawl and meet her.

Simon responded, "This fog ain't what he said 'twould be —something the sun would scoff up quick."

"No, Simon, it won't. The sun ought to do it, but this one don't seem to. I'm beginning to think there's something odd about things. We've our wits to keep about us this day." Garry let a little time pass and, in a passionate rise of his voice, usually grave and low-toned, he said, "It's ice somewhere, Simon. That's what it is, make no mistake about it. It come up on us in the night. And now it's sending a vapor of its own with this fog."

A cross sea, neither high nor heavy, struck the dory and, passing under, heaved it so smartly that the slack came out of the rope fast to the buoy.

By a silence that seemed sullen and the mournful droop of his head, it was plain that the memories of earlier struggles on the Grand Bank were hurting Simon. They had been dory-mates a long time and had been in springtime ice before. He didn't believe that he was up to any such fight and he revealed his thought by saying clearly, "I just pray to God it's not so, Garry! Not this time."

Garry thrust up his hand in a warning gesture. "You hear anything just now, Simon? I think I hear something off there. There it goes again!"

Garry had figured things out correctly. This is what he heard—an iceberg and its vast fields of ice. That new, rainy vapor had come from the berg; so had the sudden chillness of the water.

Four miles through the fog and to the southeast, the black water, in which the dory lay, became a surf beating mildly down a jagged shore of ice. To the eastward the ice field curved out in a headland that kept shifting northward in the shape of a moon's horn. To the southward and five miles from the dory, a second headland seethed forward, its horn pointed toward the first horn and swiftly approaching it.

In the main ice field there stood columns and towers the height of a foremast. Those frost-gilded structures swayed a few degrees. Each tower kept shooting a particular beam, one way or another, into the fog, and so regularly that a man might fancy each tower held an able-bodied seaman making a signal to others imprisoned. There were heaving mounds crackling under a tidal force so violent that blocks of ice frequently vaulted into the fog. In about the middle of the ice a stove boat lay, its boards all awry. It had been abandoned there by seamen long since gone away.

At times, on the farther edge of the ice field, a wind blew the vapor upward; then rose-colored clouds appeared on a blue horizon, and the berg itself, sailing at a one-knot speed, heaved grandly into the brief sunlight. Its topmost pinnacle gleamed two hundred feet above its base. Two streams, colored like a day moon, poured out of caverns below the pinnacle. Lesser peaks and round-topped hills broke the mile-long slope that slanted into the berg's wake.

In the centuries of its creation, snowfall by snowfall, upon the Greenland glacier, the berg had captured quantities of air, held in each crystal and in sealed caverns. During the passage down the Labrador Current to the Grand Bank, the deposits of air had become warmer and were rapidly expanding. Where the current began to break up, the berg entered an atmosphere gentled by sunlight and by the influence of the Gulf Stream.

In these last days the berg had driven straight down a gully of one-hundred-fathom water. When the gully shoaled abruptly, the mass of ice under the sea struck the bottom. The berg ceased its voyaging. That shock, and the more rapid expansion of air in the ice held constantly to the sun, shattered the berg. Its pinnacle swayed and crashed into the Atlantic. Clouds of splinters, shaped like arrows, soared outward and darted into the sea. The pinnacle toppled in such a massive plunge that a sea sprang halfway up the sundered walls of ice. A bellow rolled outward, filling the sky with the noise of ten thunderbolts exploding at once.

The destruction of the berg exposed the ice field to the full force of the tide. This force, and the strength of that single outward-rolling sea, changed the course of the field. It began to move to the northward. Its two headlands thrust toward each other at a faster speed. Thus the original half-moon shape took on the shape of pincers, one on either side of the dory, and both swinging into an enclosing movement.

Garry said, "Now I hear it plain—a growling off there." He pointed to the north. "And something there too." He lifted his arm to the west. For a time he stood there, his yellow jacket gleaming, his yellow Cape Ann hat running with water spilled by the fog. He looked down at the bowed figure on the thwart and said, "Stretch out, Simon, and keep out of the wind a while."

Simon lay down on the bottom boards. For a pillow he used a sack of canvas which contained bait knives and spare lines and hooks to repair their trawl.

Garry took his seat on the thwart. "You'll have a drink of tea, Simon? Cook put lots of sugar into it, the way you like it." He handed over the half-gallon water jug and Simon drank. Garry took a long swig. That was all that they carried in the way of food and drink. Such was the custom aboard those vessels, for the dorymen never were away from the schooner more than a few hours and, despite a history of losses by hunger and frost and long wanderings in fog, they had never changed.

By noon the fog had thickened to such a degree that Garry could no longer make out the trawl buoy at all. He set up their oil torch on its staff and held a match to it. The flare didn't carry far. It lighted Simon's face. He had fallen asleep so quickly that Garry became disturbed.

But he'll be all right surely, he told himself. Nevertheless, he unfurled the dory sail and spread it over his dorymate, because the chill had deepened into a frost.

Garry heard again and more distinctly the curious muffled noise that had reached his ears earlier. It became much louder. In such a din it was not possible to hear the schooner's horn. The time for her signal to begin hauling fish had long gone by. In hope, he listened for her recall signal—three blasts repeated. Because he did not hear them, he figured she was having trouble in finding the dories she had dropped last, four or five miles away from his.

He took up his conch horn and, taking care, warmed its silver mouthpiece by pressing it under his oilskins and against his woolen shirt. He began to blow an appeal to the schooner. His distinctive call, the call of Number One Dory, always began with one sweet-toned phrase, nothing more than a sea-bird's cry, then loudening to a trumpet flourish. So he began, blew, breathed deep and blew again. The first blaring note was overwhelmed by a bellowing so stupendous that it staggered him. He let his useless horn fall.

In bewilderment Simon broke out of sleep. "In God's name——"

"Ice! A berg aground and now she's busted." Garry spoke in a moderate tone because he wasn't at all sure how his dorymate would respond to a shout, to the needed alarm.

Following that uproar, a very high sea, the one caused by the toppling pinnacle, crashed out of the vapor in such force that it hurled blocks of ice against the dory. The sea hammered the dory, making it lurch, and it struck the trawl buoy so violently that the marker sank. This put a strain on the dory's painter that pitched her sharply down. Garry snatched up a bait knife and slashed the rope. Ice and breakers rolled over their trawl gear and carried it away.

Simon awkwardly made his way to the thwart. He drew the sail over him, thus making a hood from which his eyes, turned ruddy by the torchlight, stared into the jangling ice.

Garry marked the changes in the clangors of the ice. There were three chief sources of sound—a rough mooing nearby, like herds leisurely advancing; an unbroken crackling in about northeast; and the same crackling to the northwest. It took him no long time to decide that two headlands had swung toward each other and had caught the dory in a trap not to be broken by their oars nor by the *Judith*'s sails.

In all the calm that he could muster, he explained this to Simon. In answer, Simon flung the sail aside, stood up and, without a word, peered into the fog. He saw a stretch of black water, a jagged lane running into the middle of the ice field. He sat hastily to the oars and drove the dory into that opening, ever widening and yet increasingly obscured by the coming of night. The early setting of the sun had changed the color of the fog from gray to a hue like snow. For the space of an hour, Simon rowed in a channel that finally became quite straight.

"I'll spell you, Simon."

Simon shook his head and quickened his stroke. The swaying torch cast before them a murky wave of reddish light. He shouted, "Won't we make through it, Garry? Like before?"

He rowed a sharp, deep stroke for nearly another hour. He began to grunt and blow hard. The strain was telling on him when the dory struck against an expanse of solid ice. When he backed the oars, they saw that they had been closed in. The ice rolling away from her stern had already started to freeze solid again.

A groan of despair, soon shut off, came from Simon.

Garry comforted him. "We'll drink, chum." He took up the water jar. Ice clinked in it. Garry held it to the torch a while.

"Drink plenty. This ice is all old snow and can be melted." He found a warning in his own words and, after Simon had drunk, he said to him, "I'll douse the torch, Simon. We'll be needing fire before daybreak." He made Simon lie down out of the rising wind and again he covered him with the sail.

Bowed on the thwart, Garry measured the frost reaching through the wool into his body, and thus he measured its hold on his dorymate. He knew all too well how such frost subtly numbed a man's mind and he had need of thought.

He stood the night watch. From time to time he got up and beat his arms back and forth. Nothing marked the coming of day for him, except crippling spasms of hunger. Soon he could no longer bear up against the wind that now blew all over the compass, changing the crackling to shrieks and howls. He gave one last look around for the lights of the schooner and he lay down by Simon. He put the water jar under his shirt to keep it from splitting. He waited until he had rested to the point of drowsiness, and then he awakened Simon and persuaded him to drink the last sweet sips of tea.

He watched the vapor of his dorymate's harsh-taken breath. "Turn out, Simon."

"The wind is hauling, Garry."

"Aye! And it's piping up in earnest."

The wind had shifted to the southward. The fog began to swirl faster and to lift. Soon it closed in again. By noontime the Greenland ice lay freezing, block to block all around them. In the late afternoon Simon could no longer stand up. He lay under the sail. The night came on so black that Garry couldn't see Simon's face. He lighted the torch again. Its flare revealed his dorymate lying awake, his eyes too bright. Simon said, "God help us, Garry; we're in for it sure. There's no sign of her lights? She must be on the search."

"No lights, Simon. But you're right—she's after us by now, and they may see our torch."

Garry had now gone more than forty hours without food. Used to the schooner's abundant table, three or four times in a day, his body began to resist his will, yet he believed he could keep his mind fixed on his duty, sacred to him because of the tradition that had carried many a man to death itself in order that his dorymate should live. Even so strengthened by love and duty, the task dismayed him. He required food, water and shelter.

In his growing weakness, it helped him greatly when his mind changed the items to: *Shelter and food*. He counted over the tools he had at his command—oars, gaffs, knives, sail and mast, spare hooks and lines. His clear thought waned. Into the confusion of his mind there rose an image of their lost trawl, its well-baited hooks and the fat halibut thrashing far below. This image interested him too keenly; indeed, it became tantalizing, and he didn't yet know why this should be so. He tried hard to get rid of it because he knew that he should summon up new images, those that must save their lives before frost and hunger lamed him entirely. He succeeded, yet he failed to work out any plan of action.

The breaking of another day brought on a denser fog and made no change at all in the clatter of the ice around the dory. When he put out the torch, he saw Simon's lips moving in words too thin to be heard. He bent down to listen and heard him say, "I'll stay here a bit longer, Garry. I've no faith in my legs."

"All right, Simon. Rest you easy now. I'll figure out maybe what we must do."

The action of the ice made up his mind for him. It rose in a broad hump at the tholepins and it kept rising until the dory lay on a level with the wider shore of ice, a level place, not heaving. On it and nearby lay the other wrecked boat. At times Garry saw it clearly. He understood what its values might be.

"We'll go onto the ice here, Simon—lest the dory be stove in and sink under us." He took the painter in both his hands and jumped to the ice. He heaved. The dory slid forward easily. He took the sail out and laid it down. He removed his oilskin jacket and a black, high-necked sweater of Nova Scotian wool. He carried Simon to the sail. There he put the sweater on him. Simon lay calmly, his face without expression.

Garry heaved the dory up on its side and set the bottom toward the wind. He drew out all their gear and moved Simon into the shelter. He fixed the sail across the open side and lashed it with lines and nailed it with hooks.

He trudged to the wrecked boat. Its men had gone through the trouble he now faced. The thwarts and bottom boards had been taken out for a fire that had been set on a square of sheet iron. Gunwales and risings had been burned. He read the story—seal hunters had been stranded there when the ice had carried the herds down the coast of Newfoundland.

He kicked the snow aside and groped among the ashes. He found a small ax, its handle charred. He had to rest an hour. When he got up, the daylight had much improved. He knocked more pieces out of the boat and carried an armful to the dory. He did this three times. In an attempt to loosen a board, his heel rolled on an object half-buried in snow and frost. This turned out to be a small iron pot. He eagerly thrust his nose into it. Fish had been boiled in the pot. There were bones in the frost-blackened scum.

They were saved, all right. They stuck it out.

This idea gave him comfort. Indeed, before he could stop the words, he repeated them aloud in an exultant way. He struck his mouth roughly with his gloved hand. At once he became so dizzy that he had to lie down. After an even longer rest, he stood up again.

With no more than a glimmer through the vapor, the sun passed over. The wind blew harder.

Since it stayed in the same quarter, the dory protected Simon. To this protection Garry added the warmth of a fire near the dory. He lighted it by first setting a match to the torch. He melted snow in the pot. A pleasant, chowdery fragrance rose. This made him feel faint, and he had to kneel down. He couldn't stand up, so he crept to the dory, pushing the pot cleverly before him, steering it ably between humps of ice. He lifted Simon and tried to tip the liquid into his mouth.

Simon turned away, his hand wavering in vague refusal. Garry pushed the hand to one side. "It's hot, Simon. It's kind of chowderlike. A little. Now swallow some."

The answer came so clearly that Garry believed it might be the last courageous effort before death.

"You take it, Garry. Take it and live." A feverish shudder stopped his words. He whispered, "Trust me, lad. I'll not give up until I can breathe no more. I've big strength in me. Big!" He murmured about his two boys at home. Instantly his courage waned. In a desperate rise of his voice, he cried, "Hear me? We're on fish. Kill one. I'm starving, Garry, starving to sure death."

To make his own voice heard above the din of ice and tide, Garry shouted, "I will! Rest easy, Simon." To himself he said, *Why, of course—that's it.*

Taking short, careful steps, he walked to the fire, now glowing brighter in the nightfall. He gazed dreamily at the flames and held out his hands to warm them. He tried to consider the idea that had been so plain a moment earlier. He lost track of it, could only determine that he had forgotten something. He spoke in a jesting voice. "Well, don't that beat all!" He returned to the dory, took out the pot and placed it on the iron sheet. He began mumbling. In a manner close to senseless, he cocked his head as if he were trying to listen carefully to his own words. Although they were empty of meaning, he seemed to take some pride in them. In the end, he struck eagerly on the word "bait" and he droned it over and over.

This solution satisfied him. He had no idea of the problem it was supposed to solve.

He drank some of the warmed water. It had become so foul that he couldn't keep it down. Instead of weakening him, the retching cleared his heart and mind. He crawled nearer the fire and there repeated aloud, and most deliberately, the words his dorymate had uttered. Before he could go on to the next action, he had to rest again. Without meaning to close his eyes, he fell asleep.

The moon, half-full and a little more, passed over the ice field. Between the moon and the berg, a rocket slanted. It burst in a red shower. A scarlet cloud tarried aloft.

A Coast Guard cutter had fired the rocket to warn vessels away from the ice. Half an hour later, in the routine of her ice patrol, the cutter fired a second rocket. The columns of vapor, pouring out of the berg's ravines, became briefly rose-hued. A blinker on the cutter's bridge began making the signal: "Do you require assistance?"

She was speaking to the schooner, where she sailed on the far edge of the ice, her deck lighted by torches, and her cross-trees illuminated by torches and lanterns. No answering signal came from the *Judith* because she had not in her crew an able-bodied seaman; that is, a man who could read such a message and reply to it.

Garry stirred, rolled over and began to beat his heels against the ice. He got to his feet, swayed a moment and then laid wood on the fire. Because he knew he could not use the oars or thwarts, he burned them. By this fresh light he rigged a line of eight fathoms and tied on a hook. He accomplished this task, once a simple thing, so smoothly that he crowed in delight and even ran his finger along the barb.

"Sharp, eh?" Pretending that he could really size it up, he held the hook close to his eyes. His hand shook. Nevertheless, he said in a satisfied tone, "Straight too. No need of a hook-set. No, sir." These words came out poorly because his tongue had swollen and his lips had been charred by frost. He couldn't lick them. As before, he appeared to be listening attentively to himself. He became vexed.

There's something left out. He squatted and let his head hang feebly. He whispered to his hands, "Why, you have no bait!" This time he clung to the word "bait," for it seemed certain that the key to all things lay in its meaning. Unable to puzzle it out, he took up the torch, carried it to the sealers' boat and unscrewed the cap of the oil can. He sprinkled the oil over the wreck. He gazed a long time at the moon and, by the hardest kind of thought, fixed in his mind that the moon must soon set and darkness would follow.

He now tried again to center all his power of thought on his main problem—how to catch a fish. Far back in his inward murk, he heard his captain's voice cheerfully singing out the order, "Bait up! Bait up!" That had happened so long ago. Garry drove the image out of his mind and tried once more to find something that would force him on to a sound action. An image of two kneeling strangers presented itself. This displeased him. He closed his eyes against them, yet they persisted, black and bowed, in the light whirling under his eyelids. Their significance came at last—they were the Newfoundland sealers who had fought it out and had been saved.

How did they take fish, eh?

He knelt and began searching the ashes and snow with his hands. He found a length of fishing line. It had no hook.

He went back to the fire. He could not then, or ever afterward, trace the rise of the true solution. In trancelike slowness, he removed the sodden glove from his right hand. While he stared at his salt-reddened fingers, a warning rang loud and

clear through the whirligig of his thought—*Right-handed man!*
He obeyed by restoring the glove. He took the glove off his
left hand. His examination of those fingers proved something
to him. He did not perceive it at once. He nodded shrewdly
over his hand until he figured it out. The warning had not been
repeated.

But what am I up to?

This time the inevitable answer shaped itself, not in gross
excitement or in dismay or horror, but in the calmness created
by his faithful heart. He said aloud, "I'll do it in God's name.
For I am the only living thing on the ice, 'cept him."

There seemed to be nothing out of the ordinary in his decision. This may have been because the necessity of it had
been studied far within him and there accepted. He couldn't
really think about it. His unfaltering heart drove him to the
first action. When that had been done, boldly and skillfully,
and the bait provided, his heart maintained him through the
baiting of the hook and the lowering of it over the edge of
ice.

At once a fish struck and lunged. Garry set the hook by a
strong heave. He held his boot slightly over the edge so that
he could haul the line across the smooth leather and not
against jagged ice. He hauled hard until the halibut thrashed
near him. He bent over and gaffed it through the eye. He
drew the fish onto the ice, seized his gobstick and smashed its
skull. He slashed the fish's belly open, ripped out the entrails
and carved the liver into bits. He threw these fragments into
the pot and tossed in several handfuls of snow. When the
pot began to simmer, he cut three steaks out of the halibut
and laid them neatly on the glowing iron.

In order to create the strength to feed Simon, he nibbled
delicately at a steak. After he had swallowed half of it, his
body took hold of the fresh energy so forcefully that the blood

raved in his heart. He laughed boisterously and cried out, "Didn't I tell you so, kid?"

He carried the broth to Simon and fed him slowly, sip by sip, for half an hour. He ate two of the charred steaks, cut others and set them to cook. He fed one to Simon, waited a time and fed him again.

In an hour it was over. He looked again to the moon and found its rim about to vanish. He held the torch over the fire until the wick and the oil can, too, blazed. Holding it firmly in both his hands, he walked to the sealers' boat. He flung the torch onto the timbers. The oil caught fire, and soon his beacon flamed ten feet high.

Everything accomplished, he lay down, his right hand clutched over the other reddening glove. He passed into sleep. Once he cried out a phrase that had something in it about Simon's boys. After that, the tears glided to the corners of his eyes, where the frost caught them.

He came back to life in the cutter's sick bay, where sunlight, flashing off the berg's wall, filled the quiet room. To the wonderment in his eyes, the surgeon said, "Yes. You're here —aboard the cutter, mister. All's well."

From a glass vessel suspended above Garry's head, a rubber tube led to his arm and passed under bandages there. The surgeon said, "We've been feeding you some sugar, mister. And some blood—you've had that too."

"Sugar and blood." Garry thought it over a moment. "A well-found ship. I'm obliged to you." And then he asked, "My dorymate?"

"Next to you. Don't turn, please. He's come through it all right." Knowing what the other questions must be, the surgeon went on talking quietly. "The schooner's alongside. She followed us into the ice. All the other dories were picked up. A tough time. Now, mister, if you'll lie perfectly still—will you?"

"Aye."

"I'll let your skipper speak to you—a few words." He whispered, "There's one thing more I must tell you now, mister. I've told your skipper. You lost something—a little finger." He touched the bandaged left hand. "The ax, perhaps, when you broke up that boat. The frost killed the pain, eh? Well, I had a little mending to do. That's the story."

"I'm obliged to you, doctor."

The skipper of the *Judith*, a gray man, haggard now to a pitiful degree of sunken cheeks and shadowed eyes, came to the bedside. He tried a word and failed. This didn't bother him much. A change came over his face; brightness drove the shadows off, and a grave joy altered his creased forehead, gentled his lips.

"Well done, Garry. My best thanks to you. I tried hard to reach you, but the ice kept swinging in and freezing hard, and I feared I'd lose all our chums, vessel and all. Such days and nights—God spare us from such a thing!—and then your fire and the rockets."

"Simon had best lay off some trips, captain—maybe three."

"That's surely so, Garry."

"I'll take one of his boys, if he'll go dorymates with me, once I'm mended."

"An honor to him, and I hear your heart speaking again the same good tune, lad. Yes, take him, if you like, Garry. Surely." He shut off his words in the same way and for the same inward reason. He seemed like a man who had been looking for something a long, long time and had found it here. He said, "I couldn't go onto the ice, Garry. I'm too old for that. Those that took you off to me—they said you saved Simon by killing a halibut. And cooked the liver in a pot and fed it to him—so he says—and cut steaks and cooked them on that sheet iron. Eh, Garry?"

"That's so, captain; I do remember now. Forty pounds the fish was—or thereabouts."

"And I was wondering, Garry, what you did for bait? The ice being empty of everything."

"Captain, a man can always find a bait—somehow or other, if great need be."

The skipper spent a little more time in thought. He laid his hand on Garry's bandaged one. "You say true, Garry—a man can." He put ever so slight a stress on the word "man" and went away.

The Spell of Inishmore

VIVIAN CONNELL

It was my first time in Washington, and the trees looked cool and green along the summer day. The moment I was installed in my hotel room, I called John Andover at the private number he had given me last fall in Europe. A girl with music in her voice came on the line.

"My father is not home. I am sorry. Will you please say your name again."

"Conal O'Shane."

"Oh—Mr. O'Shane. Please hold on a minute. I think my mother is at home."

Then I heard a voice of the same quality, but not so young. "Mr. O'Shane? This is Mary Andover. John has talked so much about you. Listen, I am just going out to get my hair done. I should be back at half-past five. Can you come round then and have tea? John is not in Washington today. But I'll tell you all that when I see you."

I had met John Andover in Geneva. I was writing a novel, and he was representing the United States at that prolonged conference on war or peace, with East and West at the table. We found we both had started our lives farming, and on the long evenings over the lake we discussed the land and horses and compared the country lore of his own New England and my native Ireland. By the time he went home to Washington we had become close friends. And indeed it was mainly to see John again that I had come to Washington.

It was a small house for a Mr. Secretary, and it lay back from a green avenue and was as quiet as a nook in the country. There was a bell at the side and an old brass knocker on the door. From old habit in Ireland, where there is seldom a bell on a country house, I used the knocker, and the door was opened in an instant. A girl with dark hair and Atlantic-blue eyes, and wearing a pretty, white apron, opened the door with a smile and then laughed. I gave my name, and she blushed as she explained her laughing.

"I never heard the knocker used before, Mr. O'Shane. That is why I am laughing."

"Ah, I'm a country boy, and I can't get used to bells. And where do you come from?"

"From Scotland. I only came over in the spring. Oh, come in, and welcome. Miss Cathleen is waiting on you."

It was a cozy room, with their own furniture from home in New England, and the girl who was looking at pictures in a book got up with a warm smile.

"Mr. O'Shane . . . Miss Cathleen." She paused. "The scones are all piping hot, and can I bring in the tea now?"

"Yes, thank you, Sheila." Cathleen signed me to a chair. "I hope you like scones as made in Scotland, Mr. O'Shane. My mother called from the hairdresser she will be a little late."

Cathleen was a very beautiful girl, with gray eyes that turned blue when she stood in the light of the window. I had a strange feeling that I had seen her before, but her father had not shown me her picture. John did not need to carry pictures to remind him of his family. They all seemed to be with him, as he smoked in his old tweed jacket by the lake of Geneva. I remembered what he had said about Cathleen.

"She was a bit late. Ten years younger than the rest," John had said, then paused. "Like a poem that one had forgotten to make when one was young."

It was a beautiful saying, and it described Cathleen. She was a poem, with that wisdom and light often in a late child. She made me think of blue morning on the hills of Connemara, and the light of the day still on the Hebrides under the moon. She tucked in her knees and turned over a picture in a book. I saw that she had been lost in the book when I came in.

"What are you looking at, Cathleen?"

"Oh—an island. The Isle of Skye, off Scotland." Suddenly she came over with the book, and I looked at the picture of a village under a mountain. I could almost smell the heather again and hear the brook singing an old Gaelic song.

"Up there, in the crook of the mountain, is the old castle, where the ghost of the piper plays." Her voice was in a dream. "And that little house, there by the brook, that is Sheila's home." She flushed. "I haven't been there, of course, but—— Why are you smiling, Mr. O'Shane?"

I was going to answer, and then Sheila came in with the tray. She put it down and saw me looking at the picture of her native village. I looked long at her, and I remembered the doctor had married again and had a daughter.

"Is Doctor Tam still alive, Sheila? With all those trout flies in his bonnet?"

She had got a shock, and her voice was a whisper. "My father died last year."

"That old willow rod, that he made as a boy, was it buried with him, as he always said it would be?"

She blinked through her tears and nodded and then went from the room. Cathleen looked at me. Her voice was very quiet, and her eyes very searching for a girl of nineteen.

"The moment you came in the door, Mr. O'Shane, I knew something would happen—would change. . . .Tea?"

She poured the tea and gave me a hot and delicious scone from the napkin. Then she told me about Sheila.

"Sheila is over here working her way until she goes to college in the fall. She has a part scholarship, from Aberdeen. She wants to be a doctor, like her father. She works as a maid here, but she is not a maid to me." Cathleen flushed. "I apologize. I did not need to say that to you. I think she is a wonderful person, and I want to know how people like Sheila grow, in a little village, and how——"

"And you want to go to Skye?"

"Yes. For a year. All the seasons. I can stay with Sheila's mother. Sleep in her bed. But I am supposed to go to Florence. I'm doing arts. Our college has a house in Florence. And we take a year of the course there, and in Paris. And then I knew I wanted to go to Skye. My mother thinks I'm crazy—because I want to go and live a time on an island."

"Why should it be crazy?"

"Because I want to go *now*. And it breaks into college for a year. And Henry does not want me to go."

"And who is Henry?"

"Oh—I suppose he is a friend. We are not engaged. But he always seems to be there. He is doing business school at Harvard now. He believes in a career. Wall Street. But he does not believe in an island."

"Michael would laugh at that."

"Who is Michael?"

"My son. He also has a career. He is doing his doctorate in physics and math. But he wanted to go to an island. And he broke his study for a year. I never asked him why. Maybe he wanted to be alone with the moon. That might be his next island. It is a little farther away than Wall Street, and perhaps one needs solitude to prepare for such a long journey."

She turned over a page in silence. Then she spoke with her eyes on the picture. "Is Michael like you?"

"Yes, I guess he is."

"Have you got a picture of him?"

"No. I never have a picture of my family." I paused. "Besides, you can feel what Michael is like, anyway."

She did not reply and turned over the pages. We sat there far away from Washington as she turned over the pictures and I spoke of the places I knew on Skye. Then the door opened, and Mary Andover came in. She looked very smart in black and looked at her daughter and me. "Please don't move." I did move to get up. Her voice was insistent. "Just stay there, Mr. O'Shane."

She put down her handbag and sat by us. Her hair was turning gray, but the sea blue in her eyes was as fresh as the spring tide. She smiled and then gave a little laugh. "Just the way I expected to find you, from all that John has told me. One of the family." She paused. "And in the middle of a family problem already, I guess." She smiled at Cathleen, who brought her tea. "Well, have you persuaded Mr. O'Shane to find you a reason for going away to the Isle of Skye?"

"I don't believe one needs a reason to go to an island," I said. I looked hard at her, haunted by something I could not understand. "But I will tell you a story about going to an island."

"I'll listen. But I'm not going to believe a word you say, because I know you have planned all this with Cathleen!"

Why, I don't know, but I suddenly asked, "Is Cathleen a family name?"

"Why, no!" Cathleen looked startled. "There has never been a Cathleen in the family. And never an Irish name."

She turned to say something to Mary and then she saw there was a very strange look on her mother's face. And certainly a very strange feeling passed like a cool Atlantic wind over me. Cathleen looked at me with those searching eyes and then touched my hand. "Tell me the story."

"It was a long time ago," I said, "and I was only nineteen

years old, and I was going out to the island. It was a wonderful day, with an Atlantic breeze that curled the blue waves, and a clear sun that showed all the hills of Connemara in a blue light, and the boat was as light on the sea as a young horse on a green field in spring, and I was riding out and westward from Galway Bay——"

"Galway!" said Mary with a note in her voice like the pulled string of a harp.

"Yes," I said, "I was going out to the Aran Islands, and although I was Irish, I knew that I was going to a strange and foreign place. I had read a book by John Synge, and I knew I had to go to the islands. And it was a great adventure to me, because it was the first time I had gone outside my home county of Cork.

"I went up on the bridge of the *Dun Angus* with the captain, and I felt like a young Columbus looking on the sea for a new land. Then a girl came up the ladder behind me, and the captain smiled a welcome to her as she stood there, her golden hair shining in the wind and her face like a spring poem. She leaned on the rail beside me, and then she spoke.

" 'I know,' she said, 'your name is Patrick, and you write poems.'

"Well, I did write poems, but I was shy of the first American girl I had met, and I said only, 'My name is not Patrick.'

" 'Oh, it *must* be Patrick! And you *must* write poems!'

" 'All right,' I said, getting bold. 'If I am going to be Patrick, then you are going to be Cathleen.' "

"Cathleen?" said Cathleen in a startled way.

"Yes. I meant Cathleen ni Houlihan, the poet's name for Ireland. So that is how we gave each other names that were not our own, and everybody called us Patrick and Cathleen on the island. And I never got to know her own name.

"Then she told me why she was going to the island. She was studying painting and music in Florence and one day a young

Irishman showed her pictures he had painted on an island. And then suddenly she knew she had to go to that island. She knew her mother would think it crazy to go away alone to an island, so she arranged with a friend to cover her mail and her money affairs so that her mother would think she was always in Florence. So poems had called me to the island, and pictures had called her, and our sudden impulses made us friends all at once on the bridge of the *Dun Angus*.

"Now, there are three islands, and we called first to Inisheer, the smallest island. There was no pier there, and we stood off the beach in the great Atlantic swell. And there I saw the greatest picture I have ever seen, and the picture was that small beach, with the women in red skirts, the gray donkeys, the children in skirts, boys and girls in skirts, so that the bad fairies would not know the boys and steal them away, the black currachs, and the stone, the stone of the island.

"Currachs are boats of black-tarred canvas on a ribbed frame of wood, and only a sheep or a calf could be carried in the heel of the boat. So they swam the cattle out to the *Dun Angus* for the fair in Galway. One man held the head of the animal out of the water on the gunwale, while the crew pulled hard on long oars with narrow blades to cut the Atlantic winds. When they came alongside, a rope was hitched around the animal in the water, and he was hauled up by a crane.

"It was wild and exciting work, and they had a great struggle to pull out a bull through the powerful waves. The head of the bull got under water as the rope slipped, and when he was dropped into the hold, he rolled over, and blood poured out of his nose, and he died with a strange and screeching sound that whistled above the wind.

"The death of the bull was a great tragedy for the family that reared him for two years and counted to live a year mainly on his price at the Galway fair. All the women of the family came out in another currach, and they looked at the dead bull and wept and mourned for the loss of bread and cloth and turf for the fire, all bleeding away in a great pool of blood in the hold of the ship.

"This was something Cathleen had not expected from those pictures she had seen in Florence, and she looked pale and racked with the wind as she looked at the dead bull in his blood, and she held on to my hand. I remember her hand because it was trembling like strings that are still vibrating with the music, and sometimes I dream about it, and I wake up with my hand tingling and the Atlantic wind singing in my head.

"Then we called at Inishmaan, the middle island, but I do not remember anything about that call. Then finally we sailed into the bay and came alongside the pier at Kilronan, on Inishmore, the big island. And here were the great strong men of Aran, in wool jerseys spun from the oiled wool, and neither washed nor stained with dye, and weatherproof against the wind and rain. But it was their feet I looked at, in their pampooties. They are slippers made of cowskin, and the hair is on the slipper, and there were pampooties from red cows and black cows and red-and-white cows and roan cows, and the colors on the feet of the men were ancient and bright on the stone of the pier.

"There was a magnificent, tall man with silver-gray hair on the pier, and he looked hard at me when I stood ashore, and he came and shook my hand in welcome to the island. Then he saw Cathleen and welcomed her, and said he had a horse and sidecar and would drive her along the island to the small farmhouse where the Irish painter in Florence had told her to stay.

"Then he asked me, and I told him I had no plan, but I had heard there was one small hotel here in the village of Kilronan. He looked at me so long that my face burned, and then he said, 'You can't stay here, down in a hole. You need the long sea and far hills in your eyes. You'll stay in the White House up in Coolach on the crown of the island.' He turned to Cathleen and spoke to her. 'Why, this young man could read a poem a hundred miles away.' Suddenly he looked at me again. 'What is your name?'

" 'Patrick,' said Cathleen.

" 'And yours?' he asked Cathleen.

" 'Cathleen,' said I.

" 'You are both liars,' he said, 'and I think you are here on a honeymoon.'

" 'We only met on the boat,' said Cathleen.

" 'What does that matter,' he said, 'the pair of ye might have met long ago, though ye may not remember the look of the place, nor the length of the time.'

"That is how we met Con Cormac, on the pier of Inishmore. Are you listening to my story?"

"Yes," said Cathleen Andover. "But you are not telling it to me."

That answer brought a blush that looked very young on the face of Mary Andover, sitting there in formal black in a room in Washington.

"When we stepped off the pier into the street of Kilronan, a man came riding down from the hill bareback on a horse, and behind him sat a woman in a red skirt sideways on the horse, and Cathleen said, 'I'm going to ride a horse the way that woman is riding before I leave Aran.'

"She was that kind of girl, and Con Cormac smiled and knew she would learn to ride a horse that way. And then we got up on the sidecar. Now, the sidecar has two seats hanging over the wheels, and they hang loose and they rock, and Cathleen got in some practice right away for the horseback riding, for she was sitting on the sidecar in the same way as the woman on the horse.

"Con Cormac spoke in Irish to his old gray horse, and we

set up the mountain road in the light of the afternoon, with the sun gold on the small green fields all made by hand from sand and seaweed carried up by panniers on donkeys. And there was the island, all in its white stone, its white bone, beaten white by the wind and sea, and I wanted to hammer my head on that white stone and beat out my mind as clear and hard and timeless as that island.

" 'Those green fields,' said Con Cormac suddenly, 'they are just green poems that sing on the old, white silence of the island. And all those fields came up from the sea in baskets, and now they are living and green.'

"Con Cormac let the old horse walk lazily up that road, by the cottages in their yellow thatch, sweet with the smell of the turf smoke, blushing red with fuchsia, and all mirrored in the blue light of Connemara, miles away across the sea. And then suddenly Cathleen gave a strange, wild cry, and she said, 'Oh, Con Cormac, I will never be able to leave this island.'

" 'That is true,' said Con Cormac. 'You will go away, but you will never be able to leave this island.'

"Ah, and we came to the White House, up on the crown of the island, and there stood Molly O'Flaherty, with a sweetness and welcome in her smile. She took my hand and said she had a room for me, but only one room, and she was not happy that Cathleen was staying down in the hollow of Kilmoney, a mile beyond.

"Then she smiled and said, 'Ah, but ye'll be seeing each other all the time, and there will be the moon tonight and the sun tomorrow morning. 'Tis on a honeymoon ye ought to be, and make one song out of your lives.'

"I remember that because she had said the same thing as Con Cormac, and Cathleen and I were young and it made us shy of each other all the time on the island.

"Ah, the White House on the crown of Coolach! I had a little room over the kitchen that was scented by the turf smoke, and I slept on a mattress of straw, and I washed in a china bowl, and my bathroom was the sea. There was no oven, only a pot oven for making bread, that hung over the turf fire, and an iron pot that hung, that roasted the sweet mutton and boiled the fish fresh from the Atlantic. And Cathleen down in Kilmoney lived in the same way, but she had not the high and splendid view of Connemara that I had, so she came up and sat by me in the evening while I dreamed of a poem to be made, and she wondered if anybody could ever paint that light on Connemara.

"She would learn some Irish from Molly and help her with the house, while I went out with the men and learned to row a currach, with oars crossed hand over hand, to give quick leverage and ride the great waves, and I came back with my knuckles bleeding for many days. But soon I could take the stroke pair of oars and head up the hill of the wave, and by that time Cathleen could bake bread and make salted golden butter and spin wool. And every morning she came up with me in the field and stood in the dew under the gray stone wall while I milked the cow, and they called us in Irish the young people who were not strangers to the island.

"So you see," I said to Cathleen, "nothing very much happened on the island, and there was no big storm and no big story, and maybe that is why I have never written about the island, though it was the place that molded me and made me as I am.

"So the days went on, and Cathleen and I swam in the sunlight, and walked up in the moonlight to the great and mysterious fortress of stone called Dun Angus and heard the waves clashing like old shields on the rocks three hundred feet below the rampart wall.

"And then one day she got a telegram that her mother was coming over to Europe by ship, and she had to get back to Florence.

"The next morning she came up with me for the last time, to milk the cow, and she had learned an old Irish song that she sang to the cow to make the milk come sweet and free, and that morning she could not sing.

"Then we went down to the pier at Kilronan, with Con Cormac on his sidecar, and Cathleen carried a cake she herself had baked, and an old lace handkerchief that Molly had given her and that was all wet with Molly's tears.

"Just before the ship sailed, Cathleen told me that she was never going to tell anybody about the island, and I knew she never would. And that is why, I knew long later, that I could not write about the island. I was keeping her secret, too, in my silence.

"And there we stood, after all that time, and we did not know each other's name, and somehow we were afraid to ask, in that last moment, in the sheer cold terror of parting.

"It was as the *Dun Angus* pulled away that she took a locket from her neck and flung it to me on the quay.

"This is it. I always carry it with me." I handed the gold locket to Cathleen, and I said, "Her picture is in it."

Cathleen put her fingernail under the rim of the locket, and then she handed it back to me. "No, I am not going to open it." Her gray eyes were now as blue as those other eyes long ago on the pier. "I can keep a secret too." She paused. "But I'm glad I'm called Cathleen."

She got up and suddenly was quite calm, as if nothing had happened in the room. Mary did not look so calm, but she spoke in a quiet way to Cathleen. "I would like you to go to Skye."

Cathleen walked to the door and then turned and spoke to me. "Is Michael coming to Washington?"

"It was not planned that way, but I'm going to call him in Boston this evening. He will be here tomorrow. I want him to meet somebody—that I know he is waiting to meet."

She suddenly went pale and her voice was only a whisper. "Thank you."

Mary looked at me and was quite the cool Washington lady. "Who is Michael? Your son?"

"Yes."

"I see." She paused. "I am not surprised," she said in an offhand way. "I must have expected it." Then she got up. "John is down with the President. Not golf, I'm afraid. Summer ice on the Kremlin, maybe. He will be back tomorrow evening. We will have a family supper with brown eggs. Where are your suitcases?"

"Oh, at the hotel."

"Call and tell the hotel to send them here. I have to go out to a dinner. You can have supper with Cathleen. Now I must go and change. Is that all right, Patrick?"

"Fine," I said.

Prelude to Doom

THOMAS SAVAGE

Ruby lived near thirty-four hundred south on the West Side of Chicago, upstairs in one of a neighborhood of skinny two- and three-story brick tenements with gaps between, where other buildings had been condemned by whoever condemns, and razed—soot-blacked, stained, and the mortar was granular and crumbly. Entryways were cluttered with rickety baby carriages, with trash, sticks of wood and sacks of garbage bursting at their glued seams. Often a door protected the entry —a door was not really necessary except in bitter weather, for each apartment had its own door. But the wind did whisk the flinty dust inside and up the stairs, a medium for the prints of half-soled shoes.

Ruby had come from a sunny town in Iowa, a pretty girl, a big girl, with a tendency to plumpness; she could not easily pass a pastry counter or candy stores. But people liked her. She laughed, she was generous. She clowned. She could cross her eyes at will; she could imitate Donald Duck in an unintelligible tirade.

"Come on, Rube. Do your Donald Duck. . . ."

She was stoically aware of her size and knew how little

chance she had of marriage. Men do like girls with trim figures. Even men with bad figures, narrow-shouldered, pear-shaped men, feel they deserve a girl with a good figure. A surprising number of such men are not disappointed.

Men liked Ruby as a friend. They exposed their little schemes and hopes; they told how much the office manager thought of them. They called her—and rightly—a good scout, patting her shoulder. They sent her comic post cards which she conscientiously kept. But already she had learned to protect herself by a curiously attractive insouciance. "What'll you care a hundred years from now?" was a stock phrase with her, and on her lips it sounded wise and reasonable, which of course it is. She comforted a good many.

Small wonder she wept the night the slim young sailor brought her home from a dance at the Avalon. Picked up, she was—she who had gone there with the other girls expecting to sit against the wall most of the evening. But she liked the music, and a few kind men friends of her girl friends did sometimes give her a friendly whirl.

But this slim sailor, you see, told her before they parted below on the street that he loved her.

Later she lay with her head buried in the pillow of her cot in the room she shared with a pretty, intense girl who believed in stars. Weeping, her defenses were absolutely shattered. The old business of "I should care" collapsed, perhaps because she had glimpsed what life for others was.

"What am I going to do?" she said, weeping.

"Do?" her roommate asked. "Do? What would anybody do? He's a wonderful dancer!"

"But I won't see him again."

"Idiot! A man you meet doesn't say 'I love you' unless he's looking for something. He'll be back."

They danced again the following Wednesday at the Avalon. "I want you to meet my friend Alice," she told him. And

Beatrice and Mary and Trixie. She might as well, she felt, lose him now and be done with the agony. She sat against the wall —oh, familiar wall!—and watched him dance with her friends, the pretty girls, the girls with the Size four-and-a-half shoes, who had a line, who knew the words to songs. Unable to watch longer, she hid herself in the ladies' room. Distrait, she pressed her cheeks with the palm of her hand, staring at the fluorescent lights.

He was waiting near the ladies'-room door. "Gosh," he breathed, "where you been? You been in there all this time?"

"Why," she said, "I merely went inside to powder my nose. A girl's got to do that. Honest, Dick, I only——"

"Why," he said, "I looked all over. I thought you was trying to give me the slip."

She looked at him in wonder. The slip? Imagine her in a position to give a fellow like him the slip!

But proud? You talk about your proud!

But in the dark of one rainy day in winter, the raw cold smell of the lake almost suffocating, the lights reflected on the black pavement, she suddenly trusted nothing. One of these fine days he'd look at her with his eyes open and see her for what she was—a good-natured slob. Well—and she shrugged— what would it matter a hundred years from now?

But it did matter. And he did leave her. Left her for the South Pacific, a happy, hopeful, tearful, pregnant bride. The boy Pal was born while he was gone overseas.

This Dick Forbes, this sailor, the father of Pal, who loved to dance, took a test before he got out of the Navy to find out what he ought to be in civilian life. The test was given in a big room on the East Coast of the United States. He bit the pencil they gave him and looked at the little marks he'd made. The test said that he ought to be a salesman.

"Do you like people?" the test asked.

"Do you get along with people?"

"If you saw someone on the street you didn't like, would you cross the street to avoid him?" Why, sure you would. But that was maybe a trick question.

Ruby was shocked at how much thinner he was. In his letters he'd never mentioned getting so thin.

"Ah," he said, grinning accusingly, "you didn't bring the kid!"

"No, honey, he's home with the woman across the hall. It's all so noisy here. I wouldn't want him scared."

"Scared! Scared with his dad?"

"No, but little kids do get scared."

"Home!" he said, and right there out on La Salle Street—and who could blame him?—he sort of held his hands out to the city and he began to sing, "Chicago, Chicago, that wonderful town. . . ."

Smiling, he shook his head at the wonder of it.

He paused at the door of the woman who was keeping his son. He jerked his head toward the door and whispered, "He in there? Well, then," he said and started for the door.

"Dick, wait!" Ruby said anxiously. "If he should be a little shy at first——"

"Shy of his dad, hon? Kids know. Bet you six bits he knows!" He shot his hand out to her. "Six bits! Shake, hon?"

She smiled. "Now you just come along," she said. "I'll bring him in a sec."

She'd planned all this so often—Dick sitting down in his own home, maybe with a glass of beer, and then she'd bring him Pal.

"Gee," he said and looked around the little place she'd fixed all up. He stood in the center of the room and turned slowly all around. Then he strode abruptly to the window and looked down at the street. Suddenly he pressed the heels of his hands against his temples. When he turned, there she was, with his son. A spasm crossed his face. He bit his lip, and suddenly tears stood in his eyes. "Here—let me have him." He held out his arms. "Hi-ya, boy!" Grinning, he stepped forward. "I'm your daddy. You come here, son!"

Incredibly the little boy held out his arms.

"Oh, look here!" Dick Forbes said. "Oh, looky here!" Again and again he shook his head. "Your ma owes me six bits." Again the tears stood in his eyes.

"I got some nice coffee for you now, Dick," Ruby said.

He said he was just crazy about the place she'd fixed up there on the South Side of Chicago. She'd had a few things when she lived with the girl who believed in the stars. "But I'll tell you," he said and picked up a pack of cigarettes and popped one into his mouth and flipped open his lighter and talked even while he had the cigarette in his mouth so it bobbed and his talking-breath made the flame wobble. "We'll get something a lot better than this, hon."

"Listen, Dick," she said. "I'd be happy right here with you and our baby the rest of my life. And the place is cheap."

He looked pained. "It don't have to be cheap! I tell you about the test I took?"

"No, Dick."

"Well!" he said. "Well, then! Gosh, hon, there must have been maybe a thousand other guys." He paused in that cramped little room; he strode over and looked down at the street again to free his mind of the oppressive smallness of the place. True, his mind bulged with delight at his wife and son, but he was seized with an explosive need to explain how it had been in that huge, clean hall when he and these thousand other guys took tests to point out their futures, and how they said his chances were just as good as any. "A salesman can make two, three hundred a week!"

Ah, he'd learned in those years in the Navy that things were, oh, not so simple as you thought. He wished he could talk to her about when his buddy, shoulder to shoulder, side by side with him all through it said, "Dick, old boy, old boy, and what does the old test say my good friend Dick ought to get the hell out and do?"

This buddy had an interest in him all the way, shoulder to shoulder. So Dick said about the test and his being a salesman. With one mind, the two of them stopped in at a bar; with one mind, they took a booth to be away from the noise, and private.

He had bought a parting gift for his friend. He had had it gift-wrapped. "Do you want it gift-wrapped?" the girl had asked. How clearly he remembered that. Someday he must explain to Ruby about the clear, true sound of that girl's voice. Gift-wrapped.

He could hardly wait to see the look in his friend's eyes.

"Why, say!" his friend breathed. It was a silver-plated cigarette case. "Why, man, oh, man!"

"Like it?"

Big grin. "Why, hell!"

"Well," Dick Forbes had said. "That's what I think of you. That's what I'll always think." His friend looked at him and then nodded solemnly.

"And I got something for you, Dick."

"No! You didn't have to go and do that."

"I been saving it."

"No!"

"Reach down here under the table. Nobody better see." And he passed under that varnished tabletop an automatic pistol, still warm from the friend.

What a heft it had! How pleasantly it pulled on the hand at the wrist, how comfortable in the palm! "A man's just as good as any man with that in his hand, Dick."

"Why, better!"

"The old leveler," his friend said. "That's why I call it the old leveler."

Now, in this small room, he found it altogether too difficult to express, to make his wife hear his friend's voice, make her feel the presence of the men at the bar as they, there at the table, exchanged gifts. So he unclenched his fists and said, "Gee, it's sure swell to be here with you and the kid!" She gazed at him as he touched her forehead with his hands and gently pushed her hair back and kissed her sweetly and deliberately.

He bought his heart's delight—a fawn-colored suit of gabardine and wing-tipped shoes for his narrow feet. He laid the suit out on the bed, so nice, and set the shoes side by side on the floor, as if he were already standing in them. "Now," he said, his eyes expectant on her. "What else I need?"

"Shirts, Dick."

"Shirts! A dozen?"

"Well, a dozen's an awful lot."

"Well, gee!" He had hoped she would say more than a dozen, but he grinned and shrugged. "Guess you're right. All white ones?"

"Yes, I think white's best."

"You know how when you've got to be always before the public?"

"That's right, Dick. Nice white ones."

He liked this pleasant, cozy business of going over everything he was going to buy. "And what else?"

"Socks."

"Say," he said slowly. "You're right."

"And handkerchiefs?"

"Gee," he said, "sometimes I think you're a regular mind reader! I used to think if I just had some real white linen handkerchiefs with an initial on them, to pull out and show a little in your pocket. Say, if I just had those, honey, I'll bet I could sell the public like crazy!"

"Don't you worry about how you're going to sell, Dick. That part will be all right."

"No, but honest! I got a good notion to ride into the Loop and pick those handkerchiefs up right now." He watched her, tense for her reaction.

"Wouldn't you want to wait? Wait and get all the stuff at once?"

That was disappointing. Crazy, how you think you know what someone's going to say; then they say something different. "Sure, I *could*—but if I had those handkerchiefs——"

"Well, why don't you go on then? And while you're gone, I'll fix something nice for supper."

"But don't tell me what you're going to fix, hon. Know why? Because then I'll be surprised."

He came back with the handkerchiefs. They were linen, all right. But the damnedest thing had gone wrong. "You'd think they'd have an *F* for Forbes, wouldn't you?"

"It's all right, Dick. Maybe a whole lot of people wanted *F*'s."

"I know, but——" How to express being thwarted? "Well, I guess a whole lot of people use their first names instead."

On the whole, the companies who advertised in the news-papers—"See Mr. Pilkington, Room 504"—wanted men a little better educated than Dick Forbes, although some of them were kind enough to give him pointers. Also, many of the companies wanted men with cars.

"I just looked at him," he told Ruby. "I said, 'Say, I just got out of the service, how could I have a car?'"

He now shrewdly decided to circumvent the whole business of walking up flights of steps, of standing in line—afraid even to go to the bathroom or he'd lose his place. Somewhere or other he'd picked up a book of paper matches, and on the inside was a coupon you sent to a company that wanted you to sell shoes. The text of the coupon, written in the first person, was already written out, as if the fellow who read it had written it. Here's what it said.

You bet I want to make lots of money. Set me up in a BIG MONEY Shoe Business by rushing me FREE and POSTPAID, my Powerful Selling Outfit! This includes actual Air Cushion Demonstrator, featuring Comfort Shoes.

And while he waited for the powerful selling outfit to come, he spent the days at the zoo and remembered being a little boy and going there.

At last came the nice big sample case and all the stuff in it!

However, it seemed that people preferred to purchase their shoes in a store, so they could get the exact fit; they had no faith in the accurate foot-measurer on the powerful selling outfit.

And it also turned out, in the end, that the company wanted back the sample case, although he had understood he got to keep that. He had begun to feel a little hysterical when he knocked on a door; his smile pained his muscles, his hands clenched, his palms itched with sweat. And he had never hurt anybody in all his life!

"Don't you worry," Ruby told him. "You bet it's not easy to sell. Who said it was? Why, you're just getting started!" And together they'd speak of the orders he had put through. For one thing, the woman across the hall had bought a pair of shoes. "You let me rub your shoulders a little now," Ruby said. "You get all tense." She rubbed his feet, too, because of all the walking. Not everybody has the hands for rubbing. He had very narrow feet.

"That's why I never got corns or calluses," he told her proudly. "The shoes I wore were always too big." He closed his eyes and let his mind slip 'way, 'way back.

Then, in a magazine, he came on a good thing, a preparation that replated silverware. You know, it gets all rubbed off? Well, this put the silver back.

So went a year, and another, and another. Sometimes, though, he felt this terrible pressure in the back of his head; if he closed his eyes, he saw lights. "It helps most," he told her, "if you just sort of rub the back of my neck."

His best luck was with a line of Christmas cards. It is reasonable to believe people would prefer to get their cards early so they will have them and not go worrying at the last minute.

"Look," Ruby told him, "I don't mind helping out! Practically everybody's helping out these days."

"But you shouldn'ta got the job there at the Pony"—the Pony was a short-order restaurant whose exhaust fan emptied into a narrow alley off Mozart Street—"without telling me." He let her see that he was hurt. He was hurt!

"I wanted to surprise you."

"Surprise, all right! Looks like you maybe don't think I can take care of you and the boy."

"Darling! I just wanted to take the pressure off!"

Oh, he thought. The pressure. The pressure behind his eyes. "You're sure Pal's all right with the woman there? We wouldn't want to be any trouble."

"Trouble? She loves kids. And how he likes those cats of hers."

"He does? I get a kick out of that when a kid likes something. You know what? He likes cars too." Then, "Hon?"

"Dick?"

"Rub my back?"

"Sure."

He groaned, contented. "Hon, I walked by Field's, you know, by the windows on Wabash."

"I know." She went on rubbing.

"Maybe rub a little more over to the left? Well, there's a

185

little toy car there my boy would like. You know, the highest-priced car in the world is a Rolls-Royce?"

"Oh?"

"Real little scale model." He wished to describe it, the razor-like lines, the glitter of lacquer, the insolent sweep of the fenders, the tiny mascot on the radiator cap. But the perfection of the image in his mind threw his thoughts into confusion; they blurred and telescoped. Then, with difficulty, he continued, "It runs on batteries!"

"Oh," she said, "he'd get a kick, all right. But sounds expensive." As he turned his head to look at her, she made a sudden desperate little smile.

He continued to look at her and then narrowed his eyes. He didn't like something in her voice—some rejection. Now his voice rose and shook like that of a child on the verge of tears. "Hon, didn't you ever want anybody to have the best thing there is?" He blinked.

"Why, Dick, of course!" Her eyes begged him to see she would devote her life to that proposition.

"That's not what you said. You said——" But he couldn't now exactly recall what she had said. He shook his head slowly. "Hon, know what?"

"Yes, Dick?"

"I already told him—about the little car. I said, 'I'll bet you get that little Rolls-Royce for Christmas.'"

"He told me, Dick. He keeps the picture from Field's ad." She felt his muscles knot under her fingers.

Again he turned his head to look at her. "Then why did you say 'oh' back there?"

"Back where, Dick?"

"When like you didn't know I was going to get him the little car. Like it was news to you. Were you—trying to trick me or something?" He must be very careful about people's tricking him.

"Dick! I only thought maybe you shouldn't have said anything until—until you knew for sure you could afford it. You know kids."

He twisted from under her hands and spoke sharply. "Why can't I afford it?" he demanded. "Ain't my boy good as the next? Why should they think my kid can't have a little toy Rolls-Royce that really runs? Are they the only ones, out in Lake Forest and wherever, can give their kids what they want?"

Certain Navy experiences—snubs, officers' uniforms, big shiny staff cars—flooded back. "Ain't I working hard? You and me might never have a Rolls." His voice cracked, admitting this possibility. "But my kid can have the same kind of toys that their kids have." His heart was pounding; she was afraid that he was going to cry. "It'll give him something to aim at, something to shoot for. Don't you want your kid to have it better than us?"

"Of course, Dick. Darling!"

"Holy cow," he said. "Eight years selling—eight years now out of the Navy." He moved under her fingers again. "I'll get that car for him, you'll see. But I just wish you wouldn't try to trick me, not in my own place."

"I know," she said. "I'm just too cautious, I guess. Women just are more cautious. It's hard for a mother to see how much a thing like that might mean to a little boy."

"Now you're talking!" He smiled and held her eyes with his. "You're one swell girl, the way you understand."

"Crazy!"

"No, on the level." He touched her face with his fingers. "Hon, come here a minute."

"Dick?"

"Little closer now."

"Like this?"

"M'm-m-m."

"Oh, Dick."

Now, alas, he was selling a line of women's stockings—hose, as they are called—with colors like "moon mist" and "blush." The steady pressure continued behind his eyes; sometimes the entire bowl of his head welled with a diffused light, dazzling, frightening. It happened one morning late in November as he turned and looked up at the window where his wife and son waved good-by. Looking up, smiling, he waved back, walking backward toward the curb, waving and smiling.

He had begun to dread the loss of his ability to recall the past, the tunes he and his wife had danced to at the Avalon. He counted on the support of those tunes. Sometimes when he and she listened to the old portable wind-up phonograph, he found he remembered nothing. Nor could he recall the face of his old Navy pal. The figure, the stance, the gestures came on call, but not the face.

This loss of the past began to make him suspect that he was a partial man, no longer whole, and that people knew it. A waitress at a lunch counter had snatched a half-finished cup of coffee from his hand.

A man wearing an enormous diamond ring had glanced angrily at him and withdrawn a newspaper from his vision.

A woman with pearls had jabbed him with her elbow.

All this sort of thing.

"Why do they do it?" he asked Ruby. He was exhausted. Washing his face in cold water helped but little.

"If they do it, Dick, I'll tell you one thing—they're not kind."

"Why do you say 'if'? They do do it, and it ain't kind."

"Maybe thoughtless?"

He carefully weighed the word. "Maybe they think they can be thoughtless just with me. Maybe because they think I'm not worth much."

"Stop it, Dick! You're worth all the world. I think so. Pal thinks so. He talks about you all the time."

"About the little car too," he said. "But I know one thing."

"What?"

"I know one thing that makes one man just as good as another."

"So do I, Dick." She touched his face.

"No," he insisted. "There's something more."

"What?"

"Oh"—and he smiled at the corner of the room—"something." He liked having a powerful little secret, even from her; it was becoming clear that a man is really quite alone.

He began to carry with him that which was part of the past, which was not forgotten because it could be seen, gleaming and blue, and felt heavy in the pocket of his tan gabardine coat. The pistol pulled down one side of the coat, so that he had to compensate by thrusting his hand heavily in the other pocket; sometimes he simply carried the coat.

At thirty-four, then, the flood of his life narrowed and swiftened. Breathless, he abandoned the past and then the present and the "moon mist" and "blush." He clutched at the future. That, too, had narrowed—to an expensive toy in a window.

One noon he dropped in at a drugstore for coffee and a doughnut. The bowl-shaped, chrome-topped sugar bowl was quite past his reach. He found he could not ask the waitress for it, nor the man to the right of him, nor the man to the left.

Afterward, he went and stood before the Wabash windows of Field's. Imagine a father giving a thing like that to his son! The best toy in the world. Imagine the boy's face, the joy, the trust!

He went inside. "The little car in the window?" he inquired. "Runs on batteries?"

"Toy department, sir."

"Thank you," he smiled.

"I was wondering?" he asked. "The little car in the Wabash window, runs on the batteries?"

There was a Christmas tree there on the fourth floor, all bright, on a big stool thing that went round and round. And on the counters—ah, the toys that the rich bought! Chemistry sets, magic sets, steam engines with bright, polished-brass boilers that whistled, and you could buy attachments. And not just your regular electric trains, but whole railroads that went under little mountains and through little towns, real sidings with grain elevators that worked and switches and semaphores! There was a great crowd, and he saw that his shoes were not like theirs, nor his coat. His voice was high-pitched when he spoke.

"Could I see it?"

Ah, it was the finest toy of all, glittering, heavy, jewellike; even the headlights worked. Of all the toys——

"Fifty dollars," the man said.

He thought, *The man is trying to trick me.* Why, the man knew he didn't have that much. The man thought to make a laughingstock of him in a public place. What a thing to do!

He went into a movie. At any rate, all the hours of that day seemed to be used up; it must have been a movie that he went to, some movie on the North Side, probably near Thorndale, because here he was on the dark Thorndale elevated platform. The pressure was building up behind his eyes; with a rush of panic he recalled the welling of light in the white bowl of his skull.

There was going to be another baby, Ruby had said. And he couldn't so much as buy a toy for the one he had already—for the boy. There isn't much use to anything, is there, if you can't even—no, there really isn't. That's the whole thing.

Fifty dollars for a little car! And he'd promised the boy. He'd promised himself.

Underneath the overhead bracket lamp a group of girls stood laughing. Beyond, the darkness. He could hear the elevated screech around the curve down the track, the swiveling trucks under the rattly old brown cars cramped in against the sharp curve. Then the elevated started down the straight-away toward the station. The girls sobered, closed into a secretive little knot at the place they hoped one of the doors of the train would open. Why, they seemed to know exactly! He never had, never once!

It honestly surprised him that he didn't get on the train. His sudden change of purpose left him trembling and uncertain. He was alone on the platform—but not quite alone. A man stood there. This man had two expensive pigskin bags, and his face was first in shadow and then in light—as he leaned into the voluptuous flame of his lighter—and then in shadow. Either one of those bags cost a good deal more than fifty dollars.

Well, he himself had something in his pocket worth plenty —maybe a hundred—the old leveler. He had seen such side arms pass hands for more than a hundred, even.

He saw from the man's face in the glow of the lighter that he was about the same age as he was, must have been in the service, same as he; would know the worth of the old leveler and its beauty; maybe had a son, same as he.

Excitement seized him. He'd let the old leveler go for fifty dollars. That's what that fifty dollars meant to him. First he'd just strike up a conversation, and they'd get to talking, and he'd say. . . .

"I wonder could I have a light, sir?" he asked the man, for that is the way to begin a conversation. And as he approached, he reached in deep for the old leveler. The light from the bracket lamp at the end of the platform caught the cold blue of the barrel.

And now the man had hit him a blow on the Adam's apple with the rigid edge of his hand. And Dick Forbes, father of Pal, seller of ladies' hose, fell sprawling, all legs and arms and flapping gabardine coat, into the pits where the tracks and the third rail ran.

Yes, the papers made a good deal of it. The man with the pigskin bags happened to be of some importance, a young man, a promising young political figure, but the papers especially liked the paradox of it. He was not only rich and promising but had the guts to so dispatch a common hold-up man—those old Ranger tactics!

Beauty Contest at Buckingham Palace

MARY HIGGINS CLARK

Sir Winston sat patiently on the sun deck of his Riviera villa and waited for the deferential reporter across the table to begin asking questions concerning his just-published sixth volume of memoirs which encompassed the last forty years of the twentieth century.

He felt slightly chilled and gave a twist to the knob on his chair, causing the sun's rays to turn more strongly in his direction. "They got the idea for this from something called an electric blanket," he told the reporter. "But, bosh, you probably don't even remember that." He bit into his cigar, reflecting that when you got to be 146 years old, you had to remember not to refer to events or objects that belonged in the past of more than two generations ago. Otherwise people thought you were getting fey.

"Sir Winston," the reporter said, holding up his pencil, "I've read every volume of yours, with the exception of this new one. Now, looking back over your long, full life, what do you consider your moment of greatest trial? When do you feel your forces of leadership and cunning were most called to the fore? Was it during England's finest hours in World War Two?

Or perhaps when you arbitrated the squabble between Russia and the United States over who got stuck with the dark side of the moon? Or——"

Sir Winston raised his hand slowly. "My son, none of these terrible times caused my blood to run cold as did the night in 1961 when the most exalted beauty contest of the twentieth century took place."

He took a sip of brandy, shuddering at the memory. "It was during the early years of the reign of Elizabeth the Second," he said. "Jacqueline Kennedy of the United States was in the White House—as first lady, of course, not President. The first woman President wasn't elected for nearly a quarter of a century after that. Fabiola of Belgium was a recent bride. Princess Grace of Monaco was renowned for her loveliness. Sirikit of Thailand and Farah of Iran—well, someone suggested that nations meet on the basis of beauty, and out of all that a beauty contest was developed among the aforementioned ladies. The judges were Khrushchev of Russia, Nehru of India and De Gaulle of France. I knew in my bones it would be a bit of a sticky wicket, but no one would believe me; and since these ladies were to be accompanied by their husbands, it seemed a good way to have an informal summit conference in the bargain."

He reached for the brandy again. "So a first-prize medal was struck—a map of the world in miniature with precious stones outlining the borders of the countries—valued at a million pounds, it was. I was the master of ceremonies and the London *Times* dubbed me 'Sir Bert Parks'—why, I never found out. Someone had adapted a rather ghastly song, *There She Is, Miss Head of State*, to be sung to the winner. After months of preparation, all was in readiness. The ballroom at Buckingham Palace was prepared. Invitations were issued to the *crème de la crème*, and the contestants flew over in their jets. You probably don't remember about jets either."

Beauty Contest at Buckingham Palace

Sir Winston leaned back in his chair and closed his eyes. "It's as though it were yesterday," he said.

The reporter waited deferentially. He knew all about the beauty contest, of course. He'd read volumes on it. Who hadn't? It was known as Sir Winston's masterpiece.

The contestants stood in the wings, ready to walk through the crowded ballroom. The assembled ladies were dressed in high-fashion evening gowns and tiaras. For the men, white tie was *de rigueur*. Flowers filled the great hall. When Sir Winston announced the first contestant, the orchestra struck up the opening notes of *Pomp and Circumstance*. The audience didn't applaud. It bowed.

Sweeping across the room, her apricot satin gown gleaming, a million dollars' worth of jewelry sparkling on her white throat, her slim hands and her chestnut hair, was her majesty Elizabeth the Second, by the Grace of God, of the United Kingdom of Great Britain and Northern Ireland and of her other realms and territories, queen, head of the Commonwealth, defender of the Faith. She smiled dazzlingly at the assemblage, lifted her hand in her familiar gesture of greeting and took her place on the dais.

It was the first time she'd ever been involved in a beauty contest, and although she hid her nervousness behind royal aplomb, she wondered if she'd be able to add one more title to her already impressive string—"most beautiful first lady in the world." Of course, she was up against such striking girls as Grace of Monaco, Jackie of the Colonies, Sirikit of Thailand, Farah of Iran and Fabiola of Belgium, but still, she'd come a long way from the tremulous bride who'd wiggled her overample self into the love-in-the-mist-blue going-away suit that had been Norman Hartnell's creation. Dear Norman. He must have been a bit balmy to suggest that color. Really, she hadn't looked like the heiress to the empire at all. She'd looked like the empire.

She shot a quick look over to the first row where the most important dignitaries were sitting. Philip was smiling. He had a satisfied look in his eye, so she must be looking her best. She'd almost forgiven him for that day, shortly after Charles was born, when he'd looked at her quizzically and said, "Dear, you and your mummy will be able to swap clothes soon." Of course, she'd got back at him. The day some months later when he commented on her vanishing waist, she'd said. "The better to match your hairline, ducks." He hadn't minded, though. Really, it was nice to feel his pride in her.

"You're a ripping good queen, pet, probably because you enjoy it so." Well, it *was* her cup of tea, no two ways about it.

The flutter of admiration subsided, and the audience waited breathlessly for the next contestant. The English in the assemblage considered the contest over already, of course. Elizabeth had outdone even herself. It wasn't just those incredibly blue eyes, the perfect complexion, the shining hair. The girl had presence—radiance, don't you know. Shows what happens when you're born to be queen.

Sir Winston consulted the program in his hands before announcing the next contestant. Not that he needed to. Gads, that had been a harangue, trying to decide in what order they'd enter. Thank heavens, Attlee had come up with the suggestion that Elizabeth as hostess come first and the others follow in the order of the length of their reign. No delicate age problem there, and it put *the* queen at the head, which was as it should be. Trust a lamb like Attlee to turn into a dove of peace.

"Her majesty, Queen Sirikit of Thailand," he announced, managing to recapture some of the sonorous goldness of his wartime voice.

There was a gasp of admiration as slender Sirikit entered.

She'd worn a multicolored brocade with a suggestion of the Oriental culture of her country. It had straight lines and a slit in the front, revealing an ankle that would have been as at home on a chorus girl as on a queen. Her jet-black hair was piled high and soft on her head. Her even white teeth flashed as she smiled courteously to the gathering. She walked slowly across the room and up the dais, taking care to stand not too near Elizabeth.

If she could only win, she thought. These Westerners with their appalling ideas about Thailand—it was all the work of that book, *Anna and the King of Siam*. She'd actually heard someone at the airport remark, "With a queen like that, do you think the king keeps a harem too?" Harem indeed! Her dear Phumiphon. Anyone knew that if he ever fell for another girl, it would be because she played a mean sax or blew a French horn the most.

But all in all, this had been her year—on the best-dressed-women's list and now, if she won this contest, people would certainly take Thailand seriously. And not just for that damned silver jewelry that Phumpy was always asking her to wear to drum up trade.

There was excited comment among those who dared to whisper. What an impossible comparison, they were saying. Like choosing between Snow White and Rose Red. It wasn't a degree of beauty at all—it was a type. God pity the judges if the others looked half this well. Solomon himself would have been stumped today. You couldn't open windows and have bees sniff around in this kind of contest.

"Her serene highness, Princess Grace of Monaco." Sir Winston adjusted his spectacles. This was the one who worried him the most. His own queen could win hands down over the other contestants, he was sure, but these actresses had to be watched. He chuckled to himself. There'd been an actress in his past, half a century ago. Dear, dear Ethel. Smashing she'd been in

Captain Jinks of the Horse Marines. And they had a way of being regal of bearing almost beyond the ones who'd been born to the bit. He bent his head forward to get a glimpse as Princess Grace swept by. Worse than he'd expected—the girl was stunning!

She remembered not to hold her head higher than Elizabeth had done. People were always watching for that sort of thing. She was glad she'd settled on the white gown. She and Rainier had hemmed and hawed half the night before they'd decided against the blue. "You shall be the snow queen," Rainier had decreed. "Besides, the white gown will show up better on the new stamp issue."

"Oh, not another stamp issue, dear," she'd protested. "Don't you think we're beginning to have rather more stamps than letters to put them on? We still have so many left from the last issue that we had to store them in the banquet hall. Cook put her foot down on using any more of the canisters, and the basement is already heaped."

Rainier had looked crestfallen, then said hopefully, "We'll have a National Letter-Writing Week again. Last time we did that, we used up the whole atticful."

She began to ascend the dais, thinking how nice it would be to win for his sake. He did so want their country to be considered important. Those remarks that compared Monaco to Central Park certainly bugged him. And he did so much for her. Like when she'd arrived for the wedding, and he'd told her that he'd had every leak in the palace repaired in her honor. "It's a plumber's delight now," he'd said proudly.

And then he'd shown her his magnificent cactus garden. "Whenever you feel like acting, we can come out here and do a scene from *High Noon*," he'd suggested.

The last strains of *Pomp and Circumstance* died away as she took her place on the dais. *I just love that song*, she thought. *If it weren't for those* True Love *royalty checks, it would be my favorite, hands down.* She had to catch herself from humming the last line of *True Love* as she glanced quickly around. The other girls looked just great. She gazed at the first row of dignitaries and saw that Rainier was smiling from ear to ear and fairly bursting with pride. She relaxed inside. *I hope mamma remembers to send me tomorrow's Philadelphia papers,* she thought.

Farah Diba stood impatiently in the wings. She knew her eyes were sparkling and she deliberately lowered them and willed the lines of her face into the soft Mona Lisa smile that she knew people expected of her. She was wearing a pale green gown embroidered with hundreds of tiny diamonds. Her dear lord had personally placed the new tiara, valued at a king's ransom, on her head. He'd stepped back to look at her and nodded. "Unless those judges are fools, you'll have another title tonight, little one," he'd said.

She'd smiled back at him. "Have them beheaded if they go against me," she'd suggested.

He'd looked startled. "My ancestors could have done that, of course," he'd agreed. "It might not be considered good sportsmanship today." He'd linked her arm in his when they started down to the ballroom.

And the funny part of it, she'd thought, *is that you still don't know you adore me. Some little part of you believes that yesterday is with you yet.*

She remembered how she and a friend were at the Sorbonne when they'd read the shah's heartbroken message announcing his divorce from his beloved Soraya. Her friend was the sentimental kind. She'd sighed. "No matter whom he marries, he'll always weep for Soraya."

Farah remembered her answer. "Weeping willows are easily transplanted." She still believed it. Oh, granted it hadn't been easy at first. But Reza Jr. had tipped the scales in her favor. And she was six years younger than Soraya. That helped too.

"Her imperial majesty, Farah Diba, queen of Iran." She heard the opening bars of the music, started out into the great ballroom and felt unutterably sure of herself. One more thing —when she won this contest, she was fast going to see that Avenue Soraya got a new name. Oh, she wouldn't think of letting them change it till now. Better to be magnanimous, but enough was enough.

She knew the assemblage was comparing her with her predecessor. But Soraya had had a beautiful predecessor too and who mentioned her now? She strode confidently up the dais. Reza was leaning forward in his seat, smiling triumphantly. She wanted to blow him a kiss. It was the outrageous sort of thing that seemed to fascinate him, but she satisfied herself with the barest hint of a wink.

And the funny part of it all, she mused, *if it weren't for the heir to the peacock throne bit, I'd have preferred a girl.*

Sir Winston cleared his throat. He hoped the sweet young girl who'd just come through hadn't heard the whispers that compared her with her predecessors. *These Near East countries,* he thought impatiently. What in deuce was wrong with having a woman succeed to the throne? Judging from some of the kings he'd known, the queens did rather a better job of it. Speaking of queens—— He realized that the assemblage was looking at him expectantly. Oh, yes, the new little one, Fabiola of Belgium. A sweet girl really, no match for Elizabeth—but then, who was? "Her majesty, Queen Fabiola of the Belgians."

Fabiola drew in her breath sharply—but with excitement, not nervousness. She came forward in pale, shimmering pink satin, yards and yards of it, twisted and shaped into an exquisite ball gown—but no train. Dear heavens, every time she thought of that twenty-foot train she'd been married in! She'd had a stiff neck half her honeymoon from the way it pulled her back.

She walked slowly across the room, bowing slightly in response to the curtsies and cheers. She'd suggested having a comb or two in her hair and carrying a fan just to jazz her outfit with a bit of Spanish elegance. But Baudouin had looked pained. "You can wear your mantilla and combs at a costume ball sometime," he'd suggested.

She didn't pretend that she had the outstanding good looks of Grace or Jackie. *But I've got the Cinderella ingredient,* she thought. *I capture the imagination—spinster aunt of thirty-one nephews and nieces walks off with the biggest catch in Europe.* She smiled at Baudouin, who was sitting straight and proud in the first row of dignitaries, and thought of the day they'd met. It had been at a cocktail party, and he was introduced as Count Something-or-other. She'd been stunned. Did anyone really believe that the world's most eligible bachelor wasn't recognizable? She was just about to curtsy when she thought of that American contestant on some quiz program who had known the names of long-forgotten groups of islands, but not of Belgium's king. He'd had a reason for forgetting it. Some perverse quirk made her decide to play the same game.

She'd pretended complete ignorance of the count's true identity and now she thanked her stars she did. He'd been so relaxed. Maybe Baudy just got shy when he was running the country. Every once in a while he'd say, "And you really didn't know me, did you, dear?" She'd have to invite that American quiz fellow to dinner sometime. She certainly owed him a truckful of Brussels sprouts. She reached the dais and glanced around the magnificent ballroom. She felt the weight of the diamond tiara on her head and drew in her breath happily. *If this doesn't beat writing fairy tales,* she thought.

Sir Winston harrumphed loudly. Last but, by Jove, certainly not least, was the newest member of the charmed circle—that lovely Kennedy girl. Oh, these Americans—they had a way about them. Positively breath-taking! His throat cleared to his satisfaction, he waited till the expectant murmur hushed, then announced grandly, "The First Lady of the United States, Jacqueline Bouvier Kennedy."

Oleg has outdone himself, Jackie thought as she began an easy glide across the ballroom—pale gold satin, slim-lined, but with the suggestion of a train in the back. Of course, no one curtsied to her, but the deferential head-nodding was terribly flattering. She'd been telling Elizabeth this morning about how a Washington paper had sent her over to do sketches of the coronation. "I felt sorry for you that day," she'd told the queen. "All that ceremony. I didn't know then that I had an inaugural in my future."

"Well, at least you rode to it in a car," Elizabeth retorted. "That coach they drag out for me is really too much—sways like the proverbial reed and feels like the inside of a fridge."

"Yes," Jackie reminded her, "but they stick to *God Save the Queen* when you come in. Have you by any chance heard a rendition of *Jacqueline?*"

Elizabeth nodded sympathetically. "It will never make the *Hit Parade.*"

Jackie smiled to herself. The queen was really a good sport. They were going riding together in the morning too. She was passing the row of dignitaries before ascending the dais.

The President was watching her intently and he slapped his right hand firmly on his knee, so everything must be all right. If Jack stopped waving that hand, there had to be something wrong. Like the time they were in a motorcade and, after five miles of simply crawling, she'd opened her book. The minute that hand got still, she knew she was in hot water. But Chaucer was such a delight.

She walked across the dais majestically and noticed how really sweet Fabiola looked. *She's as new to this routine as I am, but she's enjoying it too,* Jackie thought. *And really, she doesn't look at all annoyed about King Baudouin's glasses.*

That had been the one bad moment of this trip. Jack had talked Philip and Reza and Baudouin and Rainier and the other boys into a quick game of touch football in the palace garden. And Jack, being Jack, played to win.

Now Philip was limping, and Baudouin was peering near-sightedly through his reading glasses, and Rainier had a sprained thumb. But what did it matter? Here she was, and that was all that counted. Pa Kennedy was so excited about this contest too. He'd promised her a check for a million dollars if she won. She stood at her appointed place and smiled into Jack's eyes. *We've got it all*, she thought. *Youth and looks and the children and each other and money and the White House. But whatever will we do for an encore?*

Sir Winston surveyed the dais intently. Never, never had such youth and beauty been present. He looked suspiciously at the judges. He'd just heard from an unimpeachable source that Nikita had offered to vote for Jackie Kennedy if the United States would sell Alaska back to him. And Nehru had promised to vote for Elizabeth if England erected a statue of Ghandi opposite the one of Queen Victoria. You'd expect De Gaulle to be above that kind of hanky-panky, but he'd been said to have promised Rainier that he'd cast his vote for Grace in exchange for the proceeds from Monte Carlo—just to tide France over till Algeria got straightened out.

Sir Winston settled his face into the bulldog look that had made it famous in the 'Forties. The contest had served its purpose. Among the husbands of the contestants and the judges, they'd have a summit meeting, the like of which the world had never seen. And he'd get it started over some fine old brandy.

He strode to the dais. "We have attempted the impossible," he thundered. "We have tried to choose between the rose and the lily, the orchid and the jasmine." He looked to the judges, who were nodding vigorously and gratefully. "We shall gather these ladies into a bouquet the like of which has never been seen. To attempt to select one from amongst them goes beyond the capabilities of the finite mind. . . ."

Sir Winston opened his eyes. It had been his moment of inspiration. The reporter was still sitting there, quietly attentive. "I thought the way you disposed of the first prize was a stroke of genius, sir," he said respectfully.

Sir Winston chuckled. "It was, young man," he admitted. "It was. I remembered the prize as I finished my speech and my eyes swept the assemblage in despair. 'Twas the grace of heaven they came to rest on Mrs. Khrushchev, who was looking quite chic in black velvet and pearls. She'd always been rather notorious for her dowdiness, you know. And after a hurried consultation with the judges, from which Nikita gracefully disqualified himself, we called it a 'greatest improvement' medal and pinned it on her."

The Beggar on
the Dublin Bridge

RAY BRADBURY

"A fool," I said. "That's what I am."

"Why?" asked my wife. "What for?"

I brooded by our third-floor hotel window. On the Dublin street below a man passed, his face to the lamplight. "Him," I muttered. "Two days ago——"

Two days ago as I was walking along, someone had "hissed" me from the hotel alley. "Sir, it's important! Sir!"

I turned into the shadow. This little man in the direst tones said, "I've a job in Belfast if I just had a pound for the train fare!"

I hesitated.

"A most important job!" he went on swiftly. "Pays well! I'll—I'll mail you back the loan! Just give me your name and hotel——"

He knew me for a tourist. But it was too late; his promise to pay had moved me. The pound note crackled in my hand, being worked free from several others.

The man's eye skimmed like a shadowing hawk. "If I had two pounds, I could eat on the way——"

I uncrumpled two bills.

"And three pounds would bring the wife——"

I unleafed a third.

"Ah, hell!" cried the man. "Five, just five poor pounds, would find us a hotel in that brutal city and let me get to the job, for sure!"

What a dancing fighter he was, light on his toes, weaving, tapping with his hands, flicking with his eyes, smiling with his mouth, jabbing with his tongue.

"Lord thank you, bless you, sir!"

He ran, my five pounds with him. I was half in the hotel before I realized that, for all his vows, he had not recorded my name.

"Gah!" I cried then.

"Gah!" I cried now at the window. For there, passing below, was the very fellow who should have been in Belfast two nights ago.

"Oh, I know him," said my wife. "He stopped me this noon. Wanted train fare to Galway."

"Did you give it to him?"

"No," said my wife simply.

Then the worst thing happened. The demon glanced up, saw us and darned if he didn't wave!

I had to stop myself from waving back. A sickly grin played on my lips. "It's got so I hate to leave the hotel," I said.

"It's cold out, all right."

"No," I said. "Not the cold. *Them.*"

And we looked again from the window. There was the cobbled Dublin street with the night wind blowing in a fine soot along one way to Trinity College, another to St. Stephen's Green. Across by the sweetshop two men stood mummified in the shadows. Farther up in a doorway was a bundle of old newspapers that would stir like a pack of mice and wish you the time of evening if you walked by. Below, by the hotel entrance, stood a feverish hothouse rose of a woman with a bundle.

"Oh, the beggars," said my wife.

"No, not just 'oh, the beggars,'" I said. "But, oh, the people in the streets, who somehow *became* beggars."

My wife peered at me. "You're not afraid of them?"

"Yes, no. Hell. It's that woman with the bundle who's worst. She's a force of nature, she is. Assaults you with her poverty. As for the others—well, it's a big chess game for me now. We've been in Dublin—what?—eight weeks? Eight weeks I've sat up here with my typewriter, studying their off hours and on. When they take a coffee break, I take one, run for the sweetshop, the bookstore, the Olympia Theatre. If I time it right, there's no handout, no my wanting to trot them into the barbershop or the kitchen."

"Lord," said my wife, "you sound driven."

"I am. But most of all by that beggar on O'Connell Bridge!"

"Which one?"

"Which one, indeed! He's a wonder, a terror. I hate him, I love him. To see is to disbelieve him. Come on."

On the way down in the elevator my wife said, "If you held your face right, the beggars wouldn't bother you."

"My face," I explained patiently, "is my face. It's from Apple Dumpling, Wisconsin, Sarsaparilla, Maine. KIND TO DOGS is writ on my brow for all to read. Let the street be empty—then let me step out and there's a strikers' march of freeloaders leaping out of manholes for miles around."

"If," my wife went on, "you could just learn to look over, around or through those people, stare them down." She mused. "Shall I show you how to handle them?"

"All right, show me! We're here!"

We advanced through the Royal Hibernian Hotel lobby to squint out at the sooty night. "Good Lord, come and get me," I murmured. "There they are, their heads up, their eyes on fire."

"Meet me down by the bookstore in two minutes," said my wife. "Watch."

"Wait!" I cried.

But she was out the door and down the steps. I watched, nose pressed to the glass pane. The beggars leaned toward my wife. Their eyes glowed.

My wife looked calmly at them all for a long moment. The beggars hesitated, creaking, I was sure, in their shoes. Then their mouths collapsed. Their eyes snuffed out. Their heads sank down.

With a tat-tat like a small drum, my wife's shoes went briskly away, fading.

From below in the buttery I heard music and laughter. *I'll run down*, I thought, *and slug me a quick one. Then, bravery resurgent——No*, I thought, and swung the door wide. The effect was much as if someone had struck a great Mongolian steel gong, once.

I thought I heard a tremendous insuck of breath. Then I heard hobnailed shoes flinting the cobbles in sparks. The men came running. I saw hands waving; mouths opened on smiles like old pianos.

Far down the street at the bookshop my wife waited, her back turned. But that third eye in the back of her head must have caught the scene: Columbus greeted by Indians; St. Francis amidst his squirrel friends with a handful of crumbs.

I was not half down the steps when the woman charged up, thrusting the unwrapped bundle at me.

"Ah, see the poor child!" she wailed.

I stared at the baby. The baby stared back. God in Heaven, did or did not the shrewd thing wink at me? *I've gone mad*, I thought; *the babe's eyes are shut. She's filled it with beer to keep it warm and on display.*

My hand, my coins, blurred among them.

"Praise be!"

"The child thanks you, sir!"

"Ah, sure. There's only a few of us left!"

I broke through them and beyond, running. My wife, without turning, saw my reflection in the bookshop window and nodded.

I stood getting my breath, brooding at my own image: the summer eyes, the ebullient and defenseless mouth. "All right, say it," I sighed. "It's the way I hold my face."

"I love the way you hold your face." She took my arm. "I wish I could do it too."

I looked back as one of the beggars strolled off in the blowing dark with my shillings.

" 'There's only a few of us left,' " I said aloud. "What did he mean, saying that?"

" 'There's only a few of us left.' " My wife stared into the shadows. "Is that what he said?"

"It's something to think about. A few of *what?* Left *where?*" The street was empty now. It was starting to rain. "Well," I said at last. "Let me show you the even bigger mystery, the man who provokes me to strange wild rages, then calms me to delight. Solve him and you solve all the beggars that ever were."

"On O'Connell Bridge?" asked my wife.

"On O'Connell Bridge," I said.

And we walked on down in the gently misting rain.

Halfway to the bridge, as we were examining some fine Irish crystal in a window, a woman with a shawl over her head plucked at my elbow.

"Destroyed!" The woman sobbed. "My poor sister. Cancer, the doctor said; her dead in a month! And me with mouths to feed! Ah, if you had just a penny!"

I felt my wife's arm tighten to mine. I looked at the woman, split as always, one half saying: *A penny is all she asks!* The other half doubting: *Clever woman, she knows that by underasking you'll overpay!* I hated myself for the battle of halves.

I gasped. "You're——"

"I'm what, sir?"

Why, I thought, *you're the woman who was just by the hotel with the baby!*

"I'm sick!" She drew back in shadow. "Sick with crying for the half-dead!"

You've stashed the baby somewhere, I thought, *and put on a green instead of a gray shawl and run the long way around to head us off here—*

My wife cut across my thoughts. "Beg pardon, but aren't you the same woman we just met at our hotel?"

The woman and I were both shocked at this rank insubordination. It wasn't done!

The woman's face crumpled. I peered close. And yes, it was a different face. I could not but admire her. She knew, sensed, had learned what actors know, sense, learn—that by thrusting, yelling, all fiery-lipped arrogance one moment you are one character; and by sinking, giving way, crumpling the mouth and eyes in pitiful collapse, you are another. The same woman, yes; but the same face and role? Quite obviously no.

She gave me a last blow beneath the belt. "Cancer."

I flinched. It was a brief tussle then, a kind of disengagement from one woman and an engagement with the other. The wife lost my arm, and the woman found my cash. As if she were on roller skates, she whisked around the corner, sobbing.

"Lord——" In awe I watched her go. "She's studied Stanislavsky. In one book he says that squinting one eye and twitching one lip to the side will disguise you. I wonder if she's nerve enough to be at the hotel later."

"I wonder," said my wife, "when my husband will stop admiring and start criticizing such acting as that?"

"But what if it were true? Everything she said? And she's lived with it so long, she can't cry any more, and so has to play-act in order to survive? What if?"

"It can't be true," said my wife slowly. "I just won't believe it. Now, here's where we turn for O'Connell Bridge, isn't it?"

The Beggar on the Dublin Bridge

"It is."

That corner was probably empty in the falling rain for a long time after we were gone.

There stood the gray-stone bridge bearing the great O'Connell's name, and there the River Liffey rolling cold gray waters under, and even from a block off I heard faint singing. My mind spun back to December.

"Christmas," I murmured, "is the best time of all in Dublin." For beggars, I meant, but left it unsaid.

For in the week before Christmas the Dublin streets teem with raven flocks of children, herded by schoolmasters or nuns. They cluster in doorways, peer from theater lobbies, jostle in alleys; *God Rest You Merry, Gentlemen* on their lips; *It Came Upon a Midnight Clear* in their eyes; tambourines in hand, snowflakes shaping a collar of grace about their tender necks. It is singing everywhere and anywhere in Dublin on such nights, and there was no night my wife and I did not walk down along Grafton Street to hear: *Away in a Manger* being sung to the queue outside the cinema or *Deck the Halls* in front of the Four Provinces pub. In all, we counted in Christ's season one night half a hundred bands of convent girls or public-school boys lacing the cold air and weaving great treadles of song up, down, over and across from end to end of the town. Like walking in snowfall, you could not walk among them and not be touched. "The sweet beggars," I called them, who gave in turn for what you gave as you went your way.

Given such example, even the most dilapidated beggars of Dublin washed their hands, mended their torn smiles, borrowed banjos. They even gathered for four-part harmonies. How could they stay silent when half the world was singing and the other half paying dearly, gladly, for just another chorus?

So Christmas was best for all; the beggars *worked*, off key, it's true; but there they were, one time in the year, busy.

But Christmas was over, and the beggars of the town, shut and glad for the silence, returned to their workless ways. All save the beggars on O'Connell Bridge who, all through the year, most of them, tried to give as good as they got.

"They have their self-respect," I said, walking with my wife. "I'm glad this first man here strums a guitar, the next one a fiddle. And there now—in the very center of the bridge!"

"The man we're looking for?"

"That's him. Squeezing the concertina. It's all right to look. Or I think it is."

"What do you mean, you think it is? He's blind, isn't he?"

These raw words shocked me, as if my wife had said something indecent. "That's the trouble," I said at last. "I don't know."

And we both in passing looked at the man standing there in the very middle of O'Connell Bridge.

He was a man of no great height, a bandy statue swiped from some country garden perhaps, and his clothes like the clothes of most in Ireland too often laundered by the weather, and his hair too often grayed by the smoking air, and his cheeks sooted with beard, and a nest or two of witless hair in each cupped ear, and the blushing cheeks of a man who has stood too long in the cold and drunk too much in the pub so as to stand too long in the cold again. Dark glasses covered his eyes and there was no telling what lay behind. I had begun to wonder, weeks back, if his sight prowled me along, damning my guilty speed, or if only his ears caught the passing of a harried conscience. There was that awful itch to seize in passing the glasses from his nose. But I feared the abyss I might find, into which my senses in one terrible roar might tumble. Best not to know if civet's orb or interstellar space gaped behind the smoked panes.

But even more, there was a special reason why I could not let the man be.

The Beggar on the Dublin Bridge

In the rain and wind and snow for two solid months I had seen him standing here with no cap or hat on his head. He was the only man in all of Dublin I saw in the downpours and drizzles who stood by the hour alone with the drench mizzling his ears, threading his ash-red hair, plastering it over his skull, rivuleting his eyebrows and purling over his glasses. Down through the cracks of his cheeks, the lines about his mouth, and off his chin the weather ran. His sharp chin shot the drizzle in a steady fauceting off in the air, down his tweed scarf and locomotive-colored coat.

"Why doesn't he wear a hat?" I said suddenly.

"Why," said my wife, "maybe he hasn't got one."

"He must have one," I said.

"Keep your voice down."

"He's got to have one," I said, more quietly.

"Maybe he can't afford one. Maybe he has bills to pay, someone sick."

"But to stand out for weeks, months in the rain and not so much as flinch, ignoring the rain—it's beyond understanding." I shook my head. "I can only think it's a trick. That must be it. Like the others, this is his way of getting sympathy, of making you cold and miserable as himself, so you'll give him more."

"I bet you're sorry you said that already," said my wife.

"I am. I am." For even under my cap the rain was running off my nose. "Sweet God in heaven, what's the answer?"

"Why don't you ask him?"

"No." I was even more afraid of that.

Then the last thing happened, the thing that went with his standing bareheaded in the cold rain. For a moment, while we had been talking at some distance, he had been silent. Now, he gave his concertina a great mash. From the folding, unfolding snakelike box he squeezed a series of asthmatic notes, which were no preparation for what followed.

He opened his mouth. He sang. The sweet, clear baritone voice which rang over O'Connell Bridge, steady and sure, was beautifully shaped and controlled, not a quaver, not a flaw anywhere in it. The man just opened his mouth. He did not sing so much as let his soul free.

"Oh," said my wife, "how lovely."

"Lovely." I nodded.

We listened while he sang the full irony of *Dublin's Fair City* (where it rains twelve inches a month the winter through), followed by the white-wine clarity of *Kathleen Mavourneen, Macushla,* and all the other tired lads, lasses, lakes, hills, past glories, present miseries—but all somehow revived and moving about, young and freshly painted in the light spring and suddenly not winter rain.

"Why," said my wife, "he could be on the stage."

"Maybe he was once."

"Oh, he's too good to be standing here."

"I've thought that—often."

My wife fumbled with her purse. I looked from her to the singing man, the rain falling on his bare head, streaming through his shellacked hair, trembling on his ear lobes. My wife had her purse open.

And then the strange perversity. Before my wife could move toward him, I took her elbow and led her down the other side of the bridge. She pulled back for a moment, giving me a look, then came along.

As we went away along the bank of the Liffey he started a new song, one we had heard often in Ireland. Glancing back I saw him, head proud, black glasses taking the pour, mouth open and the fine voice clear:

> *I'll be glad when you're dead*
> *in your grave, old man,*
> *Be glad when you're dead in*
> *your grave, old man.*

The Beggar on the Dublin Bridge

Be glad when you're dead,
Flowers over your head,
And then I'll marry the journeyman.

It is only later, looking back, that you see that while you were doing all the other things in your life, working on an article concerning one part of Ireland in your rain-battered hotel, taking your wife to dinner, wandering in the museums, you also had an eye beyond to the street and those who served themselves, who only stood to wait.

The beggars of Dublin—who bothers to wonder on them, look, see, know, understand? Yet the outer shell of the eye sees and the inner shell of the mind records, and yourself, caught between, ignores the rare service these two halves of a bright sense are up to.

So I did and did not concern myself with beggars. So I did run from them or walk to meet them, by turn. So I heard but did not hear, considered but did not consider: "There's only a few of us left!"

One day I was sure the man taking his daily shower on O'Connell Bridge while he sang was *not* blind. And the next, his head to me was a cup of darkness.

One afternoon I found myself lingering before a tweed shop near O'Connell Bridge, staring in at a stack of good thick burly caps. I did not need another cap, yet in I went to pay out money for a fine warm brown-colored cap which I turned round and round in my hands, in a strange trance.

"Sir," said the clerk. "That cap is a seven. I would guess your head, sir, at a seven and one half."

"This will fit me. This will fit me." I stuffed the cap in my pocket.

"Let me get you a sack, sir——"

"No!" Hot-cheeked, suddenly suspicious of what I was up to, I fled.

There was the bridge in the soft rain. All I need do now was walk over——

In the middle of the bridge, my singing man was not there. In his place stood an old man and woman cranking a great piano-box hurdy-gurdy which ratcheted and coughed, giving forth no melody but a grand and melancholy sort of iron indigestion.

I waited for the tune, if tune it was, to finish. I kneaded the new tweed cap in my sweaty fist while the hurdy-gurdy prickled, spanged and thumped.

"Be damned to ya!" the old man and old woman, furious with their job, seemed to say, their eyes red-hot in the rain. "Pay us! Listen! But we'll give you no tune! Make up your own!" their mute lips said.

And standing there on the spot where the beggar always sang without his cap, I thought: *Why don't they take one fiftieth of the money they make each month and have the thing tuned! If I were cranking the box, I'd want a tune, at least for myself! . . . If you were cranking the box,* I answered. *But you're not. And it's obvious they hate the begging job—who'd blame them?—and want no part of giving back a familiar song as recompense.*

How different from my capless friend. My *friend?*

I blinked with surprise, then stepped forward. "Beg pardon. The man who played the concertina——"

The woman stopped cranking and glared at me.

"The man with no cap in the rain——"

"Ah, him!" snapped the woman.

"He's not here today?"

"Do you see him?" cried the woman.

She started cranking the infernal device. I put a penny in the tin cup. She peered at me as if I'd spit in the cup. I put in another penny. She stopped.

"Do you know where he is?"

"Sick in bed. The damn cold! We heard him go off, coughing."

"Do you know where he lives?"

"No!"

"Do you know his name?"

"Now who would know that?"

I stood there, feeling directionless, thinking of the man somewhere off in the town, alone. I looked at the new cap foolishly.

The two old people were watching me uneasily. I put a last shilling in the cup. "He'll be all right," I said, not to them, but to someone—hopefully, myself.

The woman heaved the crank. The bucketing machine let loose a fall of glass and junk in its hideous interior.

"The tune," I said numbly. "What is it?"

"You're deaf!" snapped the woman. "It's the national anthem! Do you mind removing your cap?"

I showed her the new cap in my hand.

She glared up. "Your cap, man, *your* cap!"

"Oh!" Flushing, I seized the old cap from my head.

Now I had a cap in each hand. The woman cranked. The "music" played. The rain hit my brow, my eyelids, my mouth. On the far side of the bridge I stopped for the hard, the slow decision: which cap to try on my drenched skull?

During the next week I passed the bridge often, but there was always just the old couple there with their pandemonium device, or no one there at all.

On the last day of our visit my wife started to pack the new tweed cap away in the suitcase.

"Thanks, no." I took it from her. "Let's keep it out—on the mantel, please. There."

That night the hotel manager brought a farewell bottle to our room. The talk was long and good, the hour grew late, there was a fire on the hearth, big and lively, and brandy in the

217

glasses, and silence for a moment in the room perhaps because quite suddenly we found silence falling in great soft flakes past our windows.

The manager, glass in hand, watched the continual lace, then looked down at the midnight street and at last said, under his breath: " 'There's only a few of us left.' "

I glanced at my wife, and she at me.

The manager caught us. "Do you know him then? Has he said it to you?"

"Yes. But what does the phrase mean?"

The manager watched all those figures down there standing in the shadows and sipped his drink. "Once I thought he meant he fought in the Troubles, and there's just a few of the I.R.A. left. But no. Or maybe he means that in a richer world the begging population is melting away. But no to that also. So maybe, perhaps, he means there aren't many 'human beings' left who look, see what they look at, and understand well enough for one to ask and one to give. Everyone busy, running here, jumping there, there's no time to study one another."

He half turned from the window. "So you know There's Only a Few of Us Left, do you?"

My wife and I nodded.

"Then do you know the woman with the baby?"

"Yes," I said.

"And the one with the cancer?"

"Yes," said my wife.

"And the man who needs train fare to Cork?"

"Belfast," said I.

"Galway," said my wife.

The manager smiled sadly and turned back to the window.

"What about the old couple with the piano that plays no tune?"

"Has it ever?" I asked.

"Not since I was a boy." The manager's face was shadowed now. "Do you know the beggar on O'Connell Bridge?"

"Which one?" I said.

But I knew which one, for I was looking at the cap there on the mantel.

"Did you see the paper today?" asked the manager.

"No."

"There's just the item, bottom half of page five, *Irish Times*. It seems he just got tired. And he threw his concertina over into the River Liffey. And he jumped after it."

He was back then yesterday! I thought. *And I didn't pass by!*

"The poor beggar." The manager laughed with a hollow exhalation. "What a funny, horrid way to die. That silly concertina—I hate them, don't you? Wheezing on its way down, like a sick cat, and the man falling after. I laugh and I'm ashamed of laughing. Well. They didn't find the body."

"Oh, Lord!" I cried, getting up. "Oh, damn!"

The manager watched me carefully now, surprised at my concern. "You couldn't help it."

"I could! I never gave him a penny, not one, ever! Did you?"

"Come to think of it, no."

"But you're worse than I am!" I protested. "I've seen you around town, shoveling out pennies hand over fist. Why, why not to him?"

"I guess I thought he was overdoing it."

"Yes!" I was at the window now too, staring down through the falling snow. "I thought his bare head was a trick to make me feel sorry. After a while you think everything's a trick! I used to pass there winter nights with the rain thick and him there singing, and he made me feel so cold I hated his guts. I wonder how many other people felt cold and hated him because he did that to them? So, instead of getting money, he got nothing in his cup. I lumped him with the rest. But maybe he was one of the legitimate ones, the new poor just starting out this winter—not a beggar ever before; so you hock your clothes to feed a stomach and wind up a man in the rain without a hat."

The snow was falling fast now, erasing the lamps and the statues in the shadows of the lamps below.

"How do you tell the difference between them?" I asked. "How can you judge which is honest, which isn't?"

"The fact is," said the manager quietly, "you can't. There's no difference between them. Some have been at it longer than others and have gone shrewd, forgotten how it all started a long time ago. On a Saturday they had food. On a Sunday they didn't. On a Monday they asked for credit. On a Tuesday they borrowed their first match. Thursday a cigarette. And a few Fridays later they found themselves, God knows how, in front of a place called the Royal Hibernian Hotel. They couldn't tell you what happened or why. One thing's sure, though: they're hanging to the cliff by their fingernails. Poor fellow, someone must've stomped on that man's hands on O'Connell Bridge and he just gave up the ghost and went over.

"So what does it prove? You cannot stare them down or look away from them. You cannot run and hide from them. You can only give to them all. If you start drawing lines, someone gets hurt. I'm sorry now I didn't give that blind singer a shilling each time I passed. Well, well. Let us console ourselves and hope it wasn't money but something at home or in his past that did him in. There's no way to find out. The paper lists no name."

Snow fell silently across our sight. Below, the dark shapes waited. It was hard to tell whether snow was making sheep of the wolves or sheep of the sheep, gently mantling their shoulders, their hats and shawls.

A moment later, going down in the elevator, I found the

new tweed cap in my hand. Coatless, in my shirt sleeves, I stepped out into the night. I gave the cap to the first man who came. What money I had in my pockets was soon gone.

Then left alone, shivering, I happened to glance up. I stood, I froze, blinking up through the drift, the drift, the silent drift of blinding snow. I saw the high hotel windows, the lights, the shadows.

What's it like up there? I thought. *Are fires lit? Is it warm as breath? Who are all those people? Are they drinking? Are they happy? Do they even know I'm here?*

The Cathedral of Mars

WILLIAM SAMBROT

I cannot prove what I am about to tell you. I only know that much of what Kurt von Seigert told me that predawn day in Moscow has been verified by our own intelligence sources. There has been a rumor that von Seigert had vanished from Lubyanka prison, in Moscow, under mysterious circumstances; his family is known to be in North America, under heavy guard at all times. There is increased activity among American missile men, with a curious corresponding decrease in Russian missile activity.

I do have certain photographs—one an aerial photograph showing a modest little village beneath a disquieting blue-black sky, a village of stone houses, half-timbered, of an oddly medieval appearance. And there is another photograph, this one of a strange metallic object, somewhat saucer-shaped, crumpled, but recognizable as a very large artifact of quite advanced design—this lying on a low base of rough sandstone blocks, with barely distinguishable letters cut into it and running about the base out of sight. All this is within an apparently huge but crude building, with fierce sunlight streaming down from slitted embrasures high above. And I have a third photograph—of this crude building's doorway. All very odd.

222

I also know, from my scientific sources (I am a minor United States Embassy official in Moscow, with certain other duties not usually mentioned), that an unprecedented pall of radioactive material is orbiting the earth at a considerable height above the atmosphere—1025 miles, to be exact—as though a thermonuclear device had been detonated, something on the order of five megatons or so.

There was that, and what I knew about von Seigert. I was awakened one freezing dark predawn by a soft knocking on my door. I hesitated—after all, American Embassy officials in Russia have been known to disappear. But after a few moments I shrugged and padded barefooted to the door, drawing the latch. Instantly the door flew open, and a short, slim man popped in and shut the door behind him, one finger on his lips for silence. I stared at him, astonished, and then I recognized him. It was Kurt von Seigert, but not the von Seigert I'd known when, after the collapse of Germany during World War II, I'd tried to persuade him to join the other rocket experts who were coming to the West. That von Seigert was husky, shrewd-eyed, secure in the knowledge that his genius would assure a comfortable living wherever he sold his services. He'd gone to Russia.

But this von Seigert was shrunken, thin, his face so darkly tanned as to be nearly black. His eyes glowed with the familiar sharp intelligence; there was even the same faint arrogance there—and something else.

"Listen," he said sharply, "only listen. I have no time for arguments. Listen and remember. I was a fool not to have gone to America—I know that now. But——" He made a typical gesture. I fumbled for cigarettes, lighting them, staring at him. He was even more incredibly sun-tanned in the light of the match.

He stood before me, and even—I know now—with the possibility of imminent death hanging over his head, he couldn't help a faint grin as he said, "Last night I returned from the planet Mars."

I gaped at him, and he nodded seriously. "So now either one of two things will occur—the first directly dependent upon the failure of the second to happen." He held up two fingers. "A: The Russians will claim possession of the planet Mars by right of exploration and show video tapes—quite excellent ones —and complete, or nearly complete, aerial photographic maps of the entire globe, as well as photos of *Lenin I*, a nuclear-powered spaceship I personally designed and built." He waved me off as I grabbed his arm.

"To continue with A," he went on, his voice calm and unhurried, "they will go on to say that Mars is uninhabited, but is a fertile, mineral-rich planet which they claim as their own, wholly and *in toto*. And they'll express regret that upon his return from that historic flight, one of the members of the four-man expedition—Kurt von Seigert—became insane and fled from Russia, that his journey through space has caused his complete mental collapse and he is dangerous, both to himself and others, and should be immediately returned to Russia for 'hospitalization.'" He paused, his faint grin widened. "Or ——" He stopped.

"Or?" I said, intensely curious, the biting cold forgotten. I knew this man. I knew how desperately his services had been wanted by the West—how badly he'd harmed our prestige time and again by his series of brilliant rocket advances made in the name of the dark god Communism.

"Or B"—his voice dropped and became regretful—"there will be an explosion of about five megatons about one thousand and twenty-five miles above the earth"—he glanced at his watch—"in about four hours from now. In which event the Russians will say absolutely nothing about Mars or the *Lenin I*—their proof will have been vaporized. And my life will then be worth even less than it is at this moment—they know of what value I can be to the West."

I stared at him. His eyes held mine, keen, unwavering—definitely sane. He took a small plastic pouch from his pocket and opened it. "Here are some photographs, in color, I managed to salvage," he said. "In the event A happens, you must somehow manage to convey to the United Nations, indeed to all civilized people of good intentions throughout the world, that Russia has no claim on Mars because Mars is inhabited. That it has a civilization—backward in most respects, but flourishing—and that this civilization came from earth, nearly seven hundred years ago."

I reached numbly for the little packet of pictures, but he held them away, his face intent, his eyes piercing in his near-black face. "Above all," he said solemnly, "Russia must not be permitted to return to Mars without supervision. It is their intention, using my *Lenin I*, to destroy those brave struggling villages that dot that lonely planet. I repeat—Mars is inhabited and by children of earth. Mars belongs to them by prior right of colonization—no matter how accidental it might have been."

"Accidental?" I caught him as he sprang toward the window, peered out, then quickly returned. "What is this, von Seigert?" He rubbed his eyes, sat down on my bed and began to talk.

The *Lenin I*, von Seigert told me, was a nuclear-powered spaceship, built in total secrecy far above the earth. Generating a thrust of some ten million pounds—continuously—it was designed to operate only in outer space; the exhaust from its engines was highly lethal in an atmosphere. It carried a large payload: Besides the four-man crew there were a small two-man hypersonic glider for atmospheric flights and several monoatomic ram-jets—scout and survey ships, each equipped with subminiaturized TV and audio equipment as well as wide-angle precision cameras. There were also several tiny robot tanks for geological survey work.

But the *Lenin I*'s most precious cargo by far was the hundreds of spools of extremely sensitive electronic tapes and fine-grain film—all packed into heavy, lead-shielded boxes—vitally necessary to deflect the damaging impact of the high-energy radiation encountered in space flight.

The pictures these tapes and films were meant to record, of course, would be Russia's sole proof of the success of the expedition. A powerful rocket-glider, designed and built by von Seigert and manned by a crack crew, would be waiting on a launching pad in Russia, waiting to go into orbit alongside the *Lenin I* upon its successful return from Mars, specifically to take off this precious load of tapes and film, for re-entry and landing on earth.

Operating on an exceedingly tight schedule, the *Lenin I* had completed the flight to Mars in a little over forty-four days—a bit behind schedule. The intention had not been to land men at all on this flight, but merely to map the globe, pick up samples of minerals and such, by means of the remote-controlled robots, and finally, to return to earth after two days of orbiting Mars. It was a very tight schedule made necessary by the steady accretion of ash on the fuel rods in the nuclear engines.

The first results of the aerial survey exceeded their wildest hopes. The planet had an atmosphere—thin but eminently breathable. While the *Lenin I* orbited above this atmosphere, they launched their monoatomic survey ships—unique gold-catalyst ram-jets which operated by recombining "stripped" nitrogen atoms in the upper atmosphere, thereby gaining thrust and unlimited fuel.

The first few passes showed that Mars was a rich prize indeed. At some distance from the poles were great belts of trees, forests in all stages of growth, with pleasant streams meandering through broad meadows. Farther down the globe were prairies, covered with rippling vegetation resembling grain. There were immense areas near the equator that were bare, bleak deserts of sandstone and reddish sand. But mainly the planet was fertile.

On the fourth pass over a vast desert area, one of the ramjets showed a picture of something that looked too square and regular to be a mere outcropping of rock. The picture was zoomed up, and the men in the *Lenin I* cried aloud. It was a building, large and square, with curiously familiar towers and flying buttresses about it. And surrounding the building, they observed under extreme magnification, were upright stones, laid out in ordered precision. About the building were walks and meager decorations, also orderly in appearance.

All in all it looked remarkably like a graveyard about a church—a medieval church, long-abandoned, desolate.

It was decided to land at once, using the hypersonic glider. In the planet's reduced gravity, it would be possible to return to the *Lenin I*'s orbit even with the comparatively feeble thrust the small glider possessed. Because he was the smallest, von Seigert was one of the two chosen to go. The expedition commander, Evekoff, remained on the *Lenin I*. The men wore space suits, with direct communication and no switch-offs.

The landing was fast but uneventful. When they approached the great sandstone edifice, sharp and clear in the dry, dry air, von Seigert gave a gasp of disbelief. There were a single word and a date chiseled above the doorway—in writing he understood. And on each side of the word, a frieze depicting an unmistakable animal, the most common creature on earth.

Inside they paused, staring. The building was a shrine—a shrine covering a crumpled, battered metallic object, perhaps three hundred feet in diameter, that even then, pitted with ancient rust, disintegrating slowly under what must have been the impact of many hundreds of years of time's slow passage, was obviously a spaceship of incredibly advanced design. A spaceship!

"What is it?" Evekoff's harsh Russian jarred in von Seigert's ears. Calmly, as quickly as he could, von Seigert told what he was seeing, while his companion recorded it all with a minia-ture, transistorized TV camera. And from the *Lenin I* came the muffled gasps of surprise. It was all going into the tapes, he knew.

But one thing didn't go into the tapes—the crudely lettered words, carved deeply into the rough sandstone base which sup-ported the shattered remains of the spaceship. The camera re-corded the words on electronic tape, but only their image. Von Seigert stood for long moments, puzzling over the inscriptions, reading the archaic language with difficulty—but reading it to himself.

They walked about the silent empty shrine, their footfalls causing tiny tinkling sounds as bits of the spaceship fell to the ground under their tread. Outside there were names chiseled on all the many upthrust stone monuments. Names with fa-miliar ring to von Seigert, in writing he understood. He looked again at the animals carved above the door and the name chiseled there, and suddenly he shook with silent laughter. Incredible—but it was all in the books. A matter of record for all who chose to delve deeply enough—and put the pieces to-gether.

They stopped, peering about. Stretched as far as they could see was the barren desert of middle Mars. Nothing moved. Above, the dazzling sky arched overhead—blue, deep dark blue, approaching black. But empty—empty.

He'd stared once again at that enigmatic building. At that one word, that date and those identical animals. His mind whirled back through the centuries, imagining their fear, their total terror. Those who had survived the crash of that ship, being young, little by little had regained their courage. Perhaps even he—the pilot—perhaps he had survived long enough to give them some of his great knowledge; perhaps not. In any event, they'd survived; they'd built this edifice in memory of their friends, their home—and that animal which had led to their tragedy. Was it possible, after all these centuries, that some of them—their descendants—still survived?

Through his earphones he heard some rapid talk from Evekoff and an inarticulate cry from the navigator still aboard, then the distinct words: "Comrade—look! A town. Houses. People." After that, a harsh word from Evekoff and stillness. Then the order, "Return to the ship."

Evekoff listened carefully to von Seigert's rapid description of the shrine below, of the spaceship within, and he merely nodded curtly. Von Seigert said nothing about the inscription around the base of the platform supporting the spaceship. When von Seigert had finished talking, Evekoff waited for long moments, staring piercingly at him. Then he said softly, "You understand, comrade, that what you have seen is to go no farther than we four?" And looking into the hard black eyes, von Seigert remembered a fact he'd attached no significance to until now—Evekoff spoke and read and wrote German fluently.

After forty-eight hours of intensive mapping, photographing via a camera and TV-electronic-tape hookup through the survey ships—during which time von Seigert had no access to the monitors—the *Lenin I* abandoned her tiny robots to whirl endlessly about Mars, turned her sleek nose toward the sun and began the long inward plunge back to earth. And forty-four days later it began its earth orbit as silently and secretly as it had left, with only the Kremlin aware of its successful flight and the landing on Mars.

But during those forty-four days, snatching the opportunity

whenever Evekoff and the others slept, von Seigert managed to view some of the video tapes which had been kept from him by Evekoff. After viewing those tapes and hearing the open comments of the others, concerning those tapes and what they meant to Russia's hopes pertaining to Mars, von Seigert knew what he had to do.

As the *Lenin I* orbited the earth, they were told by rocket base that it would be a given number of hours before the special rocket-glider and crew, poised for final countdown on a launching pad far below, could achieve their orbit and maneuver alongside, to take off her precious cargo of heavy lead-lined boxes, each marked now with map co-ordinates.

Evekoff and von Seigert were ordered to land immediately, using the hypersonic glider. The remaining two crewmen were to assist in the transfer of the cargo and return with the rocket-glider.

And so, just before they'd prepared to leave the huge *Lenin I*, to drift in silent orbit 1025 miles above the earth, awaiting the arrival of the cargo-glider, von Seigert quietly adjusted the nuclear engines, converting them into high-yield thermo-nuclear bombs—bombs primed to detonate in a given number of hours if left unchecked.

When the two-man hypersonic glider put down at the great rocket base at Tyuratam, near the Aral Sea, KGB men—state security agents—were waiting to fly them, via fast jet, to Moscow. And as they landed at Moscow, Evekoff bluntly informed von Seigert he was under arrest, "for withholding vital information."

"He knew who they were on Mars—and where they came from," von Seigert told me softly, there in that freezing-cold room in Moscow. "He knew I would not remain silent about what the Kremlin intends to do."

"What do they intend to do?" I asked him, shifting my freezing feet.

The Cathedral of Mars

"They plan to return to Mars—this time with a load of small atomic bombs," he said. "That's why they want me out of the way—so there'd be no one to tell the world what I'm telling you: Mars is inhabited. I saw them—villages, on the tapes the ram-jets took by video, and on the film. Villages—modest villages by any standards, but still, civilization. Narrow crooked streets, cobbled; with overhanging brick and wooden-beamed homes, churches—with crosses."

He looked steadily at me. "Do you understand? Churches —surmounted by the crosses of Christianity—on Mars."

I searched his eyes again—utter sanity there. He looked at me, then slowly drew a photograph from the plastic packet. "This is the door to the shrine of the spaceship." I reached for it, but he held me off, looking intently into my face.

"Listen," he said. "There are many of them—these little medieval towns, near either pole, all with that same curiously familiar architecture." He laughed reminiscently, then went on. "Under extreme magnification, the video showed people walking around—fair, tall people, and relaxed, somehow, unhurried. No mechanization whatsoever. A few were pushing handcarts, or objects resembling wheelbarrows—so they have the wheel. They had metal, obviously, but no machines; the wheel, but no domestic animals. In fact, in all the myriad passes over Mars, under extreme magnification, no animals of any kind were observed—of any kind; not even a rodent." He smiled enigmatically at this.

"But—they'd had a spaceship once," I said.

Again that faint smile. "Agriculture they knew. Those forests were obviously being harvested and reforested at the same time. There were canals for bringing down irrigation waters from the melting polar caps. And yet there was nothing at all sophisticated mechanically. Why? It was as if a group of people with a certain experience but no real knowledge had been

231

thrown into an environment beyond their capacities—like children."

He cocked his head and looked sharply at me. I stared back, puzzled. "The date on the door above that shrine reads, ANNO DOMINI 1284—in Middle Low German script."

"But—that's impossible," I whispered, shivering, but not from the cold this time. "What people in Germany—what nation on earth in A.D. 1284 had spaceships?"

"No people—no nation—on earth," von Seigert said. "But think—throughout the ages, even Biblical times, the stories, the endless stories, of objects in the skies. Charles Fort records hundreds of them, newspaper clippings, going back for centuries. And think of the people who have vanished without a trace. Ships at sea found deserted, abandoned; whole races known to have existed—but gone. And think of one group in particular. In Germany—a calamity so great that to this day it is still commemorated, a tragic group disappearance in the year A.D. 1284."

I shook my head slowly, watching him closely. "I thought I knew my history," I said, "but that one escapes me."

"You know it, perhaps, from another sort of history book," he said quietly. He looked beyond me, to the window, where the sky was turning a bitter gray.

"It was all in the inscription around the base of the smashed spaceship," von Seigert said. "How he came to their little town in Germany—a tall, curiously dressed stranger, in search of treasure, a treasure he'd come from beyond the sun to seek. And how this stranger had performed a service for the townspeople, erasing a rodent plague that threatened them; only to learn they were unworthy of the treasure they'd possessed all along—their children."

He handed me the photograph, but for an instant I didn't look at it. I couldn't. I stared, fascinated, at von Seigert.

"The children," he said. "This stranger told them of a wonderful place, beyond the farthest sun, where children were rare and precious—and wanted. The inscription tells how the stranger had an instrument that sang an irresistible song—so they'd followed him into the mountain. And how the ship had taken off, softly, easily, rising up and beyond the earth, outward from the sun, and still they had no fear. His music was all about them. But something went wrong. They'd crash-landed on that barren place, far short of the goal. The music had stopped; the dream had ended in nightmare. And many of them had died, along with the music maker—the Pied Piper."

"Pied Piper!"

"The children of Hamelin," von Seigert said, "desperately needed on some other distant world, where a race, perhaps, was dying out. Hypnotized—kidnaped en masse, marooned on Mars by a crash-landing. But surviving—always surviving. Mars is theirs by right of colonization. Their descendants have long forgotten the shrine, abandoned in the bleak, distant desert. They are Martians now, and earth—earth is only a dim fairy tale."

Not speaking, I moved near the window to examine the photograph in the swiftly burgeoning light. It showed a doorway, opening into a great building made of sandstone, through which, dimly seen, gleamed a crumpled metal object. There was lettering over the door, clearly visible. A single word and date in medieval German script—HAMELN, A.D. 1284. And alongside these, on either side, a rough frieze of an animal, clear, unmistakable—a rat, an ordinary rat.

When I looked up—von Seigert was gone.

The Big Wheel

FRED MC MORROW

The little man did not look up from his book of poems when
the sound of the engine came through the window of his office,
a sound that had no more business being on Mechanic Street
than what it belonged to, a Jupiter Custom 12, or the kind of
man or woman a Jupiter Custom 12 would belong to, whoever
was behind the wheel.

"Sammy," the little man said, "go out and tell the man in
the Jupiter Custom 12 to come in here. Then take his car and
put it inside in the back."

Sammy looked out the window. "Now, how in hell did you
know that was a Jupiter Custom 12, Mr. Deels?" Sammy asked.
"You got eyes in your ears or something?"

"You get used to them," Mr. Deels said. "You'll catch on
when you've been with us a little longer. Go on now, before
he starts blowing his horn."

Mr. Deels went on reading his poems until, his eye jumping
to the left side of a page, he saw the hem of a camel's-hair coat
just beyond. He looked up. "Welcome," Mr. Deels said. "My
name is Mr. Deels. Hell on wheels with Mr. Deels."

"Hello, how are you," said the big man in the camel's-hair.
"I heard you had a Diana IV M around here, and I'd like to
see it."

"That's a beautiful car you've got there," said Mr. Deels.

"Yes, I know," the man said. "About the Diana IV M——"

"I can imagine the time and money it must have cost just to find that car of yours," Mr. Deels said.

"Yes. If you don't mind, I'm interested in buying your Diana IV M, if you've got one, and I'm willing to pay cash."

"I know, I know," said Mr. Deels. "Cash." He sighed and arose and closed his book and put it in a desk drawer and locked it. "I'm just curious," he said. "Do you know how many Diana IV M's there are in the world, Mr. Carmody?"

"I thought you'd recognize me," said Mr. Carmody.

"I suppose you're used to it," Mr. Deels said.

"Everybody goes to the movies," said Mr. Carmody.

"Movies?" Mr. Deels said. "Oh, yes. But I believe I asked you a question."

"All right," Mr. Carmody said impatiently, "if it makes you happy, I suppose there are fifty Diana IV M's in the world."

Mr. Deels smiled and wiped his hands, surprisingly small, clean and uncalloused for the owner of a garage on Mechanic Street, on a piece of cheesecloth and dropped it in a trash basket. "Well, Mr. Carmody," he said, "there are less than half as many Diana IV M's in the world today as there are Jupiter Custom 12's. What's the matter? Didn't you know that?"

"Why, no," Mr. Carmody said.

"I'm surprised at you," Mr. Deels said. "I'm shocked."

"What?" Mr. Carmody said.

"Yes," Mr. Deels said, "I'm shocked that a man who drives a Jupiter Custom 12 doesn't know how many Diana IV M's there are in the world."

"Well——" said Mr. Carmody.

"Why do you want the Diana, Mr. Carmody?"

"Why?" Mr. Carmody said. "Because it's a great car and I've got the money to own it, that's why. Look, you ask a lot of questions."

"I'm interested in people who go to so much trouble just to buy an automobile, coming down here and all," Mr. Deels said. "It's a little game with me. I like to find out what their motives are."

"Motives?" Mr. Carmody said, and the famous features began to flush and the nostrils quivered and grew taut. "What are you, some kind of a nut? I mean, where the devil do you get off, acting the way you do in a crazy little dump like this? I mean, this is no way to treat a customer who's willing to give you your price. I mean, you don't get customers like me every day, do you? I mean——"

"No offense," Mr. Deels said. "Really, no offense. Let's take a look at your car."

Mr. Carmody laughed. "My car?" he said. "What are you going to do, offer me a trade-in? Don't you know who you're talking to?"

"You want a Diana IV M, don't you?" Mr. Deels said. "Then let's take a look at your car. This way."

He led the way through the garage, through and between and over and past incredible piles of leaf springs and mufflers and tires and carburetors and engine blocks, and desiccated corpses of terrible old cars and trucks, to the back wall where the Jupiter Custom 12 was. Off to one side some mechanics were working on a Torquemada, apparently reconditioning it.

"Oh, I get it!" Mr. Carmody said suddenly. "Of course! Say, Mr. Deels, I'm awfully sorry. I should have realized."

"You should have realized what, Mr. Carmody?" Mr. Deels said, his eyes traveling over the Jupiter.

"Well," Mr. Carmody said, "maybe my car isn't as rare as a Diana, but it's pretty close, and you probably want it as a piece of merchandise."

"A piece of what?" Mr. Deels said, walking around the Jupiter, his hands gliding over the paint and chrome, feeling the nicks and dents.

"Merchandise," Mr. Carmody said. "You know, goods, buy and sell!"

"Oh, yes," Mr. Deels said. "Merchandise." He leaned over into the cockpit and tried an inside door handle, and it jiggled loosely, and his hand drew back as if he had touched a snake. He stepped back and looked along the right side of the car, tracing the long scar of a sideswipe or a drunken attempt to back up in a tight space.

"Get in and start the motor, will you, Mr. Carmody," Mr. Deels said, folding his arms.

Mr. Carmody jumped in and slammed the door and yanked the choke out all the way and stamped on the self-starter. The car urr-urr-urred, but would not start. "Don't worry about that, Mr. Deels," Mr. Carmody said. "She's just a little sluggish waking up, like all old girls her age." He assaulted the starter again, but the engine would not kick over. "Come on, you! Come on, damn you!" Urr-urr-urr-urr-urr. Urr-urr-urr-urr-urr. Zzzzzzzzz. "Oh, hell!" Mr. Carmody kicked at the fire wall and pounded the wheel with his fist, nostrils flaring.

"Please," Mr. Deels said. "Permit me." Mr. Carmody shrugged and got out, and Mr. Deels slid behind the wheel. He moved his hands and feet about the controls like an organist, and the Jupiter cleared her congested throat and spat and went into a rhythmic purr. Mr. Deels touched the accelerator gently, watching the tachometer and wincing as he listened to the palpitations and pings of metal fatigue and owner neglect in the engine's heartbeat. He shut off the ignition.

"I understand that you own several horses, Mr. Carmody," Mr. Deels said.

"I've got a few nags on the coast, I guess," Mr. Carmody said.

"What are their names, Mr. Carmody?"

"Their names? What's that got to do with anything?"

"And how many times have you been married, Mr. Carmody?"

"Six, though I don't see what my horses or my marriages— I mean, I don't see how it's any of your business."

Mr. Deels smiled. "You're absolutely right, Mr. Carmody," he said.

"Some of the nuts you got to put up with in this world," Mr. Carmody said. "Reading poems in a lousy little body-and-fender shop! Say, since we're getting personal, and I'm in one of the arts, you might say, and I might know something about poetry, maybe you wouldn't mind telling me what kind of poems a kooky grease monkey reads? Who wrote it? Anybody I know?"

"Not very well," Mr. Deels said.

"Well, who?"

"I did," Mr. Deels said.

"You did? I'll be damned. What's it about, the romance of grinding valves or getting crankcase oil squirted in your face or something like that?"

"Some of it," Mr. Deels said. "And about speed and touch and movement and texture. But we were getting down to business."

"It's about time."

"Let me show you the Diana," Mr. Deels said. "It's over there, through that door."

"Wait a minute," Mr. Carmody said. "What about my car?"

"What about it?" Mr. Deels said.

"Well, don't you want to drive it? Don't you want to look it over a little more? Don't you want to know what it's like, what you're getting?"

"I know what it's like," Mr. Deels said. "I know exactly what it's like. The Diana. This way."

"Some businessman," Mr. Carmody said, following the

silent Mr. Deels. "Boy, you found a home on Mechanic Street!"

Mr. Deels led Mr. Carmody into a little, one-car garage as like the main garage as a hospital operating room is like a slaughterhouse. The floor was holystone clean, the walls a subdued shade of green, indirectly lighted; along one wall hung racks of tools and spare parts that glistened like silver. In the center, her nose pointing at the street door, the Diana IV M, long, sleek, poised, waiting, alive, tensed, all of her lovely, all of her thrilling to Mr. Carmody's eyes and to his heart, her chrome seeming to blend into the ultimate midnight black of her body paint without definition as if she were, like an animal, all of a piece rather than the creation of so many components of metal, rubber and glass.

Mr. Carmody tried to say something, but he was a dreamer who tries to scream and finds his throat full of cotton. He swallowed hard and found his voice. "She's like a woman," Mr. Carmody said.

"The huntress of the night," Mr. Deels said. "The moon herself."

"My Lord," Mr. Carmody said. "Where'd *you* get her? What's she doing here? Who owned her? Have you got records on her? Papers?"

"Papers?" Mr. Deels said. "This isn't a horse or a dog, Mr. Carmody, this is a Diana IV M. This isn't something that has to be proved. She speaks for herself."

"Well, how will I know who owned the car?"

"Why should you want to know?"

"Well, I want to be able to tell people, sure, this is a Diana IV M, there's less than fifty cars like it in the whole world, a maharaja owned her, handful of diamonds, weight in gold, you know."

"That's the most important thing, isn't it, Mr. Carmody?"

Mr. Deels said. "You want to *own* her. Like you own the Jupiter."

"She's a Diana," Mr. Carmody said. "Now, look, Mr. Deels. Let's knock off all this frick-frack, frick-frack. I want the car, I've got the money, I'll pay whatever you ask and you don't have to bargain with me. Now who owned her?"

"There's only been one owner," Mr. Deels said, his hand caressing the Diana's fender as if it were the flank of a sleek black animal. "An impatient, unkind sort of man with no real appreciation or understanding of cars like this. A man who would pay thousands of dollars for a blooded horse and then shoot her if he could not break her spirit the first time he rode her."

"Why'd he get rid of the car?"

"There was an accident," Mr. Deels said. "Oh, don't worry, we repaired what damage there was. Yes, there was an accident, and her owner had no further use for her after that. He just couldn't handle a Diana. Tell me something, Mr. Carmody: How did you know about the Diana?"

"Why, I was—I mean, I heard about—wait a minute," Mr. Carmody said, and frowned. "Funny. I can't for the life of me tell you just who told me about the car—or even how to get here! Now, what do you think of that? But somehow I knew where to go, and I knew it'd be here."

Mr. Deels nodded slowly. "You've come to the right place," he said.

"How could I forget something like that?" Mr. Carmody said. "Well, never mind. I've got a checkbook here, Mr. Deels. You name the figure."

"Nothing."

"I didn't get that."

"I said the figure is nothing. Let's say it will be a simple trade. Your car for mine."

"Brother," Mr. Carmody said, "you've got yourself a deal! Except I'm not half as much of a nut as you are."

"I don't understand."

"I mean I don't buy cars just by listening to the motor. For all I know, you've got a busted-down old Model-T motor under that hood, and I'm going to see this car move before I sign anything. Now let's get in and take a little ride around the block, shall we?"

"Certainly," Mr. Deels said. He fished a set of keys out of his pocket. "Would you like to drive?"

"Later," Mr. Carmody said. "You know the neighborhood."

"You do *know* how to drive a Diana, don't you?" Mr. Deels said.

"Listen, buster," Mr. Carmody said, "I've smashed up more boats like this than you ever laid a monkey wrench to."

"I'm sure you have," Mr. Deels said. "Get in."

"I'll open the garage door for you," Mr. Carmody said.

"That won't be necessary. Get in."

"Oh, I get it. Electric eye. Pretty fancy for Mechanic Street," Mr. Carmody said. He climbed in beside Mr. Deels, and the seat seemed to come in and grip him fast, as if it had been made for his hips alone.

Mr. Carmody had never heard an engine start as the Diana's did. There was really nothing like sound, like ignition kicking off. Like an animal arising from sleep, the Diana suddenly started to vibrate, to stretch and to come to life. Mr. Deels touched the accelerator and they seemed to evaporate through the garage door into Mechanic Street.

Night had fallen and there was no traffic. The buildings were unfamiliar blurs of black, like the Diana herself. Mr. Deels wound the Diana around curves and corners of strange streets without touching the brake or gearing down, so it seemed, and she did not turn like a car but like a snake, and she kept going faster.

241

They turned onto a highway Mr. Carmody had never seen before, beyond whose lanes there was only limitless dark, a highway traveled by Diana IV M's and Jupiter Custom 12's and Zenobias and Arcturuses, all hurtling along without sound, their headlights fierce as feral eyes, and never bumping or passing one another.

The speed became so great that Mr. Carmody could not speak, and he fought to breathe as his back was pushed farther and farther into the clasp of the Diana's seat, and he seized Mr. Deels's arm and tried to communicate that he had had enough. "She's all yours now, Mr. Carmody," said Mr. Deels, his voice as clear as it had been in the garage, and he opened the driver's door. "Take the wheel. Try her," he said, and stepped into the moving dark.

Mr. Carmody managed to get behind the wheel. He tried to control the hurtling fury around and under him, but it seemed to enrage the Diana. There was a new burst of speed, and the curve which her headlights suddenly picked up, and over which she shot into a well of hopeless, bottomless black, was the last sight the mortal eyes of Mr. Carmody would ever see or need to see.

Mr. Deels did not look up from his book when the sound of the engine came through the window. "Sammy," Mr. Deels said, "go out and tell the man in the Arcturus to come in here." Mr. Deels went on reading until the stranger stood before him.

"Welcome," Mr. Deels said. "My name is Mr. Deels. Hell on wheels with Mr. Deels."

"Hello yourself," the stranger said. "I heard you had a Jupiter Custom 12 around here, and I'd like to take a look at it."

"That's a beautiful car you've got there," Mr. Deels said.

"Yes, I know," the man said. "About the Jupiter Custom 12. . . ."

Alicia Marches on Washington

ROBERT W. WELLS

The man from the outer office strode past the rows of desks, each with an Internal Revenue agent on one side, a worried taxpayer on the other, and threw open the door of the second-assistant-director's office.

"I've got a nut out here, Mr. Krutsch. I've never run into anything like it before in twenty-two years with the service. I don't know how to handle her."

Krutsch was a small, nervous man with calluses on the tips of his fingers from drumming them on his desk. He accepted the file on Mrs. Alicia Sibbison and glanced through it, frowning.

"You know the procedure if she's violent, Kimberley. Put her at a table. Have her make out triplicate copies of Complaint Form IRS-6583-Z. By the time she's finished, she'll be too exhausted for physical action."

"This one isn't violent, Mr. Krutsch. It's just that——" He paused, shaking his head. "You aren't going to believe this, but the thing she's complaining about is she got a refund and she doesn't think she's entitled to it."

The two men stared at each other. Then Krutsch arose and

folded his arms. He was, after all, an executive of an agency of the United States Government.

"I don't know what her game is, Kimberley. But send her in. I shall deal with her."

Alicia sat down. Krutsch drummed quietly on the desk for a while. Then he flashed her the moderately friendly smile prescribed in Rule IRS-856-B of the manual for dealing with taxpayers and asked her to begin at the beginning.

"Don't you want to call the others in before I start?"

"The others?"

"The rest of the brass." Alicia adjusted her hat and sighed. "I've gone through this so often I know the procedure."

"I can handle this myself, madam. Proceed. You live here in Washington, do you?"

"Oh, no. Brown Deer, Wisconsin. It's a Milwaukee suburb."

"And you came all the way to Washington to discuss your tax problem? Why didn't you go to the nearest district office?"

"I've been to the district office. I've been to the regional office. I've—but let's, as you say, start at the beginning. Eleven months ago I made out Form 1040 and sent it in with a check for twenty-three dollars and forty-two cents. That was what I figured we owed the Government in addition to the taxes withheld from Kermit's salary."

"Kermit is your husband, I take it. Did he help you make out Form 1040?"

"He kept looking over my shoulder and making suggestions, if you call that helping."

Krutsch stopped drumming with the fingers of his right hand and shifted to the fingers of his left without losing a beat. He told her to go on.

"Nothing happened for a few weeks; and then one day there was a letter from the Government in one of those brown envelopes with the window in front, and inside was my check, plus a refund check for eighty-six dollars and sixteen cents."

"I should think you'd have been delighted."

"Oh, I was at first. But then I went back and checked the figures on my copy of the tax form and rechecked them, and they still came out the same. We owed twenty-three dollars and forty-two cents, and there simply was no way in the world to make it come out so the Government owed us eighty-six dollars and sixteen cents. So I sat down and wrote a letter to the district office telling them they'd made a mistake."

"Did you return the refund check?"

"No. You know how it is in an agency as big as yours, Mr. Krutsch, things can go astray, and I didn't want to take any chances of having the Government come around later and claim I still owed the money, because it would take me months to save that much out of my grocery allotment."

Krutsch looked a little hurt about what she'd said about his agency. The system, he told her firmly, was virtually foolproof. Virtually wasn't good enough, Alicia said, not where her grocery allotment was concerned. Krutsch began drumming on the desk with the fingers of both hands.

"Go on, please, madam. What happened after you wrote and told the Government of the United States it was wrong and you were right?"

"Back came another of those brown envelopes with the window in front. Inside was a check for eighty-six dollars and sixteen cents."

Krutsch leaped to his feet. "You mean you got a second refund check?" Alicia nodded. "Let me call my superior. I want him in on this."

"I thought you would. They always do."

Krutsch gave W. A. Merriwether the swivel chair and drew up a straight-backed one for himself. He reviewed Alicia's testimony. Merriwether nodded his jowls thoughtfully and told her to go ahead.

"Well, when I got that second refund, I decided something

must have gone wrong; so I hurried down to the district office and told them all about it. They wouldn't believe me until I showed them both refund checks, and then they got all excited and told me to go home and be sure not to say anything to anybody about it, especially the newspapers, and they would get it straightened out and let me know where to send the checks. Three weeks later I got another of those brown envelopes."

Merriwether's florid face paled. "Another refund?"

"Another refund."

"Same amount?"

"Same amount. I'll say that for them. They're consistent. The checks were always for eighty-six dollars and sixteen cents."

"What happened next?" Krutsch demanded. He had the air of a man who is determined to hear the worst.

"Well, I got worried about all that money in my pocketbook that didn't really belong to me. Kermit persisted in thinking it was a big joke and making cracks about how he would visit me regularly at Alcatraz and everything, but I didn't think it was funny."

"I don't regard it as a laughing matter, either," Merriwether assured her. "Why, if Drew Pearson or one of those boys'd get hold of this——"

"Or one of those Senate committees," Krutsch suggested, shuddering.

"I thought about going back to the tax people, but then I decided I'd take it up with my congressman. When he was running for election, he kept making speeches about how we should all feel free to bring our problems to him; and if this wasn't a problem, I don't know one."

"You told a congressman about it!" Merriwether jumped to his feet. "Why didn't you say so before? This is a matter for the policy-making level then. Excuse me while I call my superior."

Warren R. Ding turned out to be a younger man with horn rims and a crew cut. He shook hands with Alicia, asked her about her family, inquired whether she was enjoying Washington, declared it was always a pleasure to meet a taxpayer and then settled back in the swivel chair and permitted Krutsch and Merriwether to brief him on the case. When they had finished, he urged Alicia not to get excited and to tell him all about it.

"I'm not excited at all. Mr. Rothrock was when I told him what had happened, though. He started waving his arms around and making speeches all over the office."

Merriwether groaned and put his head in his hands. "Don't tell me your congressman is Flinthead Rothrock?"

"That's the one. He kept saying how such things would never have happened when Andrew Mellon was running things, and I kept telling him I didn't want to make trouble for anybody, I just wanted to pay what I owed. I finally got him calmed down."

"You calmed old Flinthead down, Mrs. Sibbison?" Ding demanded. "You must have a remarkable way with men."

"I've learned from living with Kermit that if you just let a man keep talking long enough, after a while he'll realize he doesn't really have anything to say. Anyway, Mr. Rothrock said he'd take care of the matter. He kept patting me and telling me not to worry and calling me his little lady."

"And did he take care of things?" Ding asked. "But I suppose he didn't or you wouldn't be here."

"He sent me a carbon of a letter he wrote to the Internal Revenue Service. It ran for six and a half pages, single spaced, and it went into the philosophy of taxation as laid down by Alexander Hamilton and a lot of other things; but along toward the end he got around to my case, and he said it was a crying shame when an honest constituent had to beg and plead and cajole to pay her taxes and that unless instant action was forthcoming, he would see to it that heads rolled in the streets of Washington like bowling balls. It was a fine letter, except he had my name spelled wrong—only one '*b*' and 'sen' at the end instead of 'son.' But they figured out who he meant, all right."

"How do you know?"

"Well, I went out to my mailbox about a week later and——"

"Let me guess," Krutsch said. "A brown envelope. Window in front. Eighty-six dollars and sixteen cents."

Alicia nodded. The three men were staring at her, the same dazed, almost desperate, expression on each face. She felt a little sorry for them. Men always took such things so hard. She asked Ding if he'd like to rest for a while. He hesitated, then shook his head. "We've got to get to the bottom of this."

"Do you mind if I ask the taxpayer a few questions, chief?" Merriwether inquired.

"Go ahead."

"Madam, did your gross income for the year in question consist entirely of wages reported on Form W-2?"

"All except for thirty-eight dollars and forty-five cents."

"Aha. And that thirty-eight dollars and forty-five cents did not represent wages, salaries, bonuses, commissions, fees, tips or gratuities, profits from sales or exchanges of real estate, securities or other properties, industrial, civil service or other pensions, annuities or endowments?"

"It came from interest on our savings account."

"I see. And how many exemptions did you take for persons who had their home or principal place of abode with you and was a member of your household?"

"Just the two children, besides Kermit and me."

"And each of these children you claim received more than half of his or her support from you and he or she was either a citizen or alien resident of the United States or a resident of Canada, Mexico, the Republic of Panama or the Canal Zone?"

"They live right in Brown Deer with us, although once or twice Nancy stayed with a girl friend at Menomonee Falls overnight."

"And your medical and dental expenses, if claimed, did not include the amount totaling less than three per cent of your adjusted gross income and were recorded correctly on line five, page two?"

"Oh, for heaven's sake, W. A.," Ding interrupted. "The point is that this young lady kept getting refund checks every time she went to her mailbox. We'll get nowhere if you start talking about line five, page two."

"Chief," Merriwether said, a little stiffly, "that's one of the finest lines on Form 1040. It's confused a lot of taxpayers in its day, a lot of them, and I'm proud of that line. I won't hear it criticized, sir."

"I like line seven, page four," Krutsch suggested. "That's the tentative-credit line, twenty per cent of line six, for those figuring the limitation on retirement-income provision. 'Tentative credit.' The words have a certain swing to them. I wish more people got that far on the form."

Ding glared hard at his subordinates, who subsided, and turned to Alicia. He gave her a brisk nod, as prescribed in Rule IRS-841-A of the manual, and told her to go ahead.

"Now where were we?" Alicia asked. "Oh, yes. I'd seen Mr. Rothrock, and he'd promised to take care of it, and I'd opened another letter with a refund check. Well, I don't want to bore you gentlemen with all the details—in fact, they're a little hazy in my own mind sometimes—but I wrote two more letters to the district office and three to the regional office and quite a few to Washington. And each time I wrote, back came one of those brown envelopes with a check inside."

"Eighty-six sixteen?" Krutsch asked.

"Eighty-six sixteen."

"And those refunds came in each case in response to an inquiry or a communication on your part, either by mail or in person?"

"I guess they were in response. I couldn't say for sure. All I know is they kept coming."

"Did you see old Flinthead about it again?" Ding asked, leaning forward anxiously.

"Mr. Rothrock? No. But I did write to both my senators, the governor, the mayor and Charles A. Keach."

"Now you've lost me," Merriwether said. "Who is Charles A. Keach?"

"He's a friend of Kermit's who's always telling how many connections he has in Washington, and I thought—well, I was desperate by this time. But all he did was write a nice letter back saying he'd taken care of everything, and in the mailbox two days later was another refund check. It seemed like whenever I wrote a letter to anybody—it didn't matter who it was— back would come a refund check."

Ding stood up. He took a turn around the office, his hands behind his back. He removed the horn-rimmed glasses, wiped them on his handkerchief, put them on again and sank back into the swivel chair.

"I suppose you want to call for your superior?" Alicia said.

Ding shook his head. He leaned forward. He spoke softly. "Tell me, Mrs. Sibbison, how many of those refund checks have you received?"

"Twenty-eight."

"And each was for the same amount?"

"Eighty-six dollars."

"And sixteen cents," Merriwether interposed. "It may not seem like much to you, madam, but as a public servant, I must insist on accuracy to the penny."

"And sixteen cents," Alicia said.

"You seem to be a very levelheaded woman," Ding told her. "In fact, you're the only one of us who's taking this calmly."

"I'm numb."

"Tell me, how much do those twenty-eight checks total? In round numbers."

"I can tell you exactly. Two thousand, four hundred twelve dollars and forty-eight cents."

Ding leaned back and folded his arms. "Two thousand, four hundred twelve dollars and forty-eight cents. I see. And you originally tried to pay the Government twenty-three dollars you felt you owed over and above the amount withheld from your husband's salary?"

"Twenty-three forty-two, to be exact," Alicia said, with a glance at Merriwether.

"Which leaves a total amount in dispute of two thousand, four hundred thirty-five dollars and ninety cents."

"It's not in dispute as far as I'm concerned. All I want is to pay what I owe and get on a plane for Milwaukee. And to get rid of these checks before the FBI comes around and taps me on the shoulder."

She opened her handbag. She turned it upside down on the desk. The three men sat staring at the twenty-eight checks. No one made a move to touch them. Alicia stood up.

"And now I've returned them, gentlemen. If someone will give me a receipt, just in case there's ever any question. Kermit told me I ought to get a receipt, and for once I think he's right."

No one moved. Finally Ding quit staring at the checks and lifted his head. "Please sit down. Let me explain our position."

"Can't you just take them back?"

"It is not as simple as that. Let me tell you how it is. The income tax is the basic support of the American form of government. Without it there would be no money to buy missiles or surplus wheat or, heaven forbid, to pay the salaries of three of the four persons in this room. It is not a matter to be trifled with."

"I'm not trying to trifle, Mr. Ding. I'm just trying to——"

"I know. And I respect you for it. But you must realize that there are tens of millions of you taxpayers. Each of you is an individual—a living, breathing individual. But in this building each taxpayer is something else. He is a number. He is a digit. He is a set of perforations on a punch card."

"Sir," Merriwether said, "do you think it is wise? I mean, we have all come to admire Mrs. Sibbison during this crisis, but she is, after all, one of the public, one of the taxpayers; and the entire theory of the system demands——"

"I am the chief here," Ding said quietly. "There comes a time when even a taxpayer must be given credit for having common sense. I will take the responsibility." He turned back to Alicia. "Imagine, madam, what would happen if everyone who got a refund check refused to accept it."

"Would that be bad?"

"It would be disastrous. The American way of life, not to mention the economy of our country, is based on the premise that anyone who is given any money from Washington hurries right out and spends it before the Treasury Department changes its mind. The economy of our country, did I say? I will go further. I will say the economy of the free world itself!"

Alicia, for the first time, seemed shaken. She looked from one of the men to the other and back again. Could it be possible that they were right? "Do you mean it's my patriotic duty to cash these checks?"

Ding laced his fingers behind his head and stared at the ceiling. A hush came over the room. Even Krutsch stopped drumming his fingers.

"Duty, madam? It is a big word. What is duty? What is patriotism? You may say it is the thing Paul Revere carried with him in his saddlebags, the commodity that remained after the oolong was dumped into Boston harbor. But is it not also the more unspectacular sort of day-to-day citizenship—the acceptance on the part of you little people, you taxpayers, that when a check arrives from Washington the nation expects you to put your signature on the back and spend that check?" He quit looking at the ceiling. He leaned across the desk toward her and took her hand. "Madam, you are intelligent. You are attractive. You are a wife and a mother. You have your whole life ahead of you. Will you listen to the advice of a man who knows where the deepest obligation of citizenship lies?"

"I guess so."

"Then my advice is this—don't foul up the system."

Alicia hesitated for a long moment, the three pairs of male eyes watching her anxiously. But then she shook her head. "All I want is to pay the twenty-three dollars and forty-two cents I owe."

Ding leaped to his feet. His calm was gone. His hands were trembling. He strode to the door. He opened it. He beckoned to Alicia to follow him.

"Where are we going?"

"You leave me no recourse," the director said grimly. "I have tried. Heaven knows I have tried. But I have failed. Now I must take you to my superior."

"But, chief," Merriwether cried, "I thought you were——"

"You thought I was the final resort in such matters. You are wrong, W. A. I am only a cog. We are all only cogs in the system. The ultimate authority is elsewhere. Come, madam."

Alicia followed him briskly down one hall and up another, through locked doors, across crowded offices and through deserted ones. She was clutching the checks in one hand, her handbag in the other. Ding did not look back until he came to a final door. Then he paused, his hand on the knob.

"You will not change your mind, madam?"

She shook her head. He turned without a word and opened

the door. He stood aside and then followed her inside. Alicia had expected another office—a fancier one, presumably, in line with the importance of its occupant. But this was no office, but a great barnlike room with rows of machines stretching off into the distance, each with its lights blinking on and off as the machine hummed thoughtfully to itself. She turned to Ding. "I thought you were taking me to your boss."

Except for the machines, they were alone. But he spoke in a whisper. "I have, madam."

She turned and looked at the machines again. The lights were still blinking. The hum seemed to have deepened a little. In spite of herself, she found herself speaking in hushed tones, as in a cathedral. "You mean they have the final word?"

"Of course. No human brain could grasp the complexities of the system. These machines are the only ones capable of understanding what it's all about."

"Well, then," Alicia said firmly, "they've made a mistake."

She spoke in her normal tone of voice, but in the sudden stillness as the machines stopped humming, it sounded like a shout. Ding took a quick step away from her.

"They do not make mistakes. If they did——" He shook his head in horror at the thought. "But come. We will go to the very top. We will go to IRS-KCG himself."

She followed the director down the aisle past the rows of blinking machines. As she walked, she had the feeling that she was being watched from behind. But when she turned around, there was nothing there—nothing human, anyway. She clutched the checks tighter and stayed close to Ding.

They came at last to another door. This time it led into an office—or what looked like an office. But it was empty, except for IRS-KCG, who squatted in a corner, blinking his lights inquiringly.

"Don't speak unless spoken to," Ding warned her in a whisper. "He is so constructed that the human voice actuates his electronic connections."

Alicia nodded. Ding, who had brought along her records, glanced at them and then stepped up to the machine. "I introduce you to taxpayer Number 8438652-B," he said. "She is a —I mean, she has a problem."

IRS-KCG thrust out a card from a slot near his equator. Ding handed it to her. "Welcome to Washington, 8438652-B," it said. "How is your family? How do you like our city? I see you are from Wisconsin. How are the Braves doing?"

Alicia started to answer, but Ding stopped her. The questions were rhetorical ones, he explained in a whisper. IRS-KCG was merely following the manual. Actually he wasn't much interested in baseball. The lights blinked again. Another card came out.

"You have a problem, 8438652-B. Tell your problem. Speak distinctly, please."

Alicia felt like a fool standing there talking to this pile of wires and plumbing, but after a glance at Ding, she stepped forward and went through her story again, from the beginning. IRS-KCG whirred a few times, and once she was sure he grunted—it was when she got to the part about Congressman Rothrock—but mostly he just blinked thoughtfully without interrupting. Alicia began to feel, in spite of herself, that she had at last found somebody who understood her.

It took her quite a while to finish—she didn't want to leave anything out—but finally she was through. IRS-KCG thrust out a card saying, "One moment, please," and then began humming softly to himself. Once one of the lights on his panel turned from amber to red, and Ding paled; but it winked back to amber again, and the director's anxiety departed.

"You're a challenge to him, Mrs. Sibbison," he whispered. "I've never seen him hesitate so long before."

A card came out. Ding grabbed it. Alicia read it over his shoulder. "Solution: Taxpayer 8438652-B is at fault."

"Naturally," Ding said impatiently. "I didn't dream for a moment that it was our error. But be more specific, please."

"Solution, subhead A: 8438652-B's perforations wrong."

"Why, of course," Ding cried. "That explains it."

"It doesn't explain it to me," Alicia told him.

"But it's all so simple. Every time you wrote in or appeared in person, the matter was eventually referred to your index card. If something was wrong with the card——" He glanced quickly at IRS-KCG. "Through human error, of course. But if the card was wrong, naturally the result would have been the same each time—a refund check when none was due. Why didn't I think of the solution myself?"

"Too few digital connections in computor head."

"I wasn't talking to you, IRS-KCG. You're so smart, what do you suggest we do about it?"

"Feed me checks."

Ding grabbed them from Alicia's hand and thrust them into the slot on the machine. They came out in a moment marked VOID. With them was a card pointing out politely but firmly that the taxpayer owed the Government twenty-three dollars and forty-two cents and that unless she paid up promptly, the full resources of the United States Government stood ready to crack down on her delinquency. Alicia handed Ding the check she had written so many months before. Ding thrust it into IRS-KCG, who accepted it without comment.

"And now everything's settled," Ding said, turning to go. "Once IRS-KCG tackles a problem, it's solved. It was a pleasure to have met you, madam. Give my regards to the taxpayers in Minnesota."

"I'm from Wisconsin," Alicia told him, but he was already through the door and didn't seem to hear. She started to follow, but then she remembered Kermit's advice. She turned back to the machine. "May I please have a receipt for the money?"

IRS-KCG blinked in surprise. He thrust out a card. "We do not give receipts."

"But I want something to show, in case there's another mistake."

The amber lights winked red. "We do not make mistakes. To err is human."

Alicia folded her arms. "I will not leave this room until I get a receipt."

IRS-KCG whirred and grunted and fumed. But finally, bowing to the inevitable, he thrust out an envelope. Alicia grabbed it. Now that she had won, she had a panicky feeling that she had to get out of here. She half-ran through the big room past the rows of watchful machines, and it was not until she was on the plane heading back to Kermit and the children that she was able to relax.

She took out the envelope, the symbol of her triumph. Why, she wondered, did Government communications all look the same? It was so familiar, this brown envelope with the window in front. But, of course, it was ridiculous to suppose——

She tore it open with trembling hands. Then she sank back in the seat. There was no appeal. There was no place else to go. The check for eighty-six dollars and sixteen cents was signed by IRS-KCG himself.

Reprieve

BENTON RAIN PATTERSON

Because of the importance of the events which surrounded it, particularly those which followed, I, known as Eleazar, wish to relate a certain incident to which I was a witness.

I am not ashamed to say that I was in jail when I met the young man I shall tell about, for there are many who have suffered at the hands of the oppressors and have been imprisoned without just cause. So it was with me, and it was only after a considerable time spent in chains that I gained the favor of the jailer and was unshackled and placed in a cell, with a place to sleep and a bench and table and a candle to write and read by. I am now free again and have returned home; it is almost a year since it happened, but I remember it all quite well.

In my mind's eye I can see it now—the darkness, the dismal, lonely darkness of that dungeon jail. For a man outside, in the plaza, in the city's narrow streets and beyond its walls, there is sun—and moon and stars. Outside a man sees day follow the night. But down in that craggy hole all is night—always the darkness and the gloom. It is for that reason that I do not know exactly how long he was there with me. But it must have been several days, or so it seemed.

He was unruly, quite unruly, at first. He fought and struggled with the guards every step down the long stairway and through the stony corridor. Their shadows danced on the walls from the light the head guard carried. Twice the young man broke away and ran for the stairway. He must have been very strong, although he was not extraordinarily large of stature. He displayed an almost animal-like fierceness, and it required the efforts of five guards to restrain him and force him into the cell. It was the cell next to mine.

Because I had been in my cell only a short time, I did not know there was anything different about the one next to me. I wondered why the young man was not put in chains in the big, common room, as I had been. Later, when I had an opportunity to ask a guard, I was told that was where condemned prisoners were put to await execution. It was like a special cage into which the fattest hens were placed before their necks were wrung, so that there would be no mistake about which ones were to be slaughtered.

There were two others in there with him. They were a grim pair; one churlish and swaggering, the other quiet and brooding. I could not see them at all times, for there was only the light of my candle and the oil lamp attached to the corridor wall, shining weakly some distance away. When they moved to the rear of their death cell, away from the bars, they were lost to me in the blackness. It was only because of the way the cells were situated that I was able to see them at all. A stone wall divided us, but their cell faced into mine slightly because it turned a corner of the jail, ending the row of cells against a high wall of rock.

When the guards had finally hurled the young man headlong into the cell, he quickly rose to his feet and rushed at the door as it closed. The heavy, barred door slammed against him, knocking him backward. Two guards secured the latch and sighed at having at last put him away. They turned then and walked toward the stairs, and the young man shouted after them, "Swine! Filthy, foreign swine!" His words echoed down the corridor as the guard detail walked out. He grasped the bars and tried violently to shake them loose from the door timbers. The stout metal bars budged not at all, and, realizing the futility of his act, he stopped and clung thoughtfully to the door.

He seemed not to notice the others in there with him, though the boorish one taunted him about "having another try at tearing out those bars." I myself was silent, stunned actually by the intensity of the young man as he stood there, his face pressed against the unyielding bars. It was an intelligent face, I saw. The young man was obviously not of a mean background, had probably not seen the inside of a prison before. He was, I would guess, not much past his twentieth birthday. But though his unlined face bespoke youth, his dark eyes burned without brightness. There was a dull glow of embers in his eyes, not the flame of youth. He wore an expression of pain. At last he turned from the door and resignedly lay himself down on a bed of straw.

For the first hours he was there he could not let the guards come within hearing without cursing them. Whenever they came, to bring water or food or to cast in a new prisoner—it was the holiday season then, and the city must have been filled with those who had come to celebrate—he would rail at them. "Pig!" he would yell. "Damn your black soul!" Then his anger seemed to run its course. He became less belligerent, his speech less vile. His spirit seemed to relent.

But he would have nothing to do with the men who shared his cell and his fate. After a while they came to ignore him, too, even the churlish one. As I sat at my table I could see the young man's feet near the front of his cell, there in the strip of half-light at the bars. He would lie still for a long while, in either slumber or quiet thought, then at intervals would spring to his feet as if, having reached a decision, he meant to act on it. Whatever it was, those unmoving bars thwarted any action the young man had wanted to take. He was a prisoner, locked away from the world, sealed off from his companions, and he slowly but clearly came to realize it as he stood at the door. He would grip the bars and then study the hands that held them. Once, as I watched him in the dim light, I saw his eyes moisten; his thoughts had drawn tears.

It was then that I knew I must speak to him, that I must know what had put him in that death cell, that I should help him, somehow, if I could. I opened my mouth to say—— I don't know what I was going to say; but before the words could come out he turned and withdrew into the darkness.

Only occasionally did I get an opportunity to speak to a guard without being overheard. Aside from the awkwardness of speaking about someone while he is listening, I further did not want to take the risk of offending the young man and destroying any possible chance I might have later to communicate with him—although I wondered anxiously if I should approach him immediately, for there was no way of knowing how much more time he had to live. Then, a little while later, I was brought a new candle by a guard, one who had been helpful to me previously, and I motioned him over to the far side of my cell, away from the doomed men.

In a voice just above a whisper I asked the guard, "Who is he, that young fellow? What has he done?"

The guard spoke flatly, his coarse voice unable to articulate a hushed tone. "A rotten revolutionary," he said. "And a killer!"

His words, to me, seemed to boom out through the prison. I knew the young prisoner had heard it, as well as everyone else on that side of the jail. Not that it mattered to them, but it did matter to me, and I knew, too, that it mattered to the young man what was said of him. For all his earlier fierceness, he could not now hide the remorse in his heart, the anguish in his eyes.

I tried to quiet the guard. "Oh, I see," I whispered hurriedly. "Too bad. Well, thanks—many thanks." Someone in a cell at the far end of the corridor yelled to the guard, and he walked away. I was relieved to see him go. But I was sure the young man would be beyond approach now, that I had forfeited any chance I might have had to help him in the short time he had left. I sat on my bench and watched the old candle as it began to flicker.

As I watched the candle, I thought of the men in that death cell, particularly the young fellow. Their lives were now flickering, just as the candle, and soon—any time now—the light would go out, and there would be only the darkness of death. I shuddered in the chill thought of the death that awaited them. I knew the "justice" of the oppressive rulers of our land, and I wondered if these men were truly receiving their just punishment. I was certain about those two in there, a pair of cutthroats if ever I saw them. But I couldn't help thinking that somehow there must have been some mistake about the youth's having to die. I lighted the new candle and began to write. It was a letter to my dear wife.

I wrote in the bright glow of the new light, focusing my mind on the things I wished to say to my beloved. After some minutes, however, I became aware of a figure that the corner of my eye had noticed. I turned my head to see the young condemned man standing at the bars of the death cell. He stood close to the wall that separated us and was gazing intently at me as I wrote.

"Forgive me," he said as I met his eyes, and I was surprised by the calmness and the strength in his voice, "for seeming to stare; I did not mean to alarm you."

"It's all right," I told him, speaking as evenly as I could.

He moved still closer and said, "I see you are an educated

man and can write. Perhaps sometime you would be good
enough to write a letter for me." His voice then faltered, and
I saw him struggle to go on. "I am at a loss to do so for myself," he said, turning his head and extending his arm in a gesture indicating the black nothingness in his cell.

"Of course," I said. "I would be glad to. I am at your service." I wanted to go on, to say something more, but my mind,
surprised, could not supply me with words. He hesitated, his
head bowed. Then he looked up again, and I saw once more
the anguish in his eyes.

"My father, too, is a learned man," he said. "He is a teacher.
He has many students at the university."

Was it true? I wondered. There was nothing in his appearance or his speech to contradict him. But, then, did not most
men in jail speak of rich and noble families they had come
from, or the great position from which they had fallen? Mis-
fortune, a woman, bad companions—these were to blame for
their presence in prison, or else it was "the swine" who occupied our land, who had robbed them of their station, of their
fortune. I had heard many stories in jail. But this young man
was different. His words rang true.

"Is it your father you wish me to write?" I asked. He nodded, and I said, "Would you like to start now?" He must have
guessed what I was thinking, that perhaps time would run out
for him if he put it off. He nodded again.

"Yes," he said sadly. "Perhaps it would be the wise thing
to do."

Then he told me what he wished to say to his father. He
spoke slowly, and often with great difficulty. This is what I
wrote as he spoke it, and I think I have recalled it accurately.

Dearest Father: Please thank the kind friend who is writing this
for me. I am under such handicap that I am unable to write you
myself, and it is only by the goodness of my friend, to whom I am

forever indebted, that I am afforded the opportunity to convey to you the thoughts which weigh most heavily on my heart and mind. Please give him your warmest thanks, even as I so do now.

I have, regretfully, traveled some distance since last I saw you. The distance by foot is great, but could be spanned if I were free to do so. However, the distance I have strayed from honor and circumspection is irretraceable. From that good place I have wandered beyond the possibility of returning. And for that I am most deeply sorry. For though it would grieve me to leave this earth without again seeing you and wishing you well, I am so much more anguished to know that I must leave without having brought to you the honor which I ought, that instead there is disgrace.

My greatest fear now is that the news of my ignominy will soon reach your city and you consequently will suffer for my sins. If it is any solace at all to you, I wish you to know that I would give anything, would do anything, if it could be otherwise, if someway the past year could be relived.

Only a year it has been. Sometimes, as I think of home, the time seems greater; other times it seems less. Would that it were yesterday, so that I could face about now and return. After leaving home I spent several months wandering about before I came to this city. I found men who were eager to become my friends. They talked stirringly, imaginatively, excitingly. I had never heard such talk. They spoke of bold deeds, of a new order that they would establish in our country, of how they would overthrow our oppressors. I listened, and I joined them.

For a while all went well, and I was pleased with myself. Then came the time when they began to put their plans into operation, the hour to strike for freedom, they said. It was not as I had thought. Their "strikes for freedom" were the murder of innocent men and women, the slaughter of children, the burning of homes, pillaging. These were the acts of terrorists, black outlaws. I tried to withdraw from their group. They would not let me. I stayed on.

There was more killing, more burning. The government soldiers sought us night and day. We moved about constantly. Two weeks ago we planned another foray into the city, more killing. The soldiers were nearer than we thought. They surprised us, and there was much fighting. Our leader and ten others were slain; I was captured. Now I await the executioners. Except for my friend who writes for me, I am without a friend. I am alone with the thoughts of my crimes, in the blackness of my sins.

I am not afraid to die, for it is just punishment for my foul deeds. But I am sorely distressed that events have, or will, come to an abrupt end, that there is no opportunity to attempt to make amends somehow for my evil acts.

If I had all things to do over, I would, of course, do them very differently. But deeds once done cannot be undone. There is no pouring back the spilled sands of time. However, I do sincerely wish—and do earnestly desire to have you know it is my wish—that were I able, I would devote my life to repairing as I might the great harm I have done to innocents. Only God's miracle could give me that opportunity, and from Him I deserve no mercy and have not enough boldness left to ask Him.

Therefore, I bid you farewell with sincere sorrow and contrition, but knowing there is no hope for me and fearful that I have brought ruin upon you also.

He had no chance then to end the letter, for it was at that point the guards burst in on us. They drew back the latch on the death-cell door and ordered the young man out. He looked back at me, halted, then started to tell me his father's name, so that I might dispatch the letter.

"Come out, rebel scum!" a guard shouted. "Come out of there!"

The young man was calm, as though he had done all that he could to prepare for death and was now ready to face eternity.

"Wait," he said to the nearest guard, "there is one last thing"—he held out his hand to me and gestured with his fingers; I knew that he wanted to sign the letter—"I would like to do before I die."

As he stepped toward the front of my cell in the corridor, I picked up the letter and got up to meet him at the bars.

"Save it for your death day then," the guard said irritably. "This is not it."

The young man stopped short, puzzled. "Where are you taking me then?" he asked.

The guard grasped him by the arm and pulled at him. "Nowhere, you damned rebel. You're free."

The words seemed to hang in the stillness that followed them. The young man stared blankly, unbelievingly at the guards, then at me. "Free?" he said, his voice rising uncontrollably. "Me? Free?"

The guard was impatient with the young man's disbelief and his refusal to come along with them. "Yes—you!" said the guard. "You're Barabbas, aren't you?"

"Yes," the young man said, "but——"

"Well, that howling mob out there wants you. Pilate's got to give amnesty to somebody, and that mob would rather see the Nazarene dead than a black-hearted murderer like yourself. Even Pilate, the governor himself, can't understand it. Come on, get out, you."

"The Nazarene?" the young man, Barabbas, said, yielding to the guard.

"Yes—your 'king.' . . . That's a good one, ain't it?" the guard said, turning to the others. "This murdering young louse goes free, and 'the King of the Jews' takes his place on Skull Hill. Now, that's one for you to try to figure."

"I—I——" the youth stammered.

"You can tell your two playmates in there good-by," the guard said derisively, his head motioning toward the death cell. "No such luck for them. They'll be hanging on crosses along with the Nazarene before the day is out."

The young man took the letter from my hand and walked out with the Romans, speechless. He didn't look back.

After that I never saw or heard from him again. I never found out who his father was, either, or if he ever saw the letter the youth took with him. Barabbas was sincere, I know, and I often think about him. I often think also about the "miracle" which he said was the only thing that could give him the second chance he wanted so badly.

The Child Who
Was Thrown Away

STEWART TOLAND

She hadn't meant to be a thief. But then none of us do, and all of us are, stealing time and taxes and other people's laughter, if nothing worse. Thieves. For "What is mine is mine and what is thine is mine" wasn't written of angels, but of men. And women. And children.

It began with her growing up. For seven is grown up when all you've been before is six or five or even four. So she was grown up more than she'd ever been, and she was wondering about things, and wanting things, not toys that any dime might buy, but things unseen, unknown, like grownups want. She wanted to know who she was, for how can you grow up to be someone you don't know? All she was was the little girl in the third bed from the fire door, a little girl in the looking glass. And that isn't enough to be. But it was all she was, for herself was the only family she knew.

Laurie went to the washstand and looked at the little girl in the looking glass. She had big, green eyes and black, black hair; there wasn't any curl to it, but it had a shine like shoes on Sunday. She knew her eyes would be green always, and her hair black and straight, but her face was the face of a stranger.

She couldn't see the lady in it that she was going to grow to be. She pounded on the glass with her fists. She said, "Who are you? Are you pretty or ugly, fat or thin? Don't you love your little girl, or are you sick or lost? Why can't I know you? For I want to, I want to belong to you!"

But the little girl in the looking glass only pounded back with her fists that were as cold and hard and senseless as glass.

And Laurie knew she couldn't wait another day, and she ran to ask Miss Hanacher about her mother. For Miss Hanacher would have to answer her now that she was old. She couldn't say, as she had before, that Laurie was too little to understand. For Laurie knew about being poor, and sick, and lost; she was as old as that. So Miss Hanacher would have to say if Laurie's mamma was too poor or too sick. That was what most of the mothers were. They had to work, or they had to lie in hospitals, so their children lived in The Home until they got well or rich, except those who belonged to someone called The Court. But whatever it was, the children knew whom they belonged to. And Miss Hanacher knew, for she was head of The Home and knew everything about everyone.

The big girls said you couldn't have the smallest secret without Miss Hanacher's finding it out. It seemed that she could look right through you with the gray sharpness of her eyes—and if she couldn't see the secret, she could smell it with the sharpness of her nose that was so pinched it was like a finger pointing. Miss Hanacher looked like a witch, and she wasn't anybody's mother. She was just bells to tell you what to do, and rules to tell you what not to do, and she discovered secrets. And this day she told a lie.

She looked at Laurie looking at her, and said, "Laurie, your mother is dead."

Laurie knew it was a lie. She pounded on Miss Hanacher. "Why do you keep me from her? All the other little girls have mothers! Why can't I have mine?"

"Oh, Laurie!" Miss Hanacher tried to take Laurie in her arms. She said, "You're not old enough to understand how things can't always be the way we want them. But if I could give you your mother, I would!"

Which was the worst lie of all. For Laurie knew Miss Hanacher knew where her mother was. She was in the filing cabinets. Laurie looked over Miss Hanacher's shoulder at the rows and rows, a whole wall of little tin drawers. That was where the mothers were kept, and the fathers too. There were all the words in there that it took to make a mother and father. And Laurie said to Miss Hanacher, "No!" And it was hate.

It was so quick and deep a hate, it was as though it came natural to her. Miss Hanacher shivered, and Laurie twisted free and ran out the door and out of The Home and across the lawn to where the weeds began about a troubled little path leading into the willow forest that was only two trees big. But they were so great their branches swept the ground, and inside you couldn't see from their beginning to their ending, so surely it was a forest. It was a dark and secret place, where the children always came to hide when they were hurt.

Miss Hanacher went to the window and watched as Laurie disappeared beneath the trees. She said, "I must learn to lie better."

Laurie didn't cry very long. For she knew what she was going to do. The only trouble was, she couldn't read. So she sat on the edge of the willow forest and watched the big girls walking by to see if any carried a book too small and thick to be a picture book. For today was Saturday, and if someone carried a reading book when they didn't have to, it must be because they could read real good. By and by Gladys came with a book.

Gladys was ten, and she was here because her mother was sick in the hospital, but in two years they said her mother would be well, and Gladys could go home. Gladys was matter-of-fact. She said, "Of course I can read. I'm ten."

"Can you read the big words like 'mother' and street numbers?"

"Of course I can, stupid."

"Can you keep a secret?"

Gladys looked interested. "From whom?"

"From everybody."

"That can't be done. Miss Hanacher would find out."

"Would you tell her?"

"No."

"Then how would she find out?"

"Because she always does."

"Who says so? You only know about the secrets she's found out about; you don't know the secrets that are so secret she hasn't found out. I have secrets she hasn't found out."

"You have?" Gladys sat down in the lace of leaves. "What are they?"

"Cross your heart and hope to die and never visit the moon if you tell?"

Gladys crossed her heart and hoped to die and never visit the moon.

"I have the secret that I want to know who I am, and I'm going to. I have the secret that every night when Miss Hanacher takes her bath she lays her keys on the bed table, and I'm going to take them and look in the filing cabinet where the mothers are and find out who I am."

Gladys was aghast. "You'd be skinned alive!"

"Why? My mother is mine, isn't she? I have a right to her, don't I? I'm her little girl!"

"But the keys are Miss Hanacher's!"

"She won't know. She takes long baths, and it won't take you long to read my mother's name and address."

"Me?"

"Sure. That's why I'm telling you!"

Gladys rocked back and forth and thought about that. She was bored and homesick, and it would be fun to have a secret; but the best would be fooling Miss Hanacher. For how could she find out, for ladies in the bathroom always closed the door.

"When do you want to do it?"

"Tonight; she takes her longest baths on Saturday. You wait by the cabinets. Do you think you can find me in them?"

"Of course, stupid, you'll be under *L*."

"Why?"

"For Laurie, that's why. And if we get caught, I'll kill you."

Gladys got up and walked away. She didn't want her friends to see her with someone only seven.

Laurie was first in bed that night. Miss Hanacher noticed that, for she always came to say good night to everyone. She kissed Laurie to see if she had fever, but all she had was eyes —they sparkled and looked everywhere but at Miss Hanacher. They were the eyes of a little girl with a delicious secret, and Miss Hanacher was so pleased she kissed her again. That was the wonder of being only seven; yesterday's tears truly belonged to yesterday. Miss Hanacher tucked every one of the twenty little beds and turned out the lights, and by and by she said good night to the big girls, and all The Home settled down dark and still. Only Miss Hanacher couldn't settle down; she couldn't forget Laurie's eyes—the ones when she said, "No!" and the ones she took to bed with her. Maybe a nice hot bath would help.

Miss Hanacher laid her keys on her night table, just so they covered the crack in the marble, like she always did, and tested her flashlight. Then she got her slippers and gown and robe and a new book on child psychology that was supposed to answer any problem in only 560 pages, and she went into the bathroom and closed the door.

The Child Who Was Thrown Away

Laurie heard the door shut. She had had to pinch herself so many times to keep from falling asleep that she just about hurt all over. But she was awake, and she heard the door and the water running like a train going down a hill and then the swishing like a storm. Then she hardly dared breathe as she slipped down the hall and into Miss Hanacher's bedroom, where she nearly died of fright. As thieves often do. For there wasn't any noise in the tub. She almost turned and ran, but first she peeked through the keyhole, and Miss Hanacher was reading a book, which was a very odd thing to do in a tub, but it was a fine thing, for it was a very big book. Only suddenly Miss Hanacher looked around, as if sniffing the air for secrets. Laurie closed her eyes and held her breath, and in a moment she heard the soft swish of water as Miss Hanacher went back to reading. Laurie tiptoed to the table and got the keys and flashlight, and made sure the watchman wasn't coming; then she ran to Miss Hanacher's office. Gladys was waiting by the cabinets.

"Well, it's about time! Did you get the keys?"

Laurie held them out.

Gladys was a little scared, but this was the first excitement that had happened since her mother had gone to the hospital.

Besides, it really wasn't stealing, for the little individual drawer, or box, had Laurie's name on it, and if your name was on a thing, surely that made it yours—really yours.

The sixth key opened it. Laurie snatched it right out of Gladys's hands. "It's mine!" She pulled the little drawer out, and sat down on the floor and laid it in her lap, carefully, carefully, as though it weren't made of tin but glass and would break. And Gladys knelt and held the light on the box as though that were the only thing in the world that mattered, just the box and the glow it laid upon their faces, for the inside of the box was white. It was goods. Laurie picked it up;

it was a baby's slip. And on each shoulder was a little pin with four pretend pearls.

Laurie counted each one out, they were little drops of loveliness in her fingers; her hands moved so gently around them, for they were the first things she had ever known that her mother had known. For this was such a little slip it must be her mother who had pinned it on her, for she couldn't have been old enough to know anyone else.

Laurie said, "A mother would have to love her baby very much to buy such fine pins."

And Gladys said yes. "I've seen them in the five-and-dime; you only get two for twenty cents, while the regular ones are thirty for fifteen cents."

"She must be a pretty lady to love pretty things." And suddenly the little girl in the looking glass wasn't a stranger. She was pretty like her mother, with pearls on everything.

Laurie looked to see what else was hers. The next white was a diaper with two pink diaper pins pinned in it. And underneath the diaper was stiff paper, and she was so excited she just sat looking at it for a moment, for it was on paper that writing would be.

She touched it, and it made a little crackling sound, a sort of angry sound, as if it were something that mustn't be touched.

But Laurie picked it up and unfolded it until it became a shopping bag, and she stuck her head inside to see if there was anything in there. There wasn't. On the outside there was printing. And slashed beneath in black letters were the words, NOBODY BUT NOBODY.

Gladys read them out, then she read the paper that had been under the shopping bag in the very bottom of the drawer.

July 23, 1953. Infant, female, Caucasian, about three days old, weight 6 pounds 3 ounces, found abandoned in a shopping bag against the N.E. lamppost of 37 Street and Park at 3:20 A.M. The baby wore a white lawn slip with two shoulder pins of imitation pearls and a white diaper with pink diaper pins. There was no note or identification. Officer Logan gave the report. On admission to the hospital the child was listed as No. 1376421. On admission to The Home she was named Laurie.

Gladys read it very slowly, for some of the words were strange, but she knew what they said. She had read *The Little Prince*, and she knew what the word "abandoned" meant.

"What does it mean?" Laurie beat on her arm. "What does it say about my mother and father?"

"It doesn't. They aren't here. They didn't tell on themselves at all. They only threw you away. That's what 'abandoned' means, something you don't want and you throw it away like trash. You were put in a bag like trash too. I guess this one, and that's why it's here." She stuck her head in to see how it was for size. "You were left in the street against a lamppost, and your mother and father didn't put their names on you, for if they'd wanted you back, they wouldn't have thrown you away." Gladys was fascinated by the thought; she kept saying it over and over in different ways and looking at Laurie. This was the biggest secret ever.

Gladys fingered the slip, "There isn't any lace on it, so your mother must have been very poor. I guess that's why she threw you away. My baby things have lace and embroideries."

Laurie's lips were trembling so she couldn't speak. She pointed to the bag, to the printing on the outside that she wouldn't believe didn't belong to her.

Gladys said no. That was the name of a store. Her mother had taken her there once when she was little to see Santa Claus. And Nobody But Nobody wasn't a mother, it meant —— Gladys looked at Laurie, and all of a sudden she didn't see trash or even a secret. For the first time she saw a little girl who had wanted to know her mother, and knew her mother had thrown her away. And Gladys didn't know what to do about it. But then, Miss Hanacker hadn't known what to do about it either.

She stood there now in the doorway watching the darkness of the room, and the darkness of truth. For she had got there too late to stop the reading of the note, and what is read can't be unread. The flashlight lay on the floor and made a small slash of white in the night. It made ghosts of two little girls; one who didn't know what to do, just sat there hiding her mouth with her hands and staring terrified at Laurie; one who didn't do anything, just sat there with the tears running down her cheeks and making no sound at all. Miss Hanacker wanted to take her in her arms and tell her it was all right, but those weren't words you could tell to thieves in the night, or even to broken hearts.

Infinitely slowly Miss Hanacker moved back and away and out of her door. She tiptoed to her bathroom, and set up a great sloshing in the tub, for she was the one who discovered the secrets and told the lies. And after a little while, when she peeked and saw the keys back on her table, she came out and listened to the crying of the little girl who was the third bed from the fire door, a girl in a looking glass and a little girl who had been thrown away. And that was too much to know.

Miss Hanacker waited until the crying stopped. Then she went and held Laurie in her arms, not tight enough to waken her, but maybe enough so she would know in some secret place inside that there had been arms around her. And Miss Hanacker thought and thought. How could you tell a little girl who knew she had been thrown away that that was a good thing to be? How could you make a lie as big as that sound true?

Miss Hanacker laid Laurie in bed, and went and pulled the blind so the street-lamp light couldn't touch her. Then she went to her room and threw the book she had been reading into the tub and drowned it, as if it were alive and could feel and be dead. Then she cried herself to sleep, for she really was too young to have seventy children, and she was sure she was not wise enough.

Laurie had fever the next day. Miss Hanacher said she guessed it was a cold coming, but not a bad one, so she didn't make Laurie go to the infirmary, she only made her put on a sweater and told her to stay all day in the sun and drink lots of warm milk and cold juice, and she kept sending them out to her all day and the day after. Laurie didn't say she had fever only because she cried so much. She couldn't tell about the tears without telling the why, and she wouldn't tell that. Not even to Gladys would she ever tell it again. Not the word "mother." For she hated it. Hated it as much as her mother must have hated her. That was the lady in the looking glass. Hate.

And Laurie hated street lamps. Everywhere she looked she saw them, for The Home was a block square, and all around it were the lamps. Before she had thought of them as lollipops, but now she saw them as watching eyes watching her, because they knew who she was. She ran into the willow forest to hide.

That is how it happened that it was Laurie who found the kittens, because all the other children were in school. She found them in a nest of leaves, three black babies without even their eyes open, but their mouths wide and pink and yelling, with the tiniest, sharpest prickles of white teeth and real whiskers all around. Laurie knelt and was afraid even to touch them. But she did, and the baby hissed! A lion hiss just half a kitten big. It was so precious, so tiny and fierce and helpless. And all around it a great, strange world waited to pounce upon it, as worlds do on the very young.

Laurie poked the second kitten, and it hissed. She poked the third kitten, but it sniffed and grabbed her hand with all four paws and needle claws, and it sucked and sucked on her fingers, for it was the tiniest and the hungriest. Laurie had been drinking milk, and when Laurie drank milk it was sort of as if all of her were drinking it. Laurie dropped some on her hand; the drops ran down her fingers in rivers of milk, and the kittens screamed and tumbled and fought, and there were three little kittens sucking on three little fingers. Then the purring began, real cat purring just kitten size. It was like a song singing in the shadows. They sucked and sang and fell asleep, a pile of warm softness in the puddle of her lap.

Laurie waited most all day, but the mamma cat didn't come for her babies, and on account of The Home dog running loose, Laurie didn't dare leave them in the willow forest. And on account of their crying so much, for they were hungry all the time, she had to take them to bed with her, which was a warm and wonderful thing to do. Only the beds were just a table apart, and the children around heard them mewing, and they made such happy noises that Miss Hanacher came out of her room.

Everyone popped into bed, and Laurie curled about the kittens, which began to purr so loud she was sure Miss Hanacher would hear. Only Miss Hanacher had a handkerchief in her hand and was blowing her nose as she came in the door, and she saw twenty little girls lying stiff and still, and all looking at her with great, frightened eyes as though she were a witch or a man from outer space. Or as though they had a secret. Miss Hanacher blew her nose again and pulled the blinds.

"I think I'm getting a cold, so I'm not kissing anyone good night. Have you said your prayers?"

"Yes, Miss Hanacher!" It was a deafening chorus.

Miss Hanacher stopped by Laurie's bed. "How do you feel, Laurie?"

Laurie was twisted in a knot, and her eyes were about to pop out of her head, and she talked very loud and quick. "I feel fine, Miss Hanacher, and I'm sleepy, I'm almost asleep already, and I said my prayers twice and drank all the milk, and I'll just go to sleep now, thank you."

Miss Hanacher looked as if she were going to burst, but she only choked and turned out the lights and went to her room and slammed the door. It was such a loud sound it had the whole building listening, and nineteen little girls popped out of bed to crawl on Laurie's bed, and the kittens crawled over everybody's toes and tasted a few. And one little girl, whose mother had worked so hard and long she was almost rich and could give her foolish things, ran and got her doll's bottle that had a real rubber nipple with a hole in it, and they filled it with the milk Laurie hadn't drunk but hid behind her bed, and the littlest kitten lay on its back and nursed it just like a drink-and-wet doll. They put doll diapers on it, and it even wet them, and the excitement was so great one of the big girls came to see, and she knew where there were two more bottles and diapers, and before morning the entire Home knew about the kittens in Laurie's bed. And yet it was a secret!

For Miss Hanacher did have a cold. Her door never opened except to let the doctor in and great trays of warm milk and juice. And sometimes if you walked down the hall real slow you could hear sneezing, and sometimes coughing and blowing. And it was wonderful, for with her eyes watering like they must be, she couldn't see secrets; and with her nose stopped up, she couldn't smell them; and with her door closed and her inside, the whole Home was free. Because the housekeepers didn't care about secrets, so long as you didn't bother them.

So seventy little girls learned to know and love three little kittens. But the third day the biggest kitten died. It had opened one little blue eye, and it had tried to go around and see the world. It had walked the length of the dormitory where the cleaning woman had scrubbed; then it crawled into Laurie's lap and washed its feet so it would be a clean kitty, as kittens like to be. But in just a little while a terrible pain seemed to come to it, and it screamed and twisted and then lay very still. Laurie was alone, for she hadn't been sent back to classes yet, so she held the little one in her hands, trying to keep the cold that was coming from coming to it.

Then the cleaning woman came and said it was dead. She took Laurie and the kittens right into her lap and covered them with her apron, and said, "Honey, baby, The Home isn't a place for kittens. We have to keep it clean, and we have to use the things the city sends us, for none of us are rich, and the cleaning things we use are fine for cleaning floors, but they can kill kittens if they wash them off their feet. I'll tell you what, I've got a wooden box in my closet, and we'll make a little house out in the yard for them! Yards is where kittens love most of all to be."

"But the dog! What about the dog?"

"Oh, he's a nice old dog; besides you can put him on leash, and with all of you girls watching, the kittens will be safe."

Only they weren't. For even with everyone watching a thing, sometimes someone forgets. The day after the day of the funeral of the first kitten, the second kitten lay torn and dead.

Laurie couldn't stop crying. She cried so that the big girls got frightened and ran to get the nurse. All except Gladys, who once upon a time had shared a secret with Laurie. And she had thought about it a lot; she had even got up in the night to look out at the street lamp and see if there might be a shopping bag by it. But most of all she hadn't told.

Gladys dug a quick hole and buried the kitten. She snatched the last one and stuffed it down her dress. She said, "It's our secret." And she disappeared in the shadows of the willow forest.

The nurse put Laurie to bed in her own bed and called the doctor, and the doctor gave her something to make her sleep.

But first he asked for an extra blanket to make her warm; only all the blankets were being used, until the nurse remembered a new one brought into the supply room that very day, and she sent one of the girls for it. It was so new it still had the price tags and pins and was in a shopping bag. The nurse threw the tags and the bag in the wastebasket and pinned the pins in her collar. Then she spread the blanket; Laurie went to sleep.

It was past midnight when Laurie woke. She watched the fire-door light watching the night. She looked at the floor shining red as blood beneath it, and so clean it could kill. She sat up. What if Gladys hadn't understood! Laurie ran down the hall and up the stairs, and she found Gladys asleep and the kitten wandering around the floor. Laurie snatched it and ran and washed its feet in the washstand. She all but drowned it washing it and all but choked it drying it. But she waited and waited, and it didn't die. It only snuggled in the curve of her neck as if it knew it belonged there and was safe. And Laurie held it close and loved it with a heart that had waited seven years to belong to someone, and have someone belong to it. It was a fierce and powerful love, as loves that have been hurt can be. As loves that know they can't be, are.

For Laurie knew it couldn't be. That was why she had cried so. The moment she held the second dead kitten she knew there was no safe place in all her world for the little one that was left, the littlest one that had needed her more than any other. No matter how much she loved it, she couldn't keep it safe. And the strangest stirring stirred within her as she thought that out, how love isn't enough.

She would have to give the kitten away, but there wasn't anyone to give it to. She didn't know any grown person who could just keep a kitten because they wanted to but Miss Hanacher. But Miss Hanacher was the one who made the floors be so clean, and she was only rules and don'ts and filing cabinets.

Laurie sat very still as she thought of a tiny baby that had to be given away not because it wasn't loved, but because there were worse hurts to come to it than being thrown away. But it was so small it would be lost in any dark. And she thought about that. She thought of a place where there wasn't ever any night. She really didn't think it all up on her own, for she was too young to do big things like that. She could only think of things she knew. But she knew about street lamps, how they watched the night, and about babies in shopping bags.

Laurie sat cross-legged on her bed and stared at the wastebasket where, thrown half in and out and upside down, there was a shopping bag. It was new and strong. Very slowly Laurie climbed down off her bed and got the bag. She folded her sweater in the bottom, put in a doll bottle of milk and ran out the fire door.

The night was so big and dark outside that Laurie was afraid to be in it. But it wasn't as dark as the brightest day would be if the third kitten lay dead in her hand. She hugged it closer and ran across the grass to the gate she thought she would have to climb—only it was unlocked! So she slipped out to the street lamp, where the night was gone. She kissed the kitten, kissed it so hard its eyes opened, just little cracks that looked at her as though they wanted to remember how she was. Only just then there was noise. It was the watchman with his big feet and lantern, and he would find the fire door open! Laurie laid the kitten in the shopping bag and the shopping bag against the lamppost, and ran for the fire door. She didn't see Miss Hanacher standing in her window. She didn't hear her dial a number on the telephone and say one word. She said, "Now."

But Laurie didn't see or hear, she was crying so. She just ran down the dark of her room and raised the blind, and watched a shopping bag sitting by a lamppost in the middle of a night. And the strangest thing—in just a minute or so a young lady came walking down the street, even though it was so late. She was such a pretty lady, with curling hair and real high heels. She was walking so fast she would have walked by anything in the dark, but the light was so bright she stopped and looked and felt, and brought out a tiny black kitten. The lady was so surprised she laughed out loud. And she kissed it! There where anyone might see, she kissed it, and then she found the doll bottle and put it in the little mouth, and she said, "Oh, you precious, precious child!" She said it out loud, as though the night might be listening and like to hear. She let it nurse for a little, then she cuddled it in the sweater, where it would be warm and safe, and she walked on down the street and out of sight, slowly, as though the kitten slept.

Laurie was still standing there when Miss Hanacher came and put her arm around her. "Laurie, are you all right?"

Laurie said, "Oh, yes!" And she was. She could feel it inside, how all the hurt was gone, for she understood how things aren't always what they seem. She looked at Miss Hanacher, who was so rosy and rested she didn't look like she'd had a cold at all. She looked soft and pretty in the lamplight. Laurie said, "Miss Hanacher, could you leave the blind up, for with it up the light comes clear across to touch my bed, and I like to see it there."

"Do you like street lamps too?" Miss Hanacher was so pleased that Laurie could tell she liked them, and, without half thinking, Laurie hugged her, and Miss Hanacher hugged her back and picked her up, even though she was so big, and carried her to bed. She pulled the new blanket close and said, "My, this is a lovely blanket! It's soft as kitten's ears. I think we'll have to let you keep it for your very own."

Laurie petted the blanket. She touched the satin border that was softly white, as pearls shining in the night, like pearls all around her. She watched Miss Hanacher tucking it about her, and she saw her mother pinning pearls on her baby shoulders because they were the nicest things she had. She could see her mother shining in that shining light, a lovely, sparkling someone holding back the night. Her mother who had loved her as much as that, to take her from the hurts that must have been and leave her where even as tiny a baby as she couldn't ever be lost. Laurie lay there smiling, for it made such a pretty picture.

Miss Hanacher said, "Do you know, Laurie, you look lovely tonight. You're going to grow up to be a very pretty girl."

Laurie smiled and said, "Yes, I know. I'm going to grow up to be a lovely lady who loves her family."

And Miss Hanacher said, "I'd like to be that too. I'd like it most of all."

And they laughed. For they both knew Miss Hanacher was already grown and old, and she wasn't anybody's mother.

The Exiles

MARGARET LAURENCE

"No question of it," Mr. Archipelago said, snipping a wisp of hair, "I am flotsam."

"Not jetsam?" Mrs. Webley-Pryce asked, blinking watchful eyes as the scissored shreds fell down onto her face. "I always get the two confused."

Outside, the small African town was growing sluggish under the sedative sun of late morning. The one-footed beggar who squatted beside Mr. Archipelago's door had gone to sleep on the splintery wooden steps. At the shop of K. Tachie—General Merchant, Tachie himself sat beside his cash register, surrounded by boxes and barrels. Kinglike, he perched on a high stool, roaring abuse at his counter clerks. At the Africa Star Chemists, a young shopgirl dozed, propping her brown arms against a carton of Seven Seas cod-liver oil. In the government agent's office, and in the offices of Bridgeford & Knight, Exporters-Importers, Englishmen sighed and wilted and saw from their watches that they could not yet legitimately leave for lunch. Footsteps on the cracked and scorching pavement lagged. The market women walked tiredly, their head trays heavy, their bare feet pressing the warm dust into ripples and dunes. A donkey brayed disconsolately.

Mr. Archipelago riffled a comb through the winter straw of Mrs. Webley-Pryce's hair.

"Flotsam, dear lady," he said. "I looked it up in the *Concise Oxford.*"

On the other side of the room Doree glanced up from the lustrous green with which she was enameling the fingernails of her thin, white hands, knuckle-swollen from years of cleansing other women's hair.

"Can you beat it?" she said. "He looks up words all the time. What'd it say for 'flotsam,' Archipelago?"

Mr. Archipelago beamed. His shiny eyes were green as malachite. He stood on tiptoe, a plump pouter-pigeon of a man, puffing out his chest until his brocade waistcoat swelled. His hair, black as ripe olives, gave the impression of having been crimped and perfumed.

"Wreckage found floating," he said proudly. "It said— 'wreckage found floating.'"

"The very thing!" Doree cried, clapping her hands, but Mrs. Webley-Pryce looked aloof, because she did not understand.

The air in the shop was syrupy with heat and perfume. Mrs. Webley-Pryce, feeling the perspiration soaking through her linen dress, wriggled uncomfortably in her chair and tried to close her eyes to the litter all around her. Doree swept every evening at closing time, but, as her sight was so poor and she would not wear glasses, she often missed fragments of hair which gradually mingled with dust and formed themselves into small tangled balls of gray and hazelnut brown and bottled blond. The curl papers, too, had an uncanny way of escaping and drifting around the room like fallen leaves.

Sweat was gathering on Mr. Archipelago's forehead, and his fingers were becoming slippery around the comb and scissors.

"The morning beer," he announced. "It is now time. For you, as well, Mrs. Webley-Pryce?"

"I think not, thanks," she replied coldly. "Nothing before sundown is my rule. Can't you hurry a little, Mr. Archipelago?

At this rate it'll be midnight before my perm is finished."

"Pardon, pardon," said Mr. Archipelago, tilting the beer bottle. "One moment, and we fly to work. Like birds on the wing."

Out came the solutions, the flasks of pink and mauve liquid. Out came clamps and pins and curl papers, the jumbled contents of a dozen shelves and cupboards. In the midst of the debris, stirring it all like a magic potion, stood Mr. Archipelago, a fat and frantic wizard, refreshing himself occasionally with Dutch ale. He darted over to an elaborate arrangement of electrically heated metal rods, on which he placed the heavy clamps. He waited, arms folded, until the whole dangerous mechanism achieved the dull, mysterious fire which was to turn Mrs. Webley-Pryce's base metal, as it were, to gold.

"You should sell that lot," Mrs. Webley-Pryce remarked. "Any museum in Europe would give you a good price."

At once he was on the defensive, his pride hurt. "Let me tell you, dear lady, there isn't one beauty *salon* in the whole of Europe could give you a perm like this one does."

"I don't doubt that," she said.

Doree stood up, an emaciated yellow-and-white bird, a tall, gaunt crane, her hair clinging like wet feathers around her squeezed-narrow shoulders. With her long, hesitant stride she walked across the room and held out her green-lacquered hands. "Sea pearl," she said. "Kind of different, anyhow. Africa Star Chemists just got it in. Like it?"

Shuddering slightly, Mrs. Webley-Pryce conceded that it was very handsome.

" 'Pearl' reminds me," Mr. Archipelago said, restored to cheerfulness, "the *Concise Oxford* stated another thing for flotsam."

He applied a dab of spit to a finger and casually tested the heat of the clamps. "Precisely, it said, 'oyster-spawn.' Think of that. Oyster-spawn. And that is me too, eh?"

Doree laughed until she began to cough, and he frowned at her, for they were both worried by this cough, and she could not stop smoking.

"I don't see——" Mrs. Webley-Pryce probed.

"A little joke," Mr. Archipelago explained. "My father, as I may have told you, was an Armenian sailor."

"Oh, yes," Mrs. Webley-Pryce said, holding her breath as he placed the first hot clamp on her tightly wound-up hair. "Odd—Archipelago never seems like an Armenian name to me."

"It isn't."

"Oh?"

Mr. Archipelago smiled. He enjoyed talking about himself. He allowed himself a degree of pride in the fact that no one could ever be sure where the truth ended and the tinted unreality began. Also he was shrewd. He knew that his conversation was an attraction, no less than the fact that he was the only hairdresser within a hundred miles; it was his defense against home permanents.

"It would have been difficult for my mother to give me my father's name," he said, "as she never knew it. She was—I may have mentioned—an Italian girl. She worked in a wine shop in Genoa. A port town, a sailors' town. The only place I ever liked in all Genoa was the Staglieno Cemetery. I used to go there and sit beside the tombs of the rich, with the white-marble angels—so compassionate they looked, and so costly. Then I would look over at the fields of rented graves nearby. The poor rent graves for one, two, five years—I can't remember exactly. The body must be taken out if the rent cannot be paid. In death, as in life, the rent must always be paid."

"How horrible!" Mrs. Webley-Pryce said. "Look here—are you sure this clamp isn't too hot? I think it's burning my neck. It's your mother's name then?"

Doree glared. Mrs. Webley-Pryce was the wife of the government agent, but she had married late and had lived in Africa only one year—she had not yet learned that questions must always be judicious. But Mr. Archipelago did not mind her curiosity.

"No, dear lady, it is not her name. Why should a person not pick his own name? It sounds Italian. I liked it. Do you know what it means?"

"Well, of course," Mrs. Webley-Pryce said uncertainly, "an archipelago is—well, it's——"

"A sea with many islands, according to the *Concise Oxford*. That has been my life. A sea with many islands."

"This is one of them, I suppose?"

"The most enduring. Twelve years I have been here."

"You'll go back, though, someday?"

"I have no wish to go back," Mr. Archipelago answered offhandedly. "I would like to die here and be buried in my own garden. Perhaps if I were buried under the wild orchids they would grow better."

"You can't be serious," Mrs. Webley-Pryce protested. "About not going back, I mean?"

"Why not? I like it here."

"But it's so far away from everything. So far from home."

"For you, perhaps," Mr. Archipelago said, "but then, you are not a true expatriate. You may stay twenty years, but you are a visitor. Your husband, though—does he anticipate with pleasure the time when he will retire and go back to England?"

She looked at him in surprise. "No—he dreads it, as a matter of fact. His work is here, his whole life. He's been here a long time, too, you know. But it's rather different. He was sent here. He had to come."

"Did he?"

"Of course," she said. "If a person goes in for colonial administration, he must go to a colony, mustn't he?"

"Indeed he must," Mr. Archipelago said agreeably.

"But for a hairdresser," she said, "it's not the sort of place most people would exactly choose."

"Aha—now we come to it. You are one of those who believe that I was, perhaps, forced to leave my own country?"

"I didn't mean that," Mrs. Webley-Pryce floundered. "And I suppose it's a blessing for the European women that there's someone in a tiny station like this who can do hair——"

"Even if it is only Archipelago, with his equipment that belongs in a museum. Well, well. Tell me, madam—what is the current theory about me? It changes, you know. Once, I remember, I was said to have been a counterfeiter. Another time I had deserted my wife and family. Through the years it has been this and that. Perhaps one of them is true. Or perhaps not. To maintain dignity, one must have at least one secret—don't you agree?"

Mrs. Webley-Pryce gave him a sideways glance. "I have heard," she admitted, "about there having been some trouble."

But Mr. Archipelago neither confirmed nor denied. He tested a curl and began to remove the mass of iron from the hair. Mrs. Webley-Pryce, embarrassed by his silence, turned to Doree, who was applying bleach to her own long yellow hair.

"Speaking of names, I've always meant to ask you about yours, Doree. It's rather unusual, isn't it?"

"Yeh," Doree said. "I used to be Doreen."

"Oh?"

Doree spoke of herself rarely. When she did, her fabrications were obvious; she wrenched them out aggressively, knowing no one would believe her. Now she was caught off guard.

"I had my own shop once," she said in her gentle, rasping voice. "It had a sign up: DOREEN—BEAUTY INCORPORATED. Classy. Done in those gilt letters. You buy them separately and stick them up. The state of my dough wasn't so classy, though. So when the damn 'n' fell off, I figured it was cheaper to change my name to fit the sign."

Gratified, Mrs. Webley-Pryce tittered. "And just where was your shop?"

Now it was Mr. Archipelago's turn to glare. It was permissible to question him minutely, but not Doree. Customers were supposed to understand this rule. He saw Doree's eyes turn vague, and he longed to touch her hand, to comfort and reassure her. But it was better not to do such a thing. He did not want her to misunderstand his devotion or to be in any way alarmed by a realization of its existence. Instead he slithered a still-hot clamp down on Mrs. Webley-Pryce's neck, causing a faint smell of singed skin and a gasp of pain.

"It was in Montreal, if you must know." Doree said harshly.

Last time someone asked, the answer was Chicago, and once, daringly, Mexico City. Mr. Archipelago himself did not know. She had simply walked into his shop one day, and where she came from, or why, did not matter to him.

"Montreal," Mrs. Webley-Pryce said thoughtfully. "Perhaps David and I will go to someplace like that."

"You're leaving?" Mr. Archipelago asked, startled. "You're leaving Africa?"

"Yes, of course—didn't you know?"

"But why?" he asked in dismay, for recently she had been patronizing the shop regularly. "Why?"

"Dear me," she said, with an effort at brightness. "Didn't you know this colony will be self-governing soon? They don't want us here any more."

"I knew it was coming," Mr. Archipelago said, "but I had not realized it was so soon. Strange. I read the newspapers. I talk with Mr. Tachie, my landlord, who is a very political man. But—ah, well, I tend my garden, and I do the ladies' hair and drink beer and talk to Doree. I think nothing will ever change in this place—so insignificant, surely God will forget about it and let it be. But not so. How many will be going?"

"Oh, I don't know—most of the Europeans in government service; perhaps all."

He thought of the sign outside his establishment, nicely done in black and aquamarine, with elegant, spidery letters:

ARCHIPELAGO

ENGLISH-STYLE BARBER

EUROPEAN LADIES' HAIRDRESSER

"A sea with many islands," he said, addressing only himself. "Sometimes it happens that a person discovers he has built his house upon an island that is sinking."

A large green house by the shore sheltered Mr. Archipelago. Once he had lived there alone, but for the past five years he had not been alone. Doree's presence in his house had been, he knew, a popular topic of discussion in the European cantonment. He did not blame the ladies for talking, but it gave him satisfaction to know that their information was extremely slight. Neither he nor Doree had ever spoken of their domestic arrangements to customers. And their cook-steward, Attah, under the impression that he was protecting his employers' reputations, had never told a soul that the two shared only living and dining rooms, and that neither had ever entered the private apartments of the other.

Mr. Archipelago's dwelling was not close either to the white cantonment or to the African houses. It was off by itself, on a jot of land overlooking a small bay. The sprawling overgrown garden was surrounded by a high green wall which enabled Mr. Archipelago, in the late afternoons, to work outside clad only in his underwear and a round, white-linen hat. He had no wish to tame the garden, which was a profusion of elephant grass, drooping casuarina trees, frowzy banana palms, slender papaws, and all manner of unpruned flowering shrubs. Into this cherished disorder Mr. Archipelago carefully introduced wild orchids, which soon died, and pineapples, which never grew to the size sold for a mere shilling in the African market.

Just as the garden was Mr. Archipelago's special province, so the long veranda was Doree's. Here flew, uncaged, four gray African parrots, their wings tipped with scarlet. Sometimes they departed for a while and sulked in the branches of the frangipani tree. But they could not fend for themselves, and they always came back to be fed.

Doree had a chameleon, too, of which she was extremely fond, an eerie, bright-green reptile with huge eyes and a long tail. Mr. Archipelago once ventured to suggest that she might find a prettier pet. Doree's large, pale eyes squinted at him reproachfully. "What do you want me to do, anyway? Conk him on the head because he's not a damn butterfly?"

And Mr. Archipelago, appalled at his blunder, answered humbly, "Am I God, that I should judge a creature? It is not the chameleon that is ugly, but I, for thinking him so. You are right—he is beautiful."

"I don't get it," Doree said. "I never said he was beautiful."

"Well, then, I did. I do."

"You're what they call 'round the bend,' Archipelago. Never mind. Maybe I am too."

"We suit each other," he replied.

The evenings were spent quietly. They did not go out anywhere, nor did they entertain. They had always been considered socially nonexistent by the European community, while in the Africans' view they were standard Europeans and therefore apart. Mr. Archipelago and Doree did not mind. They preferred their own company.

In the evening Mr. Archipelago wore an impressive smoking jacket. It was a pale bluish-green Indian brocade, and the small cockerels on it were worked in thread of gold.

"You look just like one of those what-d'you-call-'ems—you know, sultans," Doree had once said admiringly.

He remembered the remark every time he donned the jacket. Momentarily endowed with the hauteur of Harun al-Rashid, he would saunter nonchalantly through the Bagdad of his own living room.

Frequently they brought out their perfumes, of which they had a great variety, bottles and flagons of all colors and intricate shapes. The game was to see how many could be identified by smell alone, the vessel masked, before the senses began to flag. Mr. Archipelago did not love the perfumes for themselves alone, nor even for their ability to cover the coarse reek of life. Each one, sniffed, conjured up for him a throng of waltzing ladies, whirling eternally on floors of light, their gray gowns swaying, ladies of gentle dust.

Mr. Archipelago and Doree got along well with their one servant. Attah tended to be cantankerous; he would not be argued with. They accepted him philosophically, but on one point they were adamant. They would not allow Attah's wife and family to live within the walls of the compound. Mr. Archipelago and Doree could not have endured to have the voices of children threatening their achieved and fragile quiet.

Outside the green wall, however, and far from the sugared humidity of the small shop, events occurred. Governments made reports and politicians made speeches. Votes were cast. Supporters cheered and opponents jeered. Flags changed, and newspapermen typed furiously, recording history to meet a deadline.

In the town the white men began to depart one by one, as their posts were filled by Africans. And in Mr. Archipelago's shop the whir of the hair dryer was heard less and less.

Late one night Doree came downstairs in her housecoat, an

unheard-of action for her. Mr. Archipelago, sitting in his high-back wicker armchair, glanced up in surprise.

"It's two months," Doree said, "since the Webley-Pryces left. I don't know how many are gone now. Almost all, I guess. The last perm we gave was nearly a month ago. This week only one shampoo-and-set. Archipelago, what are we going to do?"

He looked at her dumbly.

"Could we go to Liberia?" she went on. "Sierra Leone?"

Both knew they did not have sufficient money to take them anywhere.

"Please"—he hesitated—"you must not be upset, or I cannot speak at all——"

"Go on," she said roughly. "What is it?"

"Did you know," Mr. Archipelago questioned sadly, "that an expatriate without funds can go to the consulate of his country, and they will send him back?"

She lowered her head. Her yellow hair, loose, fell like unraveled wool around her, scarfing the bony pallor of her face. "I've heard that—yes."

Mr. Archipelago's incongruously small feet in their embroidered slippers pattered across the concrete floor. He returned with Dutch ale. "I have never asked," he said, "and you have never asked, and now I must break the rule. Could you go back? Could you, Doree?"

Doree lighted a cigarette from the end of the last one. "No," she replied in a strained voice.

Mr. Archipelago brought his hands together in a staccato clap. "Good. We know where we stand. Enough of this then."

"No," she said. "What about you?"

"It is very awkward," he said, "but unfortunately I cannot go back either."

She did not inquire further. For her, too, his word was sufficient. "But, Archipelago, the Africans won't let us stay if we're broke. We're not their responsibility——"

"Wait," Mr. Archipelago said. "I have just remembered something."

Beside his chair a carved wooden elephant bore a small table on its back. Mr. Archipelago groped underneath and opened a compartment in the beast's belly. He took out an object wrapped in tissue paper.

"I have always liked this elephant," he said. "See—a concealed hiding place. Very cloak-and-dagger. This necklace is one I bought many years ago—insurance against disaster. It is locally made—crude, as you can see, but heavy. Ashanti gold, and quite valuable."

Doree looked at it without interest. "Very nice," she said. "But we can't live off that forever."

"No, but it will give you enough money to leave this town and live in the city until you find work. At least it is a chance. For me, the worst would be for you not to have any chance——"

Mr. Archipelago perceived that he had revealed too much. He squirmed and sweated, fearful that she would misunderstand. But when he looked at her, he saw in her eyes not alarm but surprise.

"The necklace and all," Doree said slowly. "You'd do that —for me?"

Mr. Archipelago forgot about himself in the urgency of convincing her. "For you, Doree," he said, "of course, for you. If only it were more——"

"But—it's everything."

"Yes, everything," he said bitterly. "All I have to offer. A fragment of gold."

"I want you to know," she said, her voice rough with tears, "I want you to know I'm glad you offered. Now, put the necklace back in the elephant. We may need it worse, later."

"You won't take it?" he cried. "Why not?"

"Because you haven't told me what's gonna happen to you," Doree said. "Anyway, I don't want to go to another place."

He could not speak. She hurried on. "If I wasn't here," she said, with a trembling and apologetic laugh, "who'd remind you to put on your hat in the boiling sun? Who'd guess the perfumes with you?"

"I would miss you, of course," he said in a low voice. "I would miss you a great deal."

She turned on him almost angrily. "Don't you think I'd miss you?" she cried. "Don't you know how it would be—for me?"

They stared at each other, wide-eyed, incredulous. Mr. Archipelago lived through one instant of unreasonable and terrifying hope. Then, abruptly, he became once more aware of himself, oddly swathed in Indian brocade and holding in his fat, perspiring hands an ale glass and a gold necklace.

Doree's eyes, too, had become distant and withdrawn. She was twisting a strand of her hair around one wrist. "We're getting ourselves into a stew over nothing," she said at last. "I got a hunch we're due for a lucky break. Once I met a spiritualist—well, she told me I had natural ability. My hunches are hardly ever wrong. Shall we shake on it?"

Gravely they shook hands and drank to the lucky break. Mr. Archipelago began to tell stories about the tourists he had known in Genoa as a boy and how nervous they always were of getting goat's milk in their tea.

They talked until the pressure lamp spluttered low and the floor beneath it was littered with the broken wings of moths. Doree went upstairs then, singing a snatch of an African high-life tune in her warm, raw voice. But later Mr. Archipelago, queasy with beer and insomnia, heard once again the sound that used to be so frequent when she first came to this house, her deep and terrible crying in her sleep.

They had had no customers at all for a fortnight, but still they opened the shop each morning and waited until four o'clock to close it. One morning their landlord strolled in, prosperous in a new royal-blue cloth patterned with golden coins. Tachie was a large man; the room seemed too small to hold his brown ox shoulders, his great drum of a voice.

"Mistah Arch'pelago, why you humbug me? Two month, and nevah one penny I getting. You t'ink I rich too much? You t'ink I no need for dis money?"

Mr. Archipelago made one unhopeful effort at distracting Tachie. "Can I offer you a beer, Mr. Tachie? A light, refreshing ale at this time of day——"

Tachie grimaced. "You t'ink I drink beer which come from my shop an' nevah been pay at all? No, I t'ank you. Mistah Arch'pelago, you trouble me too much. What we do, eh?"

Mr. Archipelago's skin looked sallower than usual. Doree held out large and pitying hands toward him, but she could not speak.

"In life, as in death, the rent must always be paid," he said. "We have been dreaming, dreaming, while the world moved on, and now we waken to find it so changed we do not know what to do. We wanted only to stay and not to harm anyone, but, of course, you are right, Mr. Tachie, to remind us it is not enough. We do not have much of anything any more, but we will try to pay our debts before we move on. Perhaps a museum will buy my wave machine after all."

Doree put her hands over her face, and Tachie, horrified, looked from one to the other, unable to grasp the actuality of their despair. "You not got money—at all? De time which I come for you shop, I anger too much for you. Now angry can no stay for me. My friend, I sorry. But what I can do?"

"We do not expect you to let us stay," Mr. Archipelago said with dignity. "We are not appealing for charity."

But Tachie could not stop justifying himself. "I look-a de

shop, I see European womans all dey gone, I see you no got lucky. But I no savvy propra. I t'ink you got money which you put for bank. Now I see you no got nothing. But what I can do? I no be rich man. I got shop, I got dis place. But I got plenty, plenty family, all dey come for me, all dey say, 'Tachie, why you no give we more?' My daughtah Mercy, she big girl, all time she saying, 'Meka you buy for me one small new cloth, meka you buy powdah for face, meka you buy shoe same city girl dey wear it.'"

Mr. Archipelago peered sharply at Tachie. "Your daughter —face powder, shoes—she, too, is changed——"

"I tell you true. Mistah Arch'pelago, why you're looking so?"

Mr. Archipelago whistled a Viennese waltz, bounced across the room, grasped Doree's hand, drew her into his comprehension and his laughter. Together they waltzed, absurd, relieved, triumphant.

"Mr. Tachie, you are a bringer of miracles!" Mr. Archipelago cried. "We, even we, Doree, will make history—you will see."

Tachie frowned, bewildered. "I see it happen so, for white men, wen dey stay too long for dis place. Dey crez'. Mistah Arch'pelago, meka you drink some small beer. Den you head he come fine."

"No, no, not beer," Mr. Archipelago replied, puffing out his waistcoat. "Here—a flask kept for medicinal purposes or special celebrations. A brandy, Mr. Tachie! A brandy for the history makers!"

He and Doree laughed until they were weak. And Tachie, still not understanding, finally laughed with them and consented to drink the unpaid-for brandy.

That evening they painted the new sign. They worked until midnight, with cans and brushes spread out on the dining-room table. The sign was black and gilt, done in optimistically plump lettering:

ARCHIPELAGO & DOREE

BARBERSHOP

ALL-BEAUTY SALON
AFRICAN LADIES A SPECIALTY

The men of the town continued, naturally, to have their hair cut by the African barbers who plied their trade under the neem trees in the market. The African women, however, showed great interest in the new sign. Girls who had attended school read the words aloud to their mothers and aunts, and murmured together. But not one of them would enter the shop.

The hair-straightening equipment—obtained secondhand, and on credit, through Tachie—remained unused. Each day Doree dusted and set back on the counter the unopened packets and jars of dusky powder and cinnamon-brown make-up base which she had hurriedly ordered from the city when she discovered that the Africa Star Chemists, slightly behind the times, sold only shades of ivory and peach.

Another week, and still no customers. Then one morning, as Mr. Archipelago was opening his second bottle of Dutch ale, Mercy Tachie walked in.

"Please, Mr. Archipelago," she began hesitantly, "I am thinking to come here for some time, but I am not sure what I should do. We have never had such a place in our town before, you see. But no one wished to be the first. Then my father, he said to me today that I should be the first, because if you are having no customers, he will never be getting his money from you."

Mercy was about sixteen. She was clad in traditional cloth,

but her face was thickly daubed with a pale powder that obscured her healthy skin.

Mr. Archipelago motioned her to a chair. "Good," he said. "Doree and I welcome you. Now—can you help us to know, a little, the way you want to look?"

Mercy Tachie turned to him appealingly. "I would like to look like a city girl, please," she said.

"A city girl." Mr. Archipelago ran a finger lightly over the chalky powder on her face. "That is why you wear this mask, eh? Ladies never know when they are beautiful—strange. Ah, well. Yes, we will make you look like a city girl, if that is what you would like the most."

Mercy felt compelled to explain herself. "I was going for seven years to the mission school here, you see, and all my life I am never knowing anyplace outside this town. But someday, maybe, I will be living in some big place and, if so, I would not want to feel like a bush-girl. So I wish to know how it is proper to have my hair and what to do for the face. You do not think I am foolish?"

Mr. Archipelago shook his head. "I think the whole world is foolish," he said. "But you are no more foolish than anyone else, and a great deal less so than many."

Doree placed her splay hands on the girl's dark, wiry hair. "Not to worry," she said. "We'll straighten your hair just enough to set it and style it. We'll take that goop off your face. You got lovely skin—not a wrinkle—you shouldn't cover it up like that. We'll give you a complete make-up job. Doll, you'll be a queen."

And Mercy Tachie, her eyes trusting, smiled. "Do you think so? Do you really think it will be so?"

The air was redolent once more with the potions and unguents, the lotions and shampoos and lacquers, and the sweet, fertile fragrance of bottled scents and colognes. The snik-snik-snik of Mr. Archipelago's scissors was the theme of a small-

scale symphony; overtones and undertones were provided by
the throb of the dryer and the strident blues-chanting of Doree
as she paced the room like a priestess. Mercy began to relax.

"My friends, they also would like to come here, I think, if
they like the way I will look," she confided. "Mr. Archipelago,
you will be staying here? You will not be leaving now?"

"Perhaps we shall be staying," he said. "We must wait and
see if your friends like the way you look."

Mercy pursed her lips pensively. "Will you not go back,
someday," she ventured, "to your own country? For the sake
of your family?"

Doree glared, but Mr. Archipelago was bland. He had never
minded the curiosity of his lady customers. "The charming
questions," he said, "they begin again. Good. No—I have no
family."

"Oh, I thought it must be so!" Mercy cried.

"I beg your pardon?"

She folded her hands and looked at the floor. "I have heard,"
she said apologetically, "that you were leaving your own country many years ago because you had some bad trouble—maybe
because you thought you might go to prison. But I am never
believing that story, truly."

At last the ritual was accomplished, and Mercy Tachie
looked at herself in the yellowing wall mirror. Slowly she
turned this way and that, absorbing the details—the soft-curled
hair whorled skillfully down on to her forehead, the face with
its crimson lipstick and its brown make-up that matched her
own skin. Then she smiled.

"Oh," she breathed, "it is just like the pictures I have seen
in *Drum* magazine—the girls, African girls, who know how
everything is done in the new way. Oh, now I will know too!"

"Do you think your friends will overcome their shyness
now?" Mr. Archipelago asked. "When they have seen how
you look?"

"I will make sure of it," Mercy promised. "You will see."

They sat quietly in the shop after Mercy had left. They felt spent and drained, but filled and renewed as well. Doree stretched out her long, long legs and closed her eyes. Mr. Archipelago bulged in his carved rocking chair and cradled to and fro peacefully, his shoes off and his waistcoat unbuttoned.

The crash of noise and voices from outside startled them. They ran to the open door. Spilling down the street was an impromptu procession. Every girl in town appeared to be there, hips and shoulders swaying, unshod feet stepping lightly, hands clapping, cloths of blue and magenta and yellow fluttering around them, like the flags of nations, while they danced. A few of the older women were there, too, buxom and lively, their excited laughter blaring like a melody of raucous horns. At the front of the parade walked Mercy Tachie in newly purchased red high-heel shoes, her head held high to display her proud new hair, her new face alight with pleasure and infinite hope. Beside Mercy, as her guard and her champions, there pranced a half dozen young men, in khaki trousers and brilliantly flower-printed shirts. One held her hand—he was her own young man. Another had a guitar, and another a gourd rattle. They sang at full strength, putting new words to the popular high-life song, *Everybody Like Saturday Night.*

> *"Everybody like Mercy Tachie,*
> *"Everybody like Mercy Tachie,*
> *"Everybody, everybody,*
> *"Everybody, everybody,*
> *"Everybody say she fine pas' all . . ."*

Mr. Archipelago turned to Doree. Gravely they shook hands. "By an act of Mercy," Mr. Archipelago said, "we are saved."

They walked along the shore in the moist and cooling late afternoon. The palm boughs rustled soothingly.

"Archipelago," Doree said, "now that we're here to stay, I guess I oughta tell you."

"No," he said. "There is nothing you need tell me."

"Yes," she insisted. "You know when you asked me if I could go back, and I said I couldn't? Well, I guess I didn't give you the straight goods, in a way——"

"I know," Mr. Archipelago said quietly. "There is no troubled past. I have always known that."

"How did you know?"

He glanced at her face, at the heavy make-up that covered the aging features, ravaged and virginal. "Because," he replied slowly, "for me it was the same. I, too, had no past. The white ladies and now the brown ladies—they have never guessed. I did not intend that they should. But we know, Doree, why we are here and why we stay."

"Yes," she said. "So we don't need to talk about it any more, do we?"

"No," he promised. "No more."

"And whatever happens," she went on, "even if we go broke, you won't get any more fancy ideas about me finding a better job somewhere else?"

"The new sign—have you forgotten what it says?" he reminded her.

"That's right," she said. " 'Archipelago and Doree.' Yeh, that's right."

Mr. Archipelago sniffed the brine-laden wind. "Smell the sea, Doree? A perfume for our collection."

She smiled. "What shall we call it?"

"Oh, nothing too ornate," he said lightly. "Perhaps *eau d'exilé* would do."

They watched on the sand their exaggerated shadows, one squat and bulbous, the other bone slight and clumsily elongated—pigeon and crane. The shadows walked with hands entwined, like children who walk through the dark.

The Haunted Dancers

ARTHUR MAYSE

The holly crop paid off extra well last winter, so after Christmas we parked the kids with the grandparents and pointed our noses south, spending New Year's in San Francisco, then dropping down to Los Angeles and putting in at Vegas on the way home. Our second night there we managed to snag a table at the Twin Palms, a high-class spot that featured a dance team called The Belancas. Even though what stepping Vera and I do is pretty well confined to Chellan Golf and Country Club, we appreciate good dancing when we see it, and I tell you those Belancas were a lot better than just good.

They were into their third number—a tango, but not the kind we learned at Miss Harper's School of the Dance—when Vera said to me, "Jim, I know that girl!"

"Honey," I said, "the closest you've been to the Latins is Nick Servos's tamale parlor on Front Street. You couldn't know her."

"I couldn't," Vera said, "but I do." She had set her daiquiri down and was leaning forward with both hands clasping the new evening bag I'd given her, this being a sort of anniversary for us. "Let me think." Her voice climbed, as it does when she's excited. "Yes, of course! Jim, that's Nancy Drummond. You remember her—the gawky girl who used to live with her rich old aunt." Vera was speaking so loudly now that people had begun to stare. I shushed her, but it did no good. "And that boy is from Chellan too. Oh, dear, what was his name——"

"Hopper," I told her. "Hopper MacCutcheon." The side-burns and slicked-back hair and fancy Spanish getup changed his looks; but Vera, by golly, was right. This was the big, clumsy strawhead we'd nicknamed Clodhopper at school, shortening it to Hopper after he beat up several of us, me included.

I looked around for our waitress, feeling the need of a bracer. "Vera," I said to my wife, "there's something almighty funny about this."

"More than funny," Vera said. "It's—it's fantastic. Nan Drummond was the only girl ever to be dropped from Miss Harper's dance classes. Why, Jim, she was absolutely hope-less! She couldn't do a simple Rocking Chair without tum-bling over her feet."

"She could now, you bet!" I muttered, watching those two in their cone of golden light while I did some remembering on my own account. The one time Hopper MacCutcheon had shown up at a high-school dance—stag, of course—Vera made the mistake of feeling sorry for him and let him stomp her through a slow fox trot. She had to junk her new gold sandals and was lame for a week.

The band lit into a red-hot *rumba*. The way that pair han-dled it made you want to hop on a chair and holler, '*Ole!*' I waited till they spun close to our table, then pushed my voice under the music. "Hopper," I said. "Hey, Hopper."

For a minute I thought we must, after all, be wrong. But next time around, the girl gave us a quick little smile and the tall fair-haired guy winked at me.

They ran off hand in hand, the spot tagging them. Although I hadn't succeeded in catching the waitress, she showed up with a fresh daiquiri for Vera and a double rye for me.

"Compliments of The Belancas," she told us in a tone that

made it plain our rating had gone up a good few points, "and they ask may they join you at your table, Mr. Avery."

"Tell them we'd be honored," I said, and meant it.

They showed in about five minutes, in street clothes. I had a queer feeling that they'd shed some sort of magic along with their costumes and make-up because, except for being seven years older and a heck of a lot better dressed, Nancy and Hopper were the same awkward, odd-ball pair who had dropped out of Chellan High in their senior year. Nan crunched a fellow's foot as they edged between tables. As she stopped to apologize, Hopper bounced off her hip and spilled the champagne cocktail the fellow's girl was nursing. The way they looked at us was the same too—as if I were still the big football wheel and Vera the most popular girl in school. Anxious, if you follow me. Not too sure of their welcome.

We brought Nan and Hopper up to date on the home-town news, and learned they were married and had two children, a boy and a girl, the same as we. New York would be their next stop, and their agent was kicking a Hollywood deal around. It was plain they were big league, headed for the top of the tree.

I'd got to gabbing about our holly farm and was telling Hopper how we keep a flock of geese to take care of the weeds when Vera's curiosity reached flash point. "How on earth," she burst out, "or off it, did you two learn to dance like that? You must have sold your souls to the devil!"

Hopper glanced at his watch, managing at the same time to knock an ash tray off the table. His voice came to us muffled as he scrunched to grope for it.

"Souls," he said, "are a glut on the market these days." He came up with his hair mussed and his tie crooked. "I doubt you could give one away, much less sell it." He looked at Nan, and the magic that had been on them while they danced seemed to touch them again, turning them into a downright handsome couple.

"Very well, darling," Nan said, "tell them if you like. Only don't expect Vera and Jim to believe you."

"Certainly we will!" Vera said.

"Oh, no, you won't!" Nan answered, with her green-blue eyes smiling.

"How can you believe it," Hopper said quietly, "when we've never been able to ourselves?"

The way they laid it out for us, Nan and Hopper got their feet untangled the same night Vera and I became engaged, which was at the midwinter prom seven years ago exactly. Hopper had meant to go to that dance, but felt his courage drain away while he was still jolting along River Road in the farm jeep.

He parked a couple of blocks from Legion Hall and leaned against the jeep in his shiny blue-serge suit and thick-soled black shoes. Dance music drifted down to him from the hall; couples were passing the windows, kids he had gone to school with half his life, and he yearned so hard to be among them, be one of them, that the wanting dried his mouth. It wasn't just the clumsiness which went with a loose-coupled frame and outsize hands and feet that kept him away. His dad was Prophet MacCutcheon, a wild-eyed stump rancher who raised his family on a diet of belt leather and wrath-to-come. At eighteen turned, Hopper was too big for the Prophet to push around, and had long ago decided that dancing was no sin. But the twig had been bent. The minute he set foot on that Legion Hall floor, Hopper MacCutcheon would feel his dad's eyes drilling him, and he'd stiffen as if the Prophet's belt were about to crack across his shoulders.

Finally the pull of the music became more than flesh could stand. Hopper trudged down the empty street to the hall, eased around back and climbed the rail of the old-fashioned veranda that boxed the place. Down near the end, deep in the shadows, he spotted a shape which turned out to be Nan

Drummond standing on a bench with her arms crossed on a window sill.

"You, huh?" Hopper greeted her.

"Any law?" Nan came back at him.

Hopper didn't need to ask why she wasn't inside. The girl's aunt was one of those who are happiest when they have a young, helpless creature to torment. Other girls wore skirts and sweaters or blouses to school. Nan Drummond, at seventeen, was forced into dresses—frocks, her Aunt Bess called them—the like of which hadn't been seen on mortal back in fifty years. The only boys who ever asked Nan to a party were those whose folks owed her aunt money, and at the moment the old miser's account book must have been clear.

"Shove over," Hopper said and hoisted himself onto the bench beside her.

They peered in at the dancers, Hopper cussing himself for a coward, Nan busy with her own bitter thoughts.

"Nice band," Hopper said once, feeling he ought to make conversation for politeness's sake.

"Shut up," she told him. "I'm watching Jim Avery and Vera Hubbard. Trying to learn how they make those turns."

Hopper watched, too, elbow to elbow with Nan at the window. Inside was a world they both longed to be part of. He twisted around toward Nan. The bench jiggled, and she said, almost snarling, "Careful, you ox!"

"Well," Hopper said, "we owe but one death, as Sir Philip Sidney said, or maybe it was Sir Walter Raleigh. No point in freezing here. You want to go in and stumble around?"

The bench teetered again as Nan faced him. "Gallantly put," she said. "Sir Philip couldn't have done better." She was crying, the tears making her plain face plainer. "Thanks, Hopper. At least I can tell Aunt Bess a boy asked me without his arm being twisted. But will you please look at me? Take a *good* look!"

She flung her pinch-waisted coat wide. What Hopper saw

was a frilly white dress that might have been cute, in a quaint way, on a child of eleven.

"A blue sash goes with this little number," Nan said. "The finishing touch. I have it wadded down inside." The tears were flowing faster. "If I let you take me in, do you know what would happen?"

"I can guess," Hopper mumbled.

"In ten minutes," Nan told him in a shaking voice, "ten horrible minutes of tramping your feet and bumping other couples, my stomach, if you'll pardon a word Aunt Bess considers unladylike, would have tied itself in a knot. I'd retreat to the powder room and throw up. So you see——"

Their bench, at that point, decided to fight back. It flipped them to the veranda floor. They rolled under the rail in a tangle of arms and legs to land in an inch of January slush.

"So you see why I won't accept," Nan said drearily, as Hopper helped her to her feet. She stared at him, soaked and muddy, weeping still. "Oh, Hopper," she sobbed at him. "Clowns like us! Why don't they just take us out and shoot us!"

A long haul from Las Vegas and a feature spot at the Twin Palms. Our waitress was beside me in her little red skirt. I ordered, while Vera dabbed at her eyes with her handkerchief.

"You poor, poor kids," she said. "How cruel we all were to them, Jim. Believe me, if we'd had the least idea you were out there—I'm so glad things have turned out wonderfully for you!"

"It's as well you didn't come out," Hopper said, with his farm-boy grin. "I'd probably have picked a fight with Jim and spoiled his suit out of pure meanness. But no one came out."

They stood with the music taunting them, the jive of seven years ago, Hopper mad at himself, mad at Nan in her silly dress, at the lucky ones in the hall and the whole uncaring world. "I'm still asking you to dance," he growled at Nan, and caught her by the wrist and started off with her down the street.

"Let go!" she snapped at him. "Where do you think you're taking me?"

"To a place I know," Hopper told her, "with a better dance floor than the Legion Hall." He was striding so fast the girl had to trot or be dragged. "And this I promise you," he said as he boosted Nan into the jeep. "No one will bump us there!"

The jeep lacked top and heater, since Prophet MacCutcheon didn't hold with luxury. Hopper endured Nan's shivering till they were several miles out on River Road, then reached an arm and fetched her across the seat to huddle against him.

Dully, as if she didn't much care any more, Nan asked him again, "Where are you taking me?"

Hopper didn't answer till they were past his dad's stump ranch, off the blacktop and jouncing fast over pot-holed gravel. Then he said, "Did you ever hear of the Altenschloss?"

Nan gave him a sullen "No."

"It's a log house, a lodge I guess you'd call it, in the woods west of Black Lake. My grandpa bossed the crew that built it in 1911. I happened on it a few years ago while I was gathering cascara bark."

"Who owns it?" Nan asked without interest. But she had stopped shivering, and was fixing up her tear-streaked face from her handbag.

"Nobody, now. Count Wilhelm and Countess Maritza von Altenberg used to. He was German, an army type with a monocle and a saber scar. She was Viennese, grandpa told me. The count killed another officer in a duel over her, and they had to skip Germany with only a very few million marks for pin money."

"Romantic," Nan said, applying lipstick as best she could in the bouncing jeep. "What a nice comic-opera touch you have. So they fled to the woods and lived in a log cabin with a ballroom—happily ever after, no doubt."

"Just for two years," Hopper told her. "They'd have fifty guests at a time, mostly titled. Grandpa used to take them in by sleigh or buckboard. The parties they threw, he said, you'd have to see to believe. Dance bands from Seattle. Drinkables by the cases. Caviar and that sandwich spread they make from goose livers. Even when the count and countess were alone in the Altenschloss, life was a ball."

The gravel tongued out from under the tires. A side road bored into a black wall of timber. "Rough from here on," Hopper said, and put the jeep at the tunnel mouth. "Did I tell you they loved to dance? When I stumbled on the Altenschloss that day, their phonograph was still in the ballroom, the biggest you ever will see, an old-timer with cylinder records and a morning-glory horn." He chuckled, steadying Nan with an arm tight around her waist. "So I oiled the phonograph," he said, "swept the floor and set out to learn to dance with the broom for a partner."

"A pillow's better," Nan said. "It doesn't trip you." Her head stirred against Hopper's shoulder. "Now that you mention it, I do seem to recall something about your Prussian and his Maritza. They went home to Germany just before the First World War, didn't they? And showed up here again around 1920?"

"Uh-huh." Hopper skidded the jeep to a halt, climbed out and set to with jack and chains. When he swung back in, his suit was muddier and he sucked a skinned knuckle. "They'd lost just about everything. Crossed the Atlantic steerage and came west by day coach. Von Altenberg hoped to find work in the district, but what Chellan gave them was rotten eggs."

"And tomatoes," Nan said. "My aunt was one of the children who threw them, and how she must have enjoyed it!" She sounded almost interested now. "At least they still had each other. What happened to them, Hopper?"

"Grandpa took them out to the Altenschloss," Hopper said. He shifted on the seat, frowning into darkness that bent the headlight beams back on themselves. "Look, Nan, maybe I'd better keep my mind on the driving."

Their side road dwindled to a trail that dipped into an alder swamp and labored over a ridge. Brush flogged the jeep sides, the wheels churned unbroken snow. The track branched, then forked again. Twice, Hopper winched the jeep through stretches too tough even for chains and four-wheel drive.

"You can see why people leave the Altenschloss alone," he said after another half hour of bushwhacking.

"One reason," Nan said. She gave him an uneasy side glance. "Are you sure there isn't another?"

"You mean the yarn those deer hunters brought out seven years back?" Hopper spared the girl a grin. "What happened, they found the hidden stairs to the count's wine cellar. The shape they were in by midnight, they were ready to see anything you care to name."

Ahead, the woods thinned. Of a sudden Nan jerked erect with her spine gone broom-handle-stiff. "Hopper MacCutcheon," she squalled at him, "you turn this car around and take me out of here! I remember the rest of that story now! I'm not dancing where people have committed suicide!"

Hopper made no move to swing the jeep, although there was room and to spare on the wide, winding driveway under the wheels. "Let me tell you something, Nan," he said. "When I step onto that dance floor, something happens that doesn't anywhere else. The music moves out of my head and into my feet. All right, suppose it did end that way? There's not a thing in the Altenschloss to harm you. Just a darn good old windup phonograph and the best springy maple floor in the county." His arm tightened protectively. "You're not stupid enough to believe in ghosts and stuff like that, are you?"

"Of course not," Nan said. She ran her tongue over dry lips. The jeep was plowing through wind-drifted snow toward a great log house lovely as a fairy tale or a dream. Snow blanketed the angles and slopes of its roof. Giant icicles hung from carved gables. Moonlight turned the windows to watching eyes as the jeep labored onto the terrace that fronted the lodge.

But friendly eyes, Nan decided. "All right, Hopper," she said, "if you can take it, I can." Her mouth quirked in a bitter smile. "At least I might be an improvement on your broom!" And he—although she didn't tell him this—would be a better partner than a pillow, which was dandy to cry into, but less comforting than a husky blue-serge shoulder.

The brass-studded log door creaked open to Hopper's push. "Better stay here," he told Nan, "till I light us some candles."

Waiting, with the frost nipping at ears and nose and her nerves taut as fiddle strings, Nan heard an owl call from deep in the woods. "Oh-no . . . no-no . . . oh-no!" the owl seemed to be warning her, and she felt her courage ooze. But deep inside the house Hopper was whistling. "This way," he called, his voice booming, hollow. Nan breathed deep, swallowed twice and stepped into the Altenschloss.

The ballroom was exactly as Hopper had described it to her. The hardwood floor under her shoes was smoother than any she had ever trod. She saw the huge old phonograph with its morning-glory horn, the candles burning yellow in wall sconces and the dusty wine-red curtains drawn back from tall windows. A chandelier hung by chains from the ceiling. On the floor under it was a cross-shaped splotch, a stain too dark for any shadow. Nan, guessing what that mark was, allowed herself a shudder. Then she crossed to Hopper with her wet shoes squishing, but never a creak under her feet.

Hopper turned from cranking the phonograph. He said to her, loud and cheerful, "That crystal chandelier used to hold a hundred candles. Grandpa found the count and countess lying under it when he drove in next day with a quarter of beef and a sack of carrots and spuds. The countess wore a pink-colored gown with a low neckline and no back at all. Von Altenberg was in his dress uniform of the Black Uhlans. The way it looked, he had shot her while they were dancing—through the heart with a Luger—then killed himself." Hopper blew dust from an ancient record. "Grandpa told me the sight of them brought tears to his eyes. Even with a hole in his forehead the count was a mighty fine-looking man, and the Countess Maritza had never looked more beautiful. She died smiling."

Music, thin and scratchy, seeped into the room. "*Blue Danube,*" Hopper told Nan. "Same record that was on when Grandpa found them." He clumped forward on size-12 feet. His hand splayed against the small of Nan's back, large, warm and reassuring.

"O.K.," he said, "latch on." His left foot thumped heavily. "Let's try to hop off on the big beat."

The floor shone, the prisms of the chandelier caught the light and shattered it in diamond twinkles. They moved in a mist of moonlight and candle glow, to *The Blue Danube* and their own loud breathing and the scuff and shuffle of their shoes.

"Loosen up, will you?" Hopper said crossly in Nan's ear. "You're stiff as a mummy."

She snapped back at him through set teeth, "Lead with your left foot, dope."

They tackled a turn, and it came off, after a fashion.

"Listen," Hopper said, "you're all swelled out like a pouter pigeon. Why don't you haul that sash out and put it on? I could get a proper hold on you, your dress wouldn't slither."

Nan obliged. They resumed, becoming bolder, attempting variations they would never have dared in Legion Hall.

"Hopper," Nan said, "I do believe you're right! It's different here. The music does get into one's feet!"

"Sure," Hopper grunted. "But how do we break out of progressive? Tell me before we crash the wall."

They pulled off several waltz boxes without stumbling, a series of left turns and an almost creditable hesitation. Hopper was screwing up his nerve for a shot at a conversation corkscrew when he saw Nan's lips part and her eyes open wide and wider, until the white showed. At the same time her fingers dug at his collarbone and her other hand gripped his in a clutch gone clammy.

"Take it easy," he told her. "It's only the grandfather clock in the hall." Except it did strike him odd that the clock should be chiming like that, spaced and solemn, when the deer-hunting vandals of seven years ago had riddled it with .30-30 slugs.

He counted twelve strokes, Nan all the time gaping over his shoulder and trying to find a voice. When it came it was a rusty squeak. "Hopper. Behind you. It's them." He had a confused impression she was about to climb him like a tree. "It's the count and countess."

"Nan," Hopper said, nape prickling, "you're nuts." He bullied her into a lurching left turn. In his ears, as he finished his ragged swing, a light, amused voice made music of its own.

"Willi," it asked, charmingly puzzled, "what is it these children do?"

The answering voice was a man's, clipped and slightly guttural. "Who can say, *Liebchen?* One of the barbarous new American steps, perhaps. It seems vaguely related to the waltz."

They poised under the glittering chandelier on the dark stain which was their heartblood, arm linked through arm, a tall, scarred, monocled officer in a dress uniform all midnight black and red and a slender woman in a pink ball gown that curved from her hourglass waist in a cascade of looped flounces. Her high-piled hair was the bronze of an autumn chrysanthemum, and her eyes under arched flyaway eyebrows were the green-blue of a mountain pond. And even with his heart pounding sick and slow in his throat and Nan's wet hand crushed in his, Hopper MacCutcheon knew the Countess Maritza, or her ghost, was the loveliest creature he had seen in all his life.

"What can we do?" Nan breathed at him.

"How would I know?" Hopper croaked. The record should have played itself through long ago, the phonograph spring run down. But the horn was still giving out with Strauss; in fact it had picked up volume and a mellowness he wouldn't have believed possible from the warped old cylinder.

He muttered to Nan, "Maybe if we shifted into progressive, and danced our way to the door——" And seconds later, savagely, "Get with it, Nan! For cat's sake, will you let me lead?"

"I can't!" It hit him in an agonized whisper. "Oh, Hopper, I've forgotten the step, I can't do anything but the Rocking Chair!"

They joggled to and fro, trapped and helpless. Over the top of Nan's head, Hopper saw the countess smile at her husband.

"Ah, the poor darlings," she said in her voice that was silvery music. "Willi, come. We must introduce ourselves."

They advanced from under the chandelier, the countess's hand light on the count's arm. "I," she said, "am the late Maritza von Altenberg, and with me is my dear departed husband, Count Wilhelm Gustavus Holtzwig-Cassen von Altenberg." The turquoise eyes hinted of laughter, the rich mouth gave name and titles a dancing lilt. "You may call him Willi."

The count bowed from the waist with a soundless click of heels. Hopper ducked his head; Nan, he saw, was bobbing like a goose in a weed patch, doing her darnedest to curtsy.

"And now," the count said briskly, "since you appear to be in error on certain minor points, perhaps you will allow us to repay the honor of this visit with a—shall we say, a demonstration?"

He bowed again with the noiseless heel click, this time to his wife. Hopper watched, Nan's hand still in his, both of them enchanted beyond fear. This they were witnessing, this waltz in a mist of moon and candlelight, was perfection. It was lovelier than a flight of sea gulls, as intricately faultless as the courting play of swallows.

At the end Nan spoke to the countess with her face all aglow. "I'd sell my immortal soul," she cried, "and I know Hopper would, too, if we could dance like that!"

317

Maritza von Altenberg smiled at her. The chrysanthemum head nodded. "So? Then, my dear, let us change partners."

This part of it, his waltz with the beautiful ghost, Hopper MacCutcheon could never clearly remember. He only knew he was caught up in that same perfection, one with it and part of it, and that he could have cried like a baby when the music whispered off into silence.

He realized they were alongside the black stain under the chandelier.

"Warm work," the count said. "My man does not seem to be about. Pray excuse me."

He dimmed away, but only for a minute. Then he was standing tall at his wife's side with a monocle screwed into his eye, holding a cobwebbed enormous bottle under his arm and four crystal glasses between spread fingers.

"The best in our cellar," he said, and shot the cork so that it set the chandelier pendants tinkling. "Even for a vintage year, Maritza, it has kept its life remarkably."

They waltzed the night away, in the misted light, with vintage champagne to refresh them. Toward dawn they toasted one another in the last of the magnum.

In a gesture all grace the countess stooped to upend her glass beside the bottle. She straightened, gazing at Nan with her smile gone wistful and a brightness in her eyes that might have been tears.

"How sweet," she said through a sigh, "to be a *jeune fille* once more in a pretty white frock with a blue sash, in a warm, mortal body. To be dancing with one's first love, and hoping, knowing that after the last waltz. . . ." Her words were lost in a blush and a murmuring. Her upward glance at the count was sheer bewitchment; he cleared his throat twice, and spoke a trifle stiffly.

"In friendship," he said, "and to oblige my wife, a romantic as is every Viennese, may I prevail upon you to lend us yourselves for one waltz?" He added with the merest hint of a smile in his cold blue eyes, "I assure you we will return you unharmed."

What took place then, Nan and Hopper could remember hardly at all. Except that they were no longer an awkward stump-ranch boy and a clumsy, lonely girl but two other people—dancers with feet that moved light to the music as drifting leaves and hearts that glowed with a joy and a hope and an eager yearning they had never felt before.

Far away on River Road, a rooster crowed to the morning star, and they were Nan Drummond and Hopper MacCutcheon, waltzing together, themselves again, more or less.

"How marvelously you have improved, *mes petits*," the countess told them. "But it is always so where love is, or the seeds of love."

"Come, Maritza," the count said. "Our ball ends. A stupid convention, this of cockcrow, but rules are rules and must be obeyed."

"One moment first," the countess said gravely, but with the smile lingering. "There is the matter of two souls deeded to us, Willi."

"Return them," the count told her, with a glance at the graying windows. "Have we become—how is it said in America?—mere hucksters?"

"Very well," Maritza von Altenberg agreed. "But allow me one last small pleasure, Willi. We shall give each to the other. 'My true love hath my soul, and I have his,' as the English poet, Sir Philip Sidney, puts it."

"Heart, dearest," the count corrected her indulgently, his saber-scarred face turning again to the windows. "Heart, not soul. You're forever misquoting."

"Heart, soul," his wife said, "it makes no matter." She began to dim out like mist dissolving—eyes, smile, slim body and chrysanthemum head. Her voice touched them sweetly across a widening distance. "Not to dance for seven more long years,

Willi. So stern a penance! But perhaps at the end we shall find our young friends and waltz again."

"And that," Hopper MacCutcheon said, heaving up from our table with a lurch that sent a glass rolling, "was that. Nan and I never did go home. We hocked a case of the count's Napoleon brandy to a bootlegger down the line—we knew the von Altenbergs wouldn't mind—and took a bus to Reno and got married."

"And here we are," Nan said brightly. . . . "Hopper, we're almost on. We'd better hurry!"

They blundered off between tables to change for their second show. After a considerable silence Vera said in a testing voice, "Quite an account, Jim."

"Sure," I said. "One for the book, huh?"

"Dancing with ghosts in a haunted house," Vera said. "I suspect that bottle of champagne was tapped rather earlier than Hopper claims."

"Quiet, hon," I told her, for the music had started, *The Blue Danube*, it was, and The Belancas were waltzing in a circle of amber light. At least I guess it was they, although Hopper in the black-and-red dress uniform and Nan in a frothy pink ball gown with her hair bronze in the spotlight looked—well, like two other people. But this I was sure of as we watched them dip and whirl and glide like swallows in a mating flight—we'd never seen waltzing to match that before, and wouldn't again.

Vera didn't speak till The Belancas had gone on to their Latin numbers. Then she said all of a rush, "I don't care, I still won't believe it. Why, Jim, if I did, it would shatter me. I'd be a changed person."

I don't want my wife to change; I like her as she is. So I saw no point in telling Vera how I happened on the Altenschloss while grouse hunting last fall and found, plunk in the middle of that fine sprung-maple floor, on the cross-shaped stain under the chandelier, a champagne bottle—a magnum—and four glasses.